Formerly a BBC producer, the birth of her third child Writing, she became a tut College, where she taught She now combines writing, *Valentina*, was published by Blackbird Digital Books in 2016. Her follow up, the dark and twisting bestseller *Mother*, was published by Bookouture in November 2017 and Susie has gone on to publish gripping psychological thrillers with them ever since.

ALSO BY S.E. LYNES

Mother
The Pact
Valentina
The Proposal
The Women
The Lies We Hide
Can You See Her?
The Housewarming
Her Sister's Secret
The Baby Shower
The Ex
The Summer Holiday
The Split
The Perfect Boyfriend
Every Mother's Nightmare

THE HOUSEWARMING

S. E. LYNES

bookouture

BOOKOUTURE

First published in 2020 by Bookouture, an imprint of Storyfire Ltd.
This paperback edition published in 2026

1

A CIP catalogue record for this book
is available from the British Library.

PB ISBN 978-1-83618-795-0
EB ISBN 978-1-80019-082-5

Printed and bound in Great Britain by
Clays Ltd, Elcograf S.p.A.

Papers used by Bookouture are from well-managed forests
and other responsible sources.

Bookouture
An imprint of Storyfire Ltd.
Carmelite House
50 Victoria Embankment
London EC4Y 0DZ

An Hachette UK Company

The authorised representative in the EEA is Hachette Ireland
8 Castlecourt Centre
Dublin 15 D15 XTP3
Ireland
(email: info@hbgi.ie)

www.hachette.co.uk
www.bookouture.com

For Jackie West, with decades of love.

CHAPTER ONE

Ava

When I think about that morning, it is beat by beat, like a heart – my own heart, my daughter's, at the time so enmeshed it seemed she was part of me: my body, my tissue, my bones. She is part of me. She will always be part of me.

When I think about that morning, I watch myself, over and over, as if from above. I watch myself like you watch your children in a school play or a sports match, silently willing them to succeed, to shine, to not get hurt. I watch myself bleeding on the sidelines of slowly unfolding disaster, alive with the pain I know is coming but she, the me of that moment, does not.

I do this every minute of every hour of every day. And I have done this for almost a year.

I watch myself: there I am, making my way down the stairs with an armful of laundry. I can't see over the top. I take it slowly, both feet on one step before I lower myself to the next. Another step down, another. I am always so careful these days. I used to be care*free*, but now I see danger everywhere: an electric socket is a hazard, a glass left too near the edge of a tabletop risky, a staircase perilous.

Another step. I call her name. Abi.

'Mummy's coming,' I say.

I say, 'Mummy's just going to pop a wash on and then we'll go and feed the ducks.'

I say, 'You've been such a good girl, waiting nicely like that.'

I've always chatted away to her – from the moment she was born. At two, she loves the sound of me prattling on.

Loves. Loved.

'Mummy,' she would say. She would hold my face in her tiny hands.

'What?'

'My love you.'

'I love you too, little monkey.'

I would push the end of her nose, make a honking sound. She would throw back her head, helpless with giggles.

'Again,' she would say. 'Again, Mummy.'

Never again. Or maybe, maybe one day... She might still be out there, after all. There's a chance, isn't there? The tiniest chance? In faces of other little girls I search for her every day, but even now, her features fade from me, her smell, her warmth, the sharp arc of her paper-thin nails on my cheeks, the weight of her on my hip, the strange swing of us both when I leant forward to stir the spaghetti sauce, the anticipation on her face, waiting while I blew on the end of the spoon, her little body fraught with anticipation, knowing that in seconds she would be allowed to taste the sauce, to tell me if it was good.

That morning.

I watch myself: face full of dirty linen. I can't see my own feet.

'Abi?' I say, as yet no presentiment of disaster. 'What's the matter? Aren't you speaking, missy?'

The curved bar of her pushchair. The mesh back. Her head is not there. Her soft curling ringlets, thickening now from baby to child hair, are not there.

She is not there.

Ava, don't be a lunatic, she's leaning forward.

No, she isn't. She's not there. She's not in the buggy.

Abi is not there.

Second by second, beat by beat. A clock. The metronome that sits on my piano top, keeping time. The washing drops from my arms. I stumble, fall down the last few steps.

'Abi?' I call out, righting myself, rubbing at the pain in my hands. 'Abi?'

Another second. The prickling rise of the hairs on my arms.

'Abi? Love?'

I can see the house opposite.

I can see the house opposite.

The house opposite—

The front door is open. Oh God, I have left the front door open.

'Oh my God. Abi!'

I am on the street, scanning right, left, right again. I am calling her name, my ribcage tightening around my lungs. 'Abi? Abi? Abi!'

My heart fattens in my chest. I left Abi in the hallway and I popped upstairs.

'Wait there, darling,' I said. 'Won't be a tick.'

I did not, can't have, closed the front door. Abi was fastened into her buggy. She doesn't know how to undo the clasp. She didn't know. Yesterday she didn't know how to undo the clasp. She wasn't making any noise so I… I…

A few paces. She is nowhere on the pavement, in either direction. I have no idea which way to head. One way precludes the other, and what if she's still inside…

I dash back into the house, hearing the watery tremble of her name as it falls from my mouth. The house is held in an electric stasis. I make myself stand completely still. My ears prick. Eyes wide. The house sounds empty. It looks empty. It *feels* empty.

'Abi?' I call up the stairs. 'Abi, love? Are you in the house? Where are you? Where are you, darling?' I fight to keep the hysteria out of my voice but I, *I* can hear it.

I stride into the kitchen. The patio doors are closed. The air presses in.

'Abi?'

Silence.

I run back into the hall, open the little door under the stairs to the downstairs loo. She isn't there.

'Abi?'

Silence.

Into the living room. The piano, the metronome. The sofas, the TV, the fireplace. The coffee table.

'Abi? Are you in here?' I sweep back the curtain. 'Abi, love?'

The hard push of the window ledge against the palms of my hands. My own shuddering breath.

Silence.

I am outside again. Rain dots lead grey on the stone front path. Our house has a small patch of lawn, a rosemary hedge. There is nowhere she could hide there. She is not in front of the house. She is not on the pavement. She isn't anywhere on our side of the road, as far as I can see. Across the street, the houses are closed, impassive. Next door, on both sides, shut up and still. There is no one, no one about. Not one person.

'Abi? Abi? Aaabiii!'

I look left to the near end of the street, right to the far end. Which way? I have to go somewhere. I have to move. I jog halfway down towards the far end, towards the busier of the two larger connecting roads.

'Abi? Abi?'

I'm running back, back towards our house, aware of seconds passing, accumulating, becoming minutes. Where would she go? How long was I upstairs? I only meant to grab the laundry and come down. Abi was quiet, she was quiet so I stripped the beds – thought I may as well while she was... when I left her, she was in her buggy talking to Mr Sloth, the plush Jellycat toy that Neil and Bella gave her when she was born. She was quiet so I emptied the washing basket. You do that, every parent does – you do stuff like that while you can when you have a little one. When they're quiet. When they're not asking you for attention or food or water or...

The street is a faceless row of white arrows, roofs pointing to the sky. My heart is a blockage in my throat. I run back towards the far end, ducking my head to see under side gates, craning my neck around hedges, looking back every few seconds, back towards the house. She is not there. But she might still be in the house, behind a curtain, giggling inside a wardrobe. She might come out at any moment. If she can't hear me, she will panic. She will not know where I am.

Second by second, beat by beat... the quickening rhythm of rising panic. There's no need to panic. She'll be somewhere.

'Abi? Abi, lovey? Abi, where are you?'

My mouth dries.

Gone half past eight. When did I go upstairs? When did she leave the house? *Has* she left the house?

She wasn't making a fuss. She was contented. She was quiet. If she'd wanted me, she would have called out.

'Mummy!' she would have called. 'Mummy! My waiting!'

But she didn't. She was quiet. I was only on Facebook for a few minutes. I needed the loo, so I did a quick wee – you do, when your little one is quiet, everyone does. I sat on the loo and scrolled through Facebook, but not for long, not for that long. I only commented on a couple of threads. I only stripped the beds, emptied the washing basket. Every mum does a few quick jobs when their baby is settled and quiet, in front of the TV or in the playpen with a few toys or in the high chair with a rusk to suck on. Abi was in the hallway. She was clipped into her buggy. She had Mr Sloth to talk to. She'd had enough to eat. She was comfortable. She was fastened in. She did not know how to undo the clasp. Yesterday, she did not know.

Second by second. Beat by beat.

How unbearable it is to watch myself from today, caught in this quickening rhythm, to watch my growing despair, over and over, like an ink-black blossoming rose caught on a time-lapse film: replayed, replayed, replayed. Myself, that woman in chaos; myself, not thinking straight. But I do watch. I watch her all the time. Sometimes I admit to that moment on the toilet seat, scrolling through social media, sometimes I don't. Today I do. Today I admit that I sat there and thought: oh good, she's quiet. I'll just sit here a second. My eyes were sore. Abi wasn't a great sleeper and she could be difficult, headstrong, argumentative, even with her limited vocabulary.

Tiredness weighed in my bones and I thought, she's quiet, I'll just sit here. I'll sit here until she starts making a fuss. I'll take this break. I need this break.

Today I can look that in the eye.

But not always. Not always.

A loop. A beat. A building, building dread. I watch myself. There I am, half running a little further down our street now, head turning left, right, looking behind, in front, no clue, no clue at all which way to go for the best, mindful of the fact that my front door is open, that if Abi is hiding in the house she is now alone in there, she can now escape, and if she does, she might wander into the road looking for me. She's two. She doesn't know how to cross a road safely.

The thought of calling the police comes to me, of course it does. But no, I think. No. Be logical. It's probably only a few minutes since she actually left the house. She's round here somewhere. She escaped from the church hall toddler group once; I nearly lost my mind. Twenty minutes she was missing. Twenty. I felt every second. She'd walked all the way to Carluccio's at the far end of the high street before someone stopped her and asked where her mummy was. Children don't just disappear. They wander off, distracted, oblivious to the annihilating terror they cause. You see them sometimes: blank-faced toddlers bobbing placidly in the tight wrap of their mothers' arms, their mothers' faces still etched with the slow-fading lines of marrow-melting dread.

Logic nudges in. She might have toddled along to see Uncle NeeNee and Auntie Bel. She knows not to but she's a little tyke. In the best way. The best, best way. And my God, for such a tot, she can move fast when she wants to.

I run towards Neil and Bella's house.

'Abi?' I peer under their side gate. 'Abi! Are you there?'

Nothing. No little feet. She's wearing her red lace-up ankle boots. Kickers, ridiculously expensive for a fast-growing girl, but another gift from Neil and Bella. She loves those boots. But there's no sign of them. No sign of her little cream woolly bobble hat, her pale-blue Puffa coat.

I knock on Neil and Bella's door, ring the doorbell. Neil's van is on the street but there's no one home, of course there isn't. They'll both have left for work.

A silver Prius drifts past. I try not to wail in despair at how silent it is, how silent electric cars are. She'd never hear it. She wouldn't turn around until it was too late. The Prius turns left into the busy road. Cars are on the move. A few more minutes and the traffic will be heavier – local commuters, the school run. About a third of the cars have gone already. Many of them are big, too big – great suburban safari trucks designed to keep precious children safe inside. But what of the children on the outside? What of unthinking little ones dawdling into the road?

My breath quickens. I run back. The new neighbours will be long gone, their progeny spirited away – one to nursery, one to some private school elsewhere. At least that's what Matt and I have assumed. They only moved in a month or two ago. Their younger daughter looks to be about Abi's age. The older one, I've no idea – don't even know if it's a boy or a girl.

Adrenaline sends bitter saliva to my mouth. I cross over. I am on the pavement directly opposite our house now. That's a risk. If Abi is still inside, if she wanders out now, she might see me, she might see me and run across the road – Mummy! One of those safari trucks might come speeding round the corner. One of those silent electric cars. A motorbike. She wouldn't see it until it was too late. I run as far as I dare down this side of the street, calling her name.

'Abi! Abi?'

Hedges, front patios, side gates. No sign. Nothing. Where is everyone? Gone to work. The sweet spot between city commuters and the school run. Nausea churns in my gut, rises in my throat. I cross back to our side of the street, head towards home. I'm going round in circles. I'm wasting precious time. Seconds are becoming minutes, are already minutes, minutes are becoming... I think I need to call the police.

My hairline is wet with sweat, my armpits, my back. Abi will be somewhere – that's what's happened here. She's a wanderer. That's why I always clip her into the buggy. I thought I'd closed the front door. I'm sure I did. But I'm so tired; my brain is fog, more so these last couple of weeks. It must have banged against the catch. It does that sometimes. But I am careful. I am very careful. Even when she walks, I make her hold on to the buggy with one hand. Abi can walk all the way along Thameside Lane, all the way over the footbridge to Ham and all the way back, jabbering away, little legs going nineteen to the dozen. Cute little knees my mother has already claimed for our side of the family. Strong knees, my mum says. The Woods are excellent walkers. Can walk for days, like camels. Abi loves to walk. But she wouldn't go to the ducks on her own; there's no way she would...

'Abi?' I shout, hands a loudhailer around my mouth, turning a slow circle. 'A-a-abi-i-i-i!'

I picture the local geography in my mind's eye. Float above it. The riverside roads, parallels connected by the main artery that links my small town to the larger commercial centre of Kingston upon Thames, and the quieter Thameside Lane, a lesser road that passes the tennis courts on the way to the river, to Teddington Lock. That's the way we always walk, to the shallow slope between the chandlery and the path up to the footbridge, where the river laps and climbs when the tide is high, where ducks gather in the hope of titbits. It takes five minutes to get there, ten at most. Sometimes we head over the bridge to Ham, to the little park there, sometimes calling at the German bakery for apple cake, a big treat.

I grab my key and close the front door. If she's inside, she can't now get out.

And I'm running, calling, calling, calling her name. Flailing around, caught in the white heat of my own burgeoning panic.

At the same time, here I am, watching myself from the present, watching myself over and over, screaming at that woman, myself: *Run to the river, Ava; run to the damn river, I am begging you.*

But I don't hear my own voice. I don't hear it shouting at me from my desolate, devastated future. I don't hear it.

'Abi!' is all I hear: my own blind and desperate cry.

I run. The metallic taste of blood fills the dry cave of my mouth. Past the Parkers and the Smiths. The chap with the camper van has left. Outside my own house yet again, I stand with my hands on my hips, panting, trying to think. Next door's Mercedes has gone. She works in Surbiton, leaves early; he works in town, takes the train. The other-side neighbours' Porsche has gone; they leave together, kids in the back. Lovegood, I think their name is. I think of our own rusty Volkswagen and Neil's big white van: *Johnson's Quality Builds* written in green on the side, and I think of how Neil, Bella and Matt are more a part of this town than anyone here, though they seem like the outsiders now – their cars, their voices don't match, and I think: why am I thinking about that now?

And here, in this tortured present, what I'm thinking is: why aren't you running to the river, Ava? Why, when you were going to feed the ducks? Why haven't you thought of that?

But I do not run to the river. I am for the moment rooted to the spot. Abi will be somewhere, is what I'm thinking. She'll be in the front garden or in the house. Playing a trick. Boo! she will say. You didn't see me, did you, Mummy?

'Abi!'

Too many minutes have evaporated now into the steam of my boiling panic. Too long, too long. She should have appeared by now. I am running again. Up to the end, back again, the sense that I have done this too many times now, that I'm repeating the same action with the hope of a different outcome. Past number 76, 78, 80. Second by second. Beat by beat. The beats get louder, a pounding, drumming rhythm. My heart. My little girl's heart. Hearts beating. Clocks ticking. A metronome keeping time, a melody accelerating. Sand slipping, slipping away.

Sweat pricks on my forehead. She must be around here somewhere. She couldn't have walked as far as the main road. There's no way she'd have made it, no way she would have dared to go as far as the river.

No way.

I'm outside our house again. When did I go upstairs? Let's be logical. Let's slow this down. Eight? Five to? I clipped her into her buggy and I went upstairs. She won't have made a bolt for it immediately. If she became bored and unfastened that clasp, it would have been ten, fifteen minutes later. So she's probably been missing for maybe twenty-five minutes, maybe longer…

Crying fat rolling tears, I call Matt. Second by second, beat by beat. The long discordant ringtone. The silence. The ringtone. The silence. My own sobs bang against my ribs. The ringtone. He won't hear it. He'll be at work by now. He had a meeting at 9.30. A new project, a factory conversion somewhere in the East End. He won't hear his—

'Ava?'

'Matt!' My voice is high and shaky, my breath short. I am gasping for air, marching through the house, pulling open the kitchen cupboard doors.

'Ava? Are you OK?'

The broom cupboard is empty, the store cupboard empty.

'Matt! I can't find Abi!'

She's not under the kitchen bar. She's not under one of the stools pretending to be a lion in a cage.

'What d'you mean, you can't find her?'

'She's not under the couch!'

'Not under the couch? What?'

'She undid her buggy clasp.'

'What? OK. Ava? Ava, can you just—'

'I left the front door open. I left the door open, Matt, and she's… Oh God, the oven is empty, oh thank God.'

'Ava, slow down. Just tell me what's going on.'

'Abi's gone. She's just… disappeared. She must've wandered out. I only popped upstairs. Literally. I just went to get my

phone. There's no sign of her. There's no sign of her, Matt.'
I try the back door. Locked. I unlock it. I am in the garden.

'Abi?' I press my nose to the window of the shed. 'Abi?'

This is mad. There's no way she can access the back. But
still I scrutinise the border plants, the chaotic mass of ivy
that foams over the entire left-hand fence. Rain speckles the
sliding patio doors.

'She's probably hiding.' Matt's voice is calm, the voice of
reason. 'You know what she's like. Have you tried upstairs?'

'Not yet.' I'm back inside. My trainers pound up the stairs.
'I don't know where to look first, Matt. I don't know where
to look for the best. Should I be outside? Do you think she'd
walk as far as the main road?'

'Have you been outside?'

'Yes. She was nowhere. She's not in our bedroom.'

'Have you looked by the bins?'

'Not yet. I'm in the house. Abi! Love? She's not in our room…
she's not in her room. She's not under the bed. Oh God, oh
my God, it's been ages. Do you think I should call the police?'

'God, no, she'll be somewhere. Have you checked the
garden?'

'Yes, but the back door was locked. She's not in the bathroom. Abi, love? She's not in the washing basket. She's not
here. She's nowhere, just nowhere, like she's vanished.'

'She won't be far.'

The phone is hot at my ear. I run back downstairs, back
out of the front door. Sweat trickles down my forehead, down
the sides of my body. No sign. There is no sign of her. There
is no one on the street.

'Oh God, Matt. I feel sick. I'm going to be sick.'

'Ava?'

'I'm outside.' I can barely get the words out. 'I can't see her. I can't see her.' A pain in my sternum like the end of a broom. The rain is falling more heavily now. I shield my eyes with my hand. 'There's no sign of her. She's vanished. She's disappeared into thin air. I think I should call the police.'

'She'll be somewhere. Has she gone to Neil and Bella's, do you think?'

'She wouldn't do that. Well, she might, but I knocked and there was no one in. And if she was there, one of them would've rung me by now or brought her back. I just don't think she'd wander off like this, not for this long.'

'What about that time she wandered out of toddler group? She went miles.'

'I know, but she wouldn't do that again, would she? I was so cross with her. I shouted at her. She was really upset. I think… I mean, I don't think—'

'Look, I'm coming home,' Matt says. 'I'm not far. I got a puncture on the towpath so I'm this side of Richmond. Just keep looking, yeah? I'm turning round, OK? I'm heading back.'

CHAPTER TWO

Ava

Second by second. Beat by beat. A metronome keeps time for the frantic melody of my life's unravelling. I watch myself from above. I shout out the things I should have done, places I should have looked, the order in which I should have done it all. Really, I can be very abusive towards myself, that stupid cow there, that idiot woman who can't hear me, who is blind, blind, blind to logic, deaf to reason, numb with fear. That morning. Look at her. Look at me. Rain soaks my hair, my clothes. My dumb feet thudding on the paving stones, running to nowhere, on a wheel. I have been getting my fitness up, leaving the house with Matt when he goes to work so that I can go for long walks with Abi. Stale bread in a bag, feed the ducks, across the lock to Ham, to the little park. The German bakery, pretzels as big as her head. Fresh air makes you feel better, no matter what.

'Why don't you tell Mr Sloth what we're going to do today?' I say, clipping her into her buggy. Yes, I clip her in. I know I do because I can see us, there in the hall. I am crouched in front of her. I'm smiling at her. I'm putting Mr Sloth in her lap and I'm thinking that the silver name bracelet Neil and Bella bought her is getting a little snug around her wrist.

'Tell him we'll feed the ducks. Don't let Mr Sloth eat the bread, OK?'

She giggles. That's the last thing she does.

I only pop upstairs.

Things I would do differently. The door I would have checked before going upstairs. The two and two I would have put together. The ducks. The river. The obviousness of it all. I would have run in the right direction immediately. I would have found her hurrying towards the river, chin out, full of her own mischief, the little minx. I would have closed the damn door. I would not have scrolled through Facebook. Had I known, I would not even have looked at my phone – of course I wouldn't. God knows, I have to look at myself every day and see in my haunted reflection the ghost of my ignorant self. That morning. Almost a year ago. I see so plainly that I didn't know what was about to happen, what was happening, what had already happened. I didn't have the smallest clue and yet a prescient dread flooded my every vein. I watch myself, from here. I watch that woman sit on the loo and scroll through her phone and I shout at her, at me: 'Do not do that! Run, Ava! Run to the river! You were going to feed the ducks – why can't you think of that?'

'You need to stop shouting at yourself, Ava.' That's what my counsellor, Barbara, says. 'Try not to punish yourself. Try to forgive yourself as you would someone you love.'

Barbara is helping me limit how many times I check the front door when I get in. She tells me I didn't do what I should have done that morning because I am not psychic.

'But I should have checked the door,' I tell her.

'Sod should.'

Sod should, that's what Barbara says. There is no should. I went on my phone because since Abi was born and I cut my hours to part-time, my phone is my lifeline. My phone made me feel like I still belonged to the world. My friends were on it. My social life. My clients – the parents of the kids I teach piano to. I didn't, I don't, spend my days interacting with other professionals in a funky office space; I am no longer in a staffroom with other teachers, exchanging stories about kids in our classes or arranging to go for a drink on Friday. I don't kick off my shoes at night and sigh with the relief of not having to talk to anyone for the rest of the evening. I am often stuck at home. And yes, there are times when I have felt trapped.

So yes, I would go on Facebook or Instagram and guarantee myself a few laughs, a bit of banter, God forbid, an interesting news article, a well-articulated opinion piece.

I got lonely. I got bored. There – there's the dirty truth. I get – used to get – bored, sometimes, while I was with Abi. I would crave adult contact. While Abi was having a snack or her dinner, instead of talking to her, I would chat to my mum, too far away to pop over for a cup of tea. At the park, I got bored. I got bored with baby talk and endless domesticity and children's programmes. I got bored with nursery rhyme CDs blaring out of the car stereo. There were times when I longed to put on Chopin or Springsteen or Björk and turn the music up, up, up to drown out Abi's whingeing.

'Yes. All of that,' Barbara tells me. 'But that doesn't mean you didn't, or don't, love your little girl. It doesn't mean you couldn't, or can't, look after her.' She includes both tenses. She knows that if she talks about Abi in the past tense, I lose it. She knows I'm not ready for the past tense.

'The problem is,' I reply, 'I didn't shut the door, did I? It all comes back to that and that feels pretty insurmountable.'

'Leaving the door open or not checking it was shut is a commonplace human error that ninety-nine times out of a hundred would have no negative consequence,' Barbara says.

I don't believe her.

And so I watch myself on this endless loop. Second by second. Beat by beat. A ticking clock. A metronome. A heart-beat. A clock stopped. A melody played out. A heart broken.

That morning.

Matt is on his way home. The thought calms me. At the near end of our road, a couple of mothers are wandering past, heading down towards the primary school. They are chatting, their children a few metres in front of them, sailing along on bright plastic scooters.

'Excuse me!' I call out, but the mothers don't hear. Lost in their own conversation, they carry on walking, hoods up against the thickening rain.

I quicken my pace, scanning front gardens, peering over the tops of dwarf walls and hedges, through side gates. If she'd been knocked over there would be a scene. Sirens would be wailing. There'd be an ambulance, cars chequered blue and yellow, police waving people on. If someone saw her on her own, they would stop and ask her where her mummy was. And anyway, I wasn't upstairs that long.

'Hello!' I call again, no more than a metre away now. They turn and look at me, eyes questioning in fleeting bemusement.

'Hi. Sorry.' I'm short of breath, sweating, trying to appear rational. 'Don't suppose you've seen a little girl, have you? Did you see a little girl heading up as you were coming down?'

I level my hand above my knee, try not to sound hysterical. 'About this big. She's two. She's wearing a light blue coat and a cream woolly hat? Red ankle boots?'

They look at each other, back at me.

'No, sorry.' One of them shakes her head, digs a portable umbrella from her bag and flicks it open.

'What's her name?' asks the other. Her eyebrows rise in encouragement.

'Abi. It's Abi. Listen, if you see her, I live just there, Riverside Drive. Number eighty-eight – the first semi after that big detached one on the end there.'

They nod and smile – we've all been there, is what they say without words. Yes. We've all been there, but that doesn't make it any less frightening.

'Hate it when they run off like that,' the umbrella one says. 'Hope you find her soon.'

'I'm sure I will.' I smile. A conditioned response, but I'm off, changing direction, running now, up towards the river. Thameside Lane is wider than our suburban street. Faster, but not fast fast. But still. Cars grind up and down, pulling into spaces between other cars parked on the right. The school run is warming up. There will be more cars soon, last-minute arrivals. The cars are bigger than they were even five years ago. Newer. Even the small ones are built like bumper cars. Matt's lived here since he was eleven. He says the drivers don't give way like they used to when this was just a place, not a 'village'. These cars are too big, I think. They are bigger than they need to be. We are all protecting what is ours, enlarging what is ours, our houses, our chariots. You can't see past them – bumpers for rogue wildlife, the odd stray lion. Often they park right on the end of streets so that they are as near as possible to where they want to be, but we, we, meanwhile, can't see around the corner when we're trying to pull out, or cross over on foot. We have to step right into the road to see. If you're tiny, no chance. You'd have no chance.

I hope they're not driving too fast. I hope they're paying attention.

Stop it. If she'd been run over, there'd be an ambulance. Paramedics. You'd feel it in the air. That stillness that follows shock.

It's quarter to nine. I am yesterday and today all at once forever. I am there and I am here, shouting at the memory of myself, shouting at her, the woman that was me: 'Call the police, Ava. Call 999. Call now. Call half an hour ago. Let's go back, let's go back to when you had Abi with you. There. You have her. She is yours. She is enough. You don't need to scroll through your phone, you don't need your life. Do not answer that comment. Do not clean the bathroom. Do not strip the beds.'

There is no way on earth Abi would have got this far is what thumps in my mind to the beat of my trainers on the wet black tarmac. But she would know how is the counter-argument that slows me in my tracks. And boy, she can move fast when she has a mind to.

There are two pubs: one on the river, the Fisherman's Arms, and one a little further back, the Thames View, as if to say, we might not be on the river but we can still see it – that's what Matt said when he first took me there for a drink on our fourth or fifth date, when he was still living in a room in a shared house in Twickenham. God, that seems so long ago now.

I hear the river before I see it. I round the corner. Ducks bob on the water where the lane slopes down. The water is high after all the rain in the last few days, halfway to the blue barrier. To the right, on the other side of the footpath, the fence surrounding the Fisherman's Arms garden. Beyond, the kids' fort, endless tables and benches, all empty at this time of the morning. The rain has thinned a little, though I am wet through now anyway and don't care. I jog up the path and peer through the fence, through the pub garden to the railings on the far side, to the river, the distant white foam of the weir. Just the sight of that furious churning water makes me feel sick, but there is nothing, no sign.

I jog up to the mouth of the footbridge. Here, the river splits, becoming tidal after the lock, heading then towards Richmond, to Westminster, out to the Thames Estuary. On the far side, dog walkers disappear up the steps to the next bridge; a cyclist coming my way lifts his bike onto his shoulder. It isn't Matt.

Avoiding the white rush of the weir, I turn towards the luxury riverside flats, the boats bobbing on their moorings. Brown geese glide upriver towards Richmond. The lock-keeper's cottage stands on its little green island. The sky is bulky and grey. There is no sign of my daughter. But she could have got this far, I know that. She could be over in Ham by now. We walk this way every day and she's a bright little thing. Just because she's never done it on her own doesn't mean she can't. Like Matt said: she escaped from toddler group and got all the way down a busy high street before anyone thought to ask where her mummy was.

At the time, it frightened me out of my wits.

Now, it frightens me more.

It's after quarter to nine. The police. I need to call the police. We're too far along now. I need to call them. There is no sign of Matt and I cannot wait any longer.

Legs pumping, lungs filling and emptying, I run back. She can/she can't possibly… she could/there's no way… she's a little minx/she wouldn't wander so far without me.

The road is busier. Windscreen wipers swipe over tinted glass. The bulbous bonnets of shiny cars curve hugely, their wheels enormous, their occupants elevated like lords and ladies in horse-drawn carriages. One speck of rain and they're all driving their children to school. These children are orchids. I can't ask these people anything through their smoky windows; they can't hear me over the blast of their surround-sound stereos.

I dip into the car park of the Oasis, the private leisure centre on the river. Eyes darting across the manicured lawns, I run up to the entrance, back to the main gate. No sign. I head back to the road. Abi must have toddled into someone's back garden. It is the only answer. She'll be on some neighbour's kid's slide, having the time of her life, oblivious. Or hiding, beginning to worry now that I'll never find her.

'Boo!' she'll shout, head thrown back, giggling with relief. It will be all I can do not to yell at her.

Matt is outside the house. He must have cycled past while I was in the car park. He's wearing his lightweight raincoat, his helmet, his cycling gear. He looks down to my legs, to where Abi should be, her little hand in mine. Concern wrinkles his brow. Rain falls black on the pavement. I know it's time to call the police. It is almost nine, my God.

I burst into tears and run to him. 'Matt.'

'Hey.' He pulls me to him. 'Come on, she'll be somewhere. She can't have just disappeared.'

I wrestle myself out of his arms. 'She has though. She's just wandered off or… someone's snatched her off the street. Someone's just pulled up and thrown her in a van.'

'Don't say that. That's not… that won't have happened, come on.'

'She's been gone too long. Too, too long! We need to call the police. Oh my God, where is she, where the hell is she? This is my fault. I left the door open. I thought I'd closed it but I didn't. She was in her buggy but she's never undone the clasp herself before. Oh my God, I can't believe this is happening.'

He holds me by the arms, holds me up while I sob into his chest. 'People leave their front doors open all the time. An open door is not going to kill a kid, not in this neighbourhood, Ave. Come on – this is a safe, safe place. Let's just try and think calmly.'

I can tell by how quietly he speaks that he is rattled. He's keeping his tone level for my sake but I know him too well to be fooled.

'Matt?' My voice is a whimper. 'We need to call the police.'

His bottom lip pushes out. He doesn't say no. He doesn't say *don't be silly*. I don't want him to agree. But he is nodding. He has agreed. My throat blocks. My scalp shrinks against my head.

'You're sure you've checked the house?' he says quietly, but he is pulling out his phone.

'I'm going to check again.' I unlock the front door and fly upstairs, clearing the laundry in one great stride, taking the

stairs three at a time, calling her name, her name, her name.
'Abi? Abi. Abi. Abi. Abi.'

I look under the beds. I look in the laundry basket – empty.
I emptied it. In the wardrobes. The bath. The shower cubicle.
I have already looked.

'Abi?' I run downstairs, grab the banister and lever myself
over the last few steps. 'Abi? Please come out, love. Mummy's
getting worried.'

Matt is striding from room to room, phone at his ear. 'Abi?'
he calls out. 'Abi, come out, darling. If you're hiding, it's time
to come out now, Mummy and Daddy are getting worried.'
Then, 'Yes, hello. Yes, police, please.'

The thump, thump, thump of my heart. Everything is
white – bleached out, strange. Everything is slow.

Matt steps out of the house, stops on the square porch. I
am cringing and sobbing in the bright hall. The back of my
husband is a silhouette. How thin he looks, bent over his
phone in his black kit.

Second by second. Beat by beat. A clock. A metronome.
A heart.

His head twitches.

'Yes,' he says. 'Hello, yes, I need to report a missing child.'

CHAPTER THREE

Ava

Almost a year ago and yesterday all at once. No matter how much time passes, that day will always be yesterday and I will have to make my peace with that somehow. Yesterday and everything I should have done, would have done differently, exists in my every moment, its shadow dark and long. I'm fighting off yesterday every second of today and tomorrow and forever. The laundry tumbles from my arms. I fall after it. The pushchair is empty. The front door is open. I left it open. Me. Over and over again. My ignorant self. My stupid self. My selfish, selfish self. I have to watch myself, her. I have to stare at her from the other side of a glass wall, fingertips white: myself that morning – ignorant, stupid, selfish. I push my hands to that glass and I shout: 'Ava! Forget your online life, just today. Forget how lonely you feel. Go downstairs. Go now. Be with your little girl. She is enough.'

But she doesn't hear me shouting. She doesn't hear my fists pounding on the glass wall.

'Close the door. Close it, Ava. Please! Close the door.'

Tears are endless. I am a woman who has a daughter. I am a woman who had a daughter. Both those things are true. I live in the past; I survive in the present. I was she; I am me. My daughter is alive; she is dead. She is simply lost; she is gone forever. Her heart is the tick, tick, tick of the metronome on my piano top, stopped still in my silent living room now that all music has stopped. My daughter is a perfect cadence. My daughter is the dissonant devil's chord, that jarring combination of notes played deliberately to unsettle, to leave the listener tense, hanging. So I have been left, waiting for resolution that never comes. I am hanging – yesterday, today, forever.

The neighbours are coming out of their houses. They fold their arms. They look about. The seconds. The beats. A black weight gathering in my gut. Thickening there. Lodging there.

Each day is new. If today goes badly, tomorrow will be new again. And so on. I was ill for a time. That's the favoured term. *When you were ill.* Then I was in a clinic, my belly rounding with new life while I tried to hold on to my own. Now I am at home. My therapy sessions are down to once a week. Trauma counselling. CBT. Stop checking the door. Stop, if you can. Yesterday is a long, dark shadow. I'm trying to see my way forward in this darkness.

Fred is three months old. He keeps me alive; this is not an exaggeration. It's possible he's all that keeps me alive. His sister is a two-year-old girl in a picture frame. Matt tells me we must try to move on. He tells me that Fred will help us because we have to be strong for him. New life brings new hope, that's what Matt says. He clings to these aphorisms because he has to, and mostly I forgive him. He doesn't want me to be this sad. No one does. But if anyone else tells me that God only gives us what we can handle, or that everything happens for a reason, I swear I will punch them in the jaw. I will knock every tooth from their head. I will spit in their stupid face.

I never used to have thoughts like that.

I used to be kind, witty. Kindness has melted, wit become sarcasm. If I met me now, I would hold me at arm's length. Something edgy about her, I would think. Not sure I can trust her. I never used to understand why anyone would be mean about or to another person. Now I do.

Fred is smaller than Abi was at this age, but he will soon transfer to a buggy. His pram is the one I used for Abi before she was ready for the pushchair. I wanted a new pram for Fred, but prams are expensive and Matt is right when he says that's not how you forget the past, by throwing away everything that belonged to it. The past is a reminder, good or bad. To destroy it is to destroy its lessons. This is what he says. For me, it's not that easy.

'Thing is, I don't want to forget,' I tell Barbara, snivelling my way through entire boxes of tissues. 'I just don't want to remember every second and feel like it was my fault. I want to be able to look at her picture and stop hoping the doorbell will go and that someone will be there with her in their arms saying, here, I found her. She's safe. She's well. She was existing this whole time in some alternative reality, free from harm.'

Even as I say all this, the images come, hazy and pastel-shaded pink and blue. Abi throws back her head and laughs – how she laughs with the warm sun on her hair. How she collapses with giggles into my arms. Unharmed, untouched, happy as the day she left.

'I want to imagine her into reality,' I say to her, poor Barbara, paid to listen to all this. 'I want to stop imagining where she might be… because if she didn't die, then someone took her. If I could just remove that possibility, I could at least grieve.'

Barbara nods and listens. She knows I'm working towards a past tense. When I say the same to Matt, he listens too. But then he pushes harder. He says: 'We have to accept the facts, darling. We have to move on or we'll be living our lives in limbo.'

I don't reply. It is not a conversation I can stand to have. And I will be buying a new pushchair for Fred. There's a limit.

Fred was already on the way when Abi disappeared. I thought the foggy brain and the nausea were exhaustion from disturbed sleep and the endless activity of life with a small, bright, curious child. I took the thickening of my waist as a sign that, post-baby, it was harder now to keep the weight off, that perhaps my shape had changed. But then my period was late and so, the day before she went missing, that Sunday morning, I snuck into the bathroom and did a test and there he was: two blue lines on a white stick. I yelped, my stomach fizzing as I ran downstairs. The kitchen already smelled of the slow-roast pork Matt had put in before dawn; the vegetables were chopped and waiting in pans in cold water, the table set for Neil and Bella coming for super-late lunch. Abi was in the back garden, helping Matt with his bike, which was suspended on a stand on the lawn. It was sunny but cool outside. He had fixed her up with a bucket of soapy water and a cloth and she was washing the wheels with deadly serious intent.

'Matt!'

Our eyes met over Abi's little head. I held up the test, felt my eyes fill at the smile that spread across his face.

'What's that?' Abi was pointing at the stick. She had on her yellow wellies and pink shorts, and the front of her stripy jumper was soaking wet where she'd spilt the filthy water. Her face was a little grubby too, smudged with dirt from the bike wheel.

I shoved the test in my pocket. 'Just a toothbrush that broke,' I said, rolling my eyes, but she'd already gone back to her task.

I glanced again at Matt, saw in his eyes the promise of a snatched celebratory hug later, an excited conversation that evening after Neil and Bella had gone, lying in bed guessing at when we thought it might have happened, because back then, there were so many possibilities.

But mostly I remember that I felt joy. And if I remember it, it means I was capable of feeling it.

We were supposed to be having a barbecue that day, but September had brought a chill to the air so Matt decided on a roast dinner instead. He always took care of the food. I'm the table-setter, the washer-upper. He lets me peel and chop, but that's about it. We had drinks at the breakfast bar while Neil and Bella showered Abi with the usual attention.

'What've you got there?' Neil pointed to her chest. When she looked down, he flicked his finger up, catching her on the nose. She laughed, even though he did this every time.

'Come, NeeNee.' She grabbed his hand and dragged him off to the living room – him all eye-rolling, mugging like he was under arrest, even though we all knew he loved her wanting to monopolise him in this way. She wanted him to build her train track. He always used to make a figure of eight for her, then sit on the floor pushing the Thomas the Tank Engine set along the tracks, making choo-choo noises. He was so much better at playing with her than I was. All he needed was a bottomless supply of lager.

We weren't going to tell them so soon. But when we sat at the table and I refused a glass of red wine, Bella asked: 'Aren't you even having a glass with your meal?'

No flies on Bella. I had declined a pre-dinner fizz on the excuse of a poor night's sleep, which was part of the truth.

'Ah, no,' I said, feeling myself blush.

Bella's eyes rounded. She glanced at Matt, back at me, and smiled. 'Are you?'

I laughed.

'Oh my God, you are!' She had tears in her eyes, which I took for delight.

'Congratulations, guys,' Neil said, his glass raised. 'Really delighted for you both.'

A silence fell. I couldn't pinpoint what had happened. I still can't. But it was awkward, definitely. At the time, I thought perhaps they were offended that we'd left them to guess like that when they were our closest friends.

'We were going to wait till I was further along,' I said. It was almost an apology.

Eventually Neil made some comment about how delicious the meat was, Matt answering him hastily with some inane reply about how many hours it had been in, at what temperature, while Bella drained her glass and poured herself another. And when I think back to that day now, the thought of them coming over at all seems so alien. They haven't been to the house since that day, not like that. I was ill and then not up to it, then they came over briefly when Fred was born but I wasn't able to face polite conversation, and now, perhaps, too much time has passed.

Tragedy is like an infectious disease. People avoid you. They don't want to catch it.

Thankfully, Fred is an easy baby, easier than Abi was. Sometimes I think he was sent to heal us, that some higher force knew we would need him. And he sleeps, hallelujah! It's as if he knows that he has to tread carefully over the eggshells his parents have become.

New life brings new hope, Matt says. But it is hope that will kill me in the end.

From the pram, Fred coos softly, as if to call me back to him.

'Hey.' Matt is on the stairs. He has on his kit, ready to cycle to work, and is staring into his phone, thumbing a text. 'You were miles away.'

'Oh, sorry.'

'You OK?'

'Yes, you?'

'Just texting Neil,' he says. 'Might go for a run with him later if he's up for it.'

'Good idea.'

This is what passes for a conversation between Matt and me these days – careful exchanges in the Abi-less rooms of our home. He and Neil are training for a triathlon – childhood friends trying to stay close in the aftermath of unspeakable disaster. Not that Matt has said this; that now their friendship requires a concerted effort where once it was as natural as family.

'What's that?' Matt says.

I follow his gaze to a thick cream parchment envelope on the welcome mat. No stamp.

Mr and Mrs Atkins, it says, in an elegant purple hand.

Matt is at my shoulder by the time I've picked it up. 'What is it?'

'I don't know yet. I haven't got X-ray vision.' I'm harsh with him. I don't mean to be, didn't used to be. I tear open the envelope.

'An invitation?' Matt asks.

'Looks like it.'

Dear Neighbour,

Join us Saturday, 31 August for a housewarming party at
90 Riverside Drive.

There will be food, drink and, hopefully, merriment.

From 8 p.m. (No kids, sorry!)

RSVP

Best regards,

Johnnie, Jennifer, Jasmine and Cosima Lovegood

Under the typeface, Jennifer has written in the same flowing script as the envelope, *Hope you can make it, love, Jen.*

'Next door,' Matt states the obvious.

The paper crunches in my grip.

'A week on Saturday. We'll be able to have a nosy at their new kitch— What're you doing? Hey, don't screw it up!'

'What? You're not actually going to go?'

'Ava.' Gently he takes the ends of my fingers, prises them open and lifts the crumpled ball out of my hand. His soft brown eyes are on mine as they were that morning. *It's no one's fault, Ava. People leave front doors open all the time.* 'Come on. It might be nice. A nice thing to do.'

'You can't be serious?'

He puts the screwed-up invitation on the side before returning his gaze to me. Palms open and hovering at his waist, he leans his head a little to one side before he speaks.

'Look,' he says.

'Don't *look* me.' My words cling, trembling, to the artificially flat tone of my voice.

He raises his hands higher. 'I'm not. I'm just… I know it'll be tough; I'm not saying it won't be. I'm not saying it won't be hard, all right? All right? But just for one second, try to believe it might be… if not fun, then interesting? It might allow us to think about something else, just for a short time. I mean, it's not a trendy underground bar opening, but it *will* be the party of the year, you know, in suburban terms. Everyone's *desperate* to see inside. This whole street has been talking about the Lovegoods' refurb for months. Pete Shepherd's going to have some sort of embolism. Honestly, he's been giving me a running commentary on it since it started; he knows more about their kitchen extension than Neil does. I bet he's started getting ready already, probably got his tie on.'

He smiles but even in his smile I can see that he's disappointed not to have made me laugh even a little.

'Honestly, hon. This could be good for us. Everyone will be going.'

'Exactly! That's exactly my point. I can't face the neighbours as it is, let alone all of them in one room. What the hell am I going to say to them? What the hell are they going to say to me? What can anyone say to me? Surely you can see that?'

'I can – of course I can. But we have to talk to them sometime. Might be good to get them all out of the way in one evening. This way we can show our faces and then next time you see them it won't be so bad.'

I stare into his eyes to see if he's joking. He isn't, apparently.

'Their little one's turning three next week,' I say. 'Cosima.'

He runs his hand down the length of my arm. 'I know.'

'Abi would've been three by now.'

'Don't.'

'They would have walked to school together. Eventually.' Tears run hot down my face. A great bottomless well bubbling up, overflowing.

'The party doesn't have to be about Abi,' he almost whispers. 'It could be about us going forward, trying to make that step. And their kitchen will be spectacular, I guarantee it. Like something out of *Hello!* magazine.'

I feel so heavy. So tired. I don't care. I don't care about anything he's just said.

'I can't,' I say eventually. 'I can't go to any party. It's too soon. I'm sorry.' I press my forehead against his chest and feel his arms close around me.

'Shh.' He presses his lips to my hair. 'Don't cry. We don't have to go if you don't want to. You don't have to do anything you don't want to.'

I stay in his arms, but the walls of me are thickening, hardening. Don't have to do anything I don't want to? I have to do what I don't want to every single minute of every single day of my life. I don't want to relive the beats of that morning, but I do. I don't want to have to watch over and over the flashing film reel of it all, the constant, replaying torture. I don't want to have to put my new baby boy in his sister's pram, here in this surreal not-quite-present, knowing that he once had a sister, that he might still have a sister, somewhere out there, but that I, *I* lost her. That I left the front door open and let her wander out to who knows where. I don't want to walk out of that same front door every day, stop myself from triple-, quadruple-checking that it's locked behind me when I get home. I don't want to have to stop on the street and pass the time of day with people who know what happened, who read those horrible stories in the news, who offer kind words laced with intangible hints that plume like dark smoke around my questionable standards, my slow reactions, my fitness as a mother. I don't want to stand there trying not to listen to all that they're not saying, trying not to hear the creak of their necks as they cock their heads in sympathy that may or may not be genuine. I don't want to have to put one foot in front of the other. I don't want to have to breathe in and breathe out. I don't want to stay clean, eat, live. I don't want to wash my fucking hair.

What I want is to say all of that, now, to Matt. But I don't. It's not fair. It's me that left the door open, not him. And he has never once, in all the tears and the rage and the confusion that followed, blamed me for it.

CHAPTER FOUR

Ava

I'm taking the laundry out of the washing basket. Armfuls of sheets, shirts, pillowcases. Focusing on finding the steps one by one. The handles of the pushchair come into view, the mesh back. No Abi. I fall. Land on the bundle of dirty linen. Right myself, rub my hands. Stumble into the hall, calling her name. The house opposite. The lamp post. I can see the lamp post.

The front door. The front door is wide open.

'If only I'd shut the front door,' I sob, hours later, to Matt.

He holds me tight. We rock each other softly. 'Ava, you can't do that to yourself. Don't think about it. Come on, Ava, you'll drive yourself crazy.'

Beat by beat. Sometimes the seconds jump around. Sometimes the minutes mix themselves up. Matt stands thin and silhouetted in the doorway, making the call. He turns, slides the phone back into the hidden breast pocket of his jacket, his body slumped against the wall, his head bowed.

'They're sending someone now.'

I can see him. I see him, constantly, over and over. Second by second, lowering the phone from his ear. They're sending someone now. Face set in shock. Body a question mark. His expression my own. Endlessly.

'I thought you had to wait for someone to be considered officially missing?'

He shakes his head and replies only, 'They're on their way.'

Later, there were bite marks on my fist. Perhaps I bit my knuckles as I ran out again onto the street. Can I remember it? I'm not sure. Can I see myself running down our street, biting my own hand? I can, but maybe it's a mental image made by the marks – a deduction. What I know is that as soon as Matt called the police, I ran back to Neil and Bella's. What I can see is myself battering once again on their door, weeping frantically, full of bitter justifications for why this cannot be happening, cannot be happening to me. I have done my best, I really have. I have tried so hard to get everything right, read all the pamphlets, trained in first aid. I know how to do the Heimlich manoeuvre, how to give mouth-to-mouth, how to put someone in the recovery position.

But I didn't close the front door and no amount of safety literature can reverse that.

I bang on Neil and Bella's door again, lower my mouth to the letter box and push it open with my fingertips. 'Neil? Bel? It's Ava. Help. I need help.'

Ear to the door, I bang it with my fist. The discordant wail of a siren. Another second. I realise that sound is for me. The door opens. Neil's hair is wet. He is pulling up one strap of his white overalls, his face etched in concern.

'Ava?'

'Have you got Abi?'

He shakes his head a fraction. 'No, why? Has something happened?'

I'm backing away, stumbling a little. 'Abi's missing. I thought she might have… I've got to go. The police are here.'

'Missing?' Neil's features crowd, an expression between confusion and panic. 'Police? Christ.'

He's running with me. I can hear him panting.

'Is Matt there?' he says breathlessly.

'Yes, yes, he's come back. I knocked for you before.'

'Did you? Sorry, babe, I was in the shower.'

More neighbours have come out onto the road. Concern fills their bodies, informs their movements: arms fold, hands shield eyes from the weak sun, heads bend together, ask each other what's going on. A patrol car is parking outside my house. The blue light flashes, and stops.

'Have you seen Abi?' I ask my neighbours as we run past. 'My little girl? She's wandered off.'

'No, sorry.'

'Have you seen my little girl?'

'No, sorry.'

What do I know about that morning? Nothing. Only dread obliterating all coherent thought. Morphing time. Blurring edges. I was I am blind. I was I am deaf. I was I am senseless. Matt was Matt is talking to two police officers on our front path, the blaze of black and fluorescent yellow. The spark of radios, a blue-and-yellow-chequered car was, is parked in our road. Neil was, is with me. He has his arm around me. He is telling me to stay calm, that we'll find her.

'Don't worry, babe,' he says. 'Don't worry.'

'This is my wife, Ava,' Matt is saying now, yesterday, today, a year ago, over and over again. The uniformed police officers on my front path are one woman, one man. Their radios cough and crackle. Black and white. Fluorescent yellow. The air has thinned, shrunk my skin tight.

'Hello.' My voice is small and near, strange and far.

'And this is Neil,' Matt says. 'Our close friend. He's Abi's godfather.'

Neil holds out his hand, shakes theirs. 'All right,' he says. 'Hi.'

And then we're in the kitchen: me, Matt and the two police officers. We have had to come through the side gate because the front door has been taped off, the hallway now a potential crime scene. My hallway. Our home. The officers have radioed for more units but I don't know if I know this yet. Later, I will find out that they have called for search dogs, and for a duty officer, whose name is Bill Simmonds.

But not yet.

Now, we're sitting at the breakfast bar. I want to scream at them not to sit down, how can anyone sit down – my daughter is out there somewhere and we have no time. We have already lost so much time. The man, whose name is PC Simon Peak, has taken out a notepad. He rests it on his knee. The woman is still standing. Her radio barks with static. She takes it and wanders out through the patio doors into the back garden, around the side of the house.

'Mrs Atkins,' PC Peak says. 'If you can tell me exactly what happened.'

I begin, as best I can, but I haven't got far before Neil appears at the back door, holding out his hand. His eyes are wet, his face flushed. 'This was outside on the road.'

Lifeless in his hand slumps my daughter's plush toy. Mr Sloth.

'Oh my God.' The words leave me in a rising squeal. I cover my mouth.

Matt is on his feet. 'Where?'

'Just… at the edge of the pavement. Behind your car – out front.' Neil's brow knits. His eyes are pale blue pools of sorrow. He hands me the cuddly sloth. It is wet. I pick two mulched leaves from its fur and press the toy to my forehead, then to my nose. I inhale it but it smells cold, mossy. It doesn't smell like Abi.

'I'll need to take that,' Peak says.

I can't see. 'What's happened to her?'

'Looks like she definitely headed out,' Matt says.

'Mrs Atkins? Mrs Atkins?' Peak is looking at me. I know he has a camera on his lapel because he told me so, though when this was, I'm not sure.

'Sorry, what?' I say, thinking that Neil must have gone out again, because he isn't here anymore.

'I was asking what time she went missing – can you remember?'

'I went upstairs a little before eight. But she was perfectly happy so it would have taken her a while to become restless… she was completely settled, so let's see, I came down at about quarter past eight? I can't say exactly, not to the minute, but I'd guess the earliest she could have left would be five, ten past, but she would have called me. I would have heard her if she was getting impatient, you know? But she was definitely clipped into her pushchair. I thought I'd closed the front door but it must have banged open when I shut it.'

'Can you tell me briefly what happened?'

'I came downstairs. Her buggy was empty. The front door was open.'

He scribbles. I try not to be distracted by another siren in the street. I think I can hear Neil outside, talking to someone: businesslike, proactive, his voice sails through the open window above the sink.

'And then?' The police officer is still looking at me. Peak, his name is. 'I'm not taking a statement, Mrs Atkins, I just need to gather as much information as I can, as quickly as I can. You're doing really well.'

Sometimes the beats are episodic. Seconds go missing. Sometimes minutes get jumbled up. Matt remembers things differently. We argue as to what happened when.

It's DS Bill Simmonds now. Mid-morning. His hair is dirty blonde. We are still in the kitchen and I am aware of repeating myself. Simmonds is telling me they're conducting a door-to-door. He is explaining how they will organise the search, how it will spread progressively outwards, our home the nucleus.

'Sarge.' The woman interrupts, the one from earlier. I have forgotten her name. She is standing at the back door. Her hair is brown and tied back in a messy bun. 'The PolSA'll be half an hour.'

I look from one to the other. 'What's a PolSA?'

'It's the specialist search unit,' Simmonds tells me.

'And the dogs are on the way,' the woman adds.

'Dogs?' I say. 'Dogs, oh my God.'

This is escalating; it's escalating too quickly.

DS Simmonds shifts position. 'Try not to be alarmed, Mrs Atkins. In cases of missing children, it's procedure to make use of these resources the moment we get the call. The dogs are trained to trace your little girl, and the specialist unit are here to help find her too.'

A sob escapes me. My head pulses, hot and white. 'Oh my God. Oh my God.'

Matt is rubbing my back. He has been out on his bike, but now he is sitting on the stool next to mine. 'Shh, shh, shh, come on.' He is trying to be brave but he sounds like a boy.

DS Simmonds speaks to the female officer, low and brisk. 'Check the gardens, yeah? Garages, sheds, as well as the houses. Ask if they've seen anyone driving too fast, any cars they didn't recognise, anyone they thought looked suspicious, out of place, anyone seen a little girl, blue coat, cream bobble hat. Let's get a photo sorted. Let me know if anyone won't cooperate.'

'I think a photo's sorted, Sarge. I'll check.'

'Mrs Atkins.' He has turned back to me. I know because his voice is louder. When I glance up from my lap, he is looking at me. 'I know this is hard, but if you can try to talk us through it in as much detail as you can. We just want to make the search as effective as possible.'

I tell him, like I told PC Peak. I tell him as best I can. He scribbles, tips his head and talks into his radio.

'Wolfy,' he says, 'check for CCTV; I repeat, check for CCTV.'

'There's no CCTV,' I say. 'I don't think there is. Not on this street anyway. There might be on Thameside. It's not that kind of…' I look at Matt. There are pink tracks down his cheeks where the dust from the cycle ride has been washed away. The tense set of his shoulders makes me aware of my own. It's like we've both been dropped from a height; it's taking a conscious effort of will just to hold our bones in place.

DS Simmonds stands up, addresses himself to Matt. 'And you came back?'

'Yeah. Ava called me and I came back.'

'You saw your daughter when you left for work?'

'Yeah. Yeah. Of course.'

'And where were you when you got the call?'

'At Richmond Bridge? On the towpath. I got a puncture, otherwise I'd have been at work by then.'

He nods. 'All right, well I suggest you both stay here, in case little Abi returns or anyone tries to contact you.'

Matt takes a step forward. 'Can't I help search?'

I stand up too. 'I want to search. I need to find her. Please.'

Matt grips my arm. He's about to say something – something about me being pregnant, I'm sure – when another woman appears in the back garden, crossing in front of the glass sliding doors. She is not in uniform. She is big and tall and she is in my kitchen, but I have no idea who she is.

'Ava Atkins?' She holds out her hand when I nod. 'I'm Detective Constable Lorraine Stephens. I'm your family liaison officer.' Her hand is warm and dry. She has large dark-green eyes and short grey hair. 'I'll be here with you, all right? I'll be here with you while the police do their job and we'll keep you updated with any developments.'

Matt is following Simmonds out of the house. I hear footsteps, someone running back up the side path. Matt reappears at the back door.

'Bella's got a photo of Abi from yesterday, they're going to print it off.' His glance rests on my belly. 'Will you be OK?'

I nod, my eyes clouding over once again. 'Go.'

CHAPTER FIVE

Matt

The patrol car is parked out front. At the end of the street, the sight of blue-and-white tape winds him. There are cones on the tarmac. Three police vans have parked on Thameside Lane, their back doors open, a clutch of police officers in conference, glancing about.

Neil is with them, pointing towards the near end of the street. Another siren announces yet another police van, which parks on the double yellows a little further down, hazards flashing. Two guys in naval combats and waterproof jackets jump out of the front and make their way to the back. One of them opens the door to two German shepherds, tongues pink and lolling, eyes brown and quick.

Matt bends double, clutching at his stomach. 'Oh God.'

Neil claps him on the back. 'Come on, mate. We'll find her.'

Matt makes himself breathe. Sweat prickles all over his scalp, his face. When he's sure he's not actually going to vomit, he rises slowly.

'Sir?' One of the dog handlers is at his side. 'My name's Ian Mitchell, all right? I'm going to have to ask you for an item of your daughter's clothing. Something recently worn?'

Matt stares at him a moment. Realisation dawns. Another lurch of nausea.

'Of course,' he says.

Neil squeezes his shoulder. 'I'm going to help search, all right?'

'Sure.'

Neil jogs back into Riverside Drive. Matt follows, leading the dog handlers back to the house. He leaves them on the pavement, telling them he won't be a moment. A policewoman stands sentry beside the taped-off front door. He heads round the side, across the back of the house, to where Ava is sitting with her back to him, opposite the family liaison officer on one of the two small sofas by the patio doors.

'Matt?' His name is loaded with tears. She has turned to look at him and her face and eyes are red.

He gestures towards the interior of the house. 'I've just got to grab something.'

She nods. He runs upstairs. At the sight of Abi's room, nausea rises again, so strong it seems impossible he won't be sick. He pulls the covers from Abi's cot bed and pushes his face into the soft folds. They smell of her, though he can't say in words what that smell is. He grabs her pyjamas. Ava has folded them neatly on the mattress. Abi doesn't have a pillow; she threw it out with a scowl the first time she tried it – *me no like!* The pyjamas are pink with little grey cartoon elephants. The smell of her is more intense – her skin, her baby soap, sweat from her sleeping body, oh God.

He carries them downstairs. Ava is facing away from him, but still he hurries past, the pyjamas behind his back. She can't see this. No mother should have to see this. Even he has to look away while the dogs take turns to sniff at his daughter's pyjamas. It is an invasion. A violation. It can't be real. It cannot.

Ian, the dog handler, hands him back the pyjamas and thanks him.

Understanding himself dismissed, Matt returns to the house and somehow manages to get the pyjamas back upstairs. When he returns to the kitchen, Ava is crying. The family liaison officer – Lorraine, was it? – has moved to sit beside her and is holding her hand. It is a strangely intimate sight, a woman he doesn't know sitting so close to his wife, holding her hand.

'Do you need anything?' he asks, feeling something dropping inside him – the weight, perhaps, of his own helplessness. 'I could make some tea or something.'

Ava shakes her head. 'No. No tea.'

He hovers. He wants to say something to comfort her. More, he wants to bring Abi home, bring her home in his arms and say, look, Ava, I found her. I found our little girl.

He meets Lorraine's eye and cocks his head: *I'm going.*

She nods.

'I've got my phone,' he adds.

Outside, a German shepherd sniffs and circles at the end of the Lovegoods' drive while his handler looks on. Ian Mitchell is at the front of Matt and Ava's house, his dog sniffing and pawing at the back tyre of their old Volkswagen. The rain has started again. Not lashing down, but heavy enough. No one appears to notice.

'Have they found something?' Matt asks.

'There's a scent here.' Ian nods at the gutter. 'Your mate Mr Johnson found her toy here, is that right?'

Matt nods. 'Yes. Yes, he did. He brought it in. It's in the house. Or they might have taken it.'

'No!' It's Ava's voice. Matt turns to see her running from the side return; she is at the front of the house now, pushing past him, heading for the other dog. The other dog is sniffing the ground at the end of Johnnie Lovegood's driveway.

'You're wasting your time,' Ava is yelling, all trace of her usual cool demeanour utterly gone. 'That's where she fell. She fell there, she cut her knee right there and got blood on the pavement. Trust me, you're wasting your time; please, please, you're wasting your time.'

The dog handlers exchange a glance. Matt doesn't like what he reads there.

'Mrs Atkins, if you can just come back inside…' Lorraine is ushering his wife away with a carefully placed arm around her shoulder. The air fills with the crackle of walkie-talkies. Lorraine's persuasive tone reaches him without the sense.

Ava bucks, her arms flail, her hands close into fists. She shakes Lorraine off, turns to him, her face desperate. 'But she fell! Matt! Tell them! They could be out looking for her instead of sniffing round here. They need to search up by the river. Tell them!'

'My wife is right,' Matt says. 'She fell exactly there, this morning. I was there. She cut her knee and it bled all over. She grazed her hands too. But that was before. Look, shall I show you the way to the lock? I think it'd be better to look where she's most likely to have gone.'

Both dogs are sniffing now in the gutter; one jumps back a little, barking.

'That's where we found her toy – you know that,' he says to the handlers, fighting to keep his voice level. He knows he should let them do their job, but they're going backwards and they don't know what he knows and they're not listening, for Christ's sake, they're not hearing what Ava's telling them. 'Surely we're wasting time here?' he insists. 'Didn't you hear my wife?'

They nod, but it's a kiss-off. The dogs sniff around, trail back, back along the pavement. At the end of next door's drive they stop again, sniffing, circling, sniffing, barking. Another female officer swabs the pavement, puts the swab in a tiny vial.

'You'll find blood there, I can tell you that right now. It's Abi's. From her knee. She fell. How many times?' Feeling his temper rise, Matt bites his tongue.

The dogs and their handlers continue to the end of the road. The end of the road where he last saw his daughter. They stop at the corner, bark, sniff the ground like crazed coke addicts.

'That'll be her blood too. She sat down right there earlier this morning.'

A raindrop drips from his brow. The rain has thickened. How far could she have gone? Quite far, if she took off at a clip, if she knew she was being naughty. At the thought of her in mischievous mode, his eyes fill. That gleam in her eyes – he can see her, oh God, he can see her as if she's right there, the challenge of her cheeky smile, the smile she always gives him when he pretends to look away while she takes a bite of his toast, when he looks back and pretends to be shocked and says, 'Hey, who's been eating my toast?' Oh God, he can see her laughing hysterically, mouth full, shaking her head: not me, Daddy. Not me.

He grabs his bike and cycles towards the river, tears running with the rain. Outside a terraced house adjacent to the chandlery, two women in expensive wellies and raincoats are deep in conversation, their dogs on leads.

'Hi, hi, sorry, excuse me, I'm looking for my little girl. Have you seen a little girl? She's two years old. Blue coat. Cream woolly hat?'

They stare back, a look of mild concern. Kids wander off all the time, he reads. She'll turn up.

'We're on Riverside Drive if you see anything. Number eighty-eight. Her name's Abi.'

They nod, their expressions still little more than worry.

'Hope you find her,' one of them calls out as he rides on.

At the mouth of the bridge, brown ducks reach their beaks to the water, dip their heads beneath the surface. Abi loves to feed those ducks. The water is high, but still, still it's quite shallow. The river's calm, surely she couldn't have…

No. No.

Through a steady oncoming parade of pedestrians, he wheels his bike over the footbridge, over the bottle-green water. Yes, the river is high, very high. Abi would have no chance, she…

No.

The buzz of an engine. There, on the river, an RNLI boat speeds towards the lock.

His vision blackens. He bends and retches but nothing comes up. He spits on the ground, grips the railings while his head clears.

'Excuse me.' One of the women has crossed the bridge and is waving at him. 'Excuse me! Did you say a cream bobble hat?'

'Yes,' he says, wheeling his bike around. 'Yes, cream. Woolly hat, yes. Did you see her?'

'I think there was one on the wall.' She gestures towards Thameside Lane and together they return to where he left them. 'It was on the wall either of the Thames View or the Fisherman's Arms, or failing that...'

He doesn't hear the rest. He has clipped his feet in, is already pedalling, calling his thanks over his shoulder.

The rain is lighter now – a gently insistent mist. There is nothing on either of the pub walls. He cycles slowly, eyes on stalks, breathing shallow, past the flickering tape at the end of his road, down, down towards the school. If she did tag along with another family, she would, could possibly, have wandered down this way. But when he reaches Kingston Bridge, he turns back. This is ridiculous; she would not, could not have come this far. It wouldn't occur to her. The hat is not on any wall, not on this side, not on the other.

But it *was* there.

That means Abi left the street. It means she got at least that far. A hat doesn't fall onto a wall. That means someone found her hat on the ground and put it in a safe place, where it could be found. People round here do that; they take care of one another. No one would steal a little girl's hat. If it has gone, that means one of the searchers must have found it. If Abi has gone, it means that someone has found her. If someone has found her, lost and upset, they will have done the right thing, of course they will: taken her to a safe place. This is a neighbourhood where people put lost hats and gloves on walls. This is a neighbourhood where people return lost children. Even if Abi can't remember her address, whoever finds her will simply call the police. He has made her rehearse where she lives, is pretty sure she can give at least the road. But it will take the police a while to coordinate, budget cuts being what they are. Yes, whoever found that hat will be part of the search. No one round here would take a hat. No one round here would leave a lone toddler on her own. No one round here would take a child.

Ninety-nine per cent of people are good.

CHAPTER SIX

Matt

Matt lifts Fred and lowers him, lifts and lowers, enjoying the daft gurgling noises he makes, the way his hands clasp at his chest, his wise old man expression.

'Soon have you out on the footy field,' he says. 'Or rugby if your Uncle Neil has anything to do with it.'

He hands the baby back to Ava before stretching out his hamstrings. Last time he didn't warm up was the last time he didn't warm up – a torn hamstring hurts like hell and it actually made the skin go black on the back of his thigh.

'See you in a bit.' He kisses Ava on the head, tries not to notice the stale, oily smell of her hair, to wonder if she has changed back into her pyjamas or if she never got dressed in the first place.

Neil is already outside his house, one hand pressed against his van. When he sees Matt, he straightens up and gives a brisk wave.

Matt jogs to a standstill and waits while Neil ties his laces, one stocky, slightly porcine leg propped on the white stone slab that tops the dwarf wall in front of his house, his thick torso bent over. Now into his thirties, he's getting love handles. No time for rugby anymore, not with the hours he works, and maybe a few too many pints of a weekend, not to mention the Friday-night takeaways.

He stands, claps and chafes his hands together.

'You OK?' Matt asks.

'Knackered,' Neil says, matter-of-fact, and spits on the pavement. 'Work's been mad.' His eyes are red – yes, he looks overworked.

'We'll take it slow to start then.'

After a cursory warm-up – Neil is a quick knee-bend, spit on the ground and off we go man – they begin to jog, no faster than a brisk walk at first, heading left down Main Street.

'Job in Surbiton,' Neil says once they hit their stride. 'Loft, kitchen extension, then, get this, they want all the internal walls on the ground floor taken down. All of them. No walls at all, just the staircase. No hallway, nothing.'

'Can you do that? I mean, I know you can, but in a domestic dwelling?'

'Structural engineer's looking at it.'

'Johnnie?'

'God, no.' He spits again, as if for emphasis. 'Some guy lives up in Sunbury, seems like a good bloke actually. Thorough, you know?'

Matt nods. 'So he thinks he can do it?'

Neil sniffs, the deft head-flick of a footballer, a third spit into the gutter. 'Can't see why not. Enough steels will hold anything up. Just can't understand why they don't want a hallway. I mean, where are they going to put all the crap, the coats and shoes and all that?'

'You can go too minimalist, I suppose,' Matt offers.

'Too right. It's a house not a bloody art gallery. And it's Surbiton, not New York, know what I mean? All a bit marble floor in a council flat if you ask me.'

The residential part of the main road recedes; a bus rumbles past the scattered shopfronts, the Indian takeaway, a chippy, a nail bar and two pubs – almost the sum total of Hampton Wick village. Out on the street, it's dead, the only evidence of life a group of four old men smoking roll-ups outside the Woodcutter. Matt and Neil continue, tacitly agreeing to head under the railway bridge and back up Thameside. Any further and they'll have to cross Kingston Bridge and run up the riverbank. Which means crossing by Teddington Lock.

And that's not an option.

'We need to have you guys round,' Matt says, out of habit. 'Maybe a takeaway on Friday?'

'I'll check with Bel. Work's been mad.'

No, then. As usual. 'So you said.'

'How's your work going anyway?'

'Good. Busy.'

'You still doing that place in Kensington?'

'Almost finished. Looks good. I'll send you some pics.'

'What did you end up doing?'

Neil's interest is real. When they were at school, he used to joke that he was all good in practice; Matt all good in theory. This, in fact, has manifested itself exactly – Neil on the building side, Matt a city architect – something that amuses them both. But Matt is thankful that he's not a domestic architect. He loves Neil, he does, but Neil doesn't like being told what to do by anyone, let alone his best mate, so it would have pushed things had they worked together. As it is, they can keep their professional lives apart without any awkwardness.

It was Ava who pointed out to Matt that Neil's authority issues might stem from never having known his father, from being the man of the house since he was old enough to remember, although Matt has never spoken about this with him. Certainly it is this independent spirit more than anything that has spurred him on to work so hard and start his own business. He is – has always been – frank about wanting to be his own boss and to earn as much money as he possibly can. By twenty-eight, when Matt was barely qualified, Neil had installed his mother in a new-build riverside flat, for which he paid cash by borrowing against the mortgage he took out on the former family home. By contrast, Matt's parents sold their house to him at a ridiculously competitive price when they moved back north and helped him substantially with the deposit. As it stands, neither of them could possibly afford to move to the street they live on now had they not lived there since childhood.

'The front is all that's left of the original,' Matt says against the hum of a passing car and the whiff of stale alcohol from Neil's deepening breaths. 'The entire front is Victorian, London brick, then you go in and boom! Glass, clean lines, white colour palette; you'd think it was a brand-new building. Which it is. Apart from the front. You have to go inside to realise it's all a facade.'

'Wicked. Sounds awesome. So will that help you with the directorship?'

'Hopefully. We'll have to see. Bidding for a cool project in the East End right now, an old brewery, so we'll see if that comes through.'

Eight kilometres later, up and around Twickenham and back down again, they duck back along Thameside Lane, past the playing fields, and finally right into Riverside Drive. The Lovegoods' larger detached house stands at the end, its freshly laid York stone driveway not yet greened, its newly planted beds for the moment free from weeds. The paintwork is immaculate.

A few more strides and they're outside Matt and Ava's semi.

Matt wipes his forehead with the back of his hand and nods towards the Lovegoods' pristine house. 'Did you get the invite for their housewarming?'

Neil is panting, hands on his hips. He too looks at the house, back to Matt. 'Yeah.'

'You going?'

He wrinkles his nose. 'Bella's bending my ear about it. Wants to see the flashy kitchen and all that, so she can go one better. I'll have to stop her sneaking upstairs for a nosy round, though she won't be the only one, I don't suppose.' A grin crosses his face but falls almost instantly into a frown. 'I can do without it, to be honest. Don't think I can stand Lovecrap treating me like the staff, do you know what I mean?'

'Yeah. He's a bit—'

'Of a tw—'

'A bit superior I was going to say.' Matt holds up a palm and smiles.

'You want to try working for him – he's a bloody nightmare.'

'Ava's not keen either,' Matt cuts in. He doesn't like it when Neil gets all chippy, especially now that Matt's career is taking off. It's not the first time he's had a go at Johnnie Lovegood.

'Understandable,' Neil says.

'Too soon, she's saying, with all the neighbours, but I'm going to try to persuade her. She needs to get out.'

'Right. Not like they'll mind if she doesn't though, I suppose.'

'Of course not. But I was thinking it might do her good, you know? It's been easier for me. At work I'm not surrounded by people who were here that day, who know. If I meet a client, they don't know anything about me personally and I'm concentrating on the job, which keeps my mind off things, but it's not like that for Ava. Every time she goes out, she sees someone who knows or who helped. I completely understand that, but she can't hide from everyone forever or she'll end up never being able to go out again. I need to find a way of building her up, getting her confidence back.'

They both study the ground. It isn't lost on Matt, and he's sure it isn't lost on Neil either, that they have run for almost an hour and only now, when it is the moment to part ways, is he saying what he has intended to say since they set out. For him and Ava, the invitation has landed heavily, but it will have weighed on Neil and Bella too. It is almost a year since Abi went missing, since the past became forever entangled with the present, exerting a force so powerful that not mentioning it is always a conscious and sometimes rather exhausting act of avoidance.

'How's she doing?' Neil kicks at a weed that has sprouted between the paving stones. 'I'm sorry I've been so busy. Work's been—'

'Mad, yeah. You said. Don't worry about it. There's nothing you can do.' Matt stares for a moment at his trainers. There is a hole starting on the big toe of the right one. 'I mean, she doesn't see anyone, but you know that,' he adds, after a moment. 'I just thought if I could get her to go, even for an hour, she might... She's trying to get out during the day now, and I guess I just thought that if she could find it in herself to go, she could sit with Fred in the corner if she needs to, keep herself to herself. Perfect excuse not to be the life and soul. And it's not far to go home if she needs to duck out.' He wonders who exactly he's trying to convince.

'Sure, sure.'

'Sometimes I wish I'd told her.'

'Nah,' says Neil. 'Nothing to be gained.' He glances over at the Lovegoods' place, an expression of disgust crossing his face. 'He's a dick though. Rubber Johnnie.'

Matt laughs. 'He's not that bad. And his wife's really nice. Jennifer. It'd be great if you and Bel come. Ava might feel supported... enough to try to come for a bit. And it might be good for the four of us to get together, y'know? It's been ages.'

Neil nods. 'We could call in for an hour, I suppose. Show our faces.'

'Great. I reckon the whole street will be there. Pete Shepherd told me they spent six grand on the lighting alone, and he's seen all sorts being delivered in the last six months or so. Apparently it took four men to carry the flat screen in. Four blokes! It's like we've got our own resident rock stars.'

Neil huffs. 'Don't let Lovegoon hear you say that. He can barely get his head out of his front door as it is.'

Matt laughs. 'No, but I think people are a bit fascinated with them – well, they seem to be anyway. She's very glamorous, isn't she, the wife? Jennifer? Chic, I suppose you'd say. Classy. And I guess we're all curious to see what the best part of a year's work and vast amounts of cash can do to a place. It's bound to be a palace; well, you know what it's like better than anyone.'

Neil shrugs. 'It's big, I can tell you that. I never saw it finished, never saw the zinc effort they put in the garden, but it's just a house at the end of the day. Just bricks and cement.'

'True.' Matt knows Neil doesn't believe this any more than he does. A house is more than its material components, and an ambitious conversion is always exciting to see. Besides which, Matt is keen to meet his neighbours properly after the terrible way they were introduced.

He glances up at Neil, who is staring at the ground. He'll be fine once he gets there, Matt thinks. A few beers and he'll forget his loathing of Johnnie Lovegood, not to mention the four of them getting together for a drink for the first time since that day. It'll do them all good.

'So,' he says. 'Shall we have a livener at ours first then?'

'Sure.'

The sweat is cooling against Matt's skin. He shivers and, taking this as their cue, they lean in, clap each other on the back.

'Later, mate,' Neil calls, already a few paces down the road.

'Later,' Matt replies, without turning, sliding the key into the lock.

In the living room, Ava is watching television, Fred at her breast. It is a little after half past nine.

'Hey,' he says from the doorway, wiping his face with the bottom of his T-shirt.

'Good run?' She glances up at him, her smile wary.

'Neil didn't have a heart attack, so all good. Do you want to watch something once I've had a shower?'

She shakes her head. 'I'm going to go to bed when I've got him down.'

He nods, aware of himself nodding, of making himself stop. 'I'll grab a shower then.'

By the time he returns downstairs, Ava is settling Fred. By the time he gets to bed, she is asleep. By the time he gets to sleep, the birds are shifting on their branches, impatient to greet the dawn with sweet songs he knows are anything but. They are territorial war cries; they are warnings.

CHAPTER SEVEN

Ava

I am almost at my door after an emergency dash to the corner shop when I spot Lizzie from down the road heading towards me at full speed in her customary designer Lycra and carrying two large glossy cardboard bags with rope handles. I know it's too late to pretend not to have seen her, know it even before she calls out to me: 'Ava! Ava, hi!'

No escape. She has broken into a jog. But still I try to get to my door before she collars me.

I fail.

'Lizzie,' I say, stopping at my gate, digging in my bag for my keys.

'Hi there.' She swings her bags to and fro. One of them says L. K. Bennett on the front, the other Whistles. 'Just been into town for shoes and a frock.'

'Right.' I glance towards my front door, realise this might be rude, return my attention to her. My smile is perfunctory, but it will have to do.

'Just fancied something new to wear for the big do, you know?' She says 'big do' ironically, nodding towards the Lovegoods' house and widening her eyes. I don't believe her irony – she is clearly beside herself with an excitement that feels very real. 'Can't wait to see what they've done with the place, can you?'

'I bet it's amazing.'

This I say to appease her obviously. The fact is I couldn't give the most infinitesimal hoot. I am in the minority, however – I know that. The Lovegoods' year-long refurbishment has been the talk of the street, fuelled by an endless stream of tradespeople coming and going. I have seen them myself, from the enviable vantage point of the house next door, teams of them, like those brave DIY warriors on home-improvement shows: carpenters in goggles spraying sawdust fountains in the front garden; decorators whistling on high ladders, hair and eyelashes white with paint particles; hints of the latest colour trends glimpsed through open upstairs windows; furniture and lighting deliveries from shops I hadn't heard of; all sorts of high-tech appliances – a two-metre-wide induction hob, a flat-screen television the size of a ping-pong table, an exercise bike, a gaming chair… at least I think that's what it was, either that or the actual command seat of the Starship *Enterprise*. I'm sure I was supposed to relay all of this in breathless gushing tones to Matt when he got in from work each day, but as I say, there is no overestimating how little I care.

'Are you and Matt going?' Lizzie asks.

'Ah, I'm… I'm not sure.'

She screws up her face, her head tilting inevitably to one side. 'Of course, of course. Sorry, that was silly of me.'

'No, not at all.'

'How are things?' She adds a nose wrinkle.

'Fine.' I wish she'd straighten up her head; she's going to get a stiff neck. 'I'm fine. I'd better…' I hold up the nappies, the reason for my enforced trip out. 'Fred needs…'

'Right you are.' Her smile is a rictus grin; she looks like she's stubbed her toe. 'This little fella's grown so much! I can remember when my two were…' She looks away, possibly for an exit sign. 'Anyway,' she says, with the briefest touch to my upper arm, 'I'd better let you go. Hopefully see you at the party! Apparently they're doing Brazilian cocktails. Louise saw Johnnie. They're having a bar in the garden. Anyway, I'll let you go.'

'Yeah. Yeah. Cheers. See you.'

By the time I get to my front door, I'm sweating, frantically scrabbling around in my bag for my keys, praying no one else sees me and tries to talk to me. By the time I get inside, I'm crying. Another few seconds later, I'm sitting on the floor under my front window, sobbing violently now, dropped out of sight like a fugitive. I'm in hiding; that's how it feels – actually, that's how it is: every encounter out in the world a tense and risky business in my own self-imposed witness-protection programme.

Lizzie is not alone in being someone I dread bumping into, but she is one of the worst. I can still remember her calling round a few days after that day under the pretext of dropping off a vegan pasta bake, how her questions felt more like interrogation than concern. By then, the fact that I'd left the door open had spread like the gossip it had become. *So, you'd left the door open or it had banged open or what? I mean, I'm not saying… it could happen to anyone.* I told her I'd left milk on the stove, pretty much shut the door in her face. Suspicion is yet one more thing I have had to get used to.

That day, just hours in, I could already feel it, can still feel it coming at me in waves from Lorraine Stephens when I put myself there, as I do every day: Lorraine, that day, sitting close, holding my hand as the tea she has made me goes cold. Lorraine, beneath her veil of concern, spying on me. Moment by moment, beat by beat, how she watches for signs of anomalous behaviour, angling the conversation to discover if there is anything dysfunctional – post-natal depression, sleep deprivation, murderous intent. I am a suspect, sitting there in my despair. But she keeps it hidden.

'We're close,' I tell her when she asks about my relationship with my daughter. 'Very. She's my little girl, you know?'

She is my life, my love, she is part of me as my limbs and bones and organs are part of me. Do you have children, Lorraine? Would you ask that question if you did? What the hell do you mean, what is my relationship with my daughter? She's my daughter; I'm her mother. She's two, for God's sake… These are all the thoughts I keep hidden, even in my darkest hour. It isn't Lorraine Stephens' fault that I want to punch her in her sympathetic face.

'Does she let you sleep?'

'Most of the time.' A lie. She wakes me at least three times a night.

'You get so tired, don't you?'

'All mums get tired.'

Fuck off, Lorraine. You're not getting me that easily. The truth is, Abi often sleeps in our bed, exhaustion trumping the parenting handbook. I lie awake, pushed to the edge, body tense with the effort of not falling onto the floor while Abi and Matt sleep like angels. Sometimes this is what love is.

'They're terrors at two, aren't they?' Lorraine insists companionably, but the subtext clangs in my ears.

'She's a good girl. I never take my eyes off her, never.' I break down in front of this nosy stranger. Happy now, Lorraine? Happy now you've pushed me to yet more tears? 'I'm very careful,' I sob. 'I only went upstairs because she was clipped into her buggy. I didn't realise the front door had banged open. I'm a good mum.'

'I know you are, love.' She pats my hand.

'I always put her in the travel cot when I leave the room. I never left her on her changing table. When she rolled for the first time, I was right there. She would have fallen on the floor if I'd left her.'

The sun has moved to the side of the house. The kitchen is by turns brighter and darker as clouds pass across, bringing showers that stop as suddenly as they start. A tall woman in trousers and a lightweight black mackintosh strides slowly past my patio windows. A moment later and she's in my kitchen. My home – a public space.

'Mrs Atkins,' she says. 'I'm Detective Inspector Sharon Farnham, I'm leading this investigation. Can I sit down?'

I nod. 'Of course.'

DI Farnham sits on the opposite sofa. She pauses, brushes her chin with her thumb once, twice, three times before meeting my eye once again. Her eyes are hazel – and kind. She's older than me. Forty, forty-five. She tells me how upsetting this must be, and that she's sorry. She tells me they're doing everything they can.

'I just want to go over a couple of details,' she says. 'You told the dog handlers that your daughter fell on the pavement and that's the reason for the blood there, is that right?'

'Yes.'

'Is there any reason you left that out when you spoke to my colleagues earlier this morning?'

'I… They said they weren't taking a statement, they just needed information. I was trying to keep it relevant. I wanted them to go as quickly as they could.'

'I understand that. Of course you did. Could you tell me now exactly what happened?'

'I told DS Simmonds.'

'I know that, but can you tell me again, in your own words? Let's bring it back to when you first left the house with your husband.' She holds my gaze; it is me who breaks it. I wish Matt was here.

'I've been trying to get out for a walk when Matt leaves for work in the mornings,' I begin, 'because Abi's always up by then and I'm trying to make sure we get out and get some fresh air every day.' I shake my head, aware that I'm waffling already. 'Anyway, Abi wanted to get out and walk. I told her to wait till we'd said goodbye to Daddy, but she's stubborn and she tried to get out while we were moving. I hadn't fastened the clasp at that point and she fell and took the skin off both her knees and grazed her hands.'

DI Farnham scribbles on her notepad and looks up. 'Was she distressed? Did she cry at all?'

'Not really. She gave a shout, but not loud or anything. She was shocked, but then she was more fascinated than anything else. She's pretty feisty. She told me "My got a hurt", but she was OK.'

'But there was blood on the pavement?'

'Yes. It looked worse than it was.'

'And did you take her home at that point?'

'No, we… I mean, I was intending to but she wasn't distressed or anything so we walked Matt to the corner to wave him off.'

Only a few hours ago, my God. Matt kissing me on the lips at the end of our road, pressing his hand to my belly. Crouching down so he could be at eye level with Abi. I can still feel her hand in mine.

'Bye bye, Mr Sloth.' Matt plucked the cuddly toy from her grasp, teased her with it.

'Stobbit. Stobbit, Daddy.' Her tiny fingers reached out. They were reddish-pink with blood from her knee. 'No, Daddy. Mines.'

His grin bright and tender, he gave it back. *I love him* – I can remember that thought washing over me in a hard-rolling wave. *I love these two people more than anyone else in this world.*

I don't share this with DI Farnham. I don't tell her how, as he stood to fasten the chin strap of his silver bike helmet, I noticed the paler strip of stubble at the bottom of his sideburns where he's growing them a little longer. I don't tell her that I thought about how, in a couple of months, he would grow a moustache for Movember and how that would be a source of great amusement for us both. Zapata or goatee? Curled with oil like a Victorian or boxed like Hitler? I don't tell her that

I'm thinking now that these are questions we will never ask.
Jokes we will never share.

'And then he went,' is what I tell this grave, unflinching
woman, now, in my kitchen. A last wave and he clipped his
feet into the cleats and pushed out towards Thameside Lane.
The muscles on his calves flexed and relaxed as he powered the
bike forward. I watched him: the wide reach of his shoulders,
one dipping, then the other, in his tight red cycling top. I
watched him cross over to Kevin, on the opposite corner,
who was armed with two empty orange bags for life – an early
supermarket run, no doubt, beating the crowds.

'Kevin saw us,' I say to DI Farnham. 'I don't know his
surname but he lives just across the street so you can check
with him. Matt stopped for a quick chat. He's like that. He
always gives people the time of day.'

DI Farnham almost smiles. 'And then you took your
daughter home?'

'Well, I looked down and she was sort of painting blood
onto the paving stone with her fingers, mucky pup. That's
why there was more blood on the corner. She'll be a surgeon
one day…' My eyes fill.

'I know this is difficult, Mrs Atkins, but we're building up
as clear a picture as we can. You say your husband went to
work. What time was that?'

'It was around quarter to eight.'

'And you went home at that point?'

'Yes. I took her home and cleaned her hands and knees. She
was delighted because she was bleeding enough for a plaster.
She loves plasters. And then I went upstairs for my phone.'

'And what time was that?'

'When I went upstairs? I'd say it was a little before eight. Five to, something like that.'

'So she could have left at that time?'

I shake my head. 'No, she was settled. She had her toy and I'd told her to wait. The earliest she would have become restless would have been five past, ten past. And I would have heard her shouting. She would have shouted for me.' Why didn't she? I wonder, the question chilling my blood. Why didn't she shout for me?

'And you came down at quarter past?'

'Around then, yes. And she was gone.'

There is a pause, which DI Farnham eventually fills. 'So you said you left the clasp undone earlier, when you walked out with your husband. Do you often leave the clasp undone when your daughter's in the buggy, Mrs Atkins?' Her tone is not suspicious. Her face is open. Her eyes are on mine.

But still.

I make myself lock eyes with her. 'Not often, no. But if I know she's only going to be in there a few minutes, sometimes I might not clip her in. She's never thrown herself out of it before, but she had one on her this morning, as my mum would say. She's two. Two-year-olds can be very… stroppy, I suppose. And Abi's determined, you know? We always say it'll get her somewhere in life.' I sound defensive, I know I do. I start to cry. 'I didn't shout at her, but I… I told her off. And I know she was clipped in when we got home because I put her in there to bathe her knees and dress them and I didn't want her falling out again, only I didn't realise she knew how to unclip the clasp and I didn't realise the front door hadn't closed properly.'

'Try not to upset yourself, Mrs Atkins. We're doing everything we can. We've taken prints from the buggy, so we'll need yours and your husband's but only so we can eliminate those, plus anyone else you think might have touched it in the last twenty-four hours. I just needed to clarify how the blood came to be on the pavement. It's so we can focus the investigation in the right way, all right?'

A short silence settles upon us.

'And you say you called your husband around half past eight, quarter to nine?'

I nod.

'He works in Chiswick,' she adds. 'That's what, half an hour's cycle? But he wasn't yet at Richmond.'

I don't like her tone. I don't like it at all.

'He got a puncture,' I say, meeting her eye. 'It must have been a tricky one to fix.'

After a moment too long for comfort, the detective asks me if I know anyone who owns a green or possibly dark grey BMW sports utility vehicle.

I shake my head. 'I don't think so, why?'

'We have two witnesses who said they saw a vehicle of that description driving too fast down Thameside Lane at approximately quarter past eight. That might be a little early.'

I sit bolt upright. 'No, she could have been outside by then. The car might have come from our road?'

She nods. 'Anyone you know have a vehicle like that?'

I shake my head but my mind races. 'I don't think so, but if I think of anyone I'll let you know.'

'We also have a witness who says they saw a little girl matching Abi's description up towards the Landmark Arts Centre. One of your neighbours has set up a WhatsApp group. Your friend Mrs Johnson, Bella, is it? She's printed off photographs for distributing.' She takes out her phone, pushes her thumb to it and hands it to me.

I am staring at a photograph of my little girl. The picture blurs.

'That was taken yesterday,' I say. 'They were here for Sunday lunch, Neil and Bella. We told them I was having another baby. I'm…' I can't go on.

Lorraine rubs my back. 'All right,' she says softly.

'The Johnsons are Abi's godparents,' Farnham says. 'Is that right?'

I nod.

'Do you spend a lot of time together?'

'Yes. They're our closest friends. Well, Neil is Matt's closest friend. We often get together at weekends, as couples, you know? They dote on Abi, really dote on her.'

'Mr Johnson was at home this morning when you went for help?'

'Yes. The first time I knocked he was in the shower but he answered the second time.'

'And your next-door neighbours had also gone to work?'

'Yes.'

A buzzing sounds starts up – a phone on silent. The sofa vibrates.

Lorraine stands up, takes the call. A radio crackles, the sound drifting through the open window. *Yeah, yeah, OK, but tell the SOCO to make sure…*

'Yeah,' Lorraine says into her phone, and, 'Yeah, yeah, OK, will do. OK, bye.'

I'm glad of the distraction. I'm not sure how many times I can repeat the same words. She pockets the phone and smiles, but it isn't a happy smile.

'They've found a hat matching your description.' She returns to sit beside me. 'Nearby. On Thameside Lane, on a wall near the leisure centre.'

'The Oasis? Oh my God.' A gasp leaves me. 'I didn't see it when I went past. We were going to feed the ducks. That's on the way. I should have gone straight there. I should have called sooner.'

'Mrs Atkins, please.' Farnham is standing. 'Don't beat yourself up. If parents called us every time they lost sight of their little 'uns, we'd be overrun. You called after you'd searched, and you were right to call when you did.'

'I can't believe this is happening.'

'Try to stay calm if you can. Let us do our job. But I need to tell you that we'll be bringing the dogs into the house, if that's OK. We'll need to search the property to eliminate you from our enquiries. We might need access to the Johnsons' house too, OK?'

'OK. Whatever you need.'

She is about to leave, but Neil is there, in the doorway. He looks sweaty, though it might be rain. That it was Bella who printed out the pictures of Abi hits me only then. The two of them are so good, such good friends.

'This is Neil,' I say to DI Farnham. 'Matt's best friend.'

'All right.' Neil nods and looks at the ground, the tattoo of a swallow just visible below his left ear.

'Mr Johnson,' DI Farnham says. 'I've just mentioned to Ava that we're going to have to bring the dogs into the house. Do you have any objection if we search your house too, with the dogs?'

Neil's eyes widen slightly. This is horrible, just horrible.

'Not at all,' he says. 'I can take you there now if you like.'

'Great. It's just procedure, nothing to worry about. If you could stay around here, I'll find you when they're ready.'

'Sure.'

DI Farnham makes her move, leaving Neil and me in the newly unfamiliar space of my kitchen, with DC Lorraine Stephens, my newly appointed chaperone.

'Everyone's out there,' Neil says. 'They're checking all the houses and gardens,' he adds, looking out onto my back garden. 'Anywhere she could have wriggled through.' He takes a breath. I wait. 'I can't believe someone would take her from her own home.'

'What?'

His brow creases. He looks frightened. 'I mean, in this area, you know?'

'No, I mean how do you know she was taken?'

'I don't. I mean I can't believe someone *would* take her... not round here, that's all I meant.'

'We don't know that's what's happened, Neil. We don't know she was taken.'

He throws up his hands. 'I'm sorry, Ave, I'm sorry, I didn't mean anything by it. Come on, babe.'

I cover my face with my hands and he pulls me into his arms. He is right. It has occurred to me a thousand times that she's been taken, of course it has. But I haven't thought for one second that it might have been from inside the house. She might never have undone the clasp.

Someone else might have.

CHAPTER EIGHT

Matt

The helicopter overhead is for Abi. Matt knows it instinctively and feels the muscle of his heart spasm. The sight of the police vans on Thameside and the tape at the end of his road sends a thump of panic through him, even though he's already seen them. Further into his street, neighbours hold their hands to their mouths against the black and acid-yellow swell of police. A horrible calm. The whole atmosphere has changed. All sound has been muted.

Neil, Ava and a policeman are walking towards him. When they see him, they stop at the end of next door's driveway.

He brakes to a standstill, unclips his feet. 'Did someone hand in her hat? A woman said it was on the wall outside the pub, but there was no sign.'

Neil nods grimly. 'One of the searchers handed it in. It looks like she got as far as Thameside at least.'

Ava bursts into tears. 'What if it was a hit and run?' She pushes her head against Matt's chest. He folds his arms around her and kisses the top of her head, wonders if he's ever felt more helpless in his life.

Neil swats the rain from his face. 'I suppose she might have made it as far as the river.'

Matt shakes his head. 'Someone would have seen her. And she won't have been run over. That road's too busy. Someone would have seen.'

'You'd think.' Neil frowns.

'But people can be so focused on their own lives,' says Ava. 'Especially at that time in the morning. Parents are busy keeping an eye on their kids.'

The rain is no more than wet mist. A rainbow has formed in a sky trying to hold on to its blue. Neil claps Matt on the shoulder and leaves his arm there.

'Listen, mate,' he says, thumbing over his shoulder to the copper from earlier, PC Peak. 'I'm just going to show this guy round the Lovegoods' place, yeah? They want to check over all the houses and I've got their key. I don't think they'll mind.'

'Go for it.'

'So it was locked this morning?' Matt hears the police officer say as he and Neil wander away towards the house.

'I haven't been in yet, but yeah, it will have been.' Neil unlocks the door; their voices fade as they walk into the house.

Ava whimpers. Matt pulls her into his arms again and rests his head on hers, scanning the street, the upstairs windows. All are empty. Everyone out at work or out here, searching. On the damson trees that line the road there are already posters: Abi's face stares out, her smile incongruous, wrong. He cannot look. He cannot. Ava is sobbing hard against his chest. Lorraine comes out from the side return of his house. She strides over, one arm reaching out.

'Ava,' she says. 'Come inside, love. Come on. You'll catch a chill out here.'

Ava's body breaks slowly from his as she lets herself be turned, guided away. Matt hands her over, feeling like he's abandoning her. But she is pregnant and she can't be out here searching in the pouring rain.

He is about to take to his bike again but finds himself standing at the Lovegoods' front door, peering into their wide, generous hallway. The house is so much bigger than his and Ava's. From upstairs he can hear Neil chatting to the cop, who looked no older than eighteen.

Before he really knows what he's doing, Matt is tiptoeing into the house. A moment later, he is staring through the glass window of their kitchen door. But in the work site there is nothing, only the typically neat display of Neil's tools resting against the wall, his tool bag, the usual coffee-spattered mugs on top of the washing machine next to a filthy-looking kettle and a half-eaten packet of digestives. The space is going to be amazing – he can see that. Beyond, the absent back wall gives onto a garden no more than scrubby long grass, a dilapidated shed. This too will be landscaped, no doubt, transformed as is the way around here.

He creeps back towards the front door but is caught by Neil and the police officer returning downstairs.

'Sorry,' he says. 'I just wanted to have a quick look.'

Neil rests his hand on Matt's shoulder and together they step back out onto the street.

'Cheers,' the cop says.

'No worries.' Neil claps him briefly on the shoulder.

The cop crosses the road. Matt follows him with his eyes – watches him lean his head to one side, the way he pinches his jacket to bring his radio nearer his mouth.

'Yeah, Sarge,' he hears him say. The rest trails away.

'Matt? Matt?' Neil is staring at him. 'I was saying shall we split up and meet back here?'

'Yeah, sorry, yeah. Might be better. I'm going to try the towpath again.'

'OK. I'll head to Kingston, check Bushy Park.'

Matt stumbles towards his bike and climbs on. Heads off, as if to answer a calling, towards the river.

By early evening, it seems, the whole town is out looking for Abi. Teams of people rummage through grass in the Ham Lands, volunteers comb the towpath, search the park in long, slow lines. The air rings with her name. Acquaintances and strangers alike walk with sober expressions, their skin paling with the hours. Women weep, wipe at their eyes with white paper tissues, comfort each other in the distress they cannot help but share.

Matt cycles through them as through a mourning, murmuring sea. It is 7.30 p.m. Under a darkening sky, he reaches home just as next door's car reverses onto their drive. Outside Matt's house, a policewoman is still standing sentry, the same one from two hours ago, when DI Farnham gave a brief statement to the crowd of journalists, which has now, thankfully, dispersed.

'Hi.'

He turns to see Johnnie Lovegood's wife getting out of the far side of the car. She is tall, taller than he thought, her grey hair cut short, swept back.

'I'm so sorry,' she says, walking towards him, a tissue clutched in her hand. 'We just spoke to the policeman at the end of the road.'

'Yeah, thanks. It's—'

'Is there anything we can do? Your wife, is she… Can I… Does she need company?'

'The family liaison officer is with her. Thanks though. Her name's Ava, by the way. I'm Matt.'

'Matt. Hi. I'm Jennifer, and my husband's Johnnie. Lovegood. Do you need anything at all?'

'I'm so sorry.' Johnnie has got out of the car and is striding towards him. He too is taller, somehow, his hair the creamy pale orange of a former redhead. He stretches for a handshake but appears to reconsider. There is a thick silver bangle on his wrist. 'The police officer said she went missing first thing this morning?'

'Yeah. Just after I left for work. They think she might have got as far as the river, but they're still following up leads.'

'So, what, she just wandered out?'

Matt nods. 'Looks that way.'

'Right, right.' Johnnie shakes his head. 'God, how awful. I'm so sorry. Do you need anything? I can run up some posters in the morning.'

'Thanks. I'll let you know.'

'You must be exhausted,' Jennifer cuts in, and he notices only then her soft Irish accent. 'We'll let you go. I'm sorry we haven't… y'know… before now. I'll drop my number in tomorrow morning, OK? Just in case there's anything… anything at all. Please. Don't hesitate.'

The kindness of strangers, Matt thinks. What a way to be introduced to the neighbours.

He finds Ava hunched over on the sofa in front of a plate of untouched supermarket sandwiches. He eats one and drinks a cup of sweet tea handed to him by Lorraine, this woman who now reaches into the correct cupboard for the mugs, who knows where the teaspoons are without having to ask.

'Next door are just back,' he tells his wife. 'They said if there's anything they can do… Johnnie said if we need any more posters or anything. The wife's called Jennifer.'

Ava says nothing. It is as if only the outer shell of her exists.

At eight, the light goes. DI Sharon Farnham returns to the house, moving with that slow calm he suspects hides all manner of anxieties, to tell them that the search has been called off until tomorrow.

'I'll contact you if anything develops,' she says. 'You have my number. Call me if any new information comes to light, OK? DC Stephens will stay with you for as long as you need her.'

When she's gone, Matt wanders into the kitchen and calls Neil, who answers after two rings.

'Mate. Anything?'

'No. They've called off the search until the morning.'

'Where are you?'

'At home. You?'

'Just popped back to change into some dry clothes, I was freezing.' A pause. 'Listen, I'm going to grab my coat and head back out.'

Matt closes his eyes. 'Mate,' he says, his voice a croak. His own clothes are damp too, he realises, and, yes, he is cold and damp, his teeth chattering. 'Let me check with Ave.'

'Do you want Bella to come and sit with her?'

'She's got the family liaison woman here with her at the moment. Hold on.'

Matt goes into the living room. He holds the phone to his chest. Ava looks up. Her face is red, her eyes swollen.

'I was going to go out one last time. With Neil. He's asking if you want Bella to come and sit with you. Or would you prefer me to stay here?'

Ava glances at Lorraine, who tells them she can stay as long as they want, that she can sleep on the sofa if they need her – she doesn't mind.

'If you're sure,' Ava says, pushing her nose against the crushed tissue in her hand.

'Of course,' Lorraine replies.

Ava meets his eye. 'I think I'm fine with Lorraine. Tell Neil thanks.'

She looks as if she's been punched. It is a terrible, terrible sight. It is all, all of it, so horrible. All the times he has used the word nightmare, without thinking, and now this, this is the nightmare. It has that same thrumming, heightened surreality, the same gut-churning paralysis, the longing for consciousness, the impossibility of waking up, of ever waking up.

'Sure you don't want me to stay?' he asks.

'No, go,' Ava says, looking pleadingly at him. 'Find her. Just… find her.'

Leaden-hearted, Matt leaves her with Lorraine and returns to the hall. 'Neil? Yeah, tell Bella thanks, but the family liaison woman is going to stay until I get back.'

Quarter of an hour later, wrapped up against the chill of an early September evening, they meet outside Matt's house.

The police vans have gone; the neighbours are back inside their homes. Shell-shocked, Matt imagines, talking it through endlessly. Next door, an amber glow leaks through the Lovegoods' Scandinavian-style shutters. The car is no longer there.

Matt nods towards the house. 'I met them just now. Looks like they've gone out again.'

'Nah. Johnnie always parks in the garage. So he can remind everyone he's the only one *with* a garage.'

Matt shakes his head. 'Car like that, it's bound to get vandalised sooner or later.'

'Either way, he's a knob.'

Matt doesn't reply. Once Neil has taken against someone, it's hard to persuade him otherwise. He's the same if he decides he likes someone, as if once his loyalty is pledged, it's immutable – and God knows, Matt has been grateful for that over the years.

'Where do you want to go?' Neil hands Matt one of two powerful flashlights.

'The river,' Matt says.

Neil nods grimly, and for the first time Matt wonders what he believes, whether he knows it's a lost cause and, for the sake of their friendship, is humouring him.

They walk, updating one another on the day's efforts. Neil tells him he's cycled as far as Barnes, handing out the printed photographs, taping posters to lamp posts in Strawberry Hill, Twickenham, St Margaret's, Richmond. He is hoarse – from asking questions, calling out Abi's name, Matt supposes. He looks utterly drained. Of course. It is who he is. No one builds a business from scratch by waiting for others to do the work. Neil has created his life from nothing – with no family wealth, no father, no privilege; who else would he have relied upon if not himself?

At the lock, they head in the direction of the current, up towards Richmond, accessing the riverbank when they can, crawling through spindly trees, sharp-spoked branches, stopping, splitting up to explore the woodland on either side of the path. Matt's eyes drift always to the river. If she has fallen in, she is lost. He wonders if he knows that this is what has happened, whether his conscious mind is refusing to allow it in, misdirecting him towards wildly optimistic possibility until he is ready to accept the more probable, more obvious truth.

At Ham House, they explore the car park and the hedges, scale the locked gate and run through the ornamental gardens calling her name. Up, up again, past the wooden jetty for the foot ferry over to Marble Hill Park. Up again, back from the river, down the ginnel that leads to Petersham Nursery. Knuckles white around the black iron gates – *Do you think she could be in there? No, mate, I don't think so.* It has all been covered, by many dozens of people, and in daylight. What they are doing is senseless.

'I've searched all of this,' Matt says miserably as they tramp through the dripping gardens at the foot of Richmond Hill, rubbing at the crimson scratches on their hands and wrists. 'I biked all up this way, and back down the other side, as far as Twickenham.'

But they do it again, like some hellish penance, their torches flashing in the dark, making everything look eerie and strange. Houseboats glow from within; a few stragglers stroll along the rain-soaked path by Tide Tables, the closed-up coffee shop under the arches of the bridge.

The rain holds off – just. Two hours later, dirty and dishevelled from scrambling in the muddy bramble-strung undergrowth, they are walking back down Cross Deep. The Alexander Pope pub looms up on the right. Behind glass, under yellow lights, people drink and chat as if nothing, nothing at all has happened.

'Matt?' Neil is scrutinising him. He realises he has stopped dead. 'Have you seen something?'

'The people,' Matt says. He closes his eyes tight, opens them. 'Sorry. It just looks weird. People… out.'

Neil claps him on the back. 'Come on, mate.'

They dip into the grounds opposite – a manicured lawn with a children's park at the far end, a little café. It is where they took Abi sometimes for a change – a short bus ride, part of the fun. He and Ava would get coffee and take turns pushing her on the baby swings, or gasping with proud surprise when she reached the bottom of the slide. Neil and Bella came with them sometimes, sometimes to Bushy Park, Richmond Park, once to Garston's Farm to pick strawberries. It feels hazy, a memory of a life lived long ago, in another reality.

'I used to feel inadequate,' Matt says as they flash their torches over the sheer drop that is the edge of the path, into the water.

'What? What about?'

'When we came to the park. You and Bella always had so much energy for her. You were better at playing with her than we were. Than I was anyway.'

'Don't say that.'

'It's true. I'd see you throwing the ball for her, teaching her to catch or twirling her about, and I'd think, I should be doing that, but I was too selfish. I was too tired. I'd be reading the paper and drinking my coffee, thinking how great it was to sit down.'

'Mate.' Neil stands square on to him. 'That's rubbish – you know that, don't you? You're her parents. It's called having a break, yeah? That's what me and Bel are for; we're her godparents, aren't we? Come on! We didn't have the sleepless nights and all that lot. Don't start beating yourself up about that. You'll lose your mind.'

Matt nods, blinking away the tears that are pricking his eyes. His throat aches. Below the wall, the dark river rushes.

'Do you think she fell in?' he says, forcing himself to look Neil in the eye.

Neil frowns and glances away, across the river.

'Let's not think anything yet,' he says, but Matt knows what he means. What he means is: yes.

Quarter to midnight, and the rain hardens. Their clothes are plastered to them, their hair flat against their heads. Rain runs in fat drops down their faces, falls from their noses, their chins, the bottom of their cagoules. They have reached Thameside Lane, and Matt finds he is weeping uncontrollably. Neil too is crying; Matt feels a kick of shock in his chest. Neil is crying even as he walks, his burly rugby player's shoulders chugging with gruff, coughing sobs.

'Oh man,' he says, over and over. 'I can't believe it. I'm so sorry, mate.'

Matt puts his arm around him and together they stagger along, saying nothing. He has seen Neil lose it only once before: at school, when he missed a conversion that cost his team the match. Neil doesn't cry; he just doesn't. He is old-school: rugby captain for all five years of secondary, later a top first-team player at the local club, now a veteran, plus coaching the under twelves. His business has consumed a lot of his fitness this last year – he's been drinking more, exercising less – but back then he was the scorer of tries, the downer of pints, pass me the yard of ale, as if even in drinking beer he was the winner. When Ava first met him, she nicknamed him Action Man, and his drive to make a success of everything has been the example Matt has tried to follow. I must be an OK bloke, he still thinks sometimes, if I have the friendship of a guy like Neil.

But now all Neil's bravado is gone, as if washed away in the sheeting rain, as if it were only a superficial layer in the first place, no more a part of him than his clothes.

Matt stops walking, leans against his best mate's shoulder. 'I can't go home. How am I supposed to go home?'

They hold on to each other. There is no pretence left. After a minute or two, they return to themselves and stand apart, wiping uselessly at their faces.

'What about in there?' Neil gestures towards the hoardings of a building site between the Oasis and the pubs: two- and three-bedroomed luxury riverside flats, advertised for sale off plan.

'The police searched it,' Matt says.

'This morning they did.'

Matt breathes away the insinuation, shakes his head against the words that will not leave him: his daughter. A body.

Neil hoists himself up, hooks one work boot over the top of the plywood sheet. A grunt and he has heaved himself over.

'OK?' Matt calls.

'Yep. Throw us the lights.'

Matt throws the flashlights one by one. The board rattles against its fixings as he clambers awkwardly over. He drops down, chafes at the splinters in his hands. Together they move into the skeleton structures, their flashlights catching the glittering rain.

It is so fucking dark.

'Abi? Abi? Abi!'

Matt's light bounces off a pair of staring eyes.

'Jesus!' He almost drops the torch. But it is only a fox, which stares at him a moment before sauntering away like arrogance itself.

Further in, there is some shelter. The torturous drip-drip-drip of water falling from the steel poles above their heads. They shine their beams into the scaffolding, the half-built walls, the shallow puddles shuddering in the dug-out trenches.

'I don't know what to say to you,' Neil says, drops budding on his eyelashes. 'I don't have words, mate.'

Matt stares into Neil's wet blue eyes, sees all the love and loyalty of the past two decades. If there is one person on this earth he can tell, it is this man. And he has to tell someone.

CHAPTER NINE

Ava

Midnight. My husband and his best friend on the doorstep, their clothes saturated and filthy, raspberry pinpricks up their arms, darker red slashes. Their hands are empty. They are crying, their sobs muscular, visceral. We are not sufficiently evolved that the sight fails to shock. And it does, it shocks, especially in a man like Neil – his physical stature making up in strength what it lacks in height. He is a robust square of a man, built to lift things, to take punches, to withstand. Matt, the more effete of the two, his tall frame sagging in the middle, his dark hair slick with rain, his wretched, rectangular mouth.

'I'm so sorry. I'm sorry. I'm so, so sorry.'

The wooden floor of the hall hits my knees; the welcome mat needles the palms of my hands.

Afterwards, once Lorraine has left, Matt and I take showers. We change into jogging bottoms and T-shirts. We want to be dressed should a call come. I suppose we must fall asleep in the small hours. I remember weeping against his back. Please let her be found, I remember whispering. Please. Please. Please.

September. Almost a year ago and yesterday at once. My daughter, gone. That not knowing, that hanging chord. The rupture of selves: me there, me here. Then, the certainty somewhere not in my head but in my heart that I will search for her until the end of time; now, searching for her, still searching, until the end of time.

It isn't until the next morning that Abi's coat is found.

*

I wake up in my jogging bottoms next to Matt. For a split second everything is normal. And then it isn't.

Lorraine comes to the house early, around 8.30 a.m. She makes toast and marmalade and we eat it. We drink coffee made the way she knows we take it. Matt goes out on his bike, but not for long, I think. At around 9.30 a.m., a woman I recognise arrives. DI Sharon Farnham.

'Mrs Atkins,' she says.

I let her in. The tape is gone from the front door. That's right – they took it down last night.

'Did they find the BMW?' I ask her.

'Can we go and sit down?' The look on her face makes me think she must have something of importance to tell us. The boulder of dread in my gut hardens.

'Sure.'

Matt is coming down the stairs. He has popped back to see if I'm all right and to change his trousers, which have got soaked in yet another heavy passing shower.

'Detective,' he says, no bewilderment at all. 'Any news?'

'If we could go into the living room a moment,' she says.

And I know then with every cell of my being that she has news and that it isn't good.

'Ava,' Farnham says, 'I think it's best if you sit down.'

I lower my backside onto the sofa next to Matt. I feel the ache in my thighs, the sting of my sleepless eyes, the weight of Fred in my belly even though he is only the size of a grain of rice. The warmth of Matt beside me. The minty smell of his shower gel. The creak of the leather sofa. My feet are cold. I have not put my slippers on. Bitter saliva fills my mouth. I nod for her to tell us what she so clearly must.

'I need to tell you,' she says it quietly, though every word is as clear as a bell, 'that a coat matching the description of Abi's has been found at Richmond barrier. We've got divers in there now, the RNLI are out there and we're in touch with the coastguard, but so far nothing else has been found. Now, I need to tell you that the water is high and it's very fast – apparently due to heavy rain in Oxford over the past few days. If Abi fell in where she feeds the ducks, with her being such a small mass, it's possible her body will have surpassed Richmond barrier within an hour of her entering the water.'

The rug rushes at me, becomes a single shade of grey. Matt's fingertips push into my upper arms. I hear my name. The forward loll of my head, then back, my head against the soft velvet of the couch.

'Ava.' Matt's eyes are brown, the whites red. My bones are nothing but dust. DI Farnham closes her eyes. Matt pulls me to him and shushes me, but when he speaks, his voice is ragged and full of fear.

'But it might not be her coat,' he says. 'It won't be. She'd never jump into the river. She'd never walk that far. She'd… Can we have a look at it?'

I cannot see. All I can hear is myself, this low lupine howl. I feel myself fall as Matt leans away from me. I push the heels of my hands at my eyes. Lorraine hands me yet another tissue and tells me to be strong, not to give up hope. She rubs my back.

Matt is holding an up-to-the-minute iPhone. On the screen is a picture of a coat.

'That's Abi's,' I say. 'That's her coat. Sorry, I… I just…'

I stand up. I walk down the hall and into the kitchen. My phone is charging on the countertop. I unplug it, stretch my arm as long as it will go and bring it down hard, releasing the phone at the last second. It clatters on the tiles but doesn't smash. I open the cupboard where we keep the vacuum cleaner and a few basic tools. I pull out a screwdriver, a spanner, a hammer. A moment later, I am straddled over my iPhone. I am bringing the hammer down on it, over and over. My phone crunches, bounces, breaks.

'Ava! Ava, stop!' Matt grabs my arm as I raise it, holds me like that, like a criminal being disarmed, but then his arms are around me and we are crying into each other's necks.

'This is my fault,' I say. 'It's all my fault.'

CHAPTER TEN

Ava

I'm in my nightie and dressing gown, Fred hooked over my shoulder after his morning feed. It's 7.45 a.m., thereabouts. As I cross the kitchen, my slippers slap on the tiled floor.

Matt is standing against the counter, drinking a quick coffee before he sets off for work. He looks too thin. I don't think it's the training. Training doesn't give you black circles under your eyes. Grief does. Trauma does.

The crinkly invitation to the Lovegoods' party lies on the bar, where it has been for three days. When I avert my eyes from it, I catch Matt watching me, seeing.

'Neil said he and Bella are going to go along for a bit,' he says, sliding a cup of tea towards me. 'I said we'd maybe come with them. Just for an hour. To be polite.'

My teeth push back into my gums. I wonder if Matt can see my jaw clenching.

'I said they could come here first,' he continues. 'Might be good to see them, just the four of us? We've not socialised since… we've not seen them for ages, have we?'

We haven't socialised since the day before Abi went missing. But then Matt and I have not socialised with anyone.

'I saw Bella the other day actually,' I say, a rather obvious attempt to change the subject.

'Oh? You never said.'

'I forgot.' I cringe at the memory of the small talk we made out on the street. She couldn't get into her house fast enough.

'She was dressed immaculately as usual,' I add. 'I looked a state obviously.'

'I'm sure you didn't. Did you chat much?'

'Not really. Not like I could ask after her friends, is it? I don't even know their names. And I suppose she couldn't ask about mine.' I haven't seen any of my friends since Abi went missing, if you don't count the strained one-off visits to see the new baby, visits I cut short to spare them their palpable discomfort.

'How's the salon going?' Matt asks.

'Oh, her dad's really pleased with the new business she's bringing in with the nail bar and the sunbed.'

Matt smiles. 'That's great.'

'She said I should come in some time. She'll give me a discount. Don't know why she said that, she always gives me a discount. A good cut and colour would give me a lift, she said, which is clearly code for you look like crap. No offence, I almost replied.'

Matt doesn't reply. It's possible I'm boring him, but *c'est la vie*.

'Neil's working all the hours apparently,' I go on, boring myself now. 'Bella said she never sees him anymore. Apparently he got tons of work through Johnnie, and she reckons he'll soon be able to take three months off and work on their house for a change.' The last phrase I put in invisible quotation marks in imitation of the passive aggression in Bella's tone.

'Bella'll be happy with that,' Matt replies flatly. 'And Neil'll do a great job.'

I nod, feeling thwarted.

'She'd had her nails done,' I add. 'Some new way of doing them apparently. She was pretty serious about it.'

Matt gives me a look and I feel shitty. I never used to be like this. And I did admire them, Bella's nails.

'They're gorgeous,' I told her, though without taking her hand in mine as I would once have done.

'Come in,' she said. 'I'll get Courtney to do yours.'

I smiled, said I would. Definitely. Soon.

'She'd had some false eyelashes put in too,' I tell Matt now, unable to help myself, wickedness going neck and neck with the self-hate.

'Yeah?'

He can't possibly be interested, but I continue anyway. 'I asked if she'd had them stitched in and she thought that was hilarious. They glue them in apparently. She asked me if I liked them.'

'And did you?'

I shrug. 'I mean, she didn't look bad or anything.'

I'm trying to steer away from saying something disloyal, I am, but I can feel myself driving towards it at top speed and I've lost control of the car. Bella can't look bad is the truth of it, and yes, maybe I am a little jealous. She is so symmetrical, with full lips and dark hair, thick sculpted brows and beautiful, almost turquoise eyes that, I think, come from some Burmese ancestry on her mother's side. The amplification of the fake eyelashes had taken her expression into the realms of a cartoon. She looked astonished. I felt vaguely trippy just looking at her.

'I think it would be rude not to at least show our face at the Lovegoods,' Matt is saying now, changing – or returning to – the subject.

'Well we wouldn't want to be rude, would we?'

My sarcasm scratches like nails down a blackboard. Even I wince. But Matt perseveres. 'It'd be interesting to see their kitchen, wouldn't it? Apparently the lighting alone cost six grand.'

'Six thousand pounds? Gosh. We can't miss out on seeing that.'

He frowns, his head cocked to one side. 'Ave. Come on.'

I give the merest nod. More than anything, I want him to stop talking. 'Let me think about it, all right?'

'Sure. You can always say you have to put Fred to bed if you want to leave.'

'I said I'd think about it.'

'OK. Sorry. Just let me know.' He crosses the kitchen, walking stiffly in his cycling shoes. He grips the door and waits. I can't look at him.

It is hope that will kill us in the end.

'So,' he says, the word little more than a breath. 'Did you book a haircut then?'

I shift Fred further up my shoulder and reach for my tea. 'Bella said I should book in for next Friday, for a manicure as well. Clearly I need to up my game if she's to be seen out with me.'

'I think she was probably trying to be nice.'

I shrug. I am a horrible person, horrible.

'That's good, isn't it? A haircut? I could work from home or take the day off so I can look after Fred. Honestly, it'll be good for us to get out. We can't keep dodging the neighbours forever.'

'Matt. I said I'd think about it, and now you're... you're pushing me.'

He throws up his palms. 'Sorry! Sorry. I just think if we could normalise things—'

'Normalise things?' The blood flies into my face.

Matt's eyes widen. 'Not normalise, sorry. Sorry! I didn't mean that. I just meant... Oh my God, Ava, I didn't mean... Don't cry. Please don't cry.'

I am weeping into Fred's Babygro. Matt tries to hug me, but it's too awkward with the baby on my shoulder, and frankly, I don't want him to. I hate him and I hate myself and I don't deserve to be hugged. But still we stand there, holding on to each other as best we can.

'Ava,' he says softly. 'I didn't mean...'

'I know you didn't. I don't know why I'm like this.'

'I'm sorry.'

'Don't be. It's fine. *I'm* sorry.'

He strokes my hair, once. Finding it to be greasy, perhaps, he runs his hand down my arm.

'I know it's hard,' he says.

'Go. Go on. You'll be late for work.' I want him to go. I really want him to go.

'I hate leaving you when you're like this. Are you going to be OK?'

Of course not. 'I'm not having another breakdown, don't worry.'

'Ave,' he pleads. 'Don't.'

'Joke. It was a joke. I'll be fine. Really. I'm allowed to be sad. Being sad is the appropriate response. I just need to be on my own now, OK? Go on – go.'

'All right. Sorry.' He batters a brief drum solo on the wooden door frame. I sense him receding into the hall.

'Bye then,' he calls out a moment later, and there is such longing in the words that my eyes prickle again. He is doing his best. We both are.

CHAPTER ELEVEN

Ava

I am changing Fred upstairs in the nursery when the doorbell goes. At half past ten, I assume it must be a delivery Matt has forgotten to tell me about, since the likelihood of a friend calling round is almost non-existent.

I pick up Fred and carry him to the top of the stairs, hoping that he doesn't wee on me as often happens, his joyful response to fresh air.

'Coming,' I shout, before dashing back and quickly putting a nappy on him. With any luck, they will leave the parcel on the step.

A minute later and I can see through the frosted glass that whoever it is has not gone, but despite vaguely recognising the elegant silhouette, when I open the door it is still a shock to find Jennifer Lovegood standing on my doorstep. On a Friday.

'Jennifer! Aren't you at work?'

She smirks. 'Working from home today. I was about to make a coffee and I thought, I wonder if that Atkins woman might be skulking about, and if so, can I con her into making me a coffee instead?'

I feel myself smile. 'Well, I am and you can. Come in.'

'Grand.'

She follows me into the kitchen and takes a seat at the bar. Wordlessly I hand Fred to her and head over to the coffee machine. My face is hot. I'm delighted, I realise, thrilled, even, to see her.

'So how come you're not in the office?' I ask, pulling cups down from the cupboard.

'I had to wait in for a gourmet frozen-food delivery, would you believe? Johnnie ordered it for the party then promptly told me he had a client and couldn't be here when it came, which is classic Johnnie, to be honest. Anyway, it arrived about five minutes ago, so I thought I'd take a quick break and catch up with you.'

I smile. Her laid-back Irish delivery soothes me. Apart from my mum, she is probably the only person I am comfortable having in the house since Abi disappeared. A few days after it happened, she called round before work. I remember her beautiful trouser suit, the soft line of her red silk blouse, the green scent of her perfume.

'Ava,' she said. 'I'm Jennifer Lovegood. I'm so sorry about what's happened. How're you bearing up?'

I shook my head and wept into my hands.

She sat on the edge of the sofa next to me and took one hand in both of hers. She said nothing, nothing at all. Her hands were soft, the nails short, clean, unpainted. A white-gold wedding ring, nothing else.

'I just wish they'd find her,' I sobbed.

'Of course. Of course you do. What a terrible business.'

I didn't know her, not at all, but I leant into her shoulder and cried onto her beautiful jacket.

'Listen,' she said eventually. 'I have to get to work, but here's my number.'

She handed me a card:

Jennifer Lovegood
Lovegood and Fosketh
Specialist Family Law

A central London number, a mobile number.

'Call this one,' she said, turning the card over. On the back was another mobile number scribbled in purple ink. 'That's the bat phone, OK?'

'Thank you.'

I realise now that she must have written it out at home before coming over, that this was her way of giving me permission to disturb her.

'Text me anything you need,' she said. 'I'll call in at the supermarket on my way home. If I don't hear from you, I'll pick up some bits and pieces anyway, so don't worry about texting. You've got enough to deal with.'

And then she did something extraordinary. In her elegant clothes, she knelt – knelt – in front of me and took my hands again in hers.

'I've got to go now,' she said, her warm grey eyes filling. 'But whatever you need, don't hesitate.'

The sight of her on her knees on my kitchen floor was astonishing – as if an expensive pair of trousers was worthless to her, as if she were someone who understood, despite the trappings of wealth, what was important in life. I remember her so clearly, kneeling. But I have no memory of her leaving the house.

Since then, we've had four, maybe five cups of coffee together, always at my house, and on those occasions I have found her so easy to talk to, easier than any of my close friends. Sometimes a stranger is better. That there is no expectation of intimacy can make it come more naturally; your loneliness doesn't feel quite so acute.

I bring our coffee over to the bar.

'So, how's things?' she asks, her grey eyes searching mine.

'Oh, you know.'

We sip our coffee. Caffè latte: espresso, foamed milk. This suburban town has become a place where everyone can make perfect Italian coffee at home.

'Listen,' she says. 'I just wanted to check in and say you don't have to come to the party. Obviously I'd love you to, but you have to do what you feel comfortable with, OK? I just wanted to make sure you knew that.'

My eyes fill. 'I suppose I need to thank the neighbours for the chicken casseroles sometime.'

'You mean you didn't send home-made thank-you cards?' She raises one eyebrow. 'Rude.'

I laugh – I actually laugh. 'Matt says we have to make an effort for Fred and that sooner or later we have to face everyone. They were all so kind. I didn't even read the sympathy cards, and that was ungrateful.'

'By whose standards?' She gives a derisive snort. 'Good grief, Ava, that's a big stick you're beating yourself with there.'

Despite myself, another laugh escapes me – a little one. 'I need to wipe the ingratitude off my attitude.'

'Yeah, you spoilt bitch.'

For a miraculous third time, I laugh properly, but just as quickly my eyes fill and a moment later I'm in tears.

'Oh for God's sake,' I say. 'I'm so sorry – my eyes are incontinent.'

'Hey, hey, that's OK.' She is out of her chair. She pulls my head to her soft loose linen top. 'You need to give yourself a break. Are you still seeing the counsellor?'

I nod. 'But it doesn't change anything, that's the problem. It doesn't change that I left the door open. It doesn't change that all I want is my little girl. I just want her back so badly, unharmed, unchanged, and if that can't happen, I'm not interested in anything else and that's all there is to it. Not chicken casseroles, not lemon drizzle cakes. And I feel shitty about that, I do, but I'd rather people just said hello to me in a normal way, like you do; I can't stand the pained expressions of sympathy all the time, do you know what I mean? I just want to not hear them whispering once I've gone past them in the street, and for them to take the fear out of their eyes when they speak to me. Honestly, it's as if I have some horrible disease and they think they can catch it by standing near me or something. As if their children or grandchildren could be cursed just by having contact with me.'

'That's so shit,' she says, her accent softening the words. She is still holding my head, and even though I'm crying, it still occurs to me that I'm beyond relieved I washed my hair this morning.

'I'm sorry,' I say, pulling away and wiping my nose with the back of my hand. 'I need to start seeing people.'

'You don't need to do anything you're not up to. And you don't need to RSVP to the party invitation either. Every single person on the street has replied with a yes, which, I have to say, is a little alarming, so it's not like I'll be standing there on my own listening to the tumbleweed. Just in case you were wanting to beat yourself up about either of those things. Listen, I have a call at eleven, so I've got to scoot, but just see how you go, OK, and even if it's at the last second, you can come – or not. You won't offend me, and Johnnie's so thick-skinned he'd barely notice anyway as long as he's got someone to tell about his underfloor heating.'

'Thanks, Jennifer.' I tear off some kitchen roll and press it to my eyes.

'Jen,' she says, laying a hand on my arm. 'I always go to Jen on the fifth coffee.'

'Jen.' I laugh, blowing my nose on the kitchen roll. 'Thanks.'

When she's gone, I realise that her coming over was not, in fact, to catch up over coffee at all but to tell me that her friendship is not conditional in any way upon my attending her big, important party. When she said I didn't have to go, I believed her in a way I didn't believe Matt. And because of that, now I think I might almost want to; that wanting to is not impossible anymore.

CHAPTER TWELVE

Ava

In the bath, Fred lies on Abi's old red plastic support seat. In the shallow water, his arms and legs flail about violently. He looks like he's having a spasmodic fight with an invisible attacker while remaining completely calm.

Afterwards, I feed him downstairs on the sofa – he in a towelling Babygro, me in new light cotton pyjamas my mum sent me last week. Today has been fuelled in some strange way by Jennifer's impromptu visit. Jen. My friend, I think now, with a cosy feeling. Barbara has told me to try to focus on these small things – when something nice happens or I experience some small physical pleasure. Today, the feeling of having made a friend. Right now, in this moment, the tingle on my skin as the summer day cools into evening, the exquisite burgundy filigree of veins on Fred's tiny eyelids, his deep pink mouth. He has Matt's mouth: the same philtrum, the same Cupid's bow.

The front door rattles, clicks. Matt, returning from work. A minute later and he appears at the living-room door.

'Hey.' The word is little more than a whisper. He's never sure how he'll find me; my moods roll in like weather.

'Hey,' I say.

He blows out like the wolf on the little pig's house and his hands land on his hips, his eyes closing briefly. He's out of breath from the ride home, his kit damp with what must be sweat, since it has been baking hot all day. The hair on his legs is dusty with dry mud and, as usual, he looks drained, black-eyed, gaunt.

'You OK?' His eyebrows rise in hope.

I smile. 'Just feeding the little munchkin.'

His shoulders drop a millimetre; guilt washes over me. He is relieved to find me OK, or at least capable of pretending to be, for his sake. I want to tell him that, actually, I do feel OK; today has been a good day, and at this precise second, I feel, yes, I feel... OK.

'Have you been out today?' His eyebrows are still high. It is hope that will kill us in the end.

'Not today, no.' I avert my eyes from his face. 'But I did play the piano for an hour.'

'That's good! Great!' He is too pleased, far too pleased. 'We could go for a walk later?'

Oh, the wild optimism.

'I thought you were training with Neil?'

'I can cancel.'

'No, it's fine.' I switch my gaze to Fred's soft, dark, impossible mass of hair. 'I'll go out tomorrow, I promise. Jen came over actually.'

'Jen?'

'Jennifer from next door. She was working from home so she dropped by for a coffee.'

'That's great! That's so great!'

'I really like her.'

The air shifts. He is still at the door. I can feel him hovering. I know he wants to ask me if I've changed my mind about the party. I almost have. I think. But I don't want to give up this shelter in case my weather changes.

'I'll just get changed then,' he says after a moment. 'I can't run in these shorts.'

'Sure.'

His feet pad up the stairs. He is changing one sports kit for another. He will barely eat between now and when he goes out running, telling me he can't run on a full stomach. What began as a fitness crusade has become an obsession. He must have lost a stone since that morning and he never had it to lose.

Fred finishes feeding and lies back like a man inebriated. Like the bath, like fresh cotton on clean skin, the sight of my baby boy after a feed has the power to stir the small beginnings of joy in me: his sated obliviousness, his heavy-lidded eyes, his dopey, gummy grin. There were fears I wouldn't bond with him. My mother came down for two weeks when he was born.

'I'll look after you,' she said with the affectionate pragmatism she has given me all my life. 'You look after him.'

She was calm, she was quiet, she was there. In down times we sat together and did the crossword. Endless tea. Endless talking. Now, she calls me every day on the landline, knowing she'll find me here, at home, and this too helps, alongside the counselling, which Matt's parents insisted on paying for.

Love has not been an issue. It is not without terror, but every new mother feels a certain amount of terror, and again, thanks to Barbara, I have learnt to see this love, my ability to feel it, to give it, as a triumph on a par with a Nobel prize. With help, I have time, I think, for Fred to never see this ragged version of me. I am working on it – on her – on me. I am trying to get near to who I used to be. It is hard – gruelling, in fact – to aim for something that seems so out of reach without crucifying yourself when you miss. But Barbara talks about charging my batteries with the good moments so as to store energy for the bad. She talks a lot about being in the moment, about being kind to myself. Compassion is a word she uses a lot. Compassion for myself is necessary if I am to treat myself better. But it seems to me a tragedy both specific and cruel that all the things we might do to lift ourselves out of our lowest moments – a long walk, a carefully prepared meal, a favourite piece of music – are, in those moments, all the things we cannot face, while all the things that will make us feel worse, much worse – eating junk, drinking too many glasses of wine, staying in a room that vibrates with haunted silence – seem infinitely enticing.

Today, Jen's unexpected visit charged my batteries and gave me enough energy to play the piano for the first time since Abi's disappearance. It felt so good I am at a loss as to why I haven't played in so long. I knew, must have known, that it would soothe me. It always did. I have waited too long, but today I got there and that's what matters. I got there eventually. And if I can sit at my long-neglected mini grand, if I can feel the smooth, sliding embrace of the keys under my fingertips, if I can close my eyes to melodies forgotten, familiar and beloved – Chopin, Beethoven, Rachmaninov – and find myself coming to a kind of home, I know that there is healing here, that there can be, at least, and that one day, fresh air and people will heal me too.

Matt's footsteps return down the stairs. The moment he goes into the kitchen, he will see I haven't prepared any dinner.

It will bother him, but not for himself. He will not voice his concern, not to me at least, nor will he remind me that the supermarket delivery he ordered came only yesterday afternoon, that there is plenty to eat, even though he eats so little himself. He doesn't need to say any of it, just as he doesn't need to tell me I need to try to find a way to live despite the hanging chord of our bodyless daughter. We both do. We both know it. We both know that we know it, so what's the point?

'Do you want an omelette?' he says instead of all these things. Instead of *I will take care of you. For as long as it takes.*

'I'll make it,' I reply, instead of *I'm sorry for still being like this.*

'I don't mind.' *I am tired, so tired, but if you need me to do this, I will.*

'Don't be silly, I'll make something.' *I'm sorry I'm not looking after you.*

The clank of bottles as he opens the fridge door. 'There's some couscous. Some salad leaves and some ham and cheese?' *Sod cooking. Let's just agree to eat, at least.*

'Perfect. I might have a small glass of wine.' *See? I am returning. Please wait for me.*

'Great.' *Oh, the relief.*

'Great.' *I'm sorry.*

Great. Great. Great. Great. Great. Great.

Who knows? Who knows what anything means?

Who knows what we are saying to each other anymore?

After dinner, which I eat and Matt doesn't, he tells me to go and sit down while he cleans up the kitchen. Encouraged by my practice this afternoon, I take out the sheet music for Beethoven's *Pathétique* and prop it against the piano. Deciding the first movement is too dramatic, I opt instead for the *Adagio*.

A mistake. I don't make it past the first three bars before I can no longer see.

The doorbell rings. It will be Neil.

I wipe my eyes with my sleeves, try to compose myself. That's the trouble with beautiful music, beautiful anything: it makes you cry.

The doorbell rings again.

Fred is asleep in his Moses basket by my feet. I don't want to face Neil – things are too awkward between us – but Matt must be upstairs and I don't want the doorbell to go again in case it wakes the baby.

I haul myself off the piano stool and hurry down the hallway. 'Coming.'

Faced with Neil's bulky outline in the frosted glass, I stop, take a breath.

Another moment. I open the front door.

Shock flashes across Neil's face. He blushes, actually blushes, as he says hello.

'Hi,' I reply, trying to keep it light.

He looks at the ground. The silence between us lasts a beat too long.

'How's things?' He looks up, meets my eye for the briefest second before returning his gaze to his trainers, kicking at a seam of moss between the flagstones. He looks like he's put on weight. His face is redder than I remember, a little puffy.

'Yeah,' I say. 'You know. Keeping on.'

Behind me comes the flush of the upstairs loo.

'We're going to the Lovegoods' thing together, I think,' he says. 'Next Saturday.'

'Oh. Is that what Matt said?'

He twitches. 'Well, no, I mean, he said we might. I can't remember, to be honest. Bella said she might do your hair on Friday?'

'Oh. OK. Yes, I'll text her.'

He shrugs. 'Don't have to decide now, do we? I'm sure Johnnie Fartpants will manage without us.'

Neither of us laughs. I will Matt to return downstairs, but there is no sound.

Neil opens his mouth to speak. 'I—'

'You guys could come here first,' I say at the same time. 'We could have a drink, see where that takes us.'

'Yeah. Yeah. We'll definitely do that.' He nods. The tips of his ears glow deep pink; I hear a short breath of air escape his nostrils. How quiet this street is, especially at night. Really, you could hear a pin drop. It's as if no one lives here at all.

Matt's quick footsteps thunder on the stairs.

'Mate,' he calls. 'Sorry, I didn't hear the door.'

Thank God. He eases past, his hands warm on my shoulders. He smells of fresh laundry, a trace of sweat. He will put both kits in the machine to wash when he gets in, hang them out before he goes to bed. Quite how he keeps powering forward I have no idea.

A brief kiss on my cheek. 'See you in an hour.'

And they're off. I stand on the threshold of my house and watch them jog towards Thameside Lane. What they find to talk about, I cannot fathom. The party, obviously, which it appears we are going to whether I want to or not. Perhaps all Matt's conversations with Neil are like the ones he has with me, like everyone except Jen has with me: the conscious act of not talking about *that*. That second-by-second, beat-by-beat morning, when my life's rhythm collapsed, that yesterday last year today, when time slowed and quickened and warped in a million different ways and I left my body, never really to return. This is why I can see myself so clearly that day, as someone separate, some poor cow I am floating above, in space. Barbara calls it disassociation. A defence mechanism. Like watching a supernatural film from between your fingers – to lessen the fright.

Myself. That morning. That afternoon. Useless indoors while all around the police, my friends, my neighbours were useful outside: searching, searching for her – in parks, in hedges, in knoll-knuckled fields, on roadsides, in alleyways, gardens, allotments, in undergrowth, in bracken, on muddy riverside slopes. The beats keeping time as minutes melted into hours. The helicopter overhead. The lifeboats. The green swell of the river. The darkening sky. The time, the time, running, running, running away.

Running out.

CHAPTER THIRTEEN

Matt

They are running down the high street when Matt feels his chest tighten. He stops and, after a moment's delay, Neil stops too and looks back.

'You OK?' he calls. A moment later, he's jogged back and is now laying a hand on Matt's shoulder. 'Mate?'

'I'm all right.' Slowly the breathlessness subsides. Matt straightens up.

'Just keep breathing,' Neil says. 'Take it slow, that's it. Actually, you look knackered, mate. Eyes like piss holes. Have you been sleeping?'

Matt nods – a wordless lie.

'Keep breathing. In and out, that's it. In and out. Are you eating?'

Again, without a word, Matt nods. Another lie. He can't remember what it's like to sleep for a whole night, eat a whole meal.

Neil pulls at the elastic of his shorts, retrieves a bank card from the hidden pocket and grins.

'Sod this for a game of soldiers,' he says. 'Let's go for a pint.'

Matt grimaces. 'I didn't shower.'

'We're not on the pull, are we? It's warm enough to sit outside. Come on. You need a beer.'

Matt follows Neil to the King's Head, where, at the tables out front, small groups drink and chat. They are mostly in their forties – nicely cut clothes with no obvious logos, expensive glasses, good shoes.

'Grab us a table,' Neil says and heads into the pub.

There is a small table with one chair next to the pavement, a little way from the others. Matt grabs a spare chair from another table and sits. He stretches out his back and consciously tries to loosen his shoulders. The evening is humid and still, the sky dark blue, stars lost to the haze of street lights. From the Chinese takeaway opposite, the aroma of crispy duck makes his head spin. His mouth fills with saliva. A Pavlovian response, he thinks. He wonders if he's always this hungry actually, if this past year his brain has lost the pathway to whichever bit deals with appetite. His stomach is as hollow as a cave – he feels it, suddenly. Last time he caught sight of himself, he noticed the prominent curves of the bottom of his ribs; the premature middle-aged sag of his nipples despite all his fitness.

A grunt.

Biting two packets of crisps, Neil is putting two nut-brown creamy-topped pints on the table.

'IPA,' he says, once he's plucked the crisps from his teeth and thrown them down. 'Dunbar.'

He sits and downs half of his pint in one go. Matt does the same, closing his eyes momentarily at the taste. The beer is malty and cold, quite unbelievably delicious, and as he puts down his glass, he gasps like a bloke on a beer ad.

'Long time since I've had a proper pint,' he says.

'Me too.' Neil winks. 'Not since this morning.'

'Cheers.'

'Cheers.'

Matt takes another gulp. It is such a long time since he has sat like this, with anyone, so long it feels a little disconcerting. He resists putting the glass back to his lips a third time, knows he could easily down the rest, but he hasn't brought out his cash card. Not that this would be an issue.

They have been friends since Neil stepped in to save Matt from a highly likely black eye courtesy of Robbie Timmins, the year's hard case. It was Matt's first day at his new school after he'd moved down with his parents from Manchester. Easter: first two terms already behind them, everyone already sorted into friendship groups – excruciating for a shy, academic boy. It was only on the way home that he and Neil realised they lived on the same street. They once tried to work out how many times they must have walked the route to school together, settling eventually for *a lot*.

'Have some crisps.' Neil opens both packets and lays them flat. 'There you go. Tapas.'

A few seconds later, Matt has pretty much inhaled the lot. Good manners are all that prevent him from licking the salty grease directly from the packets. But he is hungrier now than he was a moment ago. Hungrier than he has been for... well, since that day. Since Abi. Now, the savoury waft of crispy duck is reaching torture levels and his pint has almost gone.

'Things still tough then, yeah?' Neil says.

'Yeah.' Words cannot possibly cover it.

'You did everything you could, mate.'

Matt drinks but makes himself stop, leaving a drop for form's sake. He pushes the base of his glass against the wet circle of beer on the pale beech slats of the tabletop.

'Do you think you and Bel will ever have kids?' he asks.

Neil leans back in his chair. 'Jesus. Where did that come from?'

'Sorry.' Matt grins, holds up a hand in apology. 'I suppose I was just thinking how good you were with Abi. You both were.'

Neil pushes his bottom lip up against the top and nods. 'Once I get the business established, I reckon. A year? Two?' He looks across the street, appears to study the cursive neon-green sign that reads *China Garden*. 'Just want to get to a point where I'm financially stable, we've done the house, and Bella has taken over one hundred per cent from her dad. She needs a duty manager she can trust to keep things ticking over for her. But yeah, we want kids.' He drinks, licks his lips. 'How's Ava?'

Matt shakes his head.

'She didn't seem to think she was coming to the party when I spoke to her just now,' Neil adds. 'Hope I didn't drop a bollock.'

'She said she'd think about it. She's apprehensive obviously, but I think we should aim to go and then if she doesn't, well, she doesn't. The four of us can still have a drink, can't we?'

'That's what she said, to be fair.'

'I mean, she's practically a recluse. But you know that.'

'Down to time now, isn't it?'

A weight settles on Matt's chest. He's not so sure. 'I just…'

'Just what?'

He shakes his head.

'Tell you what, mate. Let me get us another one, yeah? Then you can tell me.'

Neil scrapes his chair across the paving and disappears into the pub.

The moon sails out from behind a cloud – almost full, as it was that night – and he sees them standing in that haunted building site, him and Neil, the two of them in utter despair after their harrowing, fruitless search. Sees himself look up at that moon and think: Now? Now, at the end, when we've had need of your light for all these hours? Hears himself say: 'Mate. I need to tell you something.'

A promise. A handshake.

Ava says it is hope that will kill them. But a year later, sitting outside this pub almost fainting with year-long hunger, Matt thinks it is regret that will be the end of him. It must be possible to die of it – or guilt, or whatever it is, this black thing growing inside him. He knows his failure to admit to things comes from his fear of his father. It was Ava who cured him of the little lies he didn't even know he was telling, routinely, without thinking. She would catch him planning an excuse for not wanting to go to an event or plotting how he would wriggle out of some mistake at work.

'Just tell them you're too tired,' she would say, bewildered. Or, 'Tell them you made a mistake. It's work. You're all grown-ups and they're not your dad, Matt. If you take responsibility, no one has any comeback, do they? Just tell the truth.'

It took Ava to show him that actually the truth is almost always easier. But now here he is drinking beer when he's supposed to be running because the truth wasn't easier and now the black thing has squashed all the breath out of him, filled his stomach, taken lodging in his brain. And Neil is asking him what's the matter and he can barely stand to say that it's the same, the same guilt, the same regret. That some days all he can think about is his daughter's little blue coat being pulled from the river, himself facing the press, voice shaking, trying to hold on to a handwritten statement torn from a ring-bound notebook, while with the other hand he tried to hold up his broken wife. Her shoulders were thin, her neck collapsed into her collarbone somehow. It was as if she had been dropped. Even now sometimes when he looks at her, it seems to him that her head is lower, or her shoulders higher, or something, as if she is ducking for cover. His wife, Ava, who when he first met her laughed so much she snorted beer through her nose, then laughed so much more at that she got the hiccups. That laughing, optimistic girl is gone; he knows that. But then so is the boy he once was, the man he hoped to be. This is who they are now, who they became that day: broken shadows reading a scribbled note to a crowd of hungry journalists, a plea for information, for privacy, his eyes fixed on a dozen boom microphones like so many quivering dogs. This is who they became: those poor parents of that little girl, missing, presumed drowned.

Burying what he knows has not worked.

'Here.' Neil is back: two more pints, a bag of crisps and one of dry-roasted peanuts. He puts the pints down and throws the snacks on the table. 'Five a day.'

'Are nuts fruit?'

'Think so.' He raises his pint to his lips. 'And wheat is a vegetable.'

'No it isn't, you plank.'

They drink more slowly this time, placing their glasses back on the table in unison. For a moment neither of them says a word.

'So,' Neil says. 'What's this nothing you're not bothered about?'

Matt smiles. 'Nothing. Just tired.'

'Know what you mean. Work's been…'

'Mad?'

'Too right.' Neil's eyes are small and pale and intense. For a moment he looks like he's about to say something more, but instead he picks up his glass and drinks. The moment, and whatever it held, passes.

CHAPTER FOURTEEN

Ava

I'm watching a lame comedy on Netflix with Fred asleep on my lap when I hear the thump of first one trainer then the other landing in the basket we keep in the hall for what always seems like an inordinate amount of shoes for two people. A sigh, a couple of seconds, and Matt appears at the living-room door, his eyes a little droopy. I think I catch the smell of beer.

'Good,' he says, drumming on the door jamb, as is his way. 'You're awake.'

He's speaking clearly enough. Perhaps I'm mistaken. Perhaps he's just tired.

'Good run?' I ask.

'Went for a few beers actually.'

Ah.

'With Neil? That's unusual.'

He is staring at some distant point on the wall. 'Just had a chat. A few laughs.'

Which I can't provide is what lies beneath. I say nothing.

Matt turns away, his words trailing over his shoulder. 'I need some toast. I'm starving.'

I make myself get up off the sofa. My body is heavy, and it's not just the baby weight. It's in my legs, my arms, my gut. If

I don't fight against it, I will *become* the weight, and Matt will have no choice but to cut himself loose and float away forever.

In the kitchen, he is eating a packet of salt and black pepper Kettle Chips by the handful and watching the toaster with a determined gaze. It's the first time in… well, since… that I've seen him greet the prospect of food with anything even close to enthusiasm. In the fridge, I find the butter and a rustic-effect wooden box of Camembert that Matt must have ordered. There are herb-covered olives in a clear plastic tub, two restaurant-chain pizzas boasting roasted Mediterranean vegetables, and a pack of luxury creamy fruit yoghurts. Chorizo sausages nestle optimistically in a cardboard tray, bursting burnt orange in their tight skins. In happier, funnier times, Matt used to call them fox bollocks. Next to them, slick red peppers stuffed with feta cheese swim under oil in a jar – like specimens in formaldehyde. Matt's supermarket orders are full of food like this: French cheese, expensive salty snacks, thick biscuits in classy packaging claiming to be hand-made – incentives to keep eating, to try to enjoy food, enjoy life, if we can.

I slide the butter and cheese across the counter towards him, trying not to notice that he has no bottom at all now; the fabric of his running shorts hangs like an ice-skater's skirt.

'So did Neil have something on his mind?' I ask.

'Not at all. We were both too tired to run, and you know what he's like. Hardly had to twist his arm. I'd forgotten how fast he drinks; he's like a hoover attachment.'

'So it was your suggestion?'

'Yeah, I wasn't feeling it. I didn't sleep well last night.'

Nor any night. I know this because neither do I. I hear him: turning over, slapping the pillows, giving up and going downstairs, returning cold and tense to the bed. I should reach out to him in these moments, I know. But I pretend to be asleep – eyes closed, breathing regular. I have even faked snoring. Never something I would have imagined faking in bed, but it's incredible how convincing you can be when the need arises.

Did you talk about Abi?

Did Neil apologise for being so distant?

Did either of you come up with any new ideas as to where she might be?

Matt doesn't reply. I realise I didn't ask the questions out loud. I've asked him every question there is, over and over. Talking about it only revives the pain, he tells me, and he's right – we have to somehow find a way to go forward, to live, for our son.

'Listen,' I say as he takes a mammoth bite of toast. 'I've thought about it and I will come to the party.' I look away. It is enough that I've said it out loud without having to face the hope I know will show on his face.

CHAPTER FIFTEEN

Ava

It feels weird to be out without Fred. It's weird to have a hair appointment. It's weird to exist in any way in the world, but then I don't, I don't think. I hover over it. Swim through it maybe. Drown. Whatever, this morning, I barely know how to walk. Without the pram, my arms swing, self-consciously as a clown's. My feet look strange, the unending left, right, left, right of my white Converse absurd on the wide grey pavement. Also absurd is the memory of the me who used to covet these shoes, or any shoes, the me who, whilst not overly materialistic, I think, still derived pleasure from physical things. I remember getting these trainers home. I remember the small electric pulse when I pulled the iconic starred box from the bag, the almost illicit thrill of the tissue paper within, the *ah* that left my mouth when I pulled out the pristine canvas pumps. That person is entirely gone, I know that. This one, the me I am now, walks on surreal feet, disoriented, ethereal, too light in the heaviness of my being.

But the joyful she of that time, the time before, *is* me, I know that. Just as the wretched woman of that terrible morning is me too; just as the dazed automaton is me now, in this present. And here I am, stomach a fist, marching towards a hair appointment I'm not sure I can face for a party I don't want to go to, my mind performing its daily, hourly loops: the second by second, the beat by beat, the yesterday, last year, today. And just as the me of long, long before would try to master a fiendishly difficult piece – Liszt's Liebestraum No. 3, say, whose massive chords my hands could never hope to span, whose rushing arpeggios used to leave my fingers in knots; or Chopin's Ballade No. 1, which would make me weep with frustration at college – so the me of now tries, raging, to get to grips with my episodic memory, to make sense of the unresolved devil's chord that is my daughter's disappearance. The empty buggy in the hall, the open front door, the deserted street, the hot, swelling mass of my panicked heart. Matt's face, the sound that left me when he told me the police were on the way, the chequerboard cars, the vans, the uniforms, a little black lens on a lapel, the barking of the dogs, the neighbours, the helicopter, the clamour of the press, the flash of cameras, the quiet surrender to the darkening sky. My husband and his best friend crying on the front step at midnight.

The picture of my daughter's soaking-wet coat on DI Farnham's phone.

In the salon, Bella is waiting for me. She is solicitous, she is kind. She shows me to the waiting area as if I were a special guest, even though, since we met, I've always had my hair cut here, by her. It has been my attempt to find some common ground, for the sake of Matt and Neil's friendship. My hair-dressing needs are not great: a wash, a trim, sometimes a little longer, sometimes shorter. I had never coloured my hair, never curled it, until I met Bella. Bella persuaded me to highlight it after Abi was born to give me 'a lift'. Now, at thirty-five, there are whitish strands amid the brown roots. But I have no real opinion on them.

'Sit there, lovely.' Bella's brightness is unnatural, but I try to squash the thought. We were never so sure of our bond as to be able to tease one another. 'I'll bring you a drink. Coffee or tea? Or something stronger for a Friday? I've got some Bailey's, I could do you an iced Bailey's?' Like Matt's, her eyebrows rise.

'Oh, just tea'd be great.' I feel the apology in my smile; I cannot raise my game. 'Thanks, Bel.' Bel. There – my attempt to reassure her that I am still me, that we still know each other. I don't need to imagine how anxiety-inducing I must be to deal with; I have experienced it vicariously in the expressions of everyone I've met for a year, and see it now on my friend's too-eager-to-please face.

In the waiting area, I sit down on the red leather sofa. My arms float. I'm not sure where they should go.

'Look at some pictures.' She nods at the magazines, as if she has read my mind. 'Find something you might like, yeah? No perms though.' She giggles briefly, before downgrading to a benevolent smile. In her expression there is a trace of something – that she's proud of me for managing to come, or perhaps that she feels she can help me with her beautician's sorcery. Bella is a firm believer in appearances; I have always suspected my own isn't quite up to her standards and that this is why she doesn't invite me on nights out with her 'girls' – why she didn't, even before. Her other friends possess a specific type of glamour. Their clothes are always on a trend I haven't tuned into yet and that now I never will; their hair is always the right kind of colour and cut, the kind that looks like they've emerged from the sea or minutes earlier hiked down from a hilltop, a little bleached-out and wind-blown – a little post-coital, perhaps, is what they're going for, who knows? Women like Bella know things I don't: clothing lines, brands of make-up, new boutiques in the area; what shoes to wear with which dress. Their nails are perfection, their Instagram feeds photo shoots. I don't think she's wrong to believe in appearances – a public face is useful, essential even. Right now, it is the only thing protecting me from falling apart.

Further into the salon, hairdryers drone above commercial radio. Does the Magic newsroom have magic news? I wonder. The smell of hair and nail products pervades. I flick through magazines, try not to look too openly aghast at the misogynistic shaming of other women's bodies, the gleeful revelling in celebrity breakdowns. How can any girl grow up not hating herself? Really though, how? In the end, and in disgust, I throw down the dog-eared pages and decide to ask for a simple trim.

A young woman in a pink apron and holding a white mug of tea shows me to a styling chair and places my drink on the little shelf in front of me. In the mirror, my appearance is an assault. My brown roots are much longer, much more noticeable than I thought – they are over halfway down my head, the rest a straggly semi-blonde mess. My cheeks have hollowed; around my eyes are greyish-black pockets I have chosen not to see in the mirror at home. I am reminded of Munch's *The Scream*, the rest of me thin but not toned, my belly popping out like a moulded jelly – a snake that has swallowed a soft-boiled ostrich egg.

'So, what we having done?' It is Bella, smiling into the mirror from behind immaculate make-up and rich auburn-brown Hollywood-shiny hair. Her teeth look preternaturally white, and I see her that morning, that same immaculate appearance belying the distress and pain on her face. Running along the middle of the street in her little high-heeled ankle boots, super-skinny jeans and off-the-shoulder top, crying.

'Ava? Matt? Abi?' Her hair was aubergine back then – falling over one eye. Her forefingers propping up her eyelashes, a way of crying that, looking back, I realise prevents the make-up from running. 'Oh my God,' she sobbed. 'I can't believe it. I can't believe it. Little Abi.'

Both she and Neil were unhesitating that day. Everyone was. It has been afterwards that has been more difficult for all of us. When a child goes missing, you search. You burst into action. When they cannot be found, that agency is lost; it is hard to know what to do. And if it is hard to know what to say to a grieving parent, it is even harder to know what to say to one who cannot grieve.

But here she is, smiling at me in the mirror. This I *can* do, the smile says. I can fix the outside.

'Just a trim,' I say, pulling at the ends and letting them drop.

She looks at me through those laborious top lashes of hers. 'I think we can do better than that.' She mimes scissors with her fingers and holds them across my hair, level with my chin. 'If I chop it here, it will lift your face and show off your amazing cheekbones.'

Ah. Where I see skeletal hollows, she has seen cheekbones. 'OK.'

'I'll run three tones through it to make regrowth less obvious. You've got a few grey hairs coming in at the top, babe.'

I have no idea whether or not it is early to have grey hair. I suspect so. I realise I don't give a monkey's what she does, and the idea frees me. She's probably right: a cut might take off some of the weight.

'Whatever you think.' I smile back at her in the mirror and she goes off to mix the bleach.

Five minutes later, she is applying paste to my hair and wrapping it in foils. To her credit, she doesn't ask if I'm looking forward to the party. What she says is: 'So, do you think you'll manage an hour tomorrow night then?'

I nod. 'I'm going to try.'

'Great stuff. We're coming to yours for a drink first, aren't we? And you've got Matt, so you won't be alone.'

'I'm taking Fred. I know they said no kids, but…'

'I know, but it's not like he's going to start running round their Danish flooring or whatever, is it?'

'Is that what they have?'

She frowns. 'I think they had polished concrete in the end. I'll check with Neil. I know they had a hand-made kitchen 'cos Neil didn't have to fit it; it was some carpenter from Devon. And I know they spent a bomb on the lighting. The garden's been done now as well apparently. Apparently they have a pergola and, like, this zinc cube garden office thing. I can't wait to see it. I bet they have caterers.'

'Jen popped in the other day,' I offer. 'I know they've ordered some posh food.'

'I don't know her at all actually. Older than us, isn't she?'

'A few years, I think. She was very kind when… when Abi…' I can't go on for fear of sounding passive aggressive. The fact is, Jen has called in more often than Bella this last year. In that she has called round at all.

'She's a lawyer, isn't she?' Bella asks, wiping another blob of gunge onto my sad split ends. 'I know he's a structural engineer obviously, because of Neil.'

'She's a lawyer, yes, I think so. Divorce, possibly. He has an office on Eel Pie, I think.'

'That's right. I went there when...' She blushes, gives a vigorous stir to the paste in its black plastic bowl. 'She works up in town, doesn't she? I think they drop the kids, then he drops her at the station then drives over to Eel Pie.'

I shrug. To my shame, I haven't really met their kids. I know only that their younger daughter is about the age Abi would have been, or might still be, because I remember seeing Jen persuade her into the car once at the weekend. The older one, I have never actually seen, which seems incredible to me now I think about it. They'd only recently moved in when Abi went missing, and this last year I have deliberately designed my timetable so that I don't bump into anyone. Johnnie, like most, has kept his distance, and when Jen has come to see me, she has come alone. I suppose I should feel honoured, or something, that she's made such an effort to get to know me, especially under the circumstances. I could have asked to see her house, I suppose, and she would have gladly shown me round, but I haven't even thought of it. It's amazing how immaterial the material world can become when you lose someone who was a living part of you. And it's ironic that, in having no interest in the luxurious sheen of the street's new golden couple, I've inadvertently become closer to them than anyone else. Closer to one half of them, at least. From what Matt tells me, it would appear that every single one of my neighbours would give their right arm to be friends with the Lovegoods. Which explains why every single invitation has been accepted with such alacrity.

'The nanny brings them back apparently,' Bella is saying, and I realise I haven't been listening. 'That Volkswagen Up is hers – you know the little black one? They bought it for her. Bought the nanny a car – who does that? There's something superior about them, I think. I mean, I know it's all SUVs round here now, but a Porsche Cayenne is just showing off, isn't it, and that bright orange colour... Honest to God, d'you know what he said to Nee? He said, orange as in cayenne, you know, as in cayenne pepper, like Neil wouldn't know what cayenne pepper was.' She laughs. 'Idiot. And patronising. Like we wouldn't know what cayenne pepper was, cheeky sod. Can you believe that? I bet I can cook better than him. I did courgette flowers last week for me and Nee. I bet he'd have a heart attack if he knew. He'd be like, don't you people have egg and chips? Honestly, a Porsche just so you can go two miles down the road. I mean, I get it, mate, you're as rich as the Kardashians.' She laughs again before shaking the little plastic bowl at me and telling me she's evil, isn't she, and to hold on while she fetches the heat lamp.

She leaves me sitting in my cape, trying not to stare at my nose growing under the harsh lights, the shadows blackening under my eyes, trying not to think about how much more she knows about my next-door neighbours than I do, despite the bud of friendship with Jen so recently flowered. We are not friends, not really, I think with a flash of guilt. If we were friends, I would have asked her about herself. I would know about her children, more about her job, where she's from.

Instead, I've just let her be the shoulder I chose to cry on. I've used her, in a way. I resolve to remedy that.

Meanwhile, the fact that Bella thinks Johnnie is condescending comes as no surprise. But as far as I remember, he was kindness itself that day. It was Johnnie who let Bella use his office printer to make the extra leaflets and posters – ah yes, of course, that's what she meant a moment ago, why she blushed and moved on so quickly.

'I should have offered to pay for the ink,' I say to my reflection before stirring out of my daydream, checking that no one saw me talking to myself.

No one is looking at me. No one cares. No one really notices anything – not even a little girl wandering alone up a road, a toddler talking to the ducks at the river's edge, reaching too far, too far… falling in.

I can hear a hairdryer, but I don't know if that's because someone has just turned it on or if I have re-tuned to it. A jingle, the promise of an hour of classic love songs later. The chemical smell of hair products. The jabber of women talking. A glance into the mirror reveals a woman with my face, but thinner and older than me, her hair covered in folded strips of tin foil. She looks utterly exhausted. I am too young to look like her. I am too young to look like this.

Bella reappears wheeling a heat lamp, wide bulbs branching off like hydra heads. This she positions over my head. She is fixing the outside of me. She is putting up the scaffold, doing what she can.

We are all, all of us, doing what we can.

CHAPTER SIXTEEN

Matt

The doorbell goes at 6.30 p.m. Ava is still upstairs getting ready after Fred, apparently picking up on his mother's anxiety, was restless during his feed. Matt wishes she was here with him now; he would be able to give her a last hug before the party, a last encouraging word. She has barely spoken to him today, barely looked at him.

As it is, Fred asleep on one arm, he opens the front door to find Neil and Bella, as expected. Opening the door to them would have been nothing a year ago – it would have been Friday-night takeaway or movie night, maybe a lazy Sunday lunch. Now, the sight of them all dolled up takes him aback.

As if to emphasise the near formality of what was once so casual, Neil looks like he has come directly from the barber's. The sides of his blonde hair have been close-shaved, and his remaining hair, piled up and back, looks stiff with wax. He has on a crisp white shirt with *Superdry* embroidered on the breast pocket in navy blue, matching navy chino-style trousers and tan brogues. Neil has always been hyper-clean and smart, always freshly shaved, even on site, but since he met Bella, about six years ago now, he is immaculate. Even his overalls are white, a fresh set each day. Bella found Neil the way most people round here find their houses: great location, solid foundations but in need of TLC, to coin a favourite estate-agent term. And to be fair, she has showered her refurbishment project with plenty of tender loving care.

Bella, in a swishy dress and high-heeled sandals and smelling strongly of perfume, follows Neil into the house, handing Matt a bottle of Prosecco as he leans in to kiss her cheek.

'No need for this,' he says. 'We're only having a quick one here, aren't we? Take it with you to the party.'

'It's OK, I've got another in my bag.' She swings her hip to reveal a large white leather bag with a telltale bottle-shaped bulge. 'I've got some chocs as well. Hotel Chocolat.' She pronounces Chocolat *chockerlarr* and Matt hates himself for noticing – it is precisely the kind of educated snobbery Neil would despise, and that he himself despises.

'Thank you, that's really kind.' Matt holds up the bottle, suddenly awkward in his own skin even though he knows Bella is always over-generous. He's lost the habit of her, he realises. He discovered long ago that her over-the-top way – of giving, of dressing, of talking, of partying – is insecurity, knows that from Neil, who once told him that Bella feels she needs to do more, to be more, just to be enough. And yet to meet her, you'd think she was the most confident woman in the world.

Bella swishes past him in her thick cloud of scent. Her dress, Matt suspects, is up-to-the-minute: a soft animal print with thin shoulder straps that show off her gecko shoulder tattoo, arms tanned and muscular from the gym. He takes in her spike-heeled sandals, the painted toenails, and they bother him because he can't separate her polished appearance from how it might make Ava feel. Ava has a different style, is a completely different kind of person, but even so, of late…

'Just let me pop Fred in the basket,' he says, escaping into the living room.

When he returns, Bella is arranging her leather jacket on the back of a bar stool, complaining that it's too hot. He tries not to notice that they've chosen the places they always used to sit in, as if their seats have been saved.

'Thing is,' she says, wiggling back into her seat, 'once the sun goes down, it gets chilly, doesn't it? I just brought my leather thinking we might be in the garden later. If they've invited the whole street, there won't be room in the kitchen for everyone, will there? I mean, it's a big kitchen but it's not that big, and it can get chilly, can't it? Really chilly once the sun goes in. You don't want to be cold, do you? Nothing worse than being cold.'

She plucks at an olive and pops it into her mouth, almost as if she is telling herself to shut up. Her long nails are painted the colour of a field mouse. This must be the latest shade. Matt remembers a few years ago Bella getting very excited over a pinky-beige colour that looked to him like calamine lotion and which she'd had done at her salon. He and Ava had laughed about it afterwards, which he regrets now as he pulls four flutes down from the cupboard and places them on the kitchen bar. But the fact is, Neil and Bella are so different and sometimes he and Ava need to process it, that's all. And it's not like they themselves don't have their insecurities.

'So nice to be getting together again,' Neil says, taking charge of the bottle opening. He has rolled up his sleeves; the tips of his thumbs whiten against the cork.

S.E. Lynes

'It so is,' Bella chimes in. 'I can't wait to see their place. Do you think they'll let their kids come down for a bit? I've never even seen their kids. You have, haven't you, Nee?'

Neil shakes his head. 'Not really. I mean, in passing. I don't, like, know them or anything.'

The air changes. Ava is at the kitchen door. One look is enough to see that she is held together with glue. Her hair looks oddly voluminous; her pale and exhausted face looks too small somehow. She has on a loose denim shirt dress, which she has tied at the waist with a tan leather belt, and on her feet are her white Converse pumps, which look a little grubby. Her shins are bluish-white.

'Ava.' Bella is out of her stool. 'Your hair looks fab, babe. I love the way you've styled it.'

Ava puts a hand to her head, her cheeks flushing. 'I just pointed the hairdryer at it and hoped for the best.'

She looks up, directly at Matt, and her doubtful smile breaks his heart. He has to look away, focus on Neil's thick pink fingers on the green bottle as he fills up the glasses.

'Well, it looks fab,' Bella insists. 'And that dress… is it new?'

'It's only a maternity one.' Ava's brittle laugh fools no one. 'Just tied a belt on it. Nothing else fits.'

Undaunted, Bella reaches for two glasses and hands one to Ava.

'Well it looks really nice, babe.' She strokes Ava's arm and gulps her drink.

Matt feels a rush of affection for Bella. She's trying her best. She and Ava cannot bridge their differences with memories like he and Neil can. And since Abi went missing… since she *died*… he and Neil have taken their friendship out of their respective homes and he realises now that they must have left the two women stranded.

'Cheers anyway,' he says.

'Cheers.' The reply sounds strained, but he tells himself he is overthinking and, in his confusion, downs half a glass. The bubbles go up his nose, making him sneeze. Bella is still fussing Ava, not picking up on Ava's body language at all.

'Do you want me to do your make-up? I don't mind.'

'No,' Ava replies bluntly. And then, 'I've done it, thanks.'

'Actually, mate,' Neil says. 'Have you got a lager?'

'Sure.' It is a relief to be given a task.

'Nee,' he hears Bella say. 'Roll your sleeves down, babe.'

Matt pulls out a Stella Artois and is about to hand it to Neil, but Neil is concentrating on straightening his sleeves, not a trace of protest.

'So, how's work?' Bella asks, and Matt realises she is talking to him.

'Good, yeah.' He opens the beer bottle and hands it to Neil.

'What are you working on at the moment?' Bella insists, blinking rapidly.

He sighs, his insides dying a little. Bella never asks him about his job, is only asking now because she's been stung by Ava. A year ago, Abi would have been here, breaking what little ice there might have been with her babbling chatter. Neil and Bella always seemed keen to hear whatever funny things she had to say, and later, she would insist NeeNee take her upstairs and read her a bedtime story, and he would roll his eyes, feigning reluctance.

Matt answers Bella as briefly as he can. He has an office block to design; it's quite high-profile, exciting.

Bella nods, but he can see her eyes glazing over.

'How's the salon?' he asks, cringing. He's about as interested in her salon as he is in colonic irrigation, and is dimly aware of Neil and Ava sitting in silence.

But Bella's perfectly shaped eyebrows leap up. 'Good, yeah! Always busy this time of year – people looking forward to autumn or last-minute holidays. Doing a lot of colours, a lot of cool cuts. A lot of waxing.' She giggles and flashes a wicked grin. 'Body waxing's very popular with our male clients. I keep telling Neil he should have it done.'

'And I keep telling you that will never happen,' Neil says. 'You won't catch me getting a back, crack and sack.' He pushes the bottle to his lips and takes a long swig.

'Neil Johnson!' Bella covers her mouth and shakes her head, but she's laughing.

'What about you, Neil?' It is Ava who has spoken, no trace of mirth in her voice. The room seems to freeze. 'You've been busy?'

'Yeah, the business is doing great actually,' Neil replies, his ears reddening. 'I reckon it'll be my best year yet. Lovegood did put me forward for quite a few lucrative jobs over in Richmond in the end. Must admit, I never expected him to do that, to be honest.'

Matt tries not to notice the fact that Neil does not once look at Ava, tries to ignore the pain this causes in his chest. This is all so different from how they once were. To varying degrees, they are, all four of them, still flying backwards in the blast of what happened, arms and legs flailing. Perhaps they all still feel the strain – of the statements *just for procedure* that they knew deep down were to test if their stories checked out, of phone numbers handed over, of dogs sniffing through their private things. Yes, they all must still feel it, he feels sure, because he certainly does. Once the investigation was put under review, the heat died down; they said they'd get together soon, just the four of them. But soon became two weeks. Ava fell ill. By the time she left the clinic, weeks had become months, her belly had rounded and the landscape had changed. Neil suggested they try for a 10K, a triathlon. But they never did get together just the four of them.

Until tonight.

'Did Neil tell you we're hoping to have our kitchen done next year?' Bella says, topping up her glass with the fizz Neil has left. 'And the loft. Neil's going to take three months off, aren't you, babe?'

Neil rolls his eyes.

'Off,' he says, making Matt laugh.

Bella hits him on the knee. 'You know what I mean.' She glances up at Matt, then at Ava, as if for reassurance. 'Neil knows what I want better than anyone.'

'You still talking about the building work?' Neil quips, eliciting a mock-outraged screech from his wife.

'No, but seriously though,' she battles on. 'I can't wait to see what the Lovegoods have done with theirs. I've got my notebook with me, haven't I, Nee? And I'm gonna take photos!' She gives a wicked chuckle and Matt realises she is serious. 'Actually, do you think they'll mind if I take photos?'

'Oh, I'm sure Rubber Johnnie will love that.' Neil shakes his head, tips his beer bottle to his lips and drains it.

Matt reaches into the fridge for another and hands it to him; he takes it with a nod and a thumbs up.

Matt frowns at him. 'You OK?'

Neil shrugs. Thankfully, the women have begun their own conversation. Ava is holding Bella's fingers, her head bent forward. 'Dark taupe,' Matt overhears, and, 'A winter neutral really,' before he tunes out.

'We won't be staying long,' Neil says in a low voice.

'You really don't like him, do you?'

He shivers – actually shivers. 'I just had enough of being treated like the staff when I worked for him, d'you know what I mean? I tell you what, if he condescends to me tonight, I'll punch his lights out.'

'Condescending means talking down to people – you know that, don't you?'

Neil laughs. 'Sod off.'

'You won't punch anyone and you know it.'

'I know, but…'

'But what? You're successful, good at your job, beautiful wife, nice house. You've got everything he's got. What is it about him that gets to you so much?'

Neil moves his head about, as if to free up a stiff neck. 'I dunno. He'll, like, tell you he wants something a certain way, and when you tell him no problem, he'll tell you how to do it anyway. It's little things. Little undermining comments. Like, oh, is that how *you* do it? sort of thing, implying stuff all the time. Like, he didn't have an architect, which is fair enough. But it's the *way* he tells you he hasn't. He's all like, architects, what do they know? sort of thing.'

'Well, exactly.'

Neil smiles – just. 'He wouldn't have used you anyway, would he, but… nah… I mean, that's so him, thinking he can do someone else's job when the biggest joke of it is, he can't do his own. I saw him working out the numbers for the steels on the back of an envelope, literally, I'm not even joking – back of a flyer, anyway – and when they came they were a foot too short.'

Matt nods. 'I don't remember you mentioning that.'

'No, well, you had… you had other things to worry about, mate. I'd only just got the steels in when… But no, the guy's a knob. We had a massive bust-up about it. I was like, mate, it wasn't me who ordered the sodding beams, you know? I mean, how can that be my fault? I know I'm good, but I can't work miracles.'

'So he's slapdash?'

'Slapdash?' Neil snorts. 'What century are you in, mate? Sloppy? Is that what you mean? Too right, yeah. He's too quick, everything in a rush. I mean, how's it my fault if the beams are too short? Idiot had to be happy with feature alcoves in the end, daft git. Not like I can rebuild a steel, is it? Rebuilt his outside wall though. For free. Most extensions have a line where the new build starts, yeah? Well, I knocked it down for him so that the bricks blended in to the original house. Did he suggest that? No, that was my idea. Did he say thanks? Did he f—'

'Shall we go?' Bella is lowering herself off her stool. She pulls a mirror from her bag and pushes a lick of brown lipstick over her mouth with an impressive, deft circular sweep.

Matt meets Ava's eye. It's no more than a second before she looks away, but still, it is long enough to communicate her deep reluctance. He has betrayed her – that's how it feels. He has pushed her too hard.

But how will they ever move on with their lives if they don't start living them?

'I'll get Fred,' she says.

The moment she leaves the kitchen, Matt feels the air pressure drop.

Bella strokes his arm. And to her credit, she meets his eye, as so few people do these days. 'She looks tired. Is she OK?'

He shakes his head. 'Maybe we shouldn't go.'

'Don't be silly. It's only next door and I'll stay with her. It might take her out of herself, you know? Just an hour outside her own head.'

'Sure. Thanks.'

She gives his arm a last squeeze. Ava is in the hallway, Fred asleep in his papoose. Matt hopes she didn't hear him talking about her to Bella.

'Won't he be too hot?' he asks. 'Actually, won't *you* be too hot?'

She is staring, almost glaring, at him. 'You didn't think I was going to leave him on the floor, did you?'

'No, I—'

'Look at his little fists,' whispers Bella, her eyes shining. 'He's grown so, so much.'

'He has,' Ava concedes.

The pause that follows is heavy. The hallway seems too small, suddenly, for the five of them. Fred has done this, without speaking a word. Simply by growing, babies and small children show time passing in a way no calendar can, and as they step out of the door, Matt wonders if Neil and Bella perceive the change in Fred as he and Ava do: a constant and painful reminder of how long it is since they lost their little girl.

CHAPTER SEVENTEEN

Ava

'Welcome!' Johnnie Lovegood stands at the door, hands thrown out, dressed from head to toe in black. His shirt has a Nehru collar, his black jeans have a thin red diagonal stripe across the front pocket. I recognise the brand; it was popular, possibly still is, with urban trendies about fifteen years ago. His thick hair, mostly pushed back with some slicking product, apart from one rogue Byronic curl, flicks out from behind his neck in a discreet flourish. The first few flecks of white dapple his carefully shaped beard, and finally, his feet… are bare. The whole effect is one of trying too hard whilst trying to pretend he's not trying at all. I remember this about him – his expensive-looking charcoal suit worn over a black T-shirt. The silver bangle, which, yes, he is wearing this evening.

'Come in, come in, lovely people,' he says, and I let the others go ahead. 'We have some amazing cocktails lined up for you.'

I hang back while the others shake his hand, while he kisses Bella on both cheeks. Her verbal diarrhoea diminishes, thank God, as she heads further into the house.

'Here.' Johnnie gestures towards my rucksack and smiles warmly. 'Let me take that for you.'

'Oh, no, it's just nappies and wipes and stuff. It doesn't weigh anything.'

'Well, can I take the baby? Fred, isn't it?'

'Ava actually.'

'No, I meant…' He catches my flippancy a beat too late. 'Oh, sorry, you were joking. Let me take him for you, at least for a bit.'

'It's fine, thank you.'

'Seriously, come on. It's ages since I've worn a papoose.'

I can't quite believe how awkward this all is. Does he seriously expect me to hand over my baby, under any circumstances, let alone after having lost my daughter? Has he forgotten?

'I'm fine.' I meet his eyes, unsmiling. He has one blue and one hazel. Like Bowie. God, I bet he loves that.

He throws up his palms and backs away, his expression implying that he's tried, he really has. Neil was right: the man is immediately irritating. I'm over-critical, I know I am, but dear God, every word, every gesture, every facial tic appears laced with a kind of superciliousness, a fake kindness that is actually about showing what a great guy he is. I remember this from before, from the days following Abi's disappearance. He might not mean it. It might even be shyness. I used to give people the benefit of the doubt. But even before I hardened to this walnut shell, I remember that his questions somehow implied guilt when they were meant to convey sympathy.

'And you're sure you left the front door open? And you were upstairs for ten, twenty minutes, did you say?'

He wouldn't shut up about the door, made minutes sound like days, as if I wasn't already quite capable of torturing myself about that all on my own. But his wife had been less tactless. Jen, who is standing now in front of me in their enormous hallway.

'You came,' she says, smiling. She looks beautiful – polished yet understated in a deep grey linen maxi dress and designer flip-flops, her toenails professionally painted with coral varnish. Her grey hair is pushed back from her face in a chic French style.

'Jen, hi,' I say with relief.

She reaches out, not for the baby or my bag but for my hand. She holds it and keeps holding it after she has bent to kiss my cheek. She smells lovely – the fresh green smell I associate with her.

Another moment and she lets my hand fall but, as if conscious of even the smallest abandonment, keeps one hand light against my upper arm and asks if I'd like a drink.

'Matt brought a bottle of champagne.' I peer ahead into what looks like a gargantuan open kitchen area.

'Well, that's very naughty and very kind, but I'm asking if you want a drink, not if you brought your own.' Her dry delivery and soft Irish accent make her sound mischievous. 'I'm guessing you might need one.' She meets my gaze full-on. In her eyes there is nothing but the same kindness of this past year, of last week's visit. And more. Recognition. I see you, and I will not look away.

'Yes,' I say. 'A drink sounds good.'

'Do you trust me to bring you something delicious and alcoholic?' Her hand is still on my arm. Normally this would be starting to make me feel crowded, but somehow it doesn't.

'I'm still breastfeeding.'

She eyes the baby a moment and smiles. 'He's what, three months?'

'Almost.'

'One stiff drink won't do him any harm, and it'll take the edge off for you. I had a Guinness a day when mine were little. Generations of Gilmartins swear by the stout.' The last few words carry a stronger Irish lilt.

'Gilmartin?'

'My maiden name. I changed it when I got married, which is either old-fashioned or post-feminist, I'm not sure, but frankly I couldn't pass up on Lovegood, could I? Imagine that in court. Plus, I knew it would drive my parents mad. They hate anything pretentious, which is half the reason we landed our girls with outrageously middle-class names. Now, come with me and let me book you into the comfiest chair in the house.' She links my arm and leads me towards what I assume is the living room. 'This was the only room I was allowed to style, by the way, but honestly, you can't sit on anything Johnnie's chosen – it's all design over comfort, I'm afraid. Still, what Johnnie wants…' She laughs and rolls her eyes.

What Johnnie wants… but I don't pick up on anything coercive. If anything, Jen appears to regard her husband as a kind of man-child who requires a wry smile and a lot of indulgence, and again I kick myself for finding him so irritating when he can't help it.

Jen guides me through the door, to a dove-grey room that flickers in the light of a log fire. The last day of August, but the room isn't too hot, just cosy. Perfect. There are tasteful pictures all over the walls and amber fairy lights coiled in great glass cylinders and interesting pieces that I guess I'd have to call *objets* rather than ornaments.

'Sit here.' She gestures to a vintage leather sofa covered in soft wool blankets.

'It's so lovely in here.'

'Johnnie hates it.' She gives a brief laugh. 'Hates throws, hates fairy lights, hates the fire. Hates anything that isn't a clean line.'

'Really? Oh no! But it's so welcoming and lovely.' The sofa is soft. Fred emits one of his little baby groans and my breasts harden in response. One advantage of the papoose is that it will hide any wet marks on the front of my dress.

'Comfy?'

'God, yes, this sofa is heaven.'

There is no one else here, and for the first time this evening, as I sink into those cushions, I feel my stomach muscles unclench. I could stay here all evening. Could I stay here all evening?

'The throws are cashmere,' Jen says. 'Yikes, eh? Now, don't move. I'll be two seconds.'

And she really is, returning a moment later, though without drinks.

'Two caipirinhas are on their way.'

I am aware of my mouth, of the strangeness of a smile on it.

'I didn't think you'd come,' she says, with her customary disarming frankness, sitting beside me and picking a cream piece of fluff from her linen-draped thigh. 'I worried that by calling round and telling you not to worry about coming I'd made you feel even more obliged, and I'm guessing you need that kind of pressure like a feckin' hole in the head.'

'I didn't want to come.' The words are out before I've censored them, but she doesn't flinch.

'I'm not surprised. But you can stay in here all evening if you want, or walk out right now; like I said, you won't offend me or Johnnie, and we don't matter anyway and nor does anyone else. You don't have to think about anything other than what you want to do.'

How like Matt she sounds, except... except what?

Except she means it, perhaps.

'Thank you,' I say.

'I'm not going to ask how you are. How could you possibly be? But you're here and it really is lovely to see you and I love your hair.'

'Thanks. Bella did it. And I'm glad I came. We need to get our lives back at some point. For the baby, you know? I mean, we should.'

'Sod should.' Jennifer stands as the door opens a fraction. She lifts the drinks from a pair of seemingly disembodied hands in white gloves that make me think of the white rabbit in *Alice in Wonderland*. They've hired staff then. Bella said they would; she'll be delighted. I heard Neil complaining about being treated like the staff, in our kitchen a few minutes ago, and for one ridiculous moment I envisage him in white gloves, holding a silver tray, boiling irritation glowing red through his blonde hair.

'Here.' Jen hands me a glass of what looks like cloudy water. Two chunks of lime fight for space with a handful of ice cubes. 'It's fresh lime juice with sugar and a Brazilian white rum called cachaça. Johnnie couldn't find any Sagatiba, his favourite brand, so he had to use 51, which he was *delighted* about obviously. God knows how he'd cope in a global crisis. Cheers.'

'Sod should,' I reply, by way of a toast.

She grins. 'Sod should. My new toast.'

'My counsellor says it too.' I drink, surprised to find my throat open. 'God, that's delicious.'

'My favourite cocktail.' She pushes her hair behind her ear. 'So, tell me to shut up or don't answer if you don't want to, but I didn't have time to ask you last week where they're up to. The police. Have they closed the case?'

'They scaled back a few months ago. To be honest, I think they pretty much called it after they found Abi's coat, but DI Farnham – that's the lead detective – checks in every month and she said to call her if I need to ask her anything or if I hear anything that might shed new light on things. But I know... I feel, anyway, that they've presumed... I... Matt thinks we should say goodbye. If only for the sake of our mental health. He thinks we should have a ceremony.'

'Should. That word again. So, no suspects at all? No leads?'

'No. It's looking like a tragic accident.'

Soft music drifts from somewhere. Matt promised not to leave my side, as did Bella, and yet here they aren't.

'It's the not knowing,' I hear myself whisper into the perfect amber light. 'That's the worst.'

'Yes.'

'It's not that I wish she was dead.'

'I didn't think you meant that for a second. But you have no one to bury. No one to grieve for. And yet you're grieving every day while feeling guilty for forsaking her by even letting yourself feel that very grief.'

'That's exactly it. And guilty for ever letting her out of my sight. For leaving the door open.'

Jen puts her arm around my shoulders. I remember her holding me to her last week, how she has never shied away from the scenes I try so hard not to make. After so long feeling like I was infectious, it is a comfort to be touched by a human being who isn't my husband, son or mother. I wait for her to tell me not to beat myself up, that guilt is a wasted emotion. But she doesn't.

'How often are you having counselling?' is what she says.

'Once a week.' I take another sip of my drink. The alcohol burns but it feels good. 'It's less often now than it was. It helps, but it doesn't change anything, that's the trouble. I can pick it all apart, I can go through what happened endlessly, but I just want to know she wasn't hurt. Sorry, I'll stop talking about it – I've bored you enough.'

'Don't be silly. My shoulders are broad, believe me.'

'It's just the thought of her in the water wondering where I was as she… or worse… taken, you know?'

'I can imagine. Well, I can't. I just wish we'd been here to help that day. We had no idea.'

A log shifts in the orange fire. We contemplate it together in the silence. I have no idea why, but I feel in some small way soothed.

'Anyway, enough,' I say, straightening my back. 'This is your housewarming. I'd love to see the kitchen everyone's talking about. You've no idea how much buzz there's been surrounding your building work.'

'Oh Gawd.' She laughs. 'Sure?'

'I'm sure.'

'Ten more minutes in here, then we'll go through. And whatever you do, mention the seamless transition from indoor to outdoor space to Johnnie, will you?'

I laugh. 'Deal.'

*

The sight of what seems like the entire street gathered in one room almost has me running for the door. The space reminds me briefly of Glastonbury, or how I imagine Woodstock once was, or the Christmas lights at Kew Gardens perhaps – that same magical property, pulsating runs of coloured lights beckoning you forward, the hubbub of chatter, a soft samba vocal that sounds like Astrud Gilberto. The lights pulse, tiny pinpricks changing from red to orange to blue to green running around the perimeter. There must be floor lights too, because the polished concrete underfoot appears to glow. The work surfaces are snow white, high gloss, and the air is heavy with the sticky-sweet aroma of the cocktails, with spice, with floral scents that drift around us in a heady mix. It is almost too much, a sensory overload, and for a moment I fear I cannot go in.

But Jen is at my elbow and silently coaxes me forward. I am too hot with Fred strapped against me, but there is no alternative. I spot some neighbours I recognise: Matt is talking to Pete Shepherd, Bella is pinching the fabric of Louise Parker's top between her fingers, and Active Wear Lizzie, who is talking to Johnnie, has on what I presume is the dress she bought – a bold red frock with an overlapping ruffled neckline that puts me in mind of a pirate. They are quite taken up with one another. No one is looking at me, I tell myself. This party is about the Lovegoods and their spectacular extension, their amazing house, not about me trying to face the world again; the only person who is thinking about Abi is me.

A breeze drifts in from the garden – equally hazed in rainbow colours – cooling the sweat on my forehead. The back wall of the house is almost entirely absent; the guests spill onto the rear patio, some sitting on gargantuan deep grey velvet sofas to the rear. On the left of what I think is the end of the house is a thick graphite strip of what must be a collapsed and incredibly expensive set of floor-to-ceiling glass doors. The kitchen space itself is even bigger than I could have imagined. Bigger than the outer dimensions of the house, it seems. I say as much to Jen, who laughs.

'The joys of having a structural engineer for a husband,' she says, and then, quickly, 'And of course Neil worked miracles. Such a good builder. Johnnie recommends him to anyone who'll listen.'

As if summoned by the mention of his name, Johnnie materialises in front of us.

'Internal to external space,' he says, following my gaze. 'No boundary. Worth every penny, those doors. What do you think?'

I'm not sure whether I find him horribly brash or whether his asking what I think hints at a core of vulnerability or, actually, if I'm refreshed by his honesty. He has invited us here to admire the refurbishment – why pretend otherwise? And now he is looking at me so earnestly with his odd-coloured eyes that I don't have the heart to let him down. He is, as his wife hinted, a kid.

'It's amazing,' I oblige. 'It's so huge! But not cold, you know, in terms of atmosphere. I mean, it's modern. But it's welcoming.'

'That's the glass,' he says, throwing his arm in an arc, as if to describe a vision for an expanse of land, a settlement, say, or a kingdom. 'It's amazing what they can do now. And the colour base of whites and greys is actually green, which creates warmth within the pale colour palette without being twee; what I call your Boden brigade decor.'

'I love that you haven't boxed in the steels,' I say, saving up everything he has just said for Matt whilst admiring the great metal struts across the ceiling. 'Very industrial, in a cool way.'

He is pressing his lips tightly together in an attempt to suppress his glee. The result is even more smug than the smile would have been.

'We wanted modern,' he says. 'None of this in keeping with the period property nonsense, what I call granny extensions; no, we wanted something bold, a contrast. A statement. People will think we're mad, sure, but hey, I've always been something of a maverick.'

I nod. I feel a little dizzy, which may be the cocktail or may be the boast pummelling I've just taken to the head.

'You should speak to Matt,' I say. 'He's a commercial architect; I'm not sure if you know that. He's working on an extension for some listed buildings up in London at the moment actually.'

He flicks his hand back, just once. 'I didn't bother with an architect. Drew up the plans myself. Fat pen sketch is easy enough, then it's just the numbers, really.'

'Right.' I almost gasp, for some reason feeling like I've entered Matt into a competition of some kind without realising.

'And Neil did a great job,' he adds. 'Safe pair of hands. A solid guy, you know?'

'He speaks well of you.'

'Well that's nice to hear,' he says, missing the irony. 'Such a hard worker. Diligent. Always there bright and early before we even left for work, wasn't he, Jen?'

Jen nods. 'He was. Like clockwork. And smart too, and tidy. I liked that a lot about him. And he was so sweet with the girls.'

'Johnnie,' someone says. 'Are these LED lights?'

'Actually, they're…' Johnnie moves away, delighted to have found a willing victim.

Jen meanwhile has been collared by Louise Parker, from down the road, who is gesticulating towards the garden. For a moment, I am paralysed, my canvas pumps stuck to the floor. Everyone else seems to be talking animatedly, laughing, enjoying themselves. I am alone, utterly. I have no idea how to break into this crowd; any social skills I once possessed deserted me long ago. I glance around the enormous room. There are champagne bottles everywhere, a large silver container is filled with blue ice, stacked high with bottles of beer whose labels I don't recognise. The low lighting pulses steadily; the music is instrumental now – Cuban, I think, judging by the loose chord progressions, the salsa rhythm. I let my eyes wander over the pale grey hand-made units, the artisan snacks on small black square plates on the bar, around to the open back of the house, where, through the heads, I spot Neil, standing beneath the weeping willow that forms the centrepiece of the garden, giving the lawn the appearance of a Japanese lake. He sips from a bottle of lager and glances about him. He looks tense, as if he'd rather be anywhere else but here.

He isn't the only one.

With a jolt, I realise I have never taken the time to think about his feelings. Only by observing him now, at a distance, am I able to see that he, like me, is miserable. He is drinking fast, with intention rather than enjoyment. In this momentary parting of the clouds, I forget my own heart for a second and understand with piercing clarity that he was broken too that day – of course he was. For him, and for Bella too, socialising with us for the first time since has brought back painful memories, just as it has for us. He doted on Abi, and Abi adored him. He spoilt her rotten, used to throw her in the air and make her squeal with delight, used to make her laugh so much I'd have to tell him to stop for fear she might not be able to catch her breath. I haven't really thought about how hard that morning, that day, that night, and what followed, must have been for such a robust, capable man. To be faced with his own impotence in such a dreadful catastrophe would have offended his very masculine brand of pride at the very, very least. It will have been devastating. I can still remember his face when we asked him and Bella to be Abi's godparents. He struggled to keep it together; his eyes shone and he half coughed his thanks into his hand. It was a privilege, he said. An honour. It was a job he took almost too seriously, showering her with presents and attention as if she were his own.

My God. I have not thought about Neil at all, but now I study him and see that he is alone, alone like me in this crowded space, and I see his tortured face that day, the tears it must have cost him so much to shed, and my cheeks burn with shame. He is grieving too. There were two men broken on my front step in those black and desperate hours – Matt, the father, and Neil, the godfather. It has been worse for Matt and me, yes, yes, of course, but it has been awful for Neil too. And for Bella, who barely knows where to put herself in front of me anymore, wittering nervously over drinks just now like she didn't know us at all, trying to fix me with a haircut and colour, another layer of make-up, a manicure.

But I can't take that on. I can't take on their grief too. I have enough of my own.

My glass is empty. I know I shouldn't have more. I should stay sober.

Sod should.

CHAPTER EIGHTEEN

Ava

It's a little after 9.30 p.m. I have been here too long, spoken to maybe five people beyond the ones I came with. They are all in their small pockets of conversation, specific words melting into a dull collective roar. No one has asked me anything other than how I am. How I am coping is what they mean, and that's kind. They're right, I am defined by what has happened. The thought of talking about it here fills me with dread. The last thing I want to do is end up in a public display of tears. But I am incapable of talking about anything else and so I have nothing, nothing at all to say.

I find Bella in the garden, next to the Brazilian-themed bar, swaying to the music.

'Hi,' I say, still shy of her despite yesterday's hair appointment and our drinks earlier.

'Babe!' Bella throws her arms around me – an awkward affair with Fred in the sling – and, bizarrely, starts to cry. 'I'm so sorry,' she says, releasing me from her rather sweaty grasp.

'What for?'

'Everything.' Her eyes are red; the make-up has smudged black beneath them. In all the years I've known her, all the partying we've done together, I've never seen her with smudged make-up. 'I know we haven't been there for you and I'm sorry. I'm sorry, babe.'

Oh, this is not the time or the place. But Bella is holding on to my arm, looking up at me through her top lashes with big sorrowful eyes, and she is, without doubt, inebriated. I try to flatten a bristle of annoyance. The sight of Neil earlier has softened me, sobered me to my own self-absorption, shaken me out of my grief. Yes, Bella will have found it tough too. She was Abi's godmother and, I suspect, was the one responsible for all the expensive gifts.

'Don't worry about it,' I say. 'Really. It's been hard for you guys too – I do get that. Just because it's been worse for us doesn't mean—'

'Neil did everything he could,' Bella says miserably. 'He looked everywhere. He was broken, Ave, absolutely broken; you know that, don't you?'

'I know.'

'He's still not the same. It broke him. He's still not right.'

I glance towards the kitchen. I'm desperate to get away from her, but I don't want to offend her, not now that we've made this big step.

'I mean,' she is saying, one hand pawing my shoulder, 'he looked everywhere that night.'

'I know he did.' I humour her. 'Honestly, you guys did everything you could.'

'He looked all night, Ave. All night long he looked. He was broken, I've never seen him like that. We're… we're going through a bad patch at the minute. He's drinking a fair bit, do you know what I mean?' She pushes her fingertips to her eyes and lets out a groan.

I know I should comfort her. Instead, I step back. Horrible to admit, but I feel suffocated. Weighed down. Frankly, I wish she'd shut up, fear I might tell her to do just that.

'We should've come over more,' she goes on. 'I just feel so bad about it, but it was too difficult.'

'Bella, listen.' I lift her hand from my arm in a show of holding it before letting it drop. 'It's hard not to be able to fix things. It's hard to see your friends in pain, I understand that. But we're getting there, don't worry. Let's just… let's just try to move past it, shall we? We all need time to heal. And I won't heal, not completely, that's really what I've got to learn to navigate.'

She sniffs loudly; I wonder if she even heard. 'Just want you to know that Neil did everything, no matter what. He loved Abi, he really did, no matter what.'

'I know he did.'

'We both did. I mean, we want kids too, you know.'

'I know. Look, let's talk about this again, eh? I'm going to head off, so I'll see you tomorrow or something, OK?'

'OK, babe. Sorry, I just got a bit emotional. I get emotional, you know? I'm an emotional person.'

'I know. It's OK. I'll see you later, OK? OK.'

In the kitchen, a crescendo of chatter, the music pushes upwards in volume and tempo – a trendy remix bossa nova, I think, but can't be one hundred per cent sure. Whatever, already under the influence of strong cocktails, some of my neighbours are swaying a little to the beat, risking a head bob here and there. They want to dance. But we're in suburbia now and I doubt they'd dare.

'Ava.' It is Johnnie. He looks flushed, a little shiny.

'Hi.' I look about me, searching for Matt. Help.

'So good of you to come tonight,' he says. 'Must have taken a lot of courage.'

I glance at him. My cheeks burn. I have no idea how to respond. If Jen had said this, it would have been fine, but Johnnie is not Jen.

'Jen tells me they scaled back the investigation some months ago. Do you think they'll close it altogether once it reaches a year? It's almost a year now, isn't it?'

'Y-Yes.' My hand flies to my mouth.

'I mean,' he adds, apparently oblivious, 'I don't know how these things work, but you'd imagine a year would be long enough, what with budget cuts and so forth. Can't imagine there's much to be gained.'

My skin is alight. The room spins. I have the impression of rising into the air, that speaking is all that will keep me on the ground.

'There would be for us,' I manage to say. 'There'd be everything to gain.'

He swats the air with one hand. 'Of course, yes, I didn't mean that, I meant more in the sense that I can't imagine there'd be more evidence now, after all this time. No new leads, are there? They're not watching anyone?'

I wait. Wait to see how far he will dig before he strikes rock and breaks his shovel. Stop, I want to say, just stop talking.

'There are no new leads *at the moment*,' I say instead. 'And no, they don't have a suspect as such. But they're not closing it. Should something new come to light, they'll move quickly.'

He nods, hugely, pushes his bottom lip up so far it overlaps the top, his chin puckering beneath his highly curated stubble.

'Yes, yes,' he says, head cocked, musing like an art critic. 'Yes, I can see that, I can see that... It's just that it was reported as a tragic accident, wasn't it? I suppose because there was nothing suspicious. And they searched all the houses and gardens. The dogs were taken into Neil's place too, weren't they?'

'Only for procedure. With them being our closest friends.' The last two words sound – are – pointed. Back. Off.

'Of course, of course. But they didn't take the dogs into anyone else's home, did they?'

I narrow my eyes at him. If he picks up how aghast I am, he doesn't show it.

'They can't treat everyone as a suspect, Johnnie,' I manage. 'They'd have to have found incriminating evidence, they'd have to have good reason to justify that kind of... of violation.'

'So they had good reason? I thought you said it was procedure.'

I inhale deeply. My shoulders rise. 'I did. It was. I meant—'

'Hey.' Matt appears, hands me a drink. My third. I shouldn't. But my hands are shaking and I'm so relieved to see him, I almost down it in one go.

'Ava was just updating me on... everything,' Johnnie says.

Matt eyes him warily. 'OK.' He turns to me, must see something in my face, because his eyes flicker with concern. 'Do you want to go home soon?'

'Catch you kids later,' Johnnie says, pressing his hand to the top of my arm before he leaves us, as if in this last conversation we have established some sort of bond. My God, I think. What on earth does Jen see in him?

'Neil wasn't wrong,' Matt says under his breath once Johnnie is out of earshot.

'No. No, he wasn't.'

The music dips.

Both of us look towards the far end of the kitchen. In a half-sigh, Matt says: 'What the hell?'

CHAPTER NINETEEN

Ava

At the far end of the kitchen, cheeks even pinker now and looking for all the world like an aged cherub, Johnnie has raised his hands. He says nothing, simply stands with his arms out, confident that the talking will cease. Like Moses parting the Red Sea, I think. And sure enough, the chatter dies away. Jen is beside him, looking a little coy. Another second and I realise she is holding hands with a young girl who looks about twelve or thirteen.

When he's satisfied that the room is silent, Johnnie lowers his hands.

'Hi, everyone,' he says. 'We just wanted to say thank you for coming to our humble abode.' He smirks; no one laughs. 'It's really great to finally meet our neighbours, and yeah, hi, welcome, *willkommen*, *bienvenue*. As you know, I'm Johnnie, this is Jennifer, and these are our girls, Jasmine and Cosima, who are up way past their bedtime.'

'Past their bedtime, past their bedtime, past their bedtime,' the elder one says, stepping forward and flapping her hands in front of her chest. Her smile is so wide, it is on the edges of a laugh, which duly follows. She steps back and looks at her mother for reassurance. Jen takes both of her hands and moves them back and forth, smiling at her all the while, and in that moment I realise, with a kick to the solar plexus, that her daughter has some form of learning difficulty.

'This is Jasmine,' Jen says to the room. 'Say goodnight, Jasmine.'

'Say goodnight, Jasmine,' Jasmine calls out, and laughs again. 'Say goodnight, Jasmine, say goodnight, Jasmine.'

Shame burns through me as the guests respond in a warm chorus. I assumed the elder daughter attended an exclusive school. I have not at any point considered any other possibility for her being spirited away each morning in their big posh car. I have never asked.

'I didn't realise their eldest had special needs,' a woman behind me whispers, though loudly enough that I hear it. 'You wouldn't think, would you?'

I barely have time to consider what this even means, because at that moment Jasmine points to Kevin from across the road and says in a very loud, excited voice: 'Bicycle! Bicycle, bicycle.'

Jen and Johnnie are grinning like idiots. Their pride moves me. I have judged Johnnie harshly, but perhaps he isn't so bad after all.

'Bicycle, bicycle,' Jasmine calls out again, laughing.

'She's not wrong.' Kevin lifts his glass and addresses the room with a nod. 'I cycle to work.'

A collective murmur of affection rumbles through the room.

I cannot stop thinking that I never once asked Jen about her girls. Grief is selfish. I have become selfish as well as mean-minded and sarcastic. I used to ask people questions; I used to care. I used to be witty. Not hard. Not self-obsessed. Not like this.

'No flies on Jasmine,' Jen says, laughing and gesturing round the room. 'She's got you all pegged.'

But Jasmine has moved on and is gesticulating now at Louise Parker. She mimes headphones and runs on the spot, her fists pumping.

Louise blushes. 'Yep. I'm a runner.' She raises her cocktail in cheers. Her eyes are glassy and she looks a little drunk.

Jen throws out her hands, clearly delighted. 'What did I tell you?'

Jasmine jumps from foot to foot. She is flapping her hands quite wildly now. She takes a gasping breath and points across the crowd.

'Pockets!' she cries – a loud, joyful shout. 'Pockets, pockets, pockets.'

I follow her gaze to where Neil is skulking at the back of the kitchen. She has spotted him despite the fact that he is almost in the garden.

'Pockets,' she says again, almost beside herself. 'Pockets! Pockets!'

Johnnie puts his arm around her. 'OK, Jazzy, that's enough excitement for one night, I think. Time for bed.'

Jasmine is still pointing.

'Pockets,' she says. 'Pockets, pockets.'

Johnnie looks over at Neil. There is something in his expression I cannot read. Neil has dipped his head. The tips of his ears glow. I look back at Johnnie.

'She's wondering where your overalls are, Neil,' Johnnie calls across the heads, then redirects himself to the room at large. 'Jasmine was obsessed with Neil's overalls when he did the building work on this place, weren't you, darling?'

'Weren't you darling,' comes the echo. 'Weren't you darling, weren't you darling.'

'Oh shit,' Matt says, slipping away from my side.

My face heats. I presume Matt has headed to find Neil, but I dare not look round. *I just had enough of being treated like the staff.* Words he said in our kitchen this evening. From anyone else's lips, Johnnie's comment just now would have been innocuous, but the drawing of attention to Neil's role as labourer in Johnnie's home, under Johnnie's professional direction, with its implication of class and hierarchy, is blatant. It's possible I'm being oversensitive, overthinking, but if I am, then so is Matt.

I look out into the garden, where a group of eight or so people stand next to the bar. A little further on, under the willow tree again, is Neil, with Matt. Neil is shaking his head. Matt puts a hand on his shoulder, which he shrugs off, and from nowhere, I have the impression that something bigger has happened, bigger than being patronised in front of a room full of people. I have no idea what, but it bothers me for reasons I can't name. Reasons that have to do with Abi. Barbara tells me that everything will come back to Abi, for a long time, and so I dig into my CBT and tell myself that no, this is not about her. My *reaction* is about her, about me and my grief.

'Come on now, that's enough. Wave goodbye, Jazzy.'

My attention is called back to Johnnie, who is guiding his daughter out of the room, her voice an excited echo: wave goodbye, Jazzy, wave goodbye, Jazzy, wave goodbye, Jazzy. He appears to be handing her over to someone hidden in the hallway beyond. Back in the room, he bends out of sight, reappearing once again with a beautiful little girl in his arms.

Cosima. She looks so like Jen, has grown so much in a year, has become less of a baby, more of a little girl. Like Abi should be. Might be. Somewhere. On his hip, she grins shyly – a delighted little girl allowed to stay up late, to come and say hello to the grown-ups. My heart tightens. My eyes prick. I bite down hard on my bottom lip.

It's not enough.

My heart accelerates. My vision clouds. I stare at my trainers, focus on my breathing.

'This is Cosima,' I hear Johnnie say.

Matt has left me. He has left me on my own.

'Say goodnight, Cozzie,' Johnnie says.

I make myself stand up, almost straight, and look. Cosima giggles and sinks her head into her father's chest. A moment later, she raises her head and blows a kiss, says goodnight in a sweet little-girl voice that runs through me like a blade, and collapses into embarrassed giggles, just like Abi used to. I stare down at the floor, blinking back tears, my body white hot, my heart racing. I take deep breaths, determined to remain upright. I am stuck, stuck and alone in this hot, pounding space, while the crowd call out their goodnights, their voices soft with alcohol and affection, with memories of their own children, perhaps, at that age, children who have grown up now, who are still here.

Johnnie is handing Cosima to a middle-aged woman standing just behind them with her arms outstretched. She takes the child into her arms with a nod and a kind smile. The nanny, I guess. The one they bought a little runaround for. Cosima on one hip, Jasmine holding her hand, the three become shadows as they recede. My throat aches.

The cool bossa nova drifts back into the air. Jennifer is wielding her phone, her eyes screwed up at discreet round ceiling speakers. The volume rises. My neighbours begin to dance. They are red and jolly, animated and talkative. The party is really getting going now.

I have to go. I have to get out of here. It has to be now.

CHAPTER TWENTY

Matt

Neil is spitting bullets.

'Did you see that?' He moves to pace away, apparently decides against it, but his body bristles with the effort of simply standing still. 'Did you hear him? He couldn't *not* do it, could he?' His speech is half-whisper, half-hiss. 'Couldn't resist lording it over me in the bloody palace I built for him. Arsehole.' More expletives follow, a furious tirade that threatens to get louder and be overheard. His face pinks; the rims of his eyes redden. His scalp glows through the shaved sides of his head.

'Mate.' Matt is aware of people looking at them. 'Just keep it down, will you? He didn't mean anything by it.'

'Yes he did. Yes he did, Matt. The guy's a condescending prick. It was like this every day when I did his kitchen. Every fucking day.' At his sides, Neil's hands roll into fists.

'Mate. It was his daughter. She can't help it. She hasn't got... she doesn't speak in sentences – that's not her fault. Johnnie was just trying to... I dunno... accommodate her.'

'All right.' Neil raises one hand, nods his promise to stop making a scene. 'The thing is, it makes me laugh, because if it weren't for me, his kitchen would look like shit. It was him who got the measurements for the RSJs wrong, me and the lads that had to work around it, correct his bollocks maths. I could have done those calculations in my head.'

Matt waits. Now is not the time to say he's heard this before.

'I'd already done the maths when he first showed me the house!' Neil glances towards the kitchen and bites his bottom lip in disgust, makes a gun with his fingers and points it at his own head. 'I'd already built it, in my mind. In here! These pricks make you think it's rocket science, but it's basic... it's basic building. They think just 'cos they dossed around for a few years at uni, they think they're better. They think they know more but half the time they're useless. I'm telling you, he thinks 'cos he's got some bullshit certificate, it means no one has ever thought of doing what he's done. Leaving the steels exposed to make them look industrial?' He makes sarcastic jazz hands. 'Woo, big deal. I saw that in Peckham about five years ago. He thinks he's so edgy and cool with his zinc and his glass bullshit extension. He's a... he's a... the guy's a...' He sighs deeply, appears to cool. When he looks at Matt, there is apology in his eyes. 'I don't mean you.'

'I know you don't.'

'I don't. I know you worked hard at uni. I mean, I respect your qualifications and that. I'm not, like, chippy about it or anything.'

'I know.' Matt wonders why Neil feels the need to say this – he's never said anything like it before.

'I'm not jealous of you, that's what I'm trying to say, so don't go thinking that. I'm just pissed off, that's all. With him. I mean, I bet he couldn't get in to do architecture. I bet that's why he didn't use an architect.'

'I'm sure he was capable of doing the sketches. He was probably just sure about what he wanted.'

'All right. I know. I'm just… and I know he got me all that work and he gave me a massive tip at the end of the job – did I ever tell you that?' Neil shakes his head, continues without waiting for an answer. 'Well, no, it was… I probably never mentioned it, did I, but it was… It was difficult times, but, yeah, he gave me a five-hundred-quid tip. Five bloody ton – who does that? I said nah, but he insisted, said I'd done an exceptional job and deserved it and all that nonsense, so in the end I took it, I took it because I reckoned it was more of his patronising bullshit, do you know what I mean? Pay the little man.' He blows out a long jet of air, cools another degree. 'I dunno, it's just him, the way he is gets on my tits. But you, you were always proper brainy – you know I mean that, don't you?'

'Yeah. Yeah, of course. I'm not offended or anything.'

'That's why you were so shit at football.' He almost grins, takes a gruff swig of his beer.

'Funny.' Matt feels his chest loosen, the way it does when he spots and corrects a last-minute mistake at work.

'And at least you don't go round telling your builders how to do their job.'

'I never see the builders anymore. I'm too important.'

Neil's eyes round like he's been slapped but just as quickly crinkle. He laughs. 'Tosser.'

'Come on.' Matt lifts the empty beer bottle out of Neil's hand. 'Let's get pissed on Johnnie Lovegood's organic ale, shall we?'

He's about to head to the Brazilian-style bar that has been set up on the raised dais outside the zinc home office, but to his astonishment, Neil shakes his head.

'Nah, mate.' His eyes fix on his shoes. He kicks at something invisible on the polished concrete. 'I can't stay here. I just… I just can't.' He slaps Matt on the shoulder and walks away into the house, his head hanging low like a man bereaved.

Another moment, and he's gone.

CHAPTER TWENTY-ONE

Ava

Out on the Lovegoods' driveway, I text Matt.

Have gone home. All OK. Enjoy the party. See you in the morning. Xx

The air is cool. The sky is mottled navy, starless. The clouds have kept the evening warm. I stretch my arms out and exhale heavily into the night.

'Ava? Ave.'

Neil's voice. I shiver, turn around, wait while he jogs the few steps to join me.

'Sorry,' I say. 'I had to get out. Just…'

'Yeah. Bit intense.'

We stand a moment, awkward in each other's company, before walking to the end of the drive. Another three or four steps and I am in front of my own home. Neither of us has spoken.

'Kind of you to walk me all this way,' I say.

He shrugs. 'You know me.'

No, I don't, not anymore, I want to say. But I say nothing of the sort obviously.

'Was it complete torture tonight?' I ask instead.

He nods, his eyes flicking over to the Lovegoods' front

door, to the pavement, though not to me. 'Did you hear him? Going on about my overalls? Arsehole.'

He is slurring his words. Only slightly, but I've known him as long as I've known Matt; I know how he sounds when he's had too much to drink and how much drink that takes.

'I don't think he meant it unkindly,' I offer.

He shakes his head. 'You say that because you don't know him.'

'I think he's clumsy more than anything. Tries too hard, that's all. It'll be insecurity, underneath it all, I reckon. It usually is.'

'I wouldn't know. I'm not deep.'

'Don't say that.'

'What?'

'Don't pretend you're not smart, or that you don't feel. You are smart. You know you are. And you do feel. You feel deeply.'

I feel myself blush. The cocktails have loosened my tongue. Which is their job, I suppose.

Neil glances towards the end of the street before looking back at his shoes. The cavity of my chest heats, swells.

'Neil.' I'm hoping that by saying his name, the courage to speak plainly will follow. Cocktails or no, it is so hard to tell our closest friends when they've hurt us. There's always the fear they will resent the reproach, that nothing will be the same afterwards. But we are beyond that, I suppose.

'I know you don't like seeing us,' I begin. 'I mean, I know you find it difficult to see me.'

'Work's been mad.' He kicks at the ground but doesn't look up.

'I know. I know that. But…' Now it's me glancing around: at the damson trees that line our street, where posters once asked *HAVE YOU SEEN THIS GIRL?* 'I know how difficult it is, that's all I'm saying. And I know you're grieving too, I think I realised that tonight, properly. I know you loved her too – that's all I wanted to say.'

Somehow his gaze unglues itself from his shoes. When he looks at me, it is right into my eyes and it seems that his are full of pain – his, my own. With a jolt, I realise it is the first time he has looked at me, really looked at me, since that day.

'I did love her,' he says, his bottom lip trembling, a heart-wrenching sight in such a man. 'I did,' he repeats, looking away again. 'You've got to know that.' Overcome, he covers his eyes with his hand and lets out a gasp of distress.

I reach out, lay the flat of my hand on his arm. It is getting chilly. I have started to tremble. In the papoose, Fred sleeps on, cocooned against my chest.

'I know you loved her,' I say softly. 'I do know that, of course I do. And she adored you. I just haven't had room to… for anything else. Anyone else. And if I'm honest, I've been hurt by how distant you've been, but I understand. And I don't blame you.'

He lets out a cry. 'Oh God, Ava,' he says. 'I'm so sorry. I've let you down, I've let both of you down. I'll never forgive myself.'

'Oh, Neil, come on. It wasn't your fault. I'm the one who left the door open. It's my fault. All of it.' Tears run down my face. I push them away, into my hair, and sniff.

'Now who's talking rubbish. It wasn't your fault, all right? You've got to stop beating yourself up about that. It's killing you, I can see it is.'

He holds out his arms. I lean into him. He pulls me to him in a kind of half-hug. My head falls against his chest, Fred between us. Neil is so much thicker-set than Matt and he feels good: solid. The embrace lasts longer than either of us intend. When we pull apart, he wipes his eyes with the backs of his hands and seems about to walk away, but a moment later, I'm not sure quite how, his forehead is pressed against mine, his hand at the back of my head, keeping me there.

'I wish I could have brought her back to you,' he whispers. 'I'll never forgive myself.'

'You did everything you could,' I whisper back. 'It's me who'll never forgive myself.'

There is a beat, and it is no more than that, when a kiss is a possibility, not a kiss of friendship, nor one of two people caught up in lust for one another. Another kind of kiss, a connection too deep, a moment too intimate for what we are supposed to be to one another. I am certain he feels it too.

He breaks away, breathes out a heavy, shuddering sigh.

'I've been so wrapped up in… everything,' I rush in. 'I forgot you and Bella were suffering. I didn't think about you guys at all, really, and I'm sorry too, for that. But it's been all I can do to get through. I'm still taking it one day at a time. I didn't even know the Lovegoods' daughter had any kind of learning difficulties. Jen's my next-door neighbour, she's my friend, for God's sake, and she's been so kind to me and I didn't even… What does that make me? I'm… I'm a monster.' My eyes fill. I make myself stop.

'You're not a monster.' He takes my hand, rubs his thumb across the back of my knuckles. His skin is rougher than Matt's, a scratch in the caress, and this too feels dangerous. 'You're doing great, Ave. You've got to take it one day at a time. And I'm sorry we've not been round. Work's no excuse.'

'You've seen Matt though, haven't you?' I take my hand from his. 'I know he appreciates you getting him to do the triathlon and everything. I suppose it's hard hooking up like we used to, without Abi there. It's like there's a hole that can't be filled, and none of us have been able to face that. I just wish we knew what happened, you know? That's the worst thing – the not knowing, hanging over us all the time. I know the evidence points overwhelmingly to her drowning, but with no body… Just the thought of her being taken, being out there… suffering.' Suffering. All that is contained in that word, all that is unspeakable. 'And that I'm responsible for that. No one else. Me. How can any mother ever get over that?'

'Ava, please.' He tries to take my hand again, but I snatch it away.

'No, Neil, it's true. I wish I'd never had Fred. I wish I hadn't been pregnant. I never would have had another child, never. And I can't tell anyone how I feel because it's too awful. I haven't even told my counsellor, but the truth is, I don't deserve a baby. I'm not a good enough mother. I'm not safe.' I am weeping, and the fact of it shocks me. I have spent a year avoiding Neil, barely speaking to him, and now, now I can't stop the rush of words, of tears, pouring all over him, things I have never said out loud, have barely dared think. We are friends become strangers become friends again – almost more – crying together on the street. This is what we have needed to do, all this time. We have both known it. But it has been too frightening.

'You've been strong,' he says eventually. 'You have. I know you think you haven't, but you have. And I can understand you want to believe Abi's still alive, but…'

'Matt's the strong one,' I say, not taking on board what I know he's leading up to, what everyone wants me to accept. 'Can't even admit to using the last tea bag, never thought he'd be the rock for us both.'

'You mean the absolute world to him – you know that, don't you? He'd never leave you. He'd do anything to keep hold of you, I mean.' Now that Matt is front and centre of the conversation, I feel the danger passing, am unsure whether it was really there.

'I don't know, Nee. I'm horrible to him, just horrible, a lot of the time. If I were him, I'd leave me. God knows, I'm a misery. A misery that can't be trusted.'

Neil puffs his cheeks and blows out a long blast of air. 'You're killing me, Ave. You can't keep saying this stuff. It isn't like you think. It's not your fault, trust me, I *know* it wasn't.'

'What?' I wipe my face, meet his pale-blue eyes. My guts have folded over. 'What do you mean? What do you know?'

He shakes his head. 'Nothing. Forget I said it.'

'Neil. What do you know? If you know something, you have to tell me. You owe me that. Please, Neil. How do you know it wasn't my fault?'

'You…' His face crumples.

'Neil! Please! I'll beg you if I have to. I'll go down on my knees.'

'All right.' He raises his palms to me, looks behind him, towards the Lovegoods' house, back to me. 'But you've got to know he did it for you, all right?'

'What? Who?'

'Matt. He loves you. He'd lie down on hot coals for you – you know that, don't you? But it was him, babe.'

'Him?'

'He left the door open. It wasn't you. It was him.'

CHAPTER TWENTY-TWO

Matt

'Where's Nee gone?' Bella has materialised out of thin air and is looking all about her. 'I literally saw him here five seconds ago.'

'Bella,' he says. 'Where've you been hiding?'

'God knows. Where's Nee though, Matt?'

'He…' Matt gestures towards the kitchen but gets no further. 'I was looking for Ava, but I can't see her either.'

'Check this place out, eh?' Bella says then, the whereabouts of her husband apparently no longer a priority. She takes a sip of her tall pink drink through a black paper straw, then fixes Matt with a direct, almost flirtatious stare. She releases the straw and smacks her lips. 'I don't think I've been to a party where they have actual waiters in the house. The guy on the bar's, like, a proper mixer. I literally told him what I wanted and he mixed a cocktail just for me.' She holds up her glass and looks at it. 'This is a Pink Gin Bella! It's delicious! Try it!'

Matt shakes his head.

'Oh go on. Don't be boring.' She holds the straw to his lips and reluctantly he takes a sip.

'Nice,' he says, without knowing what he means.

'Can you taste the rhubarb?' Bella asks, eyes twinkling. 'It's got rhubarb in it.' Her brow furrows. 'Or was it gooseberries?

I can't remember. Anyway, this is my fourth, lol.' As if to prove it, her eyelids half close and she sways a little. 'Johnnie said he's going to turn the music up in a minute. He asked me to start the dancing.'

'Great,' Matt says, his gaze wandering again to the kitchen. No sign of either Neil or Ava. He has left Ava alone, as he said he would not. He went to check on Neil and when he looked round, she'd gone. Then Neil left, and he got talking to Pete Shepherd, the retired guy from over the road. He meant to look for Ava, he did. But somehow he forgot about her.

The flash of guilt amplifies in the face of another realisation: it has been a relief. To forget about her.

'Have you seen Ava?' he asks Bella.

She shakes her head. 'I saw her a while ago. Before the speeches, well, not speeches – you know what I mean.'

'I'm going to find her, OK?'

'K, babe.' Bella raises her glass. Her eyes close as she first misses then finds her lips with the end of the straw.

In the kitchen, the music is louder. The voices have amplified in such a large space. The kitchen is too big, he thinks. A garage. An aircraft hangar. The hard surfaces, the high gloss and the lack of curtains or soft furniture make the cacophony of voices bounce around, make it sound like there are a hundred people here when there are about half that. A warm smell of spices reaches him; hot snacks on square black plates spread across the ice-white kitchen bar. It is almost 10 p.m. and the atmosphere is boozy. This has happened quickly, possibly on account of the strong cocktails and perhaps because everyone is so excited to get a look *inside the Lovegoods'* – God knows, Pete Shepherd could barely contain his scandalised excitement, eyes popping as he took it all in, brain visibly exploding at his own wild estimations of the outrageous cost.

Stopping to grab another beer from the artful selection piled high on blue ice in some sort of futuristic metal trough, Matt takes the opportunity to taste what turns out to be a rice ball with melted cheese – mozzarella? – inside, delicately flavoured with… cumin? Fennel? Chilli, definitely, and salt. My God, it's good.

'Matt,' someone says.

He turns to find Jennifer Lovegood standing beside him, her features soft with alcohol and the early years of her forties, he guesses.

'This is so good,' he mumbles, holding up the… thing.

'*Supplì*, yes, they're great, aren't they? Angelo's, the Italian deli over in Barnes – do you know it? Anyway, I'm so glad you and Ava came. How are you?'

'Erm, fine,' he replies, preoccupied. 'Actually, I was looking for Ava.'

She glances about, her height allowing her to scan the room. 'She's probably in the sitting room. I showed her it earlier, in case she needed somewhere quiet to feed Fred.'

Unable to stop himself, he looks around for his wife, sees a woman he vaguely recognises with white hair, palm pressed to the top of a walking stick, in earnest debate with a tall bespectacled man with a grey Gandalf beard while Shirley, Pete's wife, listens in.

'I had a good chat with Ava,' Jennifer is saying, pulling him back. 'We stayed in the sitting room until she settled. Which she did. She's coped brilliantly.'

He meets her eye. Her soft Irish accent soothes him; it makes him want to believe everything she says, though he has no idea why that is. She has a calmness, a deep intelligence in her soft grey eyes, which is in stark contrast to her husband's rather jarring brand of being. If we're lucky, we find the person we need, he thinks. That's what Jennifer is for Johnnie, what Bella is for Neil and what Ava was for him; he can't afford to forget that. He just has to get her back to being that person. He has to make her right, make her herself again. Perhaps tonight will be the start.

'Ava said the police have scaled back the investigation,' Jennifer says, with a directness that takes him aback but somehow doesn't grate on his nerves like Johnnie does. No one apart from the Lovegoods has mentioned Abi tonight. No one ever does, unless he brings it up. Which he doesn't. Ever.

'Oh, that was months ago.' He makes himself meet Jennifer's gaze. 'They haven't closed the case, but there are no new leads for the moment.' How odd it feels to say it out loud. 'I suppose we'll always be looking for new leads. I'm trying to get Ava to move on, but…'

Jennifer is nodding gravely, but there is nothing vampiric in her attention to the open, bleeding wound of his life. 'It must be so tough.'

Such a simple statement.

'It's hell actually,' he replies. Another simple statement. What else is there? It is hell. Or purgatory, perhaps – a grim antechamber, waiting. Forever, possibly. He wants to say more, to add that he believes his daughter drowned that day, that it was an accident, not a dumping of her body after something sinister, that he has chosen to believe this for his own sanity, but he doesn't. 'The police think she drowned,' he says instead. 'They think she was feeding the ducks and got overexcited, maybe tried to pet one and lost her balance. They've said as much.' That it's the police that have said this makes it sound less like he's writing her off in one great dismissive act of callousness. Yes, he has felt callous. Feels callous. As if he wants his daughter dead. Which he doesn't obviously. But if she'd had some sort of accident, that would be better. Better than…

'Your daughters are lovely,' he says, sounding inane even to himself.

'Thank you. And your baby boy is an absolute darling. I love the name. Fred. A grandparent?'

'Chopin.'

'Ah. Of course. Ava teaches piano, doesn't she? I'd love to learn to play. I used to but I gave up – typical idiotic teenage move.'

He gets the sense that Jennifer is acknowledging his need to change the subject rather than, as is often the case around here, simply waiting until she can talk about her own children. She has been so direct with him; he figures he can return fire.

'Your elder daughter, Jasmine,' he begins but hasn't the courage to continue.

'She has Angelman syndrome,' Jennifer offers, her frankness extending, then, to herself.

He nods. 'She seems incredibly happy. She lit up the room earlier.'

Jennifer smiles. 'She does that. It's part of her condition. She smiles a lot, laughs a lot. She flaps her hands. Other things too, which you won't have noticed, like her obsession with water and shoes. She's less obsessed now that she's a teenager, but when she was little, she used to fill my slippers with water. Well, all of our shoes actually, but particularly my slippers for some reason.' She laughs.

'Wow. I've never heard of that.'

'She's echolalic too.'

Matt inclines his head in question.

'Sorry, you get used to the terms. She repeats back what people have said. An echo. Echolalic. She has limited language, but she can attach words to things or people. She can ask for things in her own way. Earlier, she said "bicycle" because we always point them out to her and she's seen Kevin so many times on his.'

'And she called Neil "Pockets".'

She grimaces. 'He seemed a bit pissed off about that.'

Matt waves it away. 'Oh, he's OK, don't worry about it. Neil's a great guy but he can be a bit… sensitive, in a way. He's one of the cleverest, smartest people I know, but he's not… he's…'

'Not academic?'

'Exactly. He's dyslexic, but he's clever. Cleverer than me in so many ways. And driven, you know? He's done it all himself, in his own way. Sometimes I feel like I've been channelled through a tube, the funnel of higher education, I suppose, whereas Neil just got out there into the world and made it happen. He didn't need channelling. The whole academic thing can be a bit in-your-face, particularly round here. It never used to be like that when I was a kid. Now, it's like it's the one true path or something. I'm not sure what I'm trying to say, to be honest. I suppose we all feel inadequate, one way or another.'

'You're obviously very proud of him.' Jennifer takes a sip of her drink. It is clear and fizzy and he suspects it's mineral water. She's not the type to get drunk, he thinks. Not the type to lose control.

'You seem very close,' she continues.

'We've been friends since we were eleven. We were each other's best man, et cetera.'

'Well, he's a good guy. Very hard worker, very reliable. I trusted him one hundred per cent in the house, which is a bigger thing than you might expect when you're having work done, especially with a vulnerable child. A lot don't seem to remember they're in someone else's home, it's just a job to them, but Neil respected my wishes without question. And Jasmine loved him.'

'Did she?'

'Pockets,' Jennifer says, smiling again. 'He used to hide her toys in one of his overall pockets, and when he saw her, he would pull out her teddy or her doll or whatever it was and say, "What's this doing in my pocket?" And she would laugh hysterically and repeat it, you know – pockets, pockets, pockets.' She shakes her head fondly. 'Sometimes she'd give him the toy and put the two together – doll pockets or teddy pockets. And he understood what she was asking and would repeat the whole thing for her – so sweet.'

That sounds so like Neil, so like the way he would tease Abi. Matt takes a sip of his beer just as one of the neighbours from the other end of the street begins to talk to Jennifer and he realises she's been waiting for a pause in the conversation. Her hands are gathered at her chest and she looks like she's queuing to meet her favourite actor. The Lovegoods have this effect on people. They possess something approaching star quality. Suburban star quality. He wonders if, whatever world you inhabit, there are always celebrities, whether it's just a question of scale.

He taps Jennifer on the arm by way of see you later and pushes through what feels like a thickening throng despite the lateness of the hour. A crowd like this he would have expected to be drifting away by ten, safe home to bed, nothing too wild.

Ava is not in the garden. There's no sign of Bella either. He doubles back into the house. No Ava, no Bella, no Neil. The rolled steel joists strike him – that they have not been boxed in by plasterboard and have been painted grey to stand out against the paler grey walls does look pretty cool, he has to admit. The edges and bolts give a trendy, urban vibe. The Lovegoods are a little ahead of the curve, and he suspects many of the people here tonight will criticise what they see, only to copy some of these ideas in the years to come.

He rests his hand against the beam and feels the strength of it. Something else too, although it could be his imagination: the rhythm of the music seems to be coming into the palm of his hand, up his wrist. The living pulse of the house. Buildings have a soul, he believes this. They transmit a feeling, almost immediately. He knows it has to do with design, with layout, with colour, and with the people in them, whether or not the guests are truly welcome, whether or not the hosts have had a blazing row five minutes before, but sometimes it feels more mysterious than that, as if the very foundations, bricks and walls are in fact a living body, the plumbing the digestive system, the electrics the veins and arteries. He looks up and only then does he notice an industrial-looking clock fixed with huge bolts to the metal beam. This is what he felt – not the music, but this, the beat of the seconds, like a heart.

And at that, a shiver passes through him. Abi, her tiny heart. Her tiny beating heart, stopped.

His eyes fill. He's a bit drunk, that's what it is. No doubt about it. If he can feel Abi with him now, it is because the drink has loosened all the things he has preferred to – has had to – keep tied up.

CHAPTER TWENTY-THREE

Ava

How blue Neil's eyes are, darker under this navy sky. He has aged this last year, I think – violently so. I have this thought before the knowledge falls into me, before it lands.

'What do you mean?' I say, beginning to understand the words but still unable to grasp their meaning fully. 'What are you talking about, I didn't leave the door open? How can it have been Matt? He wasn't there.'

Neil shakes his head. In his eyes, the passing reflection of the moon.

'I swore I wouldn't tell you,' he says. 'I shouldn't have told you. But it's going to kill you. It's going to kill all of us. You didn't leave the front door open, babe. None of this is your fault.'

He sits on the wall outside our house and covers his face with his hands. I make to sit beside him, but I can't. I can't sit down. I have to pace, two steps away, two steps back, shaking my hands as if to dry them, my fingers spread and stiff.

'But he went to work,' I whisper, the horror still peripheral, still arriving. 'He'd already gone.'

'Do you remember it was raining? Well, he popped back for his coat.'

'His coat?' I try to think. On the corner of the street. Abi taking a tumble. Blood on the pavement. Matt teasing her with Mr Sloth, kissing her, kissing me, cycling away. 'His red top,' I say, seeing it, seeing the undulating muscles in his shoulders under the stretchy fabric as he rode away, seeing him later, when he got back, when I found him standing by his bike in front of our house. I try, but I can't picture him, not then, but later, later I see him clearly, his silhouette in the doorway, phone to his ear.

'He was in his black rain jacket,' I say, to myself as much as Neil. 'When he called the police, he was in black. I didn't think it—'

'He just popped back and grabbed his jacket.' Neil's shoulders are round and his belly sticks out against his shirt, the fabric splaying between the buttons. 'He said he called ta-ta but you didn't hear him. He was running late, he said, so when he realised he'd left the door open, he just carried on to work, but only 'cos he thought you'd be back downstairs by then. He didn't do it on purpose. It was just one of those things.'

My eyes feel gritty. I blink to clear them. To see. To see, to see, to see. Opposite, the triangular roofs of the houses, so many triangles, all the same, white arrows heading away to the end of the street. Somewhere a mating vixen cries out in pain and confusion.

'Why didn't he tell me?'

Neil doesn't look up. 'He didn't tell you because you were hysterical. Everything happened too fast, everyone was panicking. He panicked too. He thought she'd turn up and it would come to nothing. And then later, when she didn't, I think he thought it was too late. The moment had gone. And he thought telling you would make things worse.'

A group of four neighbours come stumbling out of the party, laughing, making much more noise than they would normally. Seeing us, they shush each other with the theatricality of the very drunk, nod hello and stagger on their way, suppressing giggles.

'How long have you known?' I ask.

Neil stares at the ground. Chafes the soles of his brogues back and forth across the paving stones.

'How long, Neil?'

'Since that night.'

My heart hammers. My breath comes fast and shallow. 'That night?' I punch him in the shoulder, punch him again, again, again.

'Ava!' He grabs my wrists. 'Ava, stop! Ava!'

'Get off me.' I struggle against him.

'Ava, I'm sorry,' he says. 'Maybe I shouldn't have told you, but I can't stand to see you like this. I can't stand by and watch you destroy yourself. But you have to forgive him, babe. He loves you more than anything in this world.'

'Loves me? No he doesn't. Who does that to someone they love? Fuck you, Neil. Fuck both of you, you pair of fucking cowards.'

I start to run.

'Ava,' I hear him say. 'Come on. Please.'

I scrabble to find the key, find it, plunge it into the lock. Once inside, I slam the front door shut and lean against it, my head full of white noise.

Matt. Matt left the door open. My own husband is responsible for my daughter's…

I sink to the floor, my face pressed to the back of my little boy's soft head.

It wasn't you. It was him.

CHAPTER TWENTY-FOUR

Matt

His pocket is vibrating. His phone. His phone is buzzing. He didn't hear it above the music. He waves at Bella, who he eventually found in the garden an hour or so ago now. She gives him a thumbs up before staggering slightly against Pete Shepherd, who laughs and is more than happy to hold her up. He leaves them on the patio, which is now the dance floor, and wanders to the end of the garden. It is a little quieter here, in the thick dark beside the fence. On the screen is a missed call from Neil. One minute ago. A message throws up a blue speech bubble.

I had to tell her. Tried to call you. Sorry.

A feeling of unease unfurls within him. Sorry. Tell her. Tell her what? Tell who what? He checks his watch, sees that it's after eleven.

What? he thumbs and presses send.

There is another text, earlier. From Ava.

Have gone home. All OK. Enjoy the party. See you in the morning. Xx

His phone flashes. Neil.

I told her it was you who left the door open. I can explain but we need to talk. I'm so sorry, mate. I had no choice.

His guts churn. He leans his hand against the Lovegoods' back fence, worries he might be sick. Neil must have followed Ava out of the party. He should have looked harder, should have followed her himself. She's his wife. He promised he'd stick by her and he hasn't, couldn't even stay by her side and help her through the sight of the Lovegoods' little one waving goodnight.

'Shit,' he whispers. 'Shit shit shit.'

He calls Neil.

'Neil.' He pushes one hand against his ear to block out the Latin American music throbbing at full blast.

'Mate, I had to,' Neil says.

'Why?'

'She needs help, mate. She's going under. We can't do this to her, it's not right.'

Matt pinches the bridge of his nose, but the music is so loud he has to cover his ear once again to hear, to concentrate on what he wants to say. 'I don't… I wish you hadn't. Is she… how did she take it?'

'Not well. You need to get home, mate.'

'How did you even end up talking to her? Were you on your own?'

'She was outside when I left the do. She was crying, so I… I talked to her obviously. We haven't spoken since… you know, and I was just trying to calm her down. But I could see she was going mental with it, you know? The guilt is eating her up. There'll be nothing left of her if she carries on like this. So I told her. I told her you didn't tell her 'cos you love her. I explained it. Honestly, I did my best. I'm sorry, mate, I didn't know what else to do.'

Matt's head aches. He feels suddenly very sober.

'I'm sorry, mate,' Neil repeats miserably.

Someone taps him on the back. He turns to see Bella performing a drunken shimmy, mouthing at him to come back to the dance floor, miming ending the call.

He raises one finger, then turns away from her.

'No, *I'm* sorry,' he says to Neil. 'I should have told her.'

'Well you need to get home. Is Bella still there?'

Matt turns. Bella is now sitting on the floor laughing hysterically. She holds up her arms and is pulled to her feet by Pete Shepherd. By the bar, Johnnie is smoking what looks like a joint and giggling like a fourteen-year-old at a wedding. A string of fairy lights is looped around his neck. There is no sign of Jennifer.

'She's here. She's having a good time, don't worry. Listen, I'm going to go.'

'Sure. I'm sorry, OK?'

Neil rings off.

Bella is back on her feet, dancing. Matt edges around the lawn, sidles into the kitchen and through the hall. At the front door, he looks back at the utter tip that is the Lovegoods' kitchen, the perfect party lying now in ruins, as if a bomb has gone off, blowing everything to bits.

His own house is silent, save for the dull thud of the music from next door.

He takes off his shoes and tiptoes up the hall, half expecting to find Ava in the kitchen red-eyed and waiting for him. But she's not there.

He creeps up the stairs, hears the dull clank of the en suite shower door closing. She must have had a shower. She will be drying herself. If she heard the front door, she will be readying herself to face him, to confront him. An old dread bubbles up inside him. He is six. His father is throwing open the door to his bedroom, red-faced with some fresh outrage Matt has committed but as yet knows nothing about. He freezes, halfway up the stairs.

The creak of floorboard on the landing, the slightest alteration in the light, and Ava is a shadow in the bedroom doorway.

'Ava?'

She recedes into the bedroom. After a moment, he steels himself and follows.

She is sitting on the far side of the bed. Her back is to him. She is wrapped in a turquoise towel, her wet hair pushed back.

'Ava, I'm sorry.' He stays at his side of the bed, unsure of what else to do.

'What for?' She doesn't look round.

'You know what for. Neil called me. I'm sorry I didn't tell you. I'm so sorry. But that day… it all went so fast. I wanted to tell you, but the police were there and everyone was asking questions and you were hysterical, and the thing is, I never thought… I never thought we wouldn't find her. I never thought… and then the day went on and we didn't… we didn't find her and then there were dogs and the helicopter and they were talking about the river and then next thing it was dark and me and Neil—'

'And that's when you told Neil. When you told your friend but not your wife.'

He feels sick. He wants to climb across the bed and touch her but he knows he can't.

'I had to tell someone,' he says. 'And it was too late to tell you. And then they found her coat and I knew she was dead, I just knew it, and I thought if you knew it was my fault you'd… I thought you'd leave me. I didn't think you'd ever forgive me.'

She takes her nightie from under the pillow and pulls it over herself before removing the towel. The action is not lost on him.

'Ava? Talk to me. I'm so sorry.'

She lifts herself momentarily off the bed to pull the nightie down. Still she doesn't look at him.

'I'm sorry,' he says, his voice breaking.

'I should hope you are,' she says quietly. 'But sorry's not going to cover it, is it?'

His chest sinks.

'Do you know what gaslighting is?' she asks.

'What? Oh, come on. I wasn't gaslighting you.'

Her hand flies up in a stop sign. She still has her back to him; when she speaks, it is to the opposite wall.

'Gaslighting is when you encourage the belief in something you know to be untrue, to the detriment of someone's mental health.'

The effect of having only the back of her head to look at is disconcerting. He longs to tell her to turn round, to at least talk to him face to face, but he has, he knows, lost the right to object.

'Like, say,' she continues, still in this terrifying, simmering calm, 'if you tell someone they didn't post a letter when they know they did, or, to be literal, that the light is no dimmer than the day before even though you know you yourself turned down the flame and that the room is darker. Or, let me think… if you tell someone they left the front door open, a mistake that cost them the life of their daughter, when you know that actually they didn't do that. When you know that actually it was you. You left the door open. That. That's gaslighting.'

'Ava, come on. That wasn't my intention at all. I didn't do it to control you or drive you mad. I did it to save us. There was no malice, none whatsoever. I thought if you knew it was me you'd leave and then I'd have lost you and Fred as well as Abi. And *you* would lose our family too. There was too much at stake. We'd both already lost too much. Ava, I love you.'

She turns, finally, slowly, raises one knee onto the bed. This time she does look at him, she looks right at him, and he wishes she hadn't. Her eyes are small and filled with scorn.

'You might not have *meant* to drive me to losing my mind. But the fact is, you did. You did, Matt, and you've stood by and watched. And the reason you didn't tell me is much less complicated than you claim. You're a coward. That's the reason. I knew you were a coward before we were married, but I thought, with time, you'd get stronger. I thought my love would make you a braver man, but it didn't. It hasn't. You lied because you were too scared to admit to your responsibility. I know this is what you do, in life, but I never thought you'd do it to me. You've watched me drive myself into the ground with guilt, knowing that you could save me from that at least. You've watched me for a *year*. You've lied to me for a *year*, watched me come undone, watched me fight so hard to climb this fucking hill of sand without ever once holding out your hand to pull me up.' She begins to cry. 'Don't you understand?

We're done. There is nothing left of us. I will never trust you again, about anything. And so… there's nothing, nothing left.'

'Don't say that.' His chest tightens with dread. This is not an argument. This is much, much bigger. He should have known it would be like this. Perhaps he did. 'Please, Ava. I didn't lie to you, not like that. We can work through this. Maybe I need help too. I can get help.'

'That's up to you. I've had help, Matt. A lot of help. I don't go a day without using my shiny new CBT techniques to argue myself out of a crisis. I'm down to twenty milligrams a day. I'm doing ever so well.' The sarcasm drips. She climbs onto the bed, shifts herself up against the headboard.

'Ava—'

'There is nothing to work through.' She arranges a pillow behind her, sits back and folds her arms. 'All the help I've had, did you not once think that you, *you*, could have helped more than anyone? I hate you, do you understand that? I hate you. At some point you have to stand up and take responsibility, be the man you promised yourself you'd be. And you didn't. Neil has kept your shabby secret for you, but it was so grim, so difficult, he couldn't even face me. Couldn't look me in the eye. The moment he did, his compassion was too strong – his *love* was too strong – and he *had* to tell me.'

She gives a brief laugh, full of disdain. 'Didn't lie to me? Are you serious? *Oh darling, don't blame yourself. We all make mistakes. We need to move on. You* need to move on, Matt – *you* do. It's your fault. No wonder you're so keen to bury her. Of course you lied! Of course you did! You're capable of doing that to another human being, a human being you're supposed to love, when Neil… Neil had one glimpse and couldn't bear it and he's not the one who's supposed to love me more than anyone else, is he?' A tear rolls down each of her cheeks. 'He's not supposed to love me more than you.'

CHAPTER TWENTY-FIVE

Ava

Fred is moaning, a soft ack-ack. My eyes hurt, my head, my back. I reckon I have about a minute's more rest. Babies know when you haven't slept. They know like Darth Vader knows and they punish you.

His cries become more insistent. I haul myself out of bed and lift him from his crib. My limbs are heavy, my eyelids made of stone. I have a memory of birds singing but I can't remember if this is from falling asleep or waking. But no matter how empty the tank, the sight of my son fills me with relief as it does every morning. I have come to associate love with relief. He is alive, thank God. Today he is alive and I can see him, hear him, hold him, smell him, feel his warmth. He has made it through the night. He is breathing. That's what the relief – the love – is, even now.

Beside me, the bed is empty.

I remember.

My marriage is over. My now ex-husband is in the spare room.

I cradle Fred to me and weep into his soft hair. I have no idea what to do, what happens next. The only person I want to talk to, to confide in about this terrible thing, is Matt, but he's not mine, not anymore.

I take Fred with me to the bathroom and hold him to me even while I pee. In the bathroom mirror, my face is a shock. My eyelids are swollen, pink and shiny as boils. I look like I did the morning after that day. No sleep. Hours of crying. This is what despair looks like: it is ugly. It doesn't smell great. It retains water.

Downstairs, Fred over my shoulder, I make myself a strong cup of tea. My blood pressure is low, I can tell from the dizzy feeling, the stars that circled when I first stood up out of the bed. I didn't eat more than a handful of crisps last night. Drank too much. I nibble a biscuit and feel the revival of sugar hitting blood. On the sofa in the living room, I sit and feed Fred. The front of our house faces east, so I like to feed him here and watch the sun come up: learning, or relearning, to extract joy from small things.

Is that what I will continue to do now? How does this work? How bad do things have to be before mindfulness is as much use, to coin one of my mother's phrases, as a chocolate fireguard?

I wonder what Barbara will say to this fresh development, how she will guide me through the loss of my husband, my soulmate, my best friend, a year after my daughter.

Try to slow things down. Is that what she will say? *Try to savour simple pleasures. Charge your batteries with moments of pleasure, no matter how small, as best you can. Think only about what's happening now.* Really, will that be enough?

After twenty minutes, Fred lolls back, milk-drunk, dopey. I lay him on his sheepskin on the floor and cross over to the record player. Neil returns to my mind. How can he not? His intensity. His tortured face. Our foreheads touching in the deserted street. His solidity. His compassion.

I flick through the vinyl records, aware of how surreal it feels to do this. This, this now, is something I already know: the human ability to go forward with the most mundane rituals, the making of tea in the midst of a bombed-out house.

The other day I returned to the piano for the first time. Easy pieces for my rusty fingers. The first movement of the *Moonlight Sonata*, Debussy's 'Clair de Lune', the hooked-on classics everyone knows. It soothed me. I have to believe it will soothe me again. Today, on the day I wake up newly single, I am going to listen to a record. There is almost a sense of occasion, as if putting on the radio will not do. It's a long time since I have actively listened to music. I gave that up along with the teaching, the evenings out, coffee with friends, eating for pleasure, happiness. What began as a postponement has become all I can't face.

Perhaps this new crisis will send these pleasures rushing back. Perhaps, now, utterly alone, there will be a kind of numb and necessary psychopathy that will allow me to simply keep calm and carry on.

Matt always said I needed time. Time will heal. But it won't, that's my private opinion. And even if I did need time, I needed truth more. I still need it. There is still so much truth untold. The only difference between yesterday and today is the knowledge of a lie I hadn't even known about. So I am no further forward, not really. Matt's betrayal is a shock that will take me years to process; I know that. But it hasn't been a shadow – how can it have been? I had no idea. It is a new shadow, I suppose, and now I must sit in an even darker room, on my own, listening to this restless, hanging, dissonant devil's chord, waiting for a resolving note that no one seems able to play. No wonder it was associated with evil back in the eighteenth century, I think as I slide Kate Bush from her sleeve and decide, no, not quite. No wonder it was banned. The unresolved is an eternal drip torture.

I thought this was why Matt chose to believe that our baby girl had drowned, when in fact it was his way of processing guilt: to move on, to grieve. He has needed to end the cadence. I get that, I really do. I don't need to see the dark web to know what goes on there, don't even need to think about it. Matt's way of not thinking about it has been to choose death over it. It is easier to mourn the loss of our baby, to believe that her death was an accident. He knew that I had closed the door, had kept her safe, that he had opened that door, made her unsafe. So yes, it has been easier for him to think that her last waking thought would have been as vague and fleeting and full of benign joy as the falling itself, a brief moment of excitement about meeting the ducks she so loved before impact, the end, nothing.

Fast water. Such a small mass.

I need to choose a record. I'm supposed to be soothing myself, as I've been advised to do. God knows, I'm going to have to learn to do it myself.

Max Richter's *From Sleep*.

I slide it back into the stack. There is self-soothing and there is consciously choosing to make yourself fall apart.

Ditto Chopin's Prelude in E minor.

Ditto Debussy's *Prélude à l'après-midi d'un faune*.

Ditto The Carpenters.

Ditto Björk's *Vespertine*.

Hum.

Billie Holiday: a greatest hits collection that Matt gave me early in our relationship. I guess this will count as mine when we split our assets. Blue as low cloud but cathartic – sadness, yes, sorrow, absolutely, but with that crackling lacing of grit.

I guess we'll have to sell the house. We can't afford two properties.

I put the needle to the disc.

I wonder how we'll split custody?

Billie Holiday sings. Feeding Fred, I watch the sun rise. The music doesn't suit my mood perfectly, but it slows the running thoughts in my head. Last night feels like a puzzle I can't work out, like there is no puzzle, like a puzzle again. I am a puzzle. I am a mess. Less of a mess than I was but a mess nonetheless. Stop it. Listen to the music, Ava. Close your eyes. Listen. Be in the moment. That mellow bluesy wash. That phrasing. When all else fails, there is music. There is the sun that rises, there is Fred, there is tea, there is the soft sofa cushion beneath me. There is me.

I should return to teaching. Sod should. No, this is a good should. Maybe just a couple of kids after school, once a week, to start. Focusing on the children might help me escape from myself. I was deputy head of a primary school before Abi came along, responsible for the school choir, for playing the piano in assemblies and for school plays. I missed it, when I was first at home with Abi. I went back part-time, planned to build back up to full-time again before… that day. Afterwards, I could not imagine ever going back – to anything. Now, I think I could start. I could build up. Whatever has happened, wherever Abi is, I am on my own now. Fred needs me.

But even as I reason it in my mind, I am aware that this is a swing of the metronome, the weight slid to the top of the pendulum, the slowest possible beat. And as this awareness grows, so the pendulum swings back.

I have lost Matt. My love. My lover. My best friend.

Tears fall easily. I leave Fred dozing and sated on his sheepskin on the floor. I don't want to, know I shouldn't, but I check that the front door is locked, twice, before going upstairs to get dressed. It is almost eight. I push open the spare-room door a crack. Matt is sleeping, his mouth open, his chin dark with stubble. The bedroom stinks of stale alcohol, sour sweat and rank breath. The pain of what he has done returns to my chest. The trampled boundaries I cannot rebuild. I can't forgive him. I cannot.

But still, from the bathroom, I fetch paracetamol and a glass of water, which I take back to the spare room and leave on the bedside table.

Needing to keep moving, I wash my face, pull back my hair into a ponytail. I find jeans and a T-shirt on the back of a chair and put them on, grab clean socks from the drawer.

Downstairs, I try to notice how fresh the milk is, how nutty the muesli, how unctuous the yoghurt, how wonderful the word 'unctuous' sounds in my head. I do notice these things, notice myself noticing, know that it's myself outside myself, looking on, the I becoming the her. It doesn't work. A decaf coffee, made with the machine: smell the aroma, admire the burnt-caramel-coloured crema, the patterns the milk froth makes in the espresso. Yes, yes, Ava, well done.

It doesn't work. I can't imagine it ever will.

I take my coffee through to the living room. On the sofa, I sit still and tip my face to the sun. Feel the sun. Close my eyes to the warmth of the sun. No social media, no distractions, no life outside the present moment. I no longer go on my iPhone. I no longer have one, only a cheap mobile for emergency calls and texts. I am used to being alone now. Like this, utterly alone. I have no friends anymore. I had cut out most of the white noise. Now I have cut out all of it.

This will be easier. This will be my choice. No woman is an island. Wanna bet?

At 9 a.m., I pack Fred into the pram. One blanket should be enough on this, the first day of September. And Mr Sloth, of course.

It was Matt's idea to give Mr Sloth to Fred.

'Isn't that morbid?' I asked at the time, appalled. Now, of course, a darker shadow falls over it. It feels manipulative. Abusive.

'It could be a gift,' he said. 'From his older sister. It'll remind us to talk to him about Abi from the start. That way he'll absorb the knowledge over time and accept it without trauma.'

I no longer trust his reasons. I never wanted to keep the sloth. I should have burned it like I wanted to, along with this pram.

I put Mr Sloth on top of the pram. At the front door, I breathe deeply and place my hand on the catch. One glance in the hall mirror has me digging out my sunglasses. I look like I've gone ten rounds in the boxing ring.

Sunglasses on. You can do this, Ava. You've faced your neighbours once, you can do it again. Besides, it's early for a Sunday. There will be no one about.

Both feet barely on the front path and my stomach heats with anxiety at the noise of a door slamming shut. To my relief, it is only Jen emerging from her house, her two girls with her.

'Ava,' she calls and waves. She too is wearing sunglasses. Hers are large, expensive. 'A bit worse for wear this morning, I can tell you.' She laughs – she has an infectious, deep cackle I wish I could match.

I push the pram to the end of their drive. 'Thanks so much for last night,' I manage. 'I really had a lovely time. Much better than I thought, if you know what I mean. Thank you. Hi, girls.'

They smile, both reaching for their mother, one hand each.

'Sorry I left without saying goodbye,' I add.

'Oh for God's sake,' she says, waving it off. 'Don't even give it a second thought. Leaving when you did was a good move though. We got rid of the last guests at four in the morning.'

'Four? Oh my God. Who?'

'Louise – you know Louise Parker? And Pete from over the road, and your friend Bella.'

'Bella stayed till four in the morning?'

Jen nods. 'She was… she was well oiled, let's say.'

'Bloody hell. I bet Neil will have something to say about that.'

'I think he might have tried to retrieve her at about one, but she was having none of it.'

'Oh no. Did they fall out?'

Jen shakes her head. 'Bit of a drunken argument on the front step, I think, but she didn't seem upset or anything when she came back. Pete walked her home. He's such a gent.'

We smile. I wonder if she detects any strangeness in me. Because I feel very strange.

'Can I ask you something?' The words are out before I've reflected on the wisdom of saying them.

'Sure.'

'It's about Abi actually.'

She frowns. The merest glance towards her girls.

'It's nothing really,' I say. 'I was just wondering when you left that morning? Sorry, I mean the morning Abi…'

Behind her, Johnnie emerges from the house; the garage door lifts and he ducks inside. 'Erm,' Jen says, her brow furrowing. 'It will have been eight-ish. Why?'

'No real reason. I was wondering if you saw Matt at all, on his bike?' I want to say more, to add that he was coming back for his raincoat, but I don't dare.

'No, sorry. I thought he came back a bit later? Didn't he have a puncture that day?'

I nod, too quickly, too many times. 'Yes. Yes, he did.'

The Porsche comes purring out, Johnnie, in shades, at the wheel. He stops and gets out. He's dressed in black again, although he has changed to a short-sleeved linen shirt, loose long linen shorts and designer flip-flops. A sheen of sweat lies slick on his forehead, but other than that, he looks the definition of unruffled.

'Ava,' he says, picking up Cosima and opening the back door of the car.

'Johnnie. Hello.' I avert my eyes but feel the kick just the same – that easy scooping motion, how he will love the weight of her, how he will not even notice how much he loves that weight, how good it feels to scoop his child into his arms like that. My eyes prick; I am glad of my sunglasses, glad of Jasmine shouting hello now: hello, hello, hello. I match her radiant smile with my own ragged attempt. I focus hard on the beam of her happy expression. 'Hello again, Jasmine.'

'Hello again, Jasmine,' she says, smiling. 'Hello again, Jasmine.'

Unsure of how to relate to her, I smile back, pick up Mr Sloth and wiggle him. The impossibility of looking anywhere near Cosima makes my chest tight. A line of sweat runs down from each armpit. Johnnie is clipping her into her car seat, chatting to her. Her high child's voice reaches me like a thousand knives.

'Mr Sloth!' Jasmine is striding towards me, her expression one of pure joy. 'Mr Sloth, Mr Sloth!' She reaches out with both hands.

'Jasmine,' Johnnie calls out to her. 'That's not yours. That's the baby's toy, Jasmine.'

'Baby's toy, Jasmine,' she says. 'Baby's toy, Jasmine, baby's toy, Jasmine. Mr Sloth.'

'Mr Sloth is Fred's,' I say. 'But you can say hello.' I keep smiling, half wondering whether to give the toy to Jasmine, get rid of it. I can't bear it, I realise. I can't bear the sight of this toy.

Jasmine flaps both her hands.

'Pockets,' she says. She pulls out the front pocket of her baggy shorts. 'Mr Sloth pockets.'

My hair follicles tingle. I have no idea why. A buried, uneasy feeling returns, the same feeling I had when Jasmine recognised Neil at the party. I realise why only now. Neil said he never met Jen's kids. Or maybe that he didn't know them. Either way, clearly this is not true.

Jasmine is gesticulating, pulling at her pocket one moment and reaching for the toy the next.

'Mr Sloth,' she says. 'Mr Sloth pockets, Mr Sloth pockets.' She flaps her hands wildly, shifting her weight from foot to foot.

'Come on now, Jazzy,' Johnnie says with a chuckle. 'Into the car now, come on.'

But Jasmine is far too delighted by the toy and I, unsure of how to act, give it to her. It can't do any harm to let her have a moment's pleasure. It's a Sunday; there's no rush.

'Ah, now what do you say?' Johnnie says. He is so good with her, so patient. Kind. And yet...

'Do you say, do you say, do you say.' Jasmine stuffs the toy into her pocket, her face opening. She takes it out again, then, with an expression of such undiluted mischief it makes me laugh, puts it back in her pocket before taking it out once more and coyly giving it back. 'Mr Sloth pockets,' she says again, more quietly now. 'Mr Sloth pockets, pockets.' Her expression shifts, becomes earnest. 'Pockets.' She looks around, as if searching for something or someone. 'Pockets? Pockets?'

'Do you mean Neil?' I ask her. 'Is that who you mean?'

'Pockets,' the girl replies, smiling widely. 'Pockets.'

'Jasmine.' Johnnie takes hold of her shoulders and steers her towards the car. 'Come on now, darling – time to go. Say goodbye to Ava. Say goodbye, Ava.' He looks at me, his head a little to one side. 'We head to the park early to avoid the crowds, you know?'

'Say goodbye, Ava,' Jasmine repeats before I have time to answer. 'Say goodbye, Ava, say goodbye, Ava.'

'Bye, Jasmine,' I say and place Mr Sloth back on top of the pram. 'And thanks again for the party,' I call after them. 'I had a lovely time. Really lovely.'

Jennifer blows me a kiss. 'See you in the week,' she says. 'Well, next weekend, I should imagine. Why don't you come to me for coffee – maybe late Sunday morning? We can have a debrief.'

And what a debrief that will be.

'Sure,' I say. 'Thanks, I will. Eleven-ish?'

She gives me a thumbs up before ducking into the car.

Johnnie starts the engine.

Head down, I hurry past before they pull away. I am at the end of the road before I notice the tears coursing down my cheeks, my heart hammering in my chest.

CHAPTER TWENTY-SIX

Matt

Light leaks in from between the shutters, lower, brighter, warmer than it should be – it is late, later than he has woken up in a very long time. They don't have shutters. Yes, they do. In the spare room. Oh God. He sits up. His head bangs.

'Ah, Christ.'

There is water and a wallet of painkillers on the bedside table. Ava must have put them there. He wonders what that means, if he dares put any hope in it.

He takes two painkillers and drinks the water before, groaning and grunting like an old man, dragging himself into the shower. He lifts his face, lets the water pummel him. Afterwards, towelling himself dry, he catches sight of his reflection in the mirror. His ribs protrude like the bars of a glockenspiel; his eyes are red; his hair needs a cut and his chin is unshaven. He looks terrible, like a mangy, starving wolf.

He pulls on last night's black jeans and a fresh T-shirt and cleans his teeth twice before going downstairs to find Ava. She is not there, and when he sees that it is after eleven, a wash of guilt floods him. She has gone for a walk, alone. He knows all too well what that will have cost her. But as he prepares a pot of coffee, he hears the front door.

He has no idea what to say. Doesn't know if they are still together. Last night felt final, but perhaps…

'Hey,' he settles on, keen for her to know that he's up, that he's in the kitchen. He will take a shift with Fred this afternoon while she rests, he thinks. Make it up to her. They will talk.

She is at the kitchen door. She doesn't look cross, he thinks. But she is not looking at him.

'Where's Fred?'

'Asleep in the pram.'

'Coffee?' he tries. 'Decaf?'

'Actually no, I'll have a normal one for a change.'

Curt but civil. It is better than he deserves. He puts the pot and two mugs on the breakfast bar. Is about to put the milk out too when he decides to pour it into a jug.

'Very civilised,' Ava says.

He tries to ignore the feeling of discomfort this provokes in him. She always had a sarcastic streak, but it was a streak, not her default setting as it is now, and it was witty rather than bitter. He can't decide which this last was.

'Toast?'

'Sure.'

The mix of fear and uncertainty persists. He hates it, hates that he notices it, knows that you shouldn't feel like this in a relationship, knows that he never used to. And more. Knows that it is his fault. He has thrown both of them into confusion.

'Listen, I'm sorry,' he says, putting a plate of toast between them to share.

'We used to know how to have fun, didn't we? Once? That's how we started.' She sounds wistful, as if their early years together are now only a melancholy memory, part of a past she has had to put behind her. Is that what she has done?

For the moment unable to reply, he takes a bite of toast, another. He has no idea what she means. He had hoped last night would not follow them into this morning, or rather, he knew that it would but hoped it would have lessened somehow, that they would be able carefully to start building their marriage once again. He dares not speak, knows he must find words but can't, and now her face is clouding over, has darkened.

'Ava?' is what he finds to say. 'We can get through this, you know. We can get help.'

'I don't think we can,' she says, meeting his gaze briefly. She has the loveliest eyes. Soulful, intelligent, perceptive, and glazed now with unfathomable sadness. 'How on earth can we do that?'

He feels his guts plummet. 'Ava, come on. Please. I'm more sorry than I can say. I will never forgive myself.'

'I know you're sorry.' Her eyes brim, overflow. Tears run thinly down her cheeks. She dips her head and shields her face with her hand. 'I'm sorry too. I'm sorry and I'm sad and I know you'll never forgive yourself, but the trouble is, I'll never forgive you either.'

'Ava.' He rounds the breakfast bar and puts his arm around her. Miraculously, she lets him. 'Don't cry. Let's have this coffee, eh? I know we've got a lot to talk about, a lot to work through, but let's just sit together for a few minutes without crucifying ourselves.'

'You always wanted to move on,' she sobs. 'But that's because you couldn't stand your own guilt. I can't move on if I don't know what happened to her and I can't possibly be with you knowing that you lied about something so important, beyond important, and that you've reinforced that lie every day since, when at any moment you could have told me the truth.'

His throat aches. He fears he might burst into tears. He takes his arms from around her, returns slowly to his stool. 'I don't know what else I can say. Don't do this.'

'Do what? I haven't done anything. It isn't me that's broken our marriage.' She wipes her nose with the back of her hand. 'I've been walking all morning, trying to make sense of it all – us, the party.'

'The party? What's that got to do with us?' Despite the painkillers, his head pounds; his mouth tastes stale and grim.

'It's all tied up, isn't it? Abi, Neil, Bella. The Lovegoods. I saw them earlier. On their driveway.' She sighs, shaking her head. 'There are things that don't add up, Matt.'

'Like what?'

She is silent. The silence presses on his chest.

'Nothing,' she says eventually.

'Tell me,' he replies.

'Like Jasmine recognising Mr Sloth and then asking for pockets. Pockets is her name for Neil, yes? It's what she calls him.'

'What?' He can feel he has screwed up his face at her. But he doesn't know what the hell she's talking about and it scares him. 'You say our marriage is over and now you want to talk about Abi's cuddly toy and somehow pin something on my best friend? Really? You want to do this now?'

With a loud sniff, she raises her head. 'The trouble is, you want me to talk to you but then you don't listen. After everything you've done, I would've thought you'd have the grace to take me seriously, but no. Maybe this is why we can't talk to each other. Talking to each other is not who we are to one another anymore, is it? I shouldn't have even tried and, besides, you don't have the right to sit and talk to me over coffee like this. I'm not yours to talk to.'

From the hallway, Fred begins his cough-like cry.

'Ava, please. I can look after you. We can get better together.'

'No, we can't. How can we? You're no longer someone I trust. I want to trust you but I don't. I'm sorry about that, more than I can say.' Her eyes are so wounded he has to look away. He was right: last night was not an argument. It was final. Don't do this, he wants to say, over and over until she relents, but he doesn't.

'You need to pack your things,' she adds, no longer looking at him.

'Look,' he tries. 'I'll go in the morning, all right? I'll take Fred out this afternoon and you can sleep. I'm hung-over and I need to get myself sorted. I can't possibly—'

Her hand flies up. 'All right. All right. One more night. But if you're thinking I'll have changed my mind by then, I won't have. You have one more night to sort something out, but tomorrow, either book a Travelodge or sleep on someone's sofa, I don't care. I'm serious. I'll change the locks if I have to. And for the rest of the day, please just stay away from me.'

CHAPTER TWENTY-SEVEN

Ava

It's midnight. I stand at the door of the spare room and watch my husband sleep. I have no idea why I'm doing this. I am strange, I think. I have become strange.

Matt sleeps noiselessly these days. He used to snore; now it's like there isn't enough of him to produce that amount of noise – this rhythmic hushed breathing is all this skinny man can manage. Looking at him without being able to hold him makes me feel lonelier than if he weren't here at all. But I cannot touch him. We are no longer us. I always hated us falling out. Apart from Fred, he was all I had. Now I don't have him. Today we have hovered around each other like ghosts. Fred is all that's left.

I creep downstairs, fix myself a cold glass of milk and drink it standing at the front window of the living room. Opposite, Pete and Shirley's magnolia tree snakes its branches towards the never-quite-black sky. Not a soul about. On such lonely indoor night prowls as this, I am always struck by how desolate nocturnal suburban streets are. It is as if no one lives here, no one at all.

All day I have tried to turn over what Matt said to me earlier: that he can make amends, that somehow, together, we can heal. But if I can't talk to my own husband about why that bothers me, what chance is there? I have been stripped bare. Grief has unbuttoned me; betrayal has thrown away my clothes, and now there is no one to hold me, no one to throw a blanket around me and save me from the cold.

And despite all of this, despite the loneliness I have consciously chosen, still a nagging voice calls to me from deeper down. I feel it, bodily, as I feel music; hear the wrong note in the fiendishly difficult, un-spannable chord.

When struck with a fork, a glass with even a hairline crack does not chime.

I know we can all read things different ways; I'm not a fool. And I know I have been battered about, am hormonal, sleep-deprived. But I'm not paranoid. If I were paranoid, I would have suspected Neil that day. But I didn't. As late as last night, I saw in Neil only someone who loved us, loved our child, someone who would have moved heaven and earth to find her. God knows, I'm not even sure that I suspect him now, only that I can't for the life of me explain why Jasmine Lovegood would recognise Abi's toy. Something, something is off.

The loop of that morning has been replaced by the loop of Matt, of Bella, of Neil. Is that mad? Am I mad? Am I seeing things that aren't there? Neil loved Abi; I know that. And I know that my breakdown is probably why we've not seen him and Bella. But why would he follow me out of the party after barely speaking to me for a year? It's like he *had* to talk to me, like the party itself had brought his feelings to a head.

And Bella. Bella was so devoted to Abi; it seems so odd now that she hasn't doted on Fred in the same way. And like Neil, after almost a year of silence, the painful small talk at the salon, then, by contrast, at the party, it was as if she was trying to tell me something. She had the same urgency Neil had, wouldn't stop talking about how gutted he was, how it had changed him. Perhaps it was just the drink, but she wanted me to know he loved Abi *no matter what*. *No matter what* suggests something happened. It's another way of saying *despite everything*. This, and all the rest, is what I can no longer chew over with my husband. Because he is not my husband anymore, not really, and no matter what arguments and counter-arguments fall after one another, it is Jasmine's recognition of Abi's toy that is the crack in the glass, the wrong note in the chord. But it seems that I alone can hear it, me, *me*, Abi's mother, my bones, my flesh, my heart entwined forever with hers.

Idly I wander back to the kitchen. A year ago, my phone would have been here on the bar, charging, already filling up with notifications: Facebook, Instagram, the Come-and-Play mums' WhatsApp group that drove me to distraction with its endless reply-all messages: *X can't do that date because he has Monkey Music; Y has a party that day, any chance of another day?* The endless loading-up of information I didn't need, the sheer administration required just to maintain some semblance of a social life. My phone drove me bonkers, if I'm honest. It sucked my life away, made living in the moment almost impossible. But at other times, it was all that connected me in my maternal loneliness to the world. At night, in those dark and silent hours feeding Abi, I would play patience on the screen, and later, when I woke up like this, to drink milk or eat a midnight snack, my body catching up with its own hunger once Abi's needs had been met, I would sit for ten minutes with the glow of Facebook, laugh at the funnies, quip on someone's thread, reply with reassurance to someone in doubt, and yes, in those moments, I felt like I was sharing something meaningful.

Now, I cannot see how my life could ever be accommodated in a post or a comment thread. Posting on a comment thread was, in all likelihood, what I was doing when I lost my daughter. Now I have a basic mobile, a real gangster's burner. I don't look at it very often. It's in the kitchen somewhere… ah, here it is in the messy drawer beside a tin of picture hooks, a book of stamps, some gingham ribbon I must have saved from a gift.

I switch it on and search his name before I'm aware of what I'm doing. When I find it, I realise that this is why I was looking for my phone.

Hi, I thumb. *R u awake?*

The silence thickens. I wash my glass and place it upside down on the draining board. I'm about to give up and go back to bed when my phone buzzes.

Everything OK? N

No, everything is not OK. My thumb hovers. I am so tired, but I know I won't sleep until I've spoken to Neil, and I have to do that face to face so I can watch him, watch him react. And so, I text.

Can you meet me? Now?

I wait. The clock in the kitchen ticks. Twenty past twelve. The fridge hums. My phone buzzes.

OK. Where?

Outside – 5 mins?
OK.

Neil marches towards me, head down, hands pushed deep into his coat pockets. His white legs are bare but for a fringe of gingham pyjama short around the bottom of his jacket. On his feet are white Nike sliders.

'Hey.' He stops and shivers. 'You OK?'

I meet his blue eyes. I have no idea how to start. What I have to say might ruin our friendship forever. It is a betrayal of all of us, really, but what I have to know is bigger than friendship, bigger than marriage, bigger than any other thing in my life.

'Can we walk?' I suggest.

He shrugs. 'Sure.'

We pass the Lovegoods' and head towards the end of the road.

'I haven't slept since the party,' I begin. 'I mean, I didn't sleep last night and I couldn't get to sleep tonight.'

'How come?'

We turn left, into Thameside Lane. We have reached the tennis courts before I realise he is waiting for me to speak.

'Matt and I are separating,' I say.

'Oh, mate.' He stops. 'No way! Mate, I'm sure you feel like that now, but—'

I hold up my hand. 'I know what you're going to say and I know you mean well, but this is between me and Matt. I can't be with someone I don't trust, not after everything we've been through. I need someone solid or no one at all.' I continue walking, forcing him to walk too. 'I'm thinking of moving up north. I haven't spoken to my mum yet, but I imagine I'll move in with her in the short term. I can't stay here.'

'I suppose you know best what you have to do,' he says after a moment, though I don't think for one second he's accepted what I've said, more that he's realised it's pointless arguing with me in my current state, which is infuriating and depressing in equal measure. 'Is that what you wanted to talk about?'

We cross the road by the leisure centre.

'I've been thinking about that day,' I begin again. 'The day Abi… To be honest, I never think about anything else. It just goes round and round and round, you know? I don't know what I'm expecting. Maybe that if I go round enough times, I'll get a different outcome. Abi won't go missing, or she'll be found by a neighbour, or she won't reach the river, I don't know.' I am aware of myself gabbling. But he shows no sign of impatience.

We reach the Fisherman's Arms. The river is around the corner, an invisible force pulling us towards it. I wonder if he is aware of it too. If he is, he says nothing.

'I'm sorry to wake you up like this,' I say eventually. Something I should have said at the start.

'That's OK. I don't sleep well either, to be honest.'

He says it naturally. He has no idea how I might interpret his sleeplessness, with its undertones of a guilty conscience.

'I just need you to answer a couple of questions.'

We round the corner. The chandlery comes into shadowy view, the dip at the end of the lane where Abi purportedly wandered towards the ducks and to her death. At the dip, we sit on the little wall next to the footpath and stare at the shallows.

This is where my daughter died, I think.

'Come on,' he prompts. 'You can ask me anything – you know that.'

I take a deep breath. 'That morning. You were at home when I came to your house. How come?'

'What do you mean, how come? How come I was home?'

'Yes.' Shame burns in my cheeks. I cannot look at him. The enormity of what I'm asking dawns, but it is too late to go back.

'I'd been to the builders' merchants to get some stuff, why?'

'I suppose… I suppose finding out Matt lied to me has turned me inside out. I worry my memory might be playing tricks on me, that's all, and I thought maybe you could shed some light on things I probably had an explanation for at the time but have since forgotten what that explanation was, do you know what I mean?' I am gabbling, I know I am, but I press on. 'It's just… I've not seen you to talk it through, have I? Not till last night. It's just that at the party, Johnnie mentioned that you always got in early. Every day, he said, you got in before they left for work, and so I'm obviously wondering why you didn't that day, of all days.' I pause. I don't dare say any more.

Neil says nothing, so I dig myself further in.

'It's just that if Abi went missing after they left for work,' my voice shakes, 'and you were always there before they left… I don't know, I…'

'You're wondering why I wasn't there? I see. Well, now you know. I went to the builders' merchants at Apex Corner.' His tone is flat. 'Do you want me to find the receipt?'

Oh God.

'I'm not accusing you of anything, Neil. I'm just trying to piece it together in the light of my own husband…' I steel myself, determined not to let my emotions make me say something I'll regret more than I already regret coming here. 'Why did you say you didn't know the Lovegoods' kids?'

'Did I?'

'You did. Just before we went to the party.'

His mouth turns downwards, as if he hasn't a clue what I'm talking about.

'I can't remember saying that, to be honest,' he says. 'But I didn't know them, not really. They were out all day, and by the time they got back with the nanny, I was pretty much on the way out. I teased the older one a few times…'

'It's just, at the party, you reacted so violently when Jasmine called you "Pockets"…'

'No, I reacted when Johnnie Arsepain Lovegood couldn't stop himself from telling everyone I was his labourer. And I was already wound up because I didn't want to go to his stupid show-off party in the first place and Bella was bending my ear about all the fixtures and fittings and we're… we're under pressure at the moment… she was doing my head in. Where are you going with this anyway?'

'Please don't be cross. Matt says I've got to accept that Abi died that day. That she drowned. Probably right here. But it's so hard.' My throat fills with tears, the ache of them, and when I speak again, my voice is a thin, serrated edge. 'It's so hard without a body. It's so hard to believe that no one, no one saw her. I know it would only have taken her five, ten minutes to walk here, and I know it would have been before the road filled with mums and kids and all of that, I know it's just about possible, but that's all it is. *Just about possible*. And with no body, that's pretty bloody unsatisfactory.'

'I thought someone had seen her?'

'They weren't a hundred per cent sure. It came to nothing.'

'I know but they could've seen her and thought she was lagging behind or what have you. Is that it? Any more questions? It's just I've got to be up early.' He stands.

I remain on the wall, make myself look up at him. His brow is furrowed; his expression that of someone who can feel his temper shortening but is trying to hide it.

'I saw Jasmine this morning,' I say.

'Yeah?'

'She… she recognised Mr Sloth. You know, the plush toy you gave—'

'I know what you mean. Christ, Ava, you don't need to explain it.' His tone is different. Harder. 'I told Matt he should have thrown that out or kept it in a memory box or something. I don't know why he wants Fred to have it. I said we'd buy him a new one. It's… I dunno… a bit morbid if you ask me.'

'I know. I felt the same, but… why would Jasmine recognise it? Why would she know its name? That day… the Lovegoods had left the house before Abi went missing. How would she even have seen it?'

His face closes. When he looks at me, it is in a way I have never seen him look before – it is the way you look at someone when all affection for them has vanished.

The slightest shake of his head. 'Have you dragged me from my bed to accuse me of something?' He is almost whispering. 'Is that what this is? What the hell do you think I've done? Kidnapped my own god-daughter? Do you think I'm hiding her in my shed? Christ, Ava, do you think I'm a—'

'No! God, no!' The blood flashes to my head.

'Do you think I've sold her? Is that what you think? Because it'd be good for me to know, do you know what I mean? Just so we can be clear that even though I had my house and my shed and my van searched and sniffed, had my fingerprints taken like a criminal, and the police didn't suspect me of anything, even though I did all that, you, one of my best mates, you think I've got something to do with it. Christ, Ava.'

I burst into tears. 'I'm sorry. I'm a mess, I know I am, but I just have to get it straight in my mind if I'm going to have any chance of letting her go, you know? I have to accept that she's gone, forever, but the problem is, even going to that party felt like a betrayal, like we were ready to even contemplate enjoying ourselves without her, you know? I feel like I'm leaving her behind. How can I possibly do that? And then Bella said you were out all night that night. But you weren't. You came home at midnight. With Matt. You weren't out all night, so why would she say that?'

'I brought Matt back at midnight.' His voice is hoarse with exasperation, his fingers spread on outstretched hands. 'I brought him back and do you know what I did then? Do you? Have a guess – go on. I went looking for her again. I went back out there and I looked for her.' Spit flies from his mouth. The more he speaks, the angrier he gets, as if with every word he is becoming more aware of what it is I'm asking him. 'On my own. On my own, yeah? Last man standing, that's me. No one tried harder than me, Ava, no one. I tried harder than her own fucking father.'

A burning sensation runs the entire length of me, but it's too late, too late, too late. I should never have texted him. He is our closest friend. My God, what have I done?

'I was out all bloody night,' he is saying, throwing up his arms in despair. 'I was desperate to find her, all right? I can't believe this. I can't believe you're asking me this stuff. Jasmine probably saw the toy another day or that afternoon or something. I don't know. I don't know how she knew it, but she did, OK? But it doesn't mean anything. The girl's got learning difficulties, for God's sake. Just think about what you're saying, Ava!'

Deep wells of regret pool in my chest. I should never have had these thoughts. I should never have acted on them.

I sob into my hands. My nose is running, I can't see for tears. 'I just can't stop myself going over and over it. I can't bear it, Neil. I can't bear not to know. And I've lost Matt and now I've accused you, our friend, our best friend, and I just wish… I wish I didn't have Fred. I don't deserve him. I love him, but he shouldn't be forced to have someone like me for his mother. He shouldn't have to have this wreck. I don't deserve him. I'm not good enough, I'm not a good enough mother for him… for any child. Where is Abi, Neil? Where is she? Where is my little girl? I want my little girl.'

I stare out at the water. I see Neil and me on this wall. I see the streets, all the streets I used to walk with Abi, the school I would have taken her to, the parks we used to visit, the shops we used to call at on the way home. I see the slipway, now, in front of me. I see the lock. I see the moon rippling on the black river like a white silk scarf. Is this my daughter's grave? This black river? Is that where she is?

And then I am running. I am running towards the river.

CHAPTER TWENTY-EIGHT

Ava

The wet embrace of the river. The water climbs up my ankles, my shins, my knees. Soaks heavy on the hem of my nightdress.

'Ava!'

Neil's arms clamp themselves around my chest. I stumble; we fall into the deeper water. My head goes under. We come up coughing, flailing. Neil holds me up, holds me to him, drags me back onto the slipway, into the shallows. We are panting, gasping. The sky dims; the moon passes behind a cloud. The water laps gently at the slope.

We part, both sitting soaked through in the cold, wet water.

'Ava, for Christ's sake.' He keeps tight hold of my hands.

'Let go of me.' I try to pull my hands from his. 'Let me go.'

'No chance.'

'Let go. It's over. I have nothing. Nothing left. I want my daughter. I want to go to her.'

With all my weight, I lean away from him, dig my heels into the slimy floor. I get one hand free. I reach for the river, but in a strange kind of dance, he pulls me back into his arms and holds me tight, too tight; my ribcage hurts.

'Ava, come on. Don't be stupid. You have Fred. You have Matt. I know you don't think you do, but you do. He loves you. You still have a family, that's more than… it's more than enough. Matt loves you. He loves you more than anything in the world.'

Wewd, I think. That's how Neil says the word 'world'. I am soaking wet. I am sitting in the Thames. My husband's best friend says *wewd* not world. *Smow wewd*. Small world.

I begin to laugh.

'Ava?' He lets go of my hands but grips me by the biceps, at arm's length. He looks frightened. Of me.

'You rugby-tackled me,' I say, and laugh and laugh and laugh. I laugh my head off; I cannot stop. My bones are jelly. I am a rag doll, thrown aside. I am Mr Sloth, in the gutter, mulched leaves on my head.

I want to lie back in the water. I want to float away.

'Ava.' My name is a whispered plea. 'Ava, come out, darlin'. Come out of the water. Please.'

I let him take my hand. I let him pull me up.

Sober with shock, I sit on the wall. He has put his coat around me. It is dry; he must have taken it off before he ran after me into the water. I am laughing. I am crying. I am both. I am neither.

Neil is standing in front of me. He is holding out the hem of his T-shirt. Beneath, the curve of his beer belly, his thick, solid torso. 'Here.'

I dip my face to his T-shirt and wipe my nose and eyes.

After a moment, he sits beside me.

'Nutter,' he says.

Silence settles on us. I have no idea what I feel, other than a creeping sense of embarrassment, the urgent need to leave whatever just happened behind. I have been ridiculous. Paranoia has made me ridiculous. Neil is our best friend, for God's sake.

A group of lads swagger noisily from the footbridge. The air fills with the smell of weed. We wait for them to pass, neither of us wanting to draw attention to ourselves.

'Jen said you went back for Bella last night,' I say, as if to pick up on a perfectly normal conversation we were having, soaking wet, on a public wall, at midnight.

'We had a row,' he replies. 'She was pissed. She gets so bloody pissed.'

I shrug. 'She always did like to party. It's why we love her.'

'I know, but it's… she… Lately she's… we…' He puts his hand to his brow.

'Neil? What?'

'She's drinking to cope.'

'Cope? With what happened to Abi?'

He shakes his head. 'We're… we're having IVF. No one knows. Not even Matt.'

My head pounds. I feel like I've been winded.

'Oh, Neil,' I manage. 'I'm so… I'm so sorry. Have you… I mean, has it been long?'

'We had our first round last year. The day Abi disappeared we'd not long lost… we'd not long… Bel… it hadn't taken, you know? She was a mess and I couldn't… I couldn't do anything about it.'

'Oh, Neil, I'm so sorry. When did you… when did you lose the…?'

He sighs. 'It was on the Saturday. We were at yours on the Sunday.'

'On the Saturday? Oh my… and we told you we were expecting… Oh, Neil.' I attempt to pull him to me, but he wriggles out of my embrace. 'That must have been so hard.'

Their reaction to our news that day clicks into place. It was nothing, nothing I was able to put my finger on, but I felt it.

'There's been another one since. A few months ago.'

I put my arm around him, as best I can, my mind filled with how he was last night, so beside himself – it was about Abi, yes, but he had so much more going on than that.

'Poor Bella too,' I say.

No wonder she's stayed away. The sight of Fred must have been heartbreaking for her. Everything, everything about how they've been this last year is not what I thought at all.

'Don't say anything, will you?' Neil says, standing up, teeth chattering. 'She would've told you but you had enough on your plate. We didn't want to bring that into things.'

I stand up too. I offer him his jacket but he shakes his head. 'You could have told us,' I say. 'We wouldn't have taken it like that. We're friends. And I know that what's happened to us is… but it doesn't mean we don't have space for…'

'I know, but… you know what I mean. Anyway, I've told you now. Let's go home before we freeze to death, eh?'

We head home with slow, silent steps, shivering down the deserted lamplit street. Neil throws his arm around me. He talks. He talks and talks, rolls out a narration of my recent life. I suppose he's trying to bring me back to my life, back to wanting to live it.

'Matt's a good guy,' he says. 'He's the best. I know what he did was wrong, but you're everything to him, you and Fred. Abi was everything to him too.' On it goes. He is an easy talker, a businessman, a lad. I know he's handling me; I can hear it in the pacifying, near-hypnotic tone of his voice. 'Don't judge him for what he did that day, Ave. What happened happened, and everyone was panicking, yeah? Everyone. He was just trying to protect what he had. We've all got to protect what we have, haven't we? We've got to look after our own. That's all any of us can do. We build our castles and we have to defend them, yeah? Slings and arrows, no matter what. He's like me, didn't get it all handed to him on a plate, you know? He got the brains, I got the street smarts, but we've both worked hard to get to where we are, so what's he going to do, throw it all away? Do me a favour and forgive him, Ave. What's the alternative? Eh? He did what he did, we are where we are, and leaving him won't bring Abi back.'

Even his walk is solid, I think, keeping step with him, and I wonder what it must be like to walk that walk, to be that guy. The guy who takes care of everyone, who fixes things and finds solutions. But what happens when you can't take care of everyone? When you can't fix it, can't find the solution? What then? What happens then?

CHAPTER TWENTY-NINE

Matt

The strange straitjacket of a single bed. The weirdness of the white plastic origami-style lightshade against the white ceiling. He should not have stayed here. He has been hoping for reconciliation, but it has not come, and last night he should have left. He needs to leave if he is to come back; he knows that now. But, as ever, he has not done what he should have. He has not acted with integrity. He has not acted at all. And now here he is, in the spare room, thinking of his father's red face, his height, his gut-loosening bellow.

'Just admit it, lad,' his father shouts into the troubled ear of his memory – his flat Mancunian twang. 'Lying will only make it worse. Own up, for God's sake.'

He is six years old. And at that, Matt's eyes prickle, his skin heating as his body too remembers. At six, to be shouted at like that, close up, by a grown man. For what? He can't remember. He can never remember. A bike left out in the rain. A failure to help his mother with the clearing-up. A poor mark at school.

The point is, he can never remember because there is nothing a child of six can do that could possibly warrant that level of fury, the week-long ghosting, the glowering and absolute rejection that would last for days, days when his belly would be knotted in dread until, at last, at *last*, his father would give him a kind word or a joke, and Matt would feel his lungs empty, his veins drain of dread, his heart slow with sweet relief that, finally, he was out of trouble.

This is why he told Neil that night. He just wanted to confess it to someone, to share it, and feel some relief. What he was asking for was absolution, he thinks now.

'I just popped back and grabbed it from the hook,' he said as they stood there in the moonlight under the pissing rain. 'I was only in there two or three seconds. A second, literally. I just grabbed it, you know, and then I… I thought Ava would be back downstairs. I didn't think twice. I thought she'd be two seconds so I didn't think it was worth cycling all the way back.'

That horrible moment when Neil seemed to consider it, when everything seemed to be in the balance, as if he might pass some shattering final judgement and Matt would be forced to go home to his wife and tell her he was responsible, tell her and watch his entire life collapse around him. All he could do was wait, breath suspended, as his friend blinked away the rain still dripping fatly from his brow. He wanted to scream at him to say something, anything, to make him feel less wretched, but then, finally, oh God, finally, Neil rested his hand on Matt's shoulder and shook his head.

'OK, mate,' he said. 'It's OK.'

'I didn't think anything of it.' Matt could barely stop the words flushing out of him. 'But then when she called and said Abi was missing, I knew. I just knew. But when I got back, she was convinced it was her and I didn't say anything. I didn't admit it then, Nee, when I should've. I was going to but it was all… it was so… and then the moment was gone. That was my chance. I was going to tell her later, once we found Abi. I thought we'd find her straight away, I genuinely did, but then it all… and now we haven't found her, have we, we're not going to find her, and it's too late. It's too late to tell her, isn't it? How can I ever tell her? I can't lose her – do you know what I'm saying? She'll leave me. I'll lose everything. I'll lose her and the baby.'

'Baby?' Confusion wrote itself across Neil's face before it cleared. 'Oh, you mean the pregnancy?'

Matt felt his legs buckle. Another second and Neil was holding him up.

'Listen to me,' he said, his voice little more than a croak. 'So you left the front door open. And yes, you should have told her. But shit happens and you didn't say anything, all right? You didn't. We all do things without thinking. It's called being human, yeah? We make mistakes. And you regret it, of course you do. But admitting it won't get you any further, will it? It won't change what's happened. And whoever left that door open isn't whoever took Abi, so what's the point?'

'You think someone's taken her? Is that what you think? Is it?'

Neil shook his head. 'That's not what I'm saying, mate. I'm saying that *you* didn't take her, *if* she was taken. *You* didn't hurt her. *You* didn't do anything to her. Didn't you tell Ava not to blame herself?'

'Yes, but that's only because I know she *did* shut the front door. Because I had to unlock it to get my coat… Oh my God, what am I going to do? I've killed our little girl, Neil. I've killed her.'

'OK. OK. Stop. You don't know that and what you're saying, what you're saying is way too strong. Listen to me.

You love Ava, yeah? And you're right – you can't look after her and the baby if you tell her, not now. She'll leave, or she might, and what does that solve? Nothing. And it's worse for her too, yeah? She'd be on her own. She'd be devastated. So don't. Don't tell her. Don't tell her, mate. There's nothing to be gained. Are you listening? What's happened has happened and none of us can do anything about it. And when all this is over, you'll have that baby and you two can get on with being the most loved-up couple on the planet.' Neil squeezed his arms tight. 'Look at me. Look at me, mate.'

Matt made himself look up.

'Listen.' Neil's eyes were bright and clear. Focused. 'You've told me now, and that's it. It ends here. No police, no Ava, no one else. It ends here. Our secret. I've got your back. Do you get me?'

Justification. Absolution. The plastic origami light dissolves into the white ceiling. Whatever pact they made that night hasn't worked. It was wrong and now it has come out anyway and his daughter is still missing, presumed drowned, and on top of that, his marriage is over, and while he doesn't blame Neil, understands completely why he ended up telling Ava, still an old sense of injustice burns at the core of him. *Just admit it, lad. Lying will only make it worse.* It's not, it was never, fair. How, at six, could he have admitted to anything, anything at all, knowing that the punishment would be so great, that it was already upon him? Yes, yes, his father was right – if he had only confessed to… whatever it was, if he had taken responsibility and apologised, promised never to do it again, he would have been out of trouble so much quicker – yes, yes, yes. But he was a child. And, crucially, he was afraid. He panicked, always panicked; the panic rooted itself in habit, became a pattern as instinctive as running from danger. A reflex.

No matter how well Ava has helped him to understand it, he has failed to stop this pattern repeating itself. And finally, at the most crucial moment of his adult life, instinct kicked in; he failed to take responsibility; he repeated the pattern, lying by omission, letting his wife take the blame and keep taking it every day, even when he could see her unravelling. By lying he hoped to avoid Ava's fury and, ultimately, her rejection of him. By lying he hoped to maintain the life he had worked so hard to build – his castle, as Neil would say. But here, in the dark, he knows that beneath all of that is the lowest possible truth, the real truth, the what-it-all-comes-down-to truth: in the face of punishment, the reflex was to protect, above all others, himself.

CHAPTER THIRTY

Matt

He leaves for work early, exchanging a perfunctory goodbye with Ava, who is changing Fred in the nursery. In the afternoon, he calls her on the landline and three times on her mobile, but she doesn't pick up. He tries again, on the hour, but nothing. Her silence is horrible. The waiting it invokes is horrible, a horrible, anxious limbo state.

At half past four, he has done no work despite no lunch break, no idle chat by the coffee machine. Knowing that Ava must be home, he texts: *Hey. Can we talk? Xx*

Nothing.

He feels himself fall forward, at the last moment stops his head from crashing into his desk. Supporting himself with his hands, he lowers his forehead onto the hard glass surface. He is glad of his private office. He should stay and finish the sketches for the shop frontage in Aldgate to give to the team first thing tomorrow, but there is little use in him even trying. His brain is squirming like maggots, his heart a mass of crunching shards. Ava has lost her mind and that is on him – he has done this to her. He knows that her heart too will be as shattered as his and that he is responsible for this on top of everything else. It has occurred to him in these long hours that he betrayed her not only that night but every day since. Every time she has struggled, he could have held out his hand. He could have pulled her up from her hill of sand. And he didn't. He did not act. It is not what he has done but what he has not done that is unforgivable. If he'd thought about it, he would have known this. Neil should never have agreed to it, let alone offered to back him up. Neil, in whose home he will have to sleep tonight.

A buzz. She has replied after all, but the words hit him in the chest.

There is nothing to say. Please don't make this worse. I'll be contacting a solicitor. The sooner you accept it, the less painful it will be for both of us.

How quickly they have gone from what they were – two people who loved each other – to whatever this is.

I'm so sorry, he replies. *Can I at least come and grab some things? X*

Of course. We should maintain a civil relationship for Fred's sake. We have to think of him going forward.

His throat closes. God, the formality. He reads the message over and over, a stone sinking in his gut. It is as if she's someone he'd like to get to know but who is closed off to him, unattainable. He remembers thinking that about her the first time he saw her, at a client's house party in Islington. She was going out with someone else then. She was a little tipsy and was playing the piano, and when he spoke to her, he was surprised that she, like him, hailed from near Manchester.

'You're amazing at the piano,' he said to her once she'd left the keys to rumbles of drunken cries for just one more and they'd found themselves wedged in the smoky kitchen. 'You could be a concert pianist.'

She shook her head. 'Stage fright. I'm a primary school teacher. Try not to be disappointed.'

'There's nothing disappointing about that. Do you play for the kids? I bet they love you.'

'Could you talk to my mother?' She rolled her eyes, her head lolling a little, but she was blushing. 'A waste. A waste of talent.'

'Sharing your talent without any expectation of glory is not a waste.'

A week later, the client gave him her number. A week after that, he called her, with little hope of success, was amazed when she said yes, yes, sure, she'd come out to dinner.

He took her to a small dark restaurant in Soho. She seemed so sophisticated and he wanted to seem sophisticated too, but over dinner he admitted he didn't know anything about classical music.

'My parents are quite working class,' he said, by way of explanation.

'Is classical music the preserve of the middle classes?' she asked, eyes flashing. 'According to whom?'

He felt the heat in his cheeks, was glad of the dimly lit space. 'Oh, I, no, I mean...'

She laughed. 'My grandad was blue collar, as they say, but he drew the notes on a strip of cardboard and taught himself to play on an upright handed down from his father. He grew apples and rhubarb in the garden of his bungalow and made furniture for my dolls out of wood. On my father's side, they all played the piano, all of them. They used to sing round it at Christmas – one of my great-uncles had a heart attack and collapsed on the keys. Everyone laughed because they thought he was joking; it was family folklore.' She grinned, an expression that told him she wasn't done yet. 'My mum plays beautifully, used to play the *Moonlight Sonata* to lull me to sleep. My dad likes to cook, makes his own pesto, bakes his own bread. Both of them left school at sixteen, had nothing but a tiny flat when they first married, used to eat off the top of a washing machine. But classical music was all around me growing up. Honestly, people have such a weird view of what working-class people are actually like. Look at you. You went to a state school, didn't you? And now you're an architect, for goodness' sake. Hardly a geezer, are you?'

'No, but my best friend is.' He laughed, poured more wine while he worked out what to say. 'I'm sorry,' was all that came to him. 'I made an assumption. I guess I was scared we wouldn't have enough in common.'

'We don't need to have a lot in common. We just need to have what's important. Values. What's right, what's wrong. And we're both scared, so that's something else.'

'Scared?'

'I'm scared of the stage and you're scared of… well, of me, at the moment.' She laughed. 'I'm teasing. Anyway, I listen to other kinds of music. I love Bruce Springsteen.'

'So do I.' He sat back in his chair. Knew already he was in trouble. Falling.

I don't deserve her, he thought, as early as then.

He didn't. Doesn't. And he has proved it.

Now he studies her cold text, scraping through his hair with bitten fingers. She was right: he was always scared. Scared of his father, scared of the school bully, scared of success. He's a coward. But she knew it and she married him anyway. She hoped he'd change is effectively what she told him during that horrible argument after the party. What is it they say? Men marry women hoping they'll never change, but they do. Women marry men hoping they will change, but they don't. And he hasn't.

Of course, he replies. *I'll pick up some stuff after work. I'm so sorry, Ave. Really.*

She doesn't reply.

He waits.

Nothing. There is nothing to say. Sorry doesn't cover it.

CHAPTER THIRTY-ONE

Matt

Ava is in the living room watching television, Fred asleep in the crib at her feet. These last few months, he has hated finding her like this, like just anyone, slouched watching TV instead of being dynamic, being Ava, being the woman he married, the woman he would find playing Scott Joplin on the piano while Abi danced around the living room dressed in one of her pink tutus, her fairy wings strapped to her back.

'Look, Daddy.' Round and round, arms waving about, believing herself absolutely to be a ballerina. Up and down the length of the front room, around the piano, floating back to the front of the living-room area where DI Farnham sat them down and told them they'd found Abi's coat, where now Fred sleeps at his mother's feet. And Ava, his darling Ava…

'Hi,' he says, drumming the door jamb with his hands.

'Hi.' A perfunctory glance and she returns her gaze to the television.

He waits for as long as it takes him to realise there is nothing more.

'I'll go and grab a few shirts then,' he says eventually. *Please don't make me do this. Please.*

'Fine.'

How long does he stay at the door, staring at the back of her head, praying she will turn around, properly this time, and, with tears in her eyes, tell him that she can, after all, forgive him? He wants so badly to throw himself at her feet, promise her that they can get over this, but instinct tells him, *she* has told him, that the moment is not now, and that it might be never. To ask for forgiveness now would be an insult.

And so he leaves her. Upstairs he packs some shirts, pants, socks and a spare pair of trousers, some toiletries – the banality of these items bringing an acrid taste to his mouth as he places them into a sports holdall – a holdall, for Christ's sake. He returns downstairs to the still life that is his wife: transfixed or, more likely, determinedly fixing, her eyes on the screen so as not to have to look at her snivelling excuse of a husband.

'I'm off then,' he says brightly.

And then, at last, she turns. But what she has to say shocks him to the core.

'Did you know Bella and Neil were trying for a baby?'

'What?' Matt drops his bag to the floor. 'When did you find that out?'

'Last night.'

'Last night how?'

Her chin tips up. Her eyelids lower a fraction. 'You were in bed. I couldn't sleep. I texted Neil around midnight.'

'Why?'

'Because I needed to ask him about Jasmine recognising Mr Sloth.'

'Oh, Ava.' Sadness fills him.

'Don't *oh, Ava* me.'

He hears the steel in her voice.

'Neil said he was waiting until the business got up and running,' he says, trying to keep her off the topic of bloody Mr Sloth, the toy he wishes to God he'd thrown away.

'Well, they've been having IVF.'

'What?' Matt reels. 'Since when? Hang on, rewind, midnight? You were texting Neil at midnight?'

'Actually, we met up. We walked up to the lock.'

He stares at her. Her chin is still tipped up, her eyelids still low. She is his wife; he has no idea who she is.

'You were asleep,' she says, a lacing of defiance in her tone.

He shakes his head, wills himself to stay calm, above all not to shout. 'Neil didn't have anything to do with Abi, you know that. You know it, Ava.'

'I thought I knew *you*, but I didn't, did I?'

Touché. He closes his eyes, holds them closed a second, two.

'The day before Abi disappeared,' she continues, her face tight with tension, 'do you remember, that Sunday, we told them I was pregnant? Well, the night before, they'd lost a baby. A pregnancy, you know? They'd been having IVF. And it happened again a few months later.'

'Oh my God.' Matt's hand flies to his forehead. For a moment he cannot speak. Neil. His best friend. Whom he has known since he was eleven. 'Why didn't they tell us? I can't understand why they wouldn't tell us.'

She shrugs. 'I don't know. I've been thinking today that Bella did look rough that Sunday, you know, for her. I thought she was hung-over. I thought we'd offended them, maybe by not telling them, maybe they felt they'd been left to guess like strangers. And obviously, afterwards, they couldn't have told us, not on the back of our happy news – it would have

S.E. Lynes

been awful. And I suppose after Abi, they felt we had enough on our plate. I mean, it's not like I would have been much support, I suppose.'

'But he could've told *me*.'

'Maybe he feels like if he starts telling you his problems, it'd… I don't know… unbalance things.'

The subtext drifts down, settles. He is weak, that's what his wife is saying. Neil is the strong one, the one who listens and fixes and builds. That's the dynamic his far-too-perceptive wife is pointing out to him. Matt gets himself into messes he can't handle but that Neil can put right. To a certain extent Ava does this too: straightens him out. And hasn't Neil done the same with Johnnie? Sorted out his mistakes? Now he, Matt, has to walk down this road he's lived in most of his life to the man who has been his friend for all that time and pretend he doesn't know what's destroying him bit by bit because that, *that*, would reverse their roles so dramatically neither of them would know how to play their part. Instead, he will go there to be listened to and fixed and built back up after making a mess of things yet again.

'… and then when I talked to Neil after the party, he was crying,' Ava is saying, and he wonders how much he's missed.

'Poor guy.' Matt sees Neil, there in the pouring rain the night of Abi's disappearance. All that going on and there he was, solid as a rock. 'I wish he'd told me.'

Ava turns away. 'I still think there are a lot of other things he's not telling us.'

His guts flip. Surely she isn't going to keep going on about Neil. He walks slowly into the living room and sits on the sofa opposite.

She doesn't object. But nor does she speak.

'What things?' he asks after a moment, feeling suddenly incredibly tired.

She shakes her head. 'Things from the party. But what's the point? You think I'm a lunatic.'

'I don't! I… I don't. Please. I'm listening.'

She shakes her head, her bottom lip pushing petulantly against the top. But after a moment, she exhales.

'Last night at the lock, I spoke to him. And it got very intense. We sort of ended up in the river.'

'What? How the hell—'

She holds up her hand. 'I'm not getting into that now.'

He exhales, his breath shaky. It is worse than he thought. She is ill, so ill. He wants to cry, to shake her, to hold her to him, but he must not, and he must not interrupt; he has to play this carefully, very carefully indeed.

'OK,' he says.

'I believed him,' she goes on. 'Last night. But today I've been going over everything, and the thing is, I don't know if I believe him anymore. Neil's such an easy talker. But I realised, thinking about it, that when I asked him about Mr Sloth, he didn't answer me, not really. He just got defensive and started asking what the hell I thought I was accusing him of.'

'Of course he did, he—' Consciously, Matt places his left hand over his right, to remind himself to stay quiet.

She closes her eyes, that familiar tic of irritation, and opens them again.

'You don't know the whole story,' she says. 'When I saw Jen and the girls yesterday, Jasmine recognised Mr Sloth by name. By name, Matt. Think about it. The only way she could know that toy by name is through Neil. I've never even met Jasmine and neither have you. And then, and I know you don't want to hear this, she started going on about pockets, pockets, pockets, which is exactly what she called Neil at the party. That's what I've been trying to tell you, don't you see? Pockets is Jasmine's name for Neil.' She glares at him, as if to say: there.

He holds up his hand. 'Can I speak?'

She nods.

'I can explain that. At the party, Jennifer told me Neil had a game going with her. He used to hide her toys in his pocket and then pull them out – it made her laugh. That's literally it. She probably calls all her toys Mr or Mrs.'

'So why didn't he say that?'

'Because he had you in his face accusing him of having something to do with Abi's death, in the middle of the night, right by where she's supposed to have drowned. How the hell did you end up in the water anyway?'

Her eyelids flicker with irritation. He returns his hand to his wrist, squeezes it.

'Whatever,' she says. 'There are other things, things *I've* thought through properly. Like Neil being so upset at Jasmine recognising him. I know you're going to say it wasn't that, that it was Johnnie, and that's what Neil said too, but I saw you with him under the willow tree at the party and it looked like he was freaking out. His reaction was way over the top, don't you think?' She looks up. Her eyes are bloodshot. 'Don't you think?'

'Ave,' he tries. 'Listen to what you're saying. You're clutching at straws. There's no connection, none whatsoever. What you're saying is that even when Neil gives you a good reason, you don't believe him. He's our best friend, hon. Come on.'

'Please.' Once again she closes her eyes, apparently trying to keep control of this terrible rage lying immediately beneath the surface of her, as it has been for a year. 'I know you want to believe him, and I didn't put two and two together either at first. But the thing is, yesterday she was looking for Neil, calling out her nickname for him, don't you see? Before the party, in our kitchen, he said he didn't know the Lovegoods' kids. But Jasmine recognised him in front of the entire street and he reacted badly, yes? And then she recognises Abi's toy even though she's never seen it, yes? You'll forgive me if I'm starting to think something isn't right. And… and it was *Neil* who found Mr Sloth that day. He came into the house and said he'd found it on the road, do you remember? But how do we know that's true? I didn't see him pick it up. Did you? And I know he's your best friend and I know he helped—'

Matt roars; his fist smashes against the coffee table. 'For God's sake, Ava! You can't say that! You can't even let yourself think it! My God, this is Neil we're talking about!'

She is panting, chewing her lip furiously, and she looks… she looks like a caricature of madness – bulge-eyed, flushed, manic. This is who she is now. This is what unresolved grief has done to her. What *he* has done to her. His wife.

'OK,' she says, visibly trying to stay calm. 'What's going on then? Explain it. Because I asked Neil last night and he sure as hell couldn't; he just filled up the air time with what a great guy you are.'

The violence of her words, the way she says them, takes him aback. They are glaring at each other, both trembling, both shocked, and it is this shock that frightens them, calms them momentarily.

'I don't know what to say to you,' he says after a long moment, but even now he can feel the effort it takes just to keep himself from shouting. 'Except that there will be a good reason.'

'He said he didn't know those kids!'

'He only said he didn't know them well! They could still recognise him! If Neil had a little game going with the older one, it doesn't mean that he knew her well, it just means he was kind to her, and that's probably all he meant. That Jasmine remembers him and got all excited is down to Jasmine. Neil made an impact on her, which he would because he's kind and he's good with kids. And with Jasmine having learning difficulties, he was probably all the kinder because that's who he is, Ava. He's a good bloke, and he's kind and he's fair, and I know he seems tough but he's not. He's a softy underneath – the reason we're even friends is because he stepped in to defend me when we were kids. Christ, he pretty much adopted me. Ava, it's you who's talked me through so much of why I do what I do. I would've thought you'd have the emotional intelligence to realise that Neil is all heart.'

'I've always thought that.' She too is speaking quietly. She too is trembling with the effort of not screaming – or perhaps she's beginning to see just how crazy she's being. 'I love Neil. As a friend. But yesterday morning with Jasmine… and how come he miraculously found Abi's toy?'

'Oh my God, Ava, he found it on the road! On the road! A cop would have seen him pick it up; there were at least four on the street by then, one of them stationed outside the house. What do you think he did, started Charlie Chaplin whistling and somehow dropped it there in plain sight? I can't do this, Ava! *You* can't do this! You'll drive yourself mad. You *are* driving yourself mad. You're going to end up in hospital again, darling.' His eyes sting with tears, the hot steam of his rage condensing into droplets. Above all else, he feels so damn sorry for her. He has done this to her. He has broken her.

'Darling,' he tries again, softly. 'Ava, my love. Please. You have got to move on. Whatever happens to us, you can't let one stupid party when we're all a bit drunk and a bit stressed turn into this... this witch hunt. I was wrong to make you go. You weren't ready. You're not ready. I'm sorry.'

She sighs. 'There are so many things, things you haven't spotted. Like, he was so upset that night. And after not speaking to me for a year, it was like he *had* to speak to me then, and when he did, he was... I don't know how to say it, but it was like he was too upset...'

'*Too* upset? What does that even mean? He and Bella are having problems – they've lost a baby, more than one baby. That's why he's so upset.'

She sniffs, shakes her head. She won't look at him and he wonders if she's finally realised how wrong she is.

'I'm not making any accusations.' Her voice is watery. 'I tried to talk to him last night, but today I'm not convinced he answered me properly. He's very smooth. At the party Bella said he was out all night that night, and when I asked him about that, he said he'd gone back out to look for Abi, which is plausible, I suppose. But another thing that doesn't add up is that Johnnie and Jen said Neil always came to work before they left the house. Except for that morning. Why would he be at home when he was always at work by that time?'

He opens his mouth to speak, but it is like trying to board a moving train.

'When I asked him, he made some excuse about getting building supplies from Apex Corner, but don't you think that's a bit too much of a coincidence?' She is speaking faster now, her voice rising. 'I keep going over and over conversations from the party – Jen, Johnnie, Bella, Neil – asking myself why I'm feeling like this, and I remembered Bella was very insistent that Neil loved Abi no matter what. No matter what – what does that mean?'

'It's just a figure of speech.'

'They're all just figures of speech! They're all just little tiny things. Why would he go out and look for Abi all night and never tell you?' Her eyes are round; she is barely stopping for breath. 'That doesn't make sense. It's not something you'd keep secret, is it? Do you see what I'm saying? Do you?'

Matt feels his eyes prickle. His heart is breaking as surely as it did that day. He has tried not to lose her but that's exactly what's happening. He is losing her. She is losing herself. He must think, think carefully before he speaks. It's important to make her feel heard without giving her theories any credence.

'I understand,' he says slowly. 'And I can see how you can get to where you've got to. But the problem is, you're filtering it all through trauma. It was traumatic for *you* to go to that party. Being with Neil and Bella again brought back too many terrible memories and I shouldn't have made you… I shouldn't have asked you to go. It was too soon.'

'It's not about that!' she shouts, then shakes her head, as if to dispel her temper.

'I'm not saying it is,' he tries. 'I'm not saying I don't believe you or that these things weren't said, but it's all completely explainable. Neil didn't want to see Johnnie again because he hates him. He got angry because he felt patronised. They've been going through stuff we didn't know about and we were all a bit raw because it was the first time we've socialised since Abi died—'

'Died? So, what, it's definite now, is it?'

'No, I… but, Ava… we… The police say they haven't closed the case, but they have, essentially, haven't they? There's no evidence other than that she wandered up to the river, tried to feed the ducks and somehow toppled in. It's a tragedy, darling, a terrible tragedy, but—'

'But her coat was found the next morning – what if, after Neil left you, he went and threw her in the river at Richmond?'

'Oh for Christ's sake, stop!' His hands curl into fists. He is on his feet, standing over her, shouting at her. He can feel the veins in his neck, the heat in his head. He raises his fists, feels the violent grimace setting his jaw. He stops, fists falling, pressing now against his temples. My God, this is not him – it is everything he swore he wouldn't do. Wouldn't be.

'Ava,' he whispers. 'You're going to end up back in hospital.'

'You can't *not* stick up for him, can you?' Her voice is quiet, her simmering heat matching his. 'You can't *not* put him before me. I'm your wife, Matt, not him. And maybe that's the problem. Maybe that's always been the problem.'

The silence that follows is like lead. He can hear them both breathing in the quiet room.

'Ava,' he says softly.

'Please go.' She almost whispers it. 'Just… go. I've told you about their problems, that's all I intended to say, so now you know. I wish I hadn't bothered with the rest. I knew you wouldn't listen. You don't want to listen.'

His eyes fill. He can hear the hum of the fridge from the kitchen, the soft out breath of his baby boy. Don't speak, Matt. Just don't say anything.

'I'll be at Neil's,' he says.

'Of course you will.' Default sarcasm. She has turned away from him, will think him cheap, of course, not to stump up even for the Travelodge. And she'll be privately disgusted at their boys' conspiracy.

'Maybe we can talk tomorrow?'

'I doubt it.' She does not turn around.

He swallows what feels like a hard lump of air. 'Ava…'

'Matt. I'm begging you. Go. Please.'

CHAPTER THIRTY-TWO

Matt

'Mate.' Neil holds open his front door.

Matt steps out of the falling light into a house once familiar, now strange to him. It is over a year since he has been here. July, a barbecue on a Sunday afternoon. A flashing memory – Neil swinging Abi around and around by her arms as she laughed and squealed – hits him like a punch. It feels like a decade ago. It feels like yesterday. Ava was right: Neil and Bella have withdrawn. Much more than he's realised.

'You OK?' Neil's brow furrows.

'Yeah, sorry, just feel a bit weird. I don't know how I got through work today, to be honest.'

'Yeah, course.'

The pause that follows is bulky and awkward.

'Bel's made up the bed in the back bedroom,' Neil says after a moment. 'There's a clean towel. You can stick your stuff there if you want. Do you need anything else?'

'No, that's great. I'll go and dump my bag. Cheers.'

Matt plods up the stairs, feet like rocks. The spare room is clean and smells of freshly laundered bedding. On the wall is a framed architectural drawing – his own, for a converted warehouse on the South Bank, his first big commission. Neil loved this drawing.

'That's art, that is,' he said, shaking his head with pride.

'Building it is the art,' Matt replied.

Neil asked for a copy, insisted that he was serious. So, on his thirtieth birthday, Matt took it to be framed for him. Now he studies it a moment before sitting on the bed and letting his head fall into his hands, the weight of it threatening to topple him over. When he exhales, his breath is ragged. The last twenty minutes of his life have been amongst the worst, with the obvious exception of that day.

'Mate.' Neil is calling from the bottom of the stairs. 'I'm having a beer – do you want one?'

'Yep,' he calls back. 'Down in a second.'

He sighs into the damp palms of his hands. His feet are sweaty; his Marks & Spencer suit clings to his legs, his shirt wet against his armpits. He is alone in his friend's spare room, sports holdall at his stinking, sweaty feet in the Church's brogues that Ava bought him when he won a big contract, about three years ago now. Buy a better suit, she told him, she damn well told him – go to Aquascutum, she said. Or Armani. But he didn't, didn't spend the money, because, essentially, he must have known deep down that his high-street suit was good enough. When she bought him those beautiful shoes, he read pride, but what he reads now is hope, her hope that he would one day rid himself of the smallness she always saw in him, shake off the mediocrity and, with her love, become bigger, a bigger man. A better man.

A vain hope, as it turns out.

He wants to take his shoes off but he cannot stand the stink of his own feet, let alone inflict it on someone else.

He stands up and looks out of the back window onto Neil and Bella's garden while he attempts to compose himself. That sunny Sunday afternoon, a little over a year ago, seems like the most impossible idyll. Ava sitting in the shade fanning herself with a place mat. He remembers he complained about a headache when they got home. He'd been running in the morning and had not drunk enough water – it was Ava who pointed this out with weary maternal indulgence, as she would whenever he didn't take the most basic steps to look after himself. The way she looked at him then said: you are so childish, but I love you.

She loved him. Despite his limitations, she loved him. And now she doesn't.

But he loves her. He loves her, even in her reduced state, because she *was* extraordinary and he knows she can be that again. His love for her is still in the present. Hers is in the past. It ended yesterday.

So much love has been lost. There was so bloody much of it that day, here in this garden. Love between couples, between families, between friends – it didn't seem like so much then, but now… now of course the simple fact of them being together like that is everything. Abi squealing, *No, NeeNee, no!* as Neil spun her around, giggling when afterwards she couldn't stand up without falling down, Neil catching her when she fell, tickling her to the ground.

'Neil,' Ava said, breaking off her conversation with Bella. 'She's saying no. She's telling you to stop.'

He carried on. *No, NeeNee, no!*

And Ava rose from her chair. 'Neil, seriously. If she says no, you have to stop, OK?'

Only then did he stop, blowing at his hair, his face red with the exertion.

Abi ran away giggling, fell over, got up, ran back to her mum. Ava smiled and pulled her up onto her knee, made her drink some water in the shade.

Jasmine recognised Abi's toy. Ava had never seen Jasmine until the night of the party. Jasmine associated the toy with Neil. Did Neil see Abi that morning? Is it possible that he saw her, played a game, chase, maybe, meaning only to make her laugh but—

'Mate?' Neil's one-word question sails up to him, making his cheeks burn.

'Sorry,' he shouts, pulling himself away from the window. 'I'm coming now.'

CHAPTER THIRTY-THREE

Ava

The front door closes with a dull click. The sigh that leaves me is long and heavy. I feel tired. Tired and unfathomably sad.

Fred wakes and begins to cry. I lift him, put him to my breast and feel myself drift. More memories of the party come back to me in flashes: Jen's kind eyes, her naturalness, her sympathy. She has been the only stable point, outside family – standing at a distance, a point on the horizon. When the press receded, when the investigation was scaled back, when the lasagnas and casseroles and lemon drizzles ceased, she was still there, always with hand-tied flowers or a small wrap of posh chocolates, sometimes staying for coffee, sometimes not – knowing which to do out of some empathic sixth sense. She has never hidden from asking how things were, has never shied away from the bottomless dreadfulness of it all. More than once she has sat with me and held my hand, in silence, for long minutes until the depthless sadness became its own kind of peace.

I think of her and Johnnie standing together. A power couple, I suppose you'd call them. I can't put her together with him at all, but then I suppose, other people's relationships are always mysteries to those outside them.

In my silent house, Johnnie's words return to me: *Always there bright and early before we even left for work, wasn't he, Jen?*

But he wasn't. The day, the *one day* my daughter disappeared, he wasn't. He went for building supplies. Did he? It's possible. He *was* at home. I banged on his door. That morning. That ticking metronome morning. That accelerating crescendo of panic. I run out onto the street. I run about, hysterical, my chest a banging drum. Abi. Abi, Abi, Abi. Did I ring on the Lovegoods' door? I might have done. Then or later. I can't remember. I wish I'd known Jen then. She would have helped. She would have known what to do.

Abi's toy. Mr Sloth.

Could Jasmine have seen it another day? Would one of her school friends have one? Is it like Matt said, she calls all her toys Mr or Mrs?

Ava, stop. You're desperate, reading signs where there are none. Neil is your friend. He is Matt's childhood friend, his best friend.

Neil is solid. Neil is a safe pair of hands. Neil fixes problems.

I try to focus on the soft black sweep of Fred's eyelashes, the barely perceptible rhythm of him sucking. I try to keep the moment pure, but still the sense of something more presses in. How difficult that Sunday must have been for them both. Then the next morning, *that* morning, Neil's panic-stricken face when he answered the door. As if he already knew.

Ava, stop.

I lift Fred from my breast and push my face into his soft Babygro. Stop. Stop. There is nothing here, nothing at all. Look away. Neil and Bella had their own troubles that day, troubles you now know about, troubles they're still dealing with. Come on. Of *course* he looked concerned when he answered the door. You were battering on it, for God's sake, shouting through the letter box. He answered it with *precisely* the expression you would wear if someone was banging on your front door and shouting for help.

He found her toy.

Stop.

He was out all night.

Stop it, Ava.

Would Jasmine even know the word for sloth?

Stop, stop, stop.

What would Barbara say? Stay logical. It isn't about you. How others behave is rarely about you.

Against my shoulder, my baby boy's tiny body rises and falls. A human being at peace, in blissful ignorance of the horror of all that his parents have been through. What must that be like, to be at peace? Is Abi at peace? My eyes fill. Bella's tipsy face swims in my mind's eye.

Just want you to know that Neil did everything, no matter what.

A throwaway line – less, a half-line. No matter what. As if to say he did everything despite… something.

'No.' I stand up, pacing the living room, rubbing Fred's back in circular motions. 'No, no, no.'

Fred burps adorably. Outside, street lamps splash yellow on the deep blue sky. If Abi were returned to me right now, right this second, what damage would we have to repair? Could we repair her? Who would she be now? Who on earth would she be? Would she know me?

'Where are you?' I whisper, weeping softly into the strange calm that loneliness brings. 'Where did they take you, my darling girl? What did they do to you?'

Neil and Bella are our friends. I cannot seize upon throwaway comments uttered in a tearful drunken fit; I cannot. I'm starting to feel like I did after that day. Matt might be right. I might need help again. The party has been traumatic; Neil has become my focal point, my obsession, the lightning rod for my own not-quite-grief. Our foreheads touched on the empty street. He pulled me out of the water. There's a connection between us; I can feel it but I don't understand it. To suspect him is mad. I can see that; I can see it at the same time as believing that very suspicion. But our houses were searched and sniffed, for God's sake. Every house on the street, every garden, was searched. We made formal statements at the station but there was no evidence, none whatsoever, of any of us having done anything sinister. Our stories matched. That Bella had a selection of recent photos of our child on her phone was only because she took them at Sunday lunch, the day before Abi disappeared. It's possible she was hiding behind the camera while she made sense of her feelings, although I had no idea about that at the time.

It's Matt. He is to blame. Then and now. To be betrayed by the person closest to me has unhinged me. There is nothing left, nothing safe for me to hold on to, and because of that, I am unstable. But… but… there is still something I can't reach. A lost baby. A toy. Neil and Matt beneath the willow tree. Bella's drunken tears. All easily explained. And yet… like the seconds, small things accumulate. Seconds become minutes become hours. Small things become bigger things become… information?

Call me if any new information comes to light. Another whisper in the silent dusk. DI Farnham. Her number is in my phone.

But first, I'm going to talk to Bella. I rang her this morning and told her I needed a chat; she said she'd meet me in Starbucks this evening. I find my phone in the kitchen and text: *On my way.*

CHAPTER THIRTY-FOUR

Matt

Neil is in the kitchen, the air an aromatic cloud. Curry. Matt realises this is what he could smell coming into the house a few minutes ago. The back door is open and a soft breeze drifts in. Soon the weather will cool. Soon it will be the anniversary.

'Where's Bel?'

'Gone out with a couple of the girls from the salon.' Neil hands him a beer.

They touch bottles and drink. Neil has almost finished his. Matt wonders if it's his first.

'Chicken tikka masala,' Neil says. 'The rice'll be a few minutes.'

'Cool. Cheers.' Matt could not feel less like eating.

Neil busies himself with the rice. Matt takes a seat. The table has been set – properly, with place mats and glasses and, rather optimistically, a jug of water. The sight moves him. Neil is looking after him, as he always has. His and Bella's kitchen is still structured in the old-fashioned way: a small space at the back of the house with a modest pine table, no bar, no high stools, no pendant lights, no range cooker, no ample patio doors. He remembers Neil's mum in this kitchen when he came here after school, how she always asked him if he was stopping for dinner. It feels homely. Authentic. From a time when people called in on one another, when the choice was tea or coffee. Round here, they call tea 'builder's tea' – he wonders what Neil feels about that, whether he asks his clients for Earl Grey or rooibos or herbal, to make a point.

Soon, like everyone else, he and Bella will knock out the wall adjoining what estate agents would call 'the snug' at the centre of the house and open it out into this kitchen. They'll knock most of that back wall down too. *So much light!* they will say, opening out their bifold doors and clinking their flutes in celebration. It is what everyone does. It is what he and Ava did last year. Neil did the extension for them, of course. Did he ever feel like 'the staff' as he did with Johnnie? Was he irritated to be the one in overalls while Matt left for work in his suit, his hands pink, his nails white? Matt doesn't think so. Neil loves to get stuck in. Hates standing there pontificating. And it was almost a joint project – Neil altered Matt's initial sketch (improved it) and Matt did some hands-on stuff at weekends – loaded sand and cement into Neil's mixer, helped him shift the washing machine, made countless mugs of coffee and tea for him, his electrician, his plumber, running out to the corner shop to buy umpteen packets of chocolate digestives.

But if Neil could keep the huge heartache of his life hidden, has he kept other things hidden too? Resentment? Jealousy? What was it he said at the party? *They think just 'cos they dossed around for a few years at uni, they think they're better.* They.

Is Matt one of *them*?

'Do you want to talk about it?' Neil is placing two plates of chicken curry on the table. 'You're in a world of your own there, mate.' He returns to the fridge, retrieves a jar of mango chutney and a pot of Greek yoghurt and brings those over too.

'It's not the Maharajah,' he says, sitting down. 'Just from a jar, like. Sorry there's no poppadums. Bella made it before she went out. She'll tell me off for not putting this lot in little bowls.' He gestures to the condiments before shovelling a forkful of food into his mouth.

'That was kind of her.'

Bella is kind, he thinks, while Neil eats, quickly, as he always does, as if someone might snatch it away. And Neil is kind too. He is not the jealous type. Bella is materialistic, they both are, but not like that, not to the point of getting bent out of shape about it. Neil is the opposite of entitled, has always expected to work for what he has, and has always been proud of Matt's academic and professional success. He prefers to be his own boss, that's all, and is successful in his own right – it's mostly a lack of time that has prevented him from upgrading his house before now.

Isn't it? And what the hell does any of this have to do with anything anyway?

'It'll be all right, you know,' Neil says.

Matt shakes his head. Neil has cleared his plate by half; Matt's looks like he hasn't touched it. Which he hasn't.

'It's over,' he says.

'It won't be. She'll come round. People get over stuff, big stuff.'

Matt leans back from his dinner and takes a long slug of his beer.

'I should've told her,' he says, watching his friend make short work of the last mouthfuls of a meal he knows he cannot so much as touch.

Neil shrugs. 'What happened happened. You can't judge yourself on what you do in a panic. You were just trying to protect what's yours.'

'My castle,' Matt replies, the words laced with bitter irony.

'Exactly. She'll understand that once she calms down. She just needs some space, that's all.'

'I hope you're right.'

Neil grins. 'I'm always right.'

'Do you think you'll do the kitchen soon then?' Matt says, looking about him, at the pine units, the peeling corner of the lino floor.

Neil swallows his last mouthful and pushes his plate away. He takes a swig of beer and sits back in his chair.

'Think we might move, to be honest,' he says.

'Move?' Matt reels. 'Since when?'

Neil shrugs and sighs deeply. 'Might go further out. Get more for the money, you know? There's some beautiful places over by Guildford – big gardens, off-street parking, garages, the lot. One place we saw had a barn.'

'You've already looked? You never said anything.'

'Only online. It's not a definite plan, just something we're thinking about. There was nothing to say really, to be honest. But I don't want to do a load of work on this place and end up selling it. I'd rather just move to our forever home.'

Forever home. That's Bella talking. 'So you'd… you'd leave the area?'

'We're hardly moving to Australia.'

'I know, but…' But what? Matt finds himself fighting a feeling of betrayal. He swallows it. 'You always did fancy a barn, didn't you?'

'Yip.'

'And I… I suppose it'd be good to raise kids out there.' Shit. That was clumsy.

Sure enough, Neil stands, abruptly, and crosses the kitchen. 'Another beer?'

'Sure, yeah.'

Neil brings the beers, sits down. He coughs into his hand, pushes his fist to his chest, as if to rub at a pain or a morsel of food that won't go down. 'Ava told you then, did she?'

Matt nods. Another wash of guilt.

'I'm sorry,' he says.

Neil shrugs. 'Not your fault. That's why we haven't done the house yet. Treatment costs a bloody fortune. One more try and we're going to look at adopting. And if we do that, it'll be new place, new area, new start.' The sentences rattle from him, as if he wants them out in one go – and quickly.

'I see.'

From the garden, the unlikely chirrup of evening birdsong. Matt tries to remember a time when he didn't live on the same street as Neil. He cannot, not in any concrete way.

'We heard an owl the other night,' Neil says. 'They get confused with all the street lighting, birds do. You get a lot more birds further out.'

Another pause. Matt picks at the label on his bottle until Neil chinks it with his own.

'Oi,' he says. 'You can still visit.'

Later, in bed, sleep a million miles away, Matt replays what will always be known as *that day*. He had stopped doing this, but since the party, he can't help himself. The days, the weeks that followed. The latent suspicion of the police, the officer whose name he has forgotten pointing to the camera on her lapel, telling him it wasn't a formal statement, not to worry, they just needed to keep a record. Oh, but he had felt their eyes on him and Ava, their cameras recording every word and twitch, Lorraine Stephens pretending not to listen. Even if he'd wanted to tell them that it was him who left the door open, he wouldn't have – would have been a fool to change his story and risk arousing suspicion for such a small detail. It was bad enough when they piled on about the blood on the pavement.

The police were cagey with Neil too. That imperceptible layer of frost that Matt watched melt away as Neil wrapped them in his certainties, his capability, his openness. His charm.

But he hasn't been open, has he? He has hidden his troubles so deeply that Matt has not had the slightest clue.

I'm always right, Neil said at dinner.

And yes, he has always been right, has always been possessed of a kind of down-to-earth wisdom from which Matt took his lead. Neil was Matt's moral compass before Ava ever was.

But that night he wasn't right, was he? His moral compass had lost its north. That night, in the pouring rain, he insisted on shaking on the lie. It was the first time – is the only time – he has advised against honesty. Come to think of it, it was the first and only time he's suggested shaking hands. And when Matt thinks about that now, in the shadow of all that Ava has said, he wonders what need there was to mimic some gentlemen's agreement when it was already long written into the deeds of their friendship that of course Neil wouldn't have betrayed his confidence. That was a given, wasn't it? So why shake on it?

Why insist? Neil has always known the right thing to do. But not that time. That time he called it wrong. As if something had skewed his judgement.

As if he needed it to be kept secret more than Matt did.

CHAPTER THIRTY-FIVE

Ava

The September evening is a warm breath on my face. I walk the long way round so as not to pass in front of Neil and Bella's house and risk being seen by Matt. At the top of Thameside Lane, I round the corner left, my stomach clenching as it always does whenever I go near the river. Last night's scene with Neil is still fresh in my mind – of course it is: the two of us crashing into the cold water, the strange, mad intimacy of that. That Abi drowned, I know I have to accept. I am getting nearer to it, which could of course be why I am so wired – a last frenzy before the small expiry of acceptance.

But how she ended up in the river is another matter. On this, my nerves are alight. My gut tells me that if she did drown, if that has to be how her life ended, then it was not an accident.

I know nothing for certain. The only certainty I have now is that her disappearance – her death – is not my fault.

It never was.

At the sight of Bella through Starbucks' window, my stomach flares with heat. Dread – that's what I feel. I have resolved to take it slowly, but frankly, I want to grip her by the neck, push my face in close and ask her what she knows.

I back in, drag the pram in after me. The whole operation is awkward. Seated in one of two armchairs, Bella is the only one in the place apart from a spotty, lanky teenage boy at the bar. From overhead speakers, pop music mutters into the coffee-infused air. Lulled by the rhythm of the pram and a full belly, Fred has dropped off to sleep. I use the shorthand of pointing to Bella's mug and raising my eyebrows. She shakes her head, raises her mug: *I'm OK, thanks.*

'Name?' The teenager has his felt-tip pen poised.

I look about me, at the empty café, back at him. 'Really?'

He blushes and instantly I feel like a bitch. Which I am. I fancy a hot chocolate, for the sweetness, but instead order a decaf latte. When he hands it to me, I thank him profusely, by way of apology.

'Hey.' I approach my friend, wondering if *friend* is what she is now, wondering if Neil has told her about last night. *What* he has told her.

She is wearing a red and orange dress and a tiny denim jacket, drinking peppermint tea in full make-up. Her nails are painted red, not one chip, not one chewed cuticle. I look down at my own loose combat trousers, my scruffy Converse, the puke stain on my grey sweatshirt. I'm wearing no make-up; my hair is pulled back into a ponytail. I feel unfashionable, out of place and a bit manky.

'Hey.' She doesn't stand up. There will be no cheek kisses, no hugs.

I park the pram and sit down. 'I'm guessing Neil told you about last night.'

She nods slowly. Nods again when I ask if he mentioned the river incident.

'I went a bit crazy,' I say. 'I'm sorry. I shouldn't have done that.'

'He was pretty shaken up.' She sips her peppermint tea. 'Are you all right? I heard about… you and Matt.'

'Did you know?' The question flashes like a flame. I dampen my tone. 'I mean, did you know about the door?'

She shakes her head. 'No. Neil never said anything. Not a word, swear to God.'

I pour a whole sachet of sugar into my coffee, wonder why I didn't just get the hot chocolate, then how the hell I can even think about anything so trivial, so irrelevant, when elsewhere in my brain hangs the notion that someone knows something about the death of my daughter. The notion that Bella herself knows something. But I cannot grip her by the neck. Not here.

'Matt's at yours, isn't he?' are the words that find their way out of my mouth.

'It was good you rang actually. Gave me an excuse to clear out.' She sips her drink, licks her lip. 'They can have a man-to-man convo,' she adds. 'Whatever that is.'

'I have no idea.'

Incredibly, we smile at one another.

From behind me comes the clank of the barista cleaning up.

'So,' Bella says. 'What did you want to talk about?'

I study my hands. They are chapped from washing them too often, as they were when Abi was a baby. Bella will have noticed, will have wondered why I don't moisturise them. Christ, these thoughts are like bugs.

I look up, try to hold her gaze, if only for a couple of seconds.

'Remember you said Neil had been out all night,' I begin. 'The night Abi… disappeared?'

'Yeah.' She shifts: straightens her spine, lengthens her neck. 'Why?'

'Did you mean *all night* all night or just, you know, late?'

'I thought you sorted this out with Neil.' Her voice carries an edge, and when I look at her, I see that her jaw has pushed forward slightly, her mouth flat. She has told me about fall-outs with other friends that left me assuming that her friendship with those women was over, only to hear that she went out with them the following week, all sorted. I wonder what's coming, whether I can avoid the scene my insides tell me is imminent.

'I did.' I keep my tone level and quiet.

'So what's this then? Checking to see if our stories match?'

The confrontational tone almost winds me.

'I'm sorry,' I say. 'But since finding out Matt didn't close the front door, everything I've thought about that day has been turned on its head. It's not that it changes what happened so much, it's more the sense that someone I know so well could have lied to me for so long, and what that means about everything else I thought was true – do you know what I mean? I've been turned on my head, if I'm honest. That's how it feels. I've gone through it all so many times, hoping for a different outcome, but now…' I look up, but there is such hardness in her eyes, I return to the safety of the coffee I never wanted.

'Now what?'

I force myself to meet her gaze, no matter how intimidating. 'Neil said he continued looking. Can you remember what time he got back?'

Her bronzed skin yellows. Her beautiful turquoise eyes narrow. Her jaw clenches. Each alteration is tiny. Infinitesimal. But, like the inconsequential events at the party, they add up.

'Bella?'

She shakes her head. 'I don't know,' she says. 'I can't really remember. I think I just meant he was out late. I was just trying to tell you how much he cared, that's all. I mean, I was drunk, Ave. Those cocktails!' She pulls a face. Maybe she too can feel the simmering and is afraid of it.

'*In vino veritas*,' I say.

'What?' She looks at me blankly.

'Nothing. It's just that I got the impression you were trying to tell me something but you were… I don't know… afraid? I'm probably overthinking, but hey, who can blame me? You were so insistent, that's all. You were telling me how much Neil loved Abi. I know he loved Abi. But you said "no matter what" and, I don't know, it was as if… as if he'd done something terrible and you were trying to tell me he hadn't done it on purpose…'

I am watching her. I am watching her every move, her every tic, her every passing shade of skin. Beneath her tan, a rose blooms on each cheek.

'Bella?'

Her eyes fill. 'Neil would never do anything to hurt Abi. He loved her. He loved her so much.'

'I'm not saying he didn't. I'm just wondering if something happened. Maybe… maybe he was running late, maybe he was driving too fast…'

She stands up. Her chair scrapes across the floor.

'He didn't run her over, if that's what you mean. He didn't do anything.'

'I'm not saying he did.' I raise my palms to her. 'I'm not saying anything. I just want you to be honest with me, that's all. If there's anything that struck you as odd that day, anything at all. It's just that Jasmine knew the name of Abi's toy, and that's impossible. It's impossible, Bella, totally impossible, unless she saw Neil or you with it. And I know that may not sound like much, but I can't explain it, and today when I thought back to our conversation last night, I realised neither did he. So if there's something you might have noticed, something that didn't quite chime, it might not seem important to you, but it's important to me, do you see? I'm not trying to incriminate anyone, I just want to know what happened, because my little girl could still be out there, and if she is, I want her back. Surely you can understand that?' A tear snakes down each cheek almost without me noticing. And in all of this, in all of it, I'm still worried about upsetting her.

Too late. She is picking up her phone and dropping it into her tote.

'Bella, please,' I say. 'Don't take this personally. I'm in hell here – can't you see?'

She sniffs loudly, pushes her forefingers flat to her lower lashes, the way she did that day. Carefully. Conscious of her appearance even now. Conscious of it then.

'Bella, come on.' My voice rises. 'She's my baby girl. I'm her mother. You don't know what it's—'

Too late I realise what I've said.

'I don't know what? What it's like? I'm not a mum, so what, I'm some kind of psycho?'

'No.' I raise my palms to her, half stand. 'Look, I know you lost a baby,' I say gently. 'Babies. And I'm so sorry.'

Her eyes round. 'Who told you that?' Her eyes close, open, roll. 'Oh. Of course.'

'Neil was upset, that's all. It just came out.'

Her face hardens. 'Just came out, did it? One of your little chats? He always did talk to you, didn't he? Miss Classy, Miss Perfect, Miss Talented, with your piano and your nice speaking voice… so much better than the likes of me. Chavs.'

My legs straighten, almost tipping over the table. I shift, perch on the edge of the seat. 'What the hell? I would never use that word.'

'You basically think you're better than us, don't you?' Bella sneers down at me. 'You think what happened gives you the right to accuse us of doing something horrible. You're upset – I get it. You're grieving – I get that as well. Do you know why? Because I'm not as thick as you think, that's why. I can hold more than one thing in my tiny little brain. I'm gutted for myself obviously. And for Neil. But I can be gutted for you as well, you know, and I am, I really am. I find it difficult to see little Fred, but that doesn't mean I'm not pleased for you. I'm not pretending my grief is anything compared to yours, but we were devastated, me and Neil, devastated for us *and* for you. He's not been the same since that day, and we're having a terrible time, really terrible. We haven't been there for you, I know that and I'm sorry, and you haven't been there for us, but that's no one's fault. Sometimes it's no one's fault, Ava. But you don't get to go around accusing Neil of having something to do with Abi's death, all right? And I'd appreciate it if you could stop with your little midnight heart-to-hearts with him, all right? He's my husband, Ava. Mine. Not yours.'

My head throbs. 'What? Bella, what are you even saying? Where the hell is all this coming from? I'm not *after* Neil – that's nuts.'

'Why? Because he likes beer more than champagne?'

'What?' My face heats. 'This is mad! I don't look down on you; I never have. You look down on me, if anything.'

'What? No I don't.'

'You do. I never have the right clothes, for a start. I don't wear the right shoes and I don't have the right hair. All the times you go out for drinks and you've never invited me, never, in all the time we've known each other. Even before Abi went missing. I'd ruin your Instagram, wouldn't I? I'm just not glamorous enough.'

'That's not true.' Her eyes fill.

'Well neither is me being a snob. If I've seemed like that it's because just standing next to you makes me feel like I've faded to grey, like I'm an alien who'll never understand the rules. You're so… so glamorous, all the time. Look at you! It's a random Tuesday night in a deserted café and look at you! And look at the state of me! I might've felt a bit jealous on occasion, that's all. And I'm not attracted to Neil in that way, and even if I were, which I'm not, he would never do anything because he's loyal and he loves you, and I'd never do anything because I'm married to Matt.'

'Not happily though.'

My mouth drops open.

Chin tipped out, Bella shifts her bag to her shoulder, seems to be about to leave.

'Not happily?' I shout. I am shouting. In a café. Bella freezes. 'I *was* happy. I was happy until my daughter was killed or kidnapped or drowned or whatever the hell happened to her. I'm sorry, you'll forgive me if my relationship has *suffered* a little under that small amount of stress.'

Tears fall from my chin. My nose is running, I can barely see, but I do see that Bella is crying too, her chin puckered with misery, her eyes darting, shining with panic and confusion.

'I was happy,' I cry at her, even though she is visibly cringing. 'And we were getting there until I found out that my husband, my own husband, had been lying to me for a year over the small matter of the death of our daughter and who left the door open, the door that, had it been shut, would mean she would still be here today – and your husband, Mr Nice Guy, Mr Fucking Fix-It, was backing him up in some bullshit big boys' don't-tell-the-missus conspiracy. So you'll forgive me if I'm not in my right mind just now, all right?'

I gasp back a flood of grief; my head falls into my hands. 'I *don't* think I'm better than anyone, I never have. I'm just cross at everyone, that's all, and I feel grey and tired and alone, and some days I can't be bothered to wash myself, let alone my hair, and I'm not trying to accuse anyone, honestly I'm not.' I sob into my fingers. 'Well, maybe I am but I don't want to. I don't want to be this person, and I was so sorry to hear that you guys have had problems, of course I was, and of course I've got room for that, it's not that my grief is… I mean, it's not a competition. Oh God, I don't want to be like this, I don't want any of this. I don't want to fall out. I just want my daughter back. I just want my little girl so badly.'

The rolling sound of a shutter. The music dips. When I glance up, I see Bella nodding, though not at me.

'Ava,' she says quietly. 'They're closing.'

'OK.'

I wipe at my face with my fingertips. Silence presses in. A moment later, she taps my shoulder and hands me a paper napkin.

'Thanks.' I press it to my eyes, blow my nose. 'I'm sorry.'

'OK.'

'I really am.'

'I said it's OK. I am too. I didn't realise I made you feel like that.'

'Me neither.' I blow my nose.

'I think we had each other all wrong.'

'I think we did, but I've always really liked you. You're kind and you're fun and you're… you're yourself, you know?'

'And I like you, Ava. I never invited you out because I didn't think it was your scene, that's all.'

I nod. 'I'm sorry; I don't know why I said that. Let's go home, eh?'

'Actually,' she says, 'I think I'd rather walk by myself. No offence. I just need to get my head straight. But it's OK.'

'Are you sure? Well, listen, all I want to say is… if you do think of anything, even a tiny thing, please, please, please tell me, OK. I'm begging you.'

For the first time in this whole encounter, our eyes meet. And perhaps it is the intensity of the moment, but it is as if we are seeing each other for the first time. We are just women, I think, trying to survive in a world not made for any of us.

'OK,' she says, her smile watery. 'I will; I promise.'

I close my eyes, feel the pressure of her hand on my shoulder. A second, and it is gone. Another second, the squeak of the door hinge; another, the rush of a car on the high street; another, the clatter of the door. One more and the music stops. I am alone – bewildered, ostracised and alone.

CHAPTER THIRTY-SIX

Matt

Matt finds Neil eating cereal, standing feet crossed, his back against the kitchen sink, bowl cupped in one hand. It is 6.45 a.m. He is dressed for work: clean white overalls, grey T-shirt, yellow work boots. He is clean-shaven, his hair slicked back.

'Morning.' He waves his hand vaguely to indicate that Matt should help himself, the fresh smell of shower gel coming off him 'There's cereal. Or toast. Do you want tea or coffee?'

'Coffee, thanks.'

Moments later, Neil hands him a café-style latte.

'We've got one of those machines now,' he says with a note of apology. 'We'll be eating sun-dried tomatoes next.'

'You already eat sun-dried tomatoes.' Matt smiles. His face resists, his skin dry and thick as an elephant's. On no sleep, the thought of food makes him feel sick.

'Aren't you cycling?' Neil asks, eyeing Matt's suit.

'I've got a meeting in town. Embankment.'

'I can give you a lift to the station if you want. I'm in Surbiton this morning.'

'Great.'

Neil looks at his watch. 'Ten minutes?'

'Sure. Is Bella OK?'

Neil nods. 'She's fine. I took her a tea but she doesn't get up till half seven, quarter to eight.'

Matt nods, though he's not sure this explains the tear-stained mess that was Bella when she returned home last night at ten, saying she'd had a row with someone called Shannon and was going straight to bed. She barely looked at him and, horribly, he'd felt himself to be an intrusion in something difficult – difficult and private. A few minutes later, he made his excuses and went to bed so that Neil could go to her.

'I'll get a Travelodge tonight,' he says now to his friend.

'Don't be daft.' Neil throws his bowl in the sink. Matt knows that deep down Neil would prefer it if he did stay in a hotel, given the apparent state of things with Bella, but that these are not words that can be exchanged between them.

'Nah,' he says. 'I need to be on my own, I think.'

'Cool. If that's what you want to do.'

'Sure.'

Five minutes later, Matt hurries down the stairs. The front door is open and Neil is loading some gear into the back of his van.

'Shall I shut the door?' he calls out, aware of the crashing irony of the question only after it leaves him.

'Yeah. I just need one more thing.' Neil disappears into the side return, presumably to fetch more tools from his shed. Neil's is a super-shed – concrete base, reinforced and insulated, the door twice padlocked against theft. Very Neil, thinks Matt, almost smiling as he makes his way to the van, passing behind the open back doors. A glance inside reveals the electric cement mixer, a stiff yard brush, a pickaxe, a couple of spades.

He climbs up into the front of the van. A moment later, Neil walks back down the front path, singing to himself and carrying a large red tool bag the size of a small suitcase. He disappears momentarily; Matt hears the van doors slam behind him. Another second and Neil is clambering into the front.

'Right,' he says, starting the engine. A blast of music. He turns the radio down. 'All set?'

'Yep.' Matt clutches his sports bag on his lap, his rucksack with his laptop snug between his feet.

Neil pulls out of the street. As yet, the traffic is thin. Above, peach and grey clouds give way to white, September establishing itself: chilly mornings, warm days. They chat, Matt thinks later, about nothing. The weather, Neil's job, Matt's job. Neil drops him at the station, toots the horn as he drives away. Matt waves him off but turns before the van disappears out of sight.

It is only later, on the train into Waterloo, that Neil will appear again in his mind's eye, carrying his red tool bag down his front path, singing to himself. The image will release in Matt a toxic cloud of spores, which will reproduce through the cells and tissue of him until, later still, when he grabs a takeaway flat white from a bar on Villiers Street, he will pinpoint the source of the rot and discover that it wasn't words or body language or any kind of misplaced gesture but an object as innocuous as a bag, a new red tool bag, carried with perfect nonchalance down a suburban front path, and even then, it is only because of everything else that has gone before, everything that Ava said last night, that this apparently harmless detail is the one that finally sickens him.

He is early for his meeting. In the public garden at the back of the Embankment, he sits on a bench and sips his coffee in the sun. Commuters bustle by – urgent, purposeful. He thinks back to that day, to Neil showing the cop around the Lovegoods' kitchen extension.

'Listen.' Neil placed a hand on Matt's arm, his voice quiet and low. 'We're just going to check Johnnie's place.'

He was so natural, so open. Matt remembers the policeman, who looked about eighteen.

Sitting now in the sun, he remembers too how he went inside to look for himself. He has not stopped to wonder why, why he would check after Neil had checked. Was there a subconscious lack of trust even then? He doesn't think so. Abi was his daughter; it was normal to rest his bike against the wall and step into his next-door neighbours' house. It was normal to creep up the hall, listening out for Neil and the police officer talking on the first floor. It was normal to stand at the kitchen door and stare through the glass to Neil's work site.

But there was almost nothing there – only the shell of a large hangar-like room, the ceiling held up with great rolled-steel joists, the back wall to the garden almost entirely gone. A house on stilts. Venetian, he thought then, or a Tudor jetty. He remembers thinking it, even in that charged moment, remembers how random thoughts like that came to him that day, as if from some earlier version of himself. Standing there staring, he remembered his and Ava's kitchen looking like that – a smaller model – when Neil did their extension. Two brooms, two spades and a pickaxe leant against the right-hand wall, a neat pile of rubble at their base. Neil was always a tidy worker. A tool bag lay at the far side next to the open-mouthed, frog-like drum of Neil's electric mixer, the same one in which Matt had helped him mix concrete. A lone washing machine stood over to the left, connected to a standpipe. On top of the washing machine, a mud-splashed radio, a half-eaten packet of digestive biscuits, a kettle, also spattered with dried muddy water and three grotty white mugs with the Radio Jackie logo just about visible under streaks of dried coffee.

Hearing voices coming down the stairs, he hurried back to the front door, though too slowly to avoid being caught in the hallway by Neil and the cop.

'Sorry,' he said. 'Just needed to look for myself, you know?'

Neil *volunteered* to show the policeman round, he thinks now, trying to fit it all together with this horrible poisonous feeling. He himself double-checked. But what bothers him, what bothers him now, is that in amongst the brushes, the spades, the heavy tools and the cement mixer, the mugs and the kettle, the radio and the half-eaten packet of biscuits on the top of the lone washing machine was Neil's tool bag. Neil's brand-new black tool bag, the white stitching still bright. The size of a small suitcase. He didn't think about it at the time; it wasn't one of the thousand random thoughts he had that day, but now he remembers that Neil told him it cost a couple of ton. Two hundred pounds. The Rolls-Royce of tool bags.

But it was black, with white stitching, still bright. It was new. And it was not red.

Afterwards, Neil suggested they split up.

'I'll head to Kingston,' he said. Said he would check Bushy Park.

Did he?

A wave of nausea threatens to bring up the coffee he has just drunk. He puts his head between his knees and feels the sun on the back of his neck. His forehead pricks with perspiration and all he can see is that bag. The size of it. The brand-new condition of it. The size. The size, the size, the size.

When Ava knocked for Neil, he was at home, which was unusual but not alarm-bell-ringing. Later, when the more unpleasant glimmer of suspicion fell upon them and their best friends, the dogs sniffed their way around their house too and found nothing. Nothing. Because Abi wasn't – had never – been there. Afterwards, he and Neil separated again. They only hooked up in the evening – Neil said he'd been as far as Barnes, handing out the printed photographs and taping posters to lamp posts from Strawberry Hill to Richmond.

Had he?

No idea. Matt knows only that they searched until midnight. Abi's jacket was found the next morning.

But Bella told Ava that Neil was out all night, which means he didn't go home, not then.

Once the jacket was found, there were no further household searches. The divers went into the Thames, found nothing. Neil and Bella, Ava and himself all gave their statements. Other leads ran to nothing – the BMW, the witness who wasn't sure, mobile-phone data, CCTV. The investigation was scaled back, put under review. DI Farnham left her direct line: *call me if any new information comes to light.*

There is no new information.

On its own, the tool bag is not information.

On its own, Jasmine's recognition of Mr Sloth is not information.

On its own, Neil's being out all night is not information.

Every detail, on its own, is not information.

But together…
He calls Ava.

CHAPTER THIRTY-SEVEN

Ava

I am alone, alone with my boy and with something rushing in, something taking shape. I am watching the street wake up, watching front doors open, my neighbours walking in the direction of the station, cars drifting away to local jobs. I am watching them and thinking about Sunday morning, talking to Jen on the street. The garage door opening behind her. Johnnie emerging in his car.

I am thinking about that beat-by-beat morning, about Matt returning home for his raincoat just before 8 a.m.

Eight-ish, Jen said she and Johnnie left for work.

His car wasn't on the drive.

But Johnnie keeps his car in the garage.

If their car was in the garage, it was not visible.

If their car was not visible, their house would have seemed closed, empty.

If they left at eight, and if Matt grabbed his coat just before, it's possible the Lovegoods were still home.

Which means it's possible that they were still there when he left the door open.

If Abi left moments later, carrying Mr Sloth, it's possible they saw her and that she told them his name.

Jasmine would have seized upon the name, put it together with Neil in her mind because Neil had a game going with her cuddly toys.

Neil wasn't there; he was at home. Which means the Lovegoods, not Neil, were there that morning.

They must have spoken to her.

They must have seen her.

Seen her and said nothing.

My mobile is ringing. I find it in the kitchen drawer and see what I already know – Matt calling, doubtless all hand-wringing and apologies after the fact. I have no desire to speak to him; I need to process all that I'm now thinking and am frankly appalled that he can't just leave me alone. But if I don't answer, he will ring again and again. So I pick up.

'Matt.'

'Ava. Ava, don't hang up. It's not… I'm not calling about us.'

Something stirs within me, something that is not quite premonition.

'It's about Abi,' Matt says, his tone wretched. 'It's about Neil.'

Instinctively I wander into the living room to check on Fred. He is sitting in a sling chair and cooing at the archway of plastic toys that dangle over him.

'Go on.' I am looking out at the street, which is waking up at this time as it did that day, minutes too late.

'I don't know what to think.' He sounds fraught.

'What? What do you mean? Have you found out something else?'

He sighs. 'It's probably nothing. But maybe it's like you said. All the little things, you know?'

'Matt, I can hear you're upset, but if you've called me for a game of charades, I'm afraid I—'

'Stop!' His breath staggers down the line. 'Stop… let me…'

I nod, even though he is not here to see me.

'I've been thinking,' he says, still out of breath. 'I've been thinking about Neil and how he's always been my adviser in life, you know? What I mean is, I always knew he was shooting from the hip; he never had any ulterior motive. And because of that, his was always good advice. No agenda, you know?'

'What has this got to—' I interrupt but make myself shut up.

'But that night,' Matt ploughs on, 'he told me not to tell you about the door. It was the wrong advice. I'm not blaming him. It was my fault I didn't tell you. I didn't have to take his advice, even though I always have. I should have told you. I should have had the strength to ignore him and do the right thing.'

'Matt—'

'No, wait. Let me finish. What I'm trying to say is that it's the first time he's given me bad advice. And it's the first… no, it's the *only* time he's told me to be dishonest. About anything.'

'And?'

'He insisted we keep it between us. It was like some sort of pact. But… any pact we've had, we've had since we were kids. It's an unspoken thing. And that night, he made us shake on it, Ave. It's not that he acted suspiciously or weirdly, he just didn't act like *himself*, that's all. So I was wondering if it suited *him* for me to lie – but I can't figure out why that would be, and all this on top of Mr Sloth.' He sighs. 'And then this morning, I saw he had a new tool bag.'

'What do you mean? What's a new tool bag got to do with anything?'

Another heavy sigh. I can see him, see the angle of his head, the sorrowful set of his dark eyes. 'That morning. When Abi… disappeared. I looked in at the work site – next door's extension – while he was upstairs. And his tool bag was there and it was black. And it was new. And I remembered just now it was really expensive. Only it was the size of it.'

'The size.' I feel sick. 'What do you mean, the size?'

'It was big, you know? Big enough.'

A sob leaves me. I sit down on the sofa, my hand across my eyes.

'And this morning,' Matt goes on, 'he had a *red* bag. A new red bag. And I don't even know what it means. If it means anything. I'm being paranoid. His black one is probably in the shed. I'm paranoid. Sorry… Ava? Are you still there?'

'I'm here.' I'm here and I am trembling.

'I… Look, I'm just going to say this, OK? It's going to sound really woo-woo, but you know at that party? I can't explain it, but I felt like she was there. I was leaning against the steel and I felt her pulse. Like it was beating through the house. I mean, I realised it was the clock, and I was drunk, but for those few seconds, it was like I felt her. Her heart. The beat of it.'

I am aware of myself breathing – regularly, heavily, as if I'm pretending to myself that I'm asleep. But I am not asleep.

'Are we being mad?' he asks.

I hear the catch in his voice.

'Maybe,' I reply, remembering the unbearable sight of Cosima in Johnnie's arms, how I couldn't get Abi out of my mind. 'It was a tough night, hard to shake off. Look, come over tonight and we'll talk. I'm not saying stay, OK? But I've had some thoughts too. My mind's a mess.'

'OK,' he says. 'But, Ava?'

'Yes?'

'Mostly what I want to say is that I believe you, all right? I didn't, and I'm sorry I didn't, but I do now. I don't know what it is, but you're right, it's something. Something's off.'

'Thank you.'

An hour later, I'm about to put Fred in the pram when a text comes in. Bella.

Can you talk?

Like oil under a lit match, my body fills with burning dread. I ring her immediately.

'Bella?'

All I can hear is background noise: a radio, talking, the hum of a hairdryer.

'Bella?'

The noise fades. I hear the clunk of a door closing.

'Ava?' She says. 'Hi, it's me.'

'I know. Are you at work?'

'Yeah. I've come into the loo.'

I wait. A second passes, two. I hear a sniff.

'Bella? Are you OK?'

A sob. I stay silent – it is all I can do to not speak.

'I'm only going to say this once,' she whispers. 'And I'll never say it again, do you hear me?'

'OK.'

'And I'm not saying it means anything, OK?'

'OK.'

'And you can't tell anyone I told you.'

'All right.'

She sighs. I wait, my breath held in my chest.

'OK,' she says after a long moment. Another deep sigh. 'When I got back from the salon the morning Abi… that morning, I went home to change into my trainers so I could help look.'

I nod, realise I'm holding my breath.

'And… Neil's clothes were in the washing machine. His overalls and that. I didn't think anything of it, I just put them in the dryer and went to get changed. But the next morning, there was another set of clothes in there that he'd washed in the night. And I didn't think anything of that either. I knew he'd been out and thought he must have got muddy, that's all. I didn't think anything of anything, I swear to God I didn't.' Another sniff.

'Bella?' I whisper, desperate to comfort her but scared of interrupting in case I frighten her back into silence.

'OK,' she says, her voice trembling. 'I didn't think anything, only a bit of surprise maybe that he'd washed his gear himself, like. But you said anything, no matter how small, and now… I mean, this year he's not been himself at all. He never used to shout at me or anything, he was always sweet. He never used to drink during the week. I mean, I just thought it was the stress of the IVF…'

I listen, floating, unable to believe the fact of her telling me this, less than an hour after Matt. It isn't coincidence – of course it isn't. It is simply that the party has pulled the plug on the weird, stagnant pond of our lives, has drained the water from details half submerged, which lie now in the shallows, exposed.

'He's not been himself,' Bella repeats, the words fraught with meaning. 'It was understandable, but now…' Her voice is little more than a squeak; the rest follows in a tearful rush. 'Thing is, that morning, before I went to work, there were no dirty clothes in the washing basket. None. I did them at the weekend, I always do. And even if there were, Neil never washes his clothes. Never. I do them. I'm not saying he did anything, all right? But if I don't tell you what I know and it turns out he knew something, well, I'll never forgive myself. Never.'

'Bella?'

The line dies. I sit back, winded, thoughts racing. I had believed, or thought it was possible to believe, that Neil had nothing to do with it. I had even got as far as the Lovegoods. But even as I think of them, the sense that I was clutching at straws grows. It was a wild hypothesis wrought from desperation, desperation not to accept a much more horrible, unthinkable possibility. Neil.

I call Matt.

'Ava?'

'Bella just called. You need to come home now. I'm calling Sharon Farnham. I'm calling the police.'

CHAPTER THIRTY-EIGHT

Ava

Matt taps everything into his phone while I drive to the police station, trying not to rant at the wheel. We start low, make a sensible list: the sloth toy, the odd behaviours, Neil's washing in the machine, the tool bag. But hysteria rises exponentially, up and away to febrile theories worthy of later seasons of television dramas fresh out of ideas. In one, Abi is being looked after by a contact of Bella's in a country far away, Neil and Bella waiting until the dust settles, when they will collect their visas and fly to live under aliases with her as their own child. In this theory, their kitchen extension is being put on hold not because of spiralling fertility fees but because they're saving money for this midnight flit into obscurity.

'Unless,' I say.

'Unless what?'

'Do you know the monkey experiment?'

He shakes his head. I pass through the lights, take a left.

'I read about it once. They put a monkey and her baby in a cage and slowly turn up the heat on the cage floor. The mother picks up her baby to protect it from the heat. She holds her baby up, keeping it off the floor while the heat increases, burning her feet. She hops from foot to foot until at last—'

'She lies down?'

'No. That's the thing. She puts the baby on the floor and stands on it.'

'Oh for God's sake.' Matt looks appalled. 'What the hell did you tell me that for?'

'Bella.' I glance at him.

'Bella?'

'Think about it. Bella is the only other person who knew the name of the toy. And when Abi went missing, she was nowhere to be seen. What if… what if she did something terrible in a jealous rage and Neil covered for her? And what if, now the heat has been turned up too high, she's thrown him on the floor to protect herself?'

He shakes his head. 'No. Stop. We need to stop.'

I nod. We're being mad. Suspicion has driven us both mad.

'The fact is,' I say, 'we don't know anything at all.'

'We do. Just nothing that, alone, is worth mentioning. But it's not about one piece of information, is it?'

'Right. But we don't want to appear mad. So, no conspiracy theories, just the facts. And maybe not mention that we felt her presence at the housewarming party?'

Incredibly, this makes us laugh – a dark spark of grim connection, muscle memory long forgotten.

Detective Inspector Sharon Farnham leads us into an interview room made to look like a living room and asks us to sit down on a firm beige sofa. On the phone, she offered to come to us, but I said no, that we preferred to come here. I didn't want Neil or Bella to see a police car outside our house.

Matt lets me do the talking, which I do whilst feeding Fred and with a nasty, creeping sense of treachery. Matt takes over and I listen with a terrible stillness, a block in my guts. If we are wrong, what remains of our life is lost; we deserve to be excommunicated from our closest friends and anyone who ever loved us.

If we are right, it is worse.

DI Farnham listens, the device on the table recording every word.

'And then I saw the bag,' Matt is saying now. 'And I remembered I hardly saw him that day. I mean, that's the thing when everyone's concentrating on a common task... the focus is elsewhere. I thought he was with other neighbours. Ava thought he was with me. I didn't even think about where Bella might be.' He looks at me. 'We didn't think about any of that, did we? We had no reason to suspect either of them.'

I glance at Farnham, whose expression gives nothing away. She must think we are insane. Or rats, betraying our closest friends like this with no more than scraps to go on. Whatever she feels, she is staying quiet. Perhaps she is indulging us, nothing more. Perhaps she is trained simply to listen in the hope that, sooner or later, someone will say something that leads to a solution, to an arrest, to a conviction. Perhaps it's us she's waiting for: a fatal slip of the tongue that will allow her to click the cuffs around our wrists.

'The thing is,' Matt continues, 'the dogs never went inside the Lovegoods' kitchen, did they? So if she was in that bag...' He covers his mouth; his eyes close.

'There was no reason for them to take the dogs in,' Farnham says. 'We don't treat people like criminals until we have reason to do so. The site and garden were checked on the day and there was no evidence to suggest Abi had been inside, no access points to the property. Mr Johnson was at home, as witnessed by yourself, and the Lovegoods had already left. As it is, it's still difficult to see how Abi could've accessed the house. Mr Johnson's data still places him at home until much later, when you called for him…' She passes her hand across her chin before glancing first at Matt, then at me. 'Do either of you remember seeing the Lovegoods when you left for work that first time? Is it possible they could have been in the house?'

'Yes,' I say.

'I'm pretty sure they left around eight.' Farnham looks at her notes, passes her hand once, twice, three times across her chin. 'They would have been gone by the time Abi left the house between five past and quarter past eight…'

'Thing is,' Matt says, glancing at me, back at Farnham. 'It could have been earlier. That Abi left. I didn't say this on the day and I should have done. But I went back to the house that morning to pick up my jacket.'

Farnham stares at him as if he's lost his mind.

'I should've said and I'm sorry. I didn't think it was relevant and everything was going so fast and Abi was still there in the hall when I went back and she was there when I left the house.' He breathes in deeply, exhales. His eyes are wet and my heart constricts at what this is costing him. 'But it was me who left the door open. Not Ava. Me.' He gasps, his hand flying to his mouth. 'Oh God, now I'm thinking it's possible that seeing me, seeing the door open, was what made her run out. She would've wanted to follow me. I never thought about that. Oh God, she ran out after me.' He pushes his face into his hands and sobs.

I rest my hand on his back. If there is anyone who knows how he feels, it is me.

Impassive, Farnham writes everything down. 'So, this will have been before eight?'

Matt pulls his hands away from his face and nods. 'A little before, yes.'

'And were the Lovegoods home at that time?'

'No, they'd gone.'

'Not necessarily,' I say.

Matt looks at me; his brow furrows.

Farnham transfers her attention to me.

'I was thinking about this earlier,' I say. 'But I dismissed it after Bella called. The thing is, the Lovegoods could still have been at home. Matt thought they'd gone because there was no car on the drive, but it could have been in the garage. They keep it in there. And if Matt's appearance prompted Abi to follow him, she would have followed him immediately, so it's possible she left our house before the Lovegoods left theirs.'

'So, we have a new timeline.' Farnham scribbles more notes, bites her lip, taps the end of her pen against her teeth. A long moment passes. She leans back, reads it out at arm's length. 'You both left at seven forty-five.' She glances at me. 'Ava, you return just after ten to eight, patch up your daughter's knees and head upstairs at around five to, around the same time Matt returns for his jacket. But you don't hear him because you go into the loo – either the door slams or you flush the chain or whatever. When you come out of the loo, Abi isn't making any noise so you assume she's all settled – does that sound right?'

I nod.

She looks briefly at Matt before continuing. 'You ride away, Abi follows you but you've gone. She then sees either your friend Neil or a member of the Lovegood family, but whoever she sees, she's got the sloth toy with her. By the time you come downstairs, Ava, at quarter past, Abi is gone.'

Neither of us says a word.

'Did you ask Neil where the old tool bag was?' she asks Matt eventually.

He shakes his head. 'I didn't think of it till later. But it was definitely in the work site that day. And I've never seen it since. And as we've said, so many things don't add up.'

I feel like I need a shower. I need to clean my damn teeth. Regret and betrayal have made a sour mix in my mouth. I wonder if Matt can taste it too.

'For me it's about the toy,' I add pointlessly. 'Mr Sloth and Jasmine. It's possible Abi could have explained who Mr Sloth was to the Lovegoods, but she didn't know them at all; I don't think she'd have chatted to them like that. But she knew Neil was working in their house, and there's only us and Neil and Bella who call the toy Mr Sloth.' I make myself shut up, push my foot flat to the floor to stop my leg from jackhammering.

By contrast, Farnham stays quite still, one hand across her mouth. After what seems like an age, she swipes her hand away and leans forward.

'All we can do is bring them in for questioning,' she says, with the air that she was going to say more but has decided against it.

Matt glances at me. I return his gaze and realise I can't find the hate I have for him. I know it's there, but all I can see is my companion in this immense loss, someone who believes me absolutely, someone who has admitted fully to his fault in all this. Without him, I am utterly alone. My husband, who has let me down so badly, but who is here now.

'I'm sorry,' he says.

I take his hand and squeeze it. 'I know.'

He wipes his eyes, turns towards the detective and nods.

'If there's any way of keeping us out of it,' he says, 'that would be better. But if you need to name us, then I'll take full responsibility.'

I drive us home in silence. Park up. Unclip the seat belt and lift Fred out in his car seat. It is after 5 p.m. The street is quiet, so quiet. I wonder if we will have to move away. Regardless of what happens now, I can't imagine living here anymore.

We walk up the short pathway. At our door, Matt glances down the road, towards Neil and Bella's house.

'Do you think they've taken them in?' he asks.

I shrug. 'No idea. Do you think they'd do that?'

'I don't know.' His face is stretched. Grim. 'I've never turned in my best mate before. I'm not sure how it works.'

I touch him on the arm. 'Try not to think about it.'

'Oh, OK then.'

I turn away from his sarcasm and open the front door. Together we go inside. I have no idea what happens next. I am in a different kind of limbo. We both are. In this together but separate; floating but tethered to the same hook. We make tea. We make sandwiches. We pour fruit juice, which we leave. We open a bottle of red wine, which we drink. Just like the day our daughter went missing, all we have is this: waiting, waiting and the small domestic rituals of our life.

At around 8.30 p.m., the phone rings. I hear it from upstairs. I leave Fred in his crib and run downstairs. Matt is in the living room, on the phone.

'No,' he says. 'Yes, thank you.'

He rings off. A long moment passes. I open my mouth to say his name but he crouches, bends over his knees and moans. His hands come up, cradle the back of his head. His knuckles are white knots.

'Matt?' My body fills with the familiar heat of dread.

'Oh God.' He begins to cry. 'Oh God oh God oh God.'

'What?' I say, heart banging. 'Was it Farnham?'

'Yes.'

'And?' My chest is tight. 'Matt? Can you tell me? Matt, hon?'

'Oh God oh God oh God.' Slowly he straightens up, paces to the window, back to me. His face is red, glazed with tears, his eyes small. His arms are still cradling his head.

'What? It's not him, is it? It's not Neil?'

'It is.' He meets my eyes, a sob breaking from him. 'He's confessed. Neil killed our little girl.'

CHAPTER THIRTY-NINE

Neil

His street slides past the windows of the police car; the place where he built his life flickers like a crude cartoon made from the corner of a notepad: houses become one sole house, overlaid and overlaid again – different-colour doors, different shrubs, different curtains.

This is my home, he thinks. *This is my town.*

And as the town too slips by in the same flicking of a thumb, he knows that it is not his, not any longer – it is the place he was born and raised, the place where he laid the foundations and built his castle brick by brick, only to send a wrecking ball through it and bring the whole thing crashing down. That day. That terrible, terrible morning. Thirty-five years living as a good bloke, minding his own business, meeting Bel, proposing to her on holiday in the Seychelles, marrying her, working hard, never asking anything of anyone, only ever wanting as much as the next man without doing anybody over, trying to be a good mate to Matt, to encourage him, get him to believe in himself…

It doesn't matter. *He* doesn't matter. He is nothing. By doing what he has done, he has obliterated not only his castle but himself and anything he might have stood for, any good he might have done.

He tries to pinpoint when exactly he became nothing. The first seconds he can attribute to panic. The conscious part, he thinks, was the moment he pulled the zip over her pale and sleeping face. But maybe not. Maybe he was still senseless then. Blind. Deaf. Numb. Yes, maybe he was. Maybe it was later, when he emerged in fresh overalls from his home and began the great pretence.

It doesn't matter. He doesn't matter. Who the hell cares what he thinks?

He closes his eyes to the buzzing of the police radio, the rising hum of the gears, the bleeping of the pedestrian crossing, and sees himself standing over the bag in the cavernous shell of a half-built kitchen extension. It is out of his control now. There is nothing he can do to make this right. There is no going back; there never was. It is almost a relief. It was killing him, one day at a time, stripping him out from the inside. Better to have it out in the open, and some hours from now, it will be, once and for all. Matt and Ava will know what he's done. Everyone will know what he's done.

He wonders what Bella knew. If she suspected. Last night, she came in all upset, and when he went up to bed, she was propped up against the headboard waiting for him.

'Why are Matt and Ava suspicious of you?'

'What?'

'Ava said you and Matt got back at midnight the night little Abi went missing. You didn't get back at midnight. Where were you?'

'I went back out.' He pulled off his clothes and climbed into bed. 'I thought I could find her. I told her that.'

'Why did you do a wash load that morning?'

'Wash load? What? What are you going on about?'

'I had to lie for you,' she said. 'It was horrible.'

'I haven't done anything though. They're just paranoid. Something about that party set them off. Ava especially. I told you. She's gone mental, needs some proper help, that's all. Come here. Come on. What you need is a cuddle.'

'You always defend her.'

'Come here.'

He talked her round like he always did. She liked to be persuaded out of a bad mood like that, used to pretend she was angry about something or other – he was pretty sure she did it on purpose – so they could end up like they did last night, one thing leading to another. It was the best sex they'd had in ages – spontaneous instead of thermometers and ovulation kits and all that crap. It was, he thinks, the last sex they'll ever have. Wonders now if she knew that, if she was saying goodbye.

The police car pulls up outside the station. He waits for the cop to open the door. He believed he could move past it. He thought, with time, it would become no more than a bad feeling. But he knows – has always known – that if it comes out, it will define him. And now that day has come. He is about to become Neil Johnson, the guy who killed his best friend's child.

CHAPTER FORTY

Ava

'He had a plausible story,' Farnham is saying, sitting at one end of the sofa while Lorraine Stephens sits pushed up against the opposite arm. 'It matched what he said at the time, and there was nothing to put him in the frame. When we spoke to Mrs Lovegood, she told us he wasn't at their home when they left for work and that he texted to say he'd be in later, that he had to go to the builders' merchants for equipment. Mr Johnson's wife confirmed that he wasn't in the house when she left for work but that didn't put him at the Lovegoods necessarily. His phone data had him at home the whole time.'

Matt's leg presses against mine, our hands a knot between us.

Farnham leans forward and folds her hands together.

'But he couldn't explain the toy,' she says. 'I asked Mrs Lovegood whether Jasmine would recognise a sloth and be able to name it as such if she hadn't seen the toy before, or whether she had a sloth toy herself. She said most definitely not, to both, that the nearest she'd get would be a monkey. There was no record on Mr Johnson's bank statement of buying equipment earlier that morning, to which he initially replied that they were out of stock. We pushed him on the toy and in the end he admitted that he was at the Lovegoods' property at

7 a.m. He'd left his mobile at home. He was working in the utility room while the family were getting ready to leave. The Lovegoods didn't know he was there.'

'He was in their downstairs loo?' I cut in.

'Yes. But he couldn't give us any explanation why he'd lied about that. Then of course we have a missing large tool bag and a missing… person.'

A small mass, I think. A large bag.

Farnham continues. We listen to the second-by-second, beat-by-beat rhythm of a different melody all together. Except this one will not end in taunting and tantalising but in one terrible closing note.

'We put it to him that, according to Mrs Lovegood, the only way Jasmine could have known that toy by name is if she'd had it named for her. Ava, you said that Jasmine had called the toy not sloth but *Mr* Sloth, the name you and your husband had given it. This name would most likely only have been used by yourselves and your friends the Johnsons. We put this to Mr Johnson.'

'And he couldn't explain it,' I say.

'No, he couldn't. The change in timelines was significant. If Abi left your home nearer 8 a.m., and Neil arrived at the Lovegoods' house a little after seven, it was possible for Abi to have seen him inside the property and for Jasmine to have not only seen Abi's toy but had it named for her by Neil. It was possible that Jasmine was the only member of the Lovegood family who saw Neil. And later that morning he handed the toy to you, Ava. He found it on the road, which of course means he could have planted it there earlier.'

'So he confessed?' Matt interrupts.

Farnham performs her now familiar mannerism of brushing her hand across her chin. 'Sometimes you get the impression that, no matter how much a suspect is resisting, actually they want to confess. There's a kind of inevitability to it, as if you and they know that's where you're all headed. An innocent person will tend to be very insistent. They can get physical. But throughout, Mr Johnson seemed like he was going through the motions, like he'd lost the will or couldn't or didn't want to lie anymore. And once we had him against the wall, as it were, he admitted that, yes, Jasmine had seen him and he'd shown her the toy… and that's when he broke down.' She looks up, first at Matt, then at me.

'So he definitely killed her?' Matt's disbelief is palpable. 'I mean, he said it with his own mouth, not under duress or anything?'

Farnham nods. 'I'm afraid so. I'm so sorry, I know this must be terribly hard to hear. There are two detective constables with your neighbours just now, explaining the situation. And tomorrow morning we'll be excavating the site.'

'The site? I thought she was in the river?'

'That was the working theory, yes, and I'll give you a full account of the sequence of events as we understand them in a moment, but tomorrow we're going to have to excavate your next-door neighbours' kitchen floor with a view to accessing the trench immediately to the rear of the kitchen entrance.'

'No,' I say. 'No, no, no, no, no.'

She sighs heavily, glances up at us both. 'I'm so sorry.'

CHAPTER FORTY-ONE

Neil

He gets in early, as usual. The Lovegoods are upstairs: the clank of crockery in the makeshift kitchen they've set up on the landing, the flush of water from the upstairs bathroom, the screech and sing-song of the girls. He's fitting the boiler himself because Rick, his plumber, has let him down at the last minute. Adam is due later on, at which point they'll concrete in the beams. He's in the utility, minding his own business, concentrating. Strictly speaking, he's not qualified to fit a boiler, but Rick will check it later in the week before signing it off. It's silent in the little room. He works steadily, but after a while, he notices the silence. It starts to bug him; he could do with some tunes. He pats his overalls, realises he's left his phone in the work site. Or at home – yeah, he can see it charging on the kitchen table. Not to worry. There's a radio; he can use that – he'll pop back for the phone once the boiler's in.

He puts the screwdriver on the cistern and opens the door of the utility space.

Straight away, straight away, he sees it: he's left the bloody kitchen door open.

A soft whistle leaves him, eyes rolling, checking the stairwell.

But they're still upstairs. He can hear the buzz of an electric toothbrush.

Jennifer made him fit a lock to the kitchen door the day the building work started. Wouldn't let work commence until that was done. Told him in the smiling, certain terms he's used to from his clients that if she ever found that door open while the kids were in the house, she would fire him on the spot. Did he understand? Too right he did. He does.

But now, in the hallway, he can hear Jennifer and the kids upstairs, so at this point he's only annoyed with himself. He's been distracted. Bella got so upset last night and again this morning, and now he's all over the place. He's told her they'll get there, that they'll keep trying as many times as it takes, but it breaks his heart to see her like that, it really does.

The throaty purr of Johnnie's Porsche reaches him from the drive. Sometimes he honks the horn to hurry Jennifer and the kids along, but Neil knows it's not about that – it's about wanting to show off to the neighbours, make sure they've seen him and know what a big cheese he is. Idiot.

He hurries into the site and kicks the door shut behind him. Danger over. No more sloppiness from here on in. This job is worth a fortune. It'll pay for another round of IVF, and if Johnnie is pleased, he said he'll recommend Neil to all his clients going forward. This job will be the making of him.

The radio is on top of the washing machine.

He takes a step, glancing down to judge where his feet are. Last thing he needs is to go falling into the trench.

Time slows.

Abi's cuddly toy is on the ground. The one he and Bella bought and took into the hospital the day she was born. What the hell is it doing in here?

He swallows, takes one more step, and peers into the trench.

He tastes vomit, swallows it down. Falls. The shock of the fall sends pain shooting into his knees.

'No,' he whispers. 'No, no, no, no, no.'

Abi. Little Abi. His darling little girl. The set of her limbs, the slackness of her mouth, her skin. A cellophane bag lies by her head, just beyond her tiny fist – in it, two slices of bread. Two enormous plasters cover her little knees.

She's dead; he knows it in his bones before he jumps in, before he jumps in and presses his fingers to her soft and tiny neck, to her impossibly thin white wrists, moaning, crying at her to be alive.

'No, Abi. No, no, no, no. Come on, baby girl. Breathe. Breathe for your Uncle Nee. Come on, babe, come on.'

There is no pulse. No beat of her little heart. Head thumping, skin burning, he lifts her. Presses his face to her little blue coat, holds her in his arms.

'Abi, darling. Darling, no.'

He can barely see. But he casts about, sees his tool bag against the wall and knows with a terrible clarity that will return to him over and over for the rest of his days that it is big enough. It will hide her.

Here in this cell, staring at the grey ceiling in his depthless misery, he knows that his panic was blind – morally blind, unthinking, a kind of deafening, reverberating buzz drowning out all but action. He knows that this is what happened. He wishes he could play it out again and do it differently, but he can't. He can't; he couldn't then, even ten minutes later, and he can't now and that's that.

But that doesn't stop him picking at it. Thinking about how, gladly, without a moment's hesitation, he would give all that he owns to reverse time, to go back, to put it right. Bella, yes, even Bella. He would start his life again from scratch. He knows how to do it, knows he can. The castle he built is rubble at his feet. It wasn't, was never, worth this. Every time he closes his eyes, he's back there, back to that terrible morning, that dusty shell of a room, picking up Abi's tiny body, running, cradling her, laying her gently in the bag. Her pale, lifeless face; the touch of her eyelids on the ends of his fingers. The worst is pulling the zip closed over her, half choking, her face blurring. That terrible, terrible morning.

'Oh God. My little darling; my beautiful little girl.'

He stands, wipes his eyes, takes shallow breaths, over and over, gasping for air. He crosses the site and looks back. All he can see is a work site, tools, a tool bag. He will figure out what to do in a moment. He just needs the Lovegoods to leave.

He picks up the toy, leaves the site, locks the door behind him. One hand on the kitchen door handle, he pushes his forehead against the glass and lets out a long, ragged breath.

'Pockets.'

Startled, he turns. Jasmine, her face alight with that smile of hers, her mischievous way. He has such a soft spot for her, the way she repeats everything he says, the fact that he has to do so little to make her laugh. It is all he can do to compose himself. His heart batters against his ribs. It feels like it's about to come right out of his chest.

'Hello, Jasmine,' he manages.

'Hello, Jasmine, hello, Jasmine.' She shifts from foot to foot, waving her hands at him and smiling.

Beyond her, he can hear Jennifer out on the drive, bustling little Cosima into her car seat.

'Pockets!' Jasmine is pointing at the toy.

'This is Mr Sloth,' he replies helplessly, tears running down his face now. 'Say hello to Mr Sloth.'

'Say hello to Mr Sloth, say hello to Mr Sloth, say hello to Mr Sloth.'

He knows the word for this; Jennifer told him last week: echolalia.

'Mr Sloth. Mr Sloth. Pockets.' Jasmine throws back her head and laughs.

'Jasmine?' Jennifer calls from the driveway.

Neil pushes his finger to his lips. 'Shh,' he says. 'I can't do Mr Sloth pockets today, darling, I'm sorry.' He waves. 'I'll do Mr Sloth pockets another day.' He slides into the utility room, closes himself inside, silently. Ear pressed to the door, he listens.

'Mr Sloth pockets another day,' Jasmine is almost singing, repeating, her voice coming closer, closer now.

He grabs the door handle just in time. Feels it shudder in his hand as she tries to open the door from the other side.

'Mr Sloth pockets another day,' she says, shaking the door handle. 'Pockets, pockets, pockets.'

A line of sweat runs from his forehead.

'Pockets isn't here yet, darling.' Jennifer's voice is near. She's come back into the house. She's right on the other side of the door. He clamps his mouth shut, closes his eyes.

'Pockets, pockets,' Jasmine says. The door handle trembles, loosens against the palm of his hand.

'We'll see him later, darling.' Jennifer sounds like she's back at the front door, coaxing her daughter outside. 'Come on, darling – let's get in the car now. Daddy's waiting.'

'Pockets.' Jasmine too is quieter. She's heading out of the house.

The front door slams shut. A long breath leaves him. He thinks he hears Jasmine half singing his nickname over and over again before the car door closes with a thunk. Another few seconds and the deep roar of serious horsepower fades to nothing.

He gasps, sobs against the door. What has he done what has he done what has he done?

Professional negligence, manslaughter, his lifelong friendship over, his wife a stranger, his business ruined, his reputation in tatters, his place in the town he's lived in all his life gone forever. His castle. Everything he's built, he will lose.

He will lose Bella.

He will lose Matt, his mates, his mum, his sister, his niece and nephew.

He will lose everything.

All he can do now is take control.

All he can do now is fix it.

All he can do now is… is what?

He creeps down the hall, opens the Lovegoods' front door a crack.

There is no one about. He checks the upstairs windows. No, no one. He runs as far as the kerb, throws the toy into the gutter, legs it back inside. He closes the door, pushes his hands to his knees and slides to the floor. He is hyperventilating, crying and cringing. Please God let no one have seen him do that. Please God don't let this be the end of him. Little Abi, his darling little Abi, it's not possible, it can't have happened, it can't be happening. For a moment, she is still alive. He's got it wrong. When he goes back and checks, she will wake and look at him in confusion.

'NeeNee,' she will say. She will wonder what she's doing there.

He will take her in his arms and carry her back to her mother. Here, Ava, look who I found, cheeky monkey. No. No, he won't, because she's gone; he knows it's impossible just as he knows it's true. But nothing good can come of coming clean. Nothing nothing nothing good can come of coming clean nothing good can come nothing good nothing nothing oh God oh God oh God.

'Abi!'

Ava. Ava is on the street. He checks his watch. Holy Christ, he's been here over ten minutes, caught in some sort of daze.

'Abi? Abi, darling, where are you?'

A rivulet of sweat runs from his forehead; the salt and grease sting his eyeballs. His breath comes fast, faster; the air thin.

'Abi? Abi!'

This is hell. This is what hell is and he's in it. There is no way out. All he can do now is fix it. All he can do now is take control. He has to work fast.

Back in the work site, he clears the trench in one stride and studies the bag. He'll have to get it out of here but the street is too risky. The back of the house is open. The gardens on this street are long. Should he take the bag now? Whatever, he can't be here. No one apart from Jasmine knows he's here.

The bag.

He picks it up, weighs it. It is heavy. Big. There's no way he'll get it to his own house if he goes the back way – he'll have to sneak behind the sheds and that'll be a tight squeeze as it is, and there's no way he can throw her over the fences. No way. On his own, he can, he reckons, get back to his house. He's done it enough times as a lad, fence-hopping through gardens much smaller than these for a dare.

He puts the bag back on the concrete floor, the beginnings of a plan forming in his mind.

The police will be here soon enough. Ava will start to panic. And only now does he wonder how the hell Abi got into the Lovegoods' house.

The front door, of course. That wasn't him; that was fucking Johnnie, fucking idiot. She would have seen it open and she would have known he was in here because she's seen him coming in and out these last few weeks. She must have toddled in looking for him. For him, oh God. For Uncle NeeNee. It must have all happened in seconds, split seconds. But how did she get out of her own house, unless… unless Ava left her front door open too.

Not one door left open then. Not two. But three.

And he's only to blame for one of them. There's no way he could have known. If it's his mistake, it's Ava's too. And Johnnie's.

Enough.

None of that matters.

What matters is now, what he does now.

Think. Think, Neil.

He studies the bag. Steels himself. Opens it and removes Abi's hat. Then, cringing, her little coat. He needs to lay a trail. A plan forms in his mind. The coat he wraps in a dirty work towel and stuffs it into the washing machine. It is too big, too blue to hide in his pocket. He'll come back for it later. The hat. The hat he can place. But he needs to be quick.

He runs out of the open work site, climbs over the Lovegoods' back fence, lands in the flower bed of the flats beyond. His heart bangs. If Johnnie for some reason comes back to check on him…

Stop thinking. Just act.

He crouches and runs, like that, eyeing the windows of the flats. It is the work of seconds and he is out on Thameside Lane, almost opposite the Oasis. He could drop the hat here and run back. The traffic is light. He spots a young mother pushing a buggy, her son in a school uniform on a scooter about five metres ahead. They're early. Some pre-school club maybe. He waits.

When they're far enough down towards the school, he walks calmly across the road. Sits on the wall by the leisure centre. A car passes. Then nothing. All he needs is this second. He drops the hat and he's back, back across the road, back into the flats' bushy overgrowth. He scales the fence. Back in the Lovegoods' garden, he studies the work site. It looks normal, like nothing has happened, but still, a doubt about the bag has him running back. It's closed. He closed it. It will have to hide in plain sight. There's no way he can risk being seen carrying it out now.

He's about to grab the coat and get the hell out when he glances down at the trench. He should wash it, he knows. If they bring forensics in here, they could pick up some trace of something he can't see. Yes. He should wash it. Quickly.

He detaches the washing machine from the standpipe and uses it to fill his bucket, along with some of the Lovegoods' detergent. Down on his hands and knees, he sponges the sides of the trench, the base of the trench, rubbing hard, hoping the water dries before anyone looks in. He can't see any blood – she must have cracked her head and that was it. He washes the floor of the site, washes the hallway, up to the front door.

Sweating hard, he empties the bucket into the flower bed and stashes it back behind the washing machine. The detergent he places carefully, adjusts it, thinks it's in exactly the same position. He reconnects the washing machine, stands back and takes one last look.

It looks OK. He could walk out now, but no, someone will see him. It's better if he was never here. If he goes the back way, he can return for her later, walk straight in the front door, as if to collect his tools. Hopefully before the police get here. It's not perfect but it's all he's got.

He runs to the back fence, hides a moment behind the dilapidated shed. A quick scan of the bedroom windows – no one, so far as he can make out. There's no time to wait; he'll have to take his chance.

He climbs, jumps, lands in Ava and Matt's back garden. He is behind their shed, panting, when he hears Ava again, this time close by.

'Abi? Are you in the garden?'

She is metres away. He hears the crackle of something underfoot as she paces up the lawn.

'Abi?' She is closer still.

He holds his breath, his palms flat against the sap-sticky back of the shed. Oh God.

'Abi?' Her voice alters as she pushes her face to the window of the shed. She is so near. The urge to make himself known, to throw himself at her feet and tell her what's happened almost overwhelms him. A wincing sound escapes him. He closes his eyes tight, as if by not seeing he will become unseen. Her footsteps recede, her calls growing distant. A moment later, the back door slides shut with a low roll and a soft thud.

'Oh God,' he breathes.

Another second, sweating, panting, he clears the next fence. Again he is hidden behind a shed, the cramped space strung with cobwebs and dropped pine needles. He was right. These spaces are small, too small to bring the bag over this way. And he cannot wait until dark. He will have to take it out later in plain sight, as if it's simply a bag of tools. There's no choice. He'll have to stash it somewhere until the heat dies down. It. Her. Abi. His little darling.

One, two, three, seven, eight, ten fences. He is crying, he is sweating, his T-shirt drenched, his overalls torn where he caught them on a nail. He reaches his own back garden – his super-shed on its perfectly level concrete base, his garden furniture, the brick barbecue he made.

Bella will have left for work.

He hopes.

He digs his keys from his overalls pocket, unlocks the back door, opens it. The house is still, silent. But even so, he calls out to his wife.

No reply.

His phone is on the table. He texts Adam, his labourer, tells him the concrete mix hasn't arrived, to not bother coming till Wednesday. Two days, to be sure.

Another idea comes to him. He thumbs a WhatsApp to the group Jennifer set up.

Hi J and J. Just to let you know I'll be in a bit later today – have to pick up some stuff from the builders' merchants. Best, N.

He studies it a moment. It sounds like him, yes; he's pretty sure it sounds like him. He presses send.

He strips naked and loads every item into the washing machine, finds where Bel keeps the detergent and sets it to wash. Up the stairs three at a time. Under the shower, he scrubs himself near raw, biting down hard on his bottom lip, forcing himself to stay in the moment. He can't lose it. He has to keep focused.

He dries himself and puts on fresh clothes, clean white overalls. He is still panting like a racehorse, still crying, still stopping himself from crying. Everything is loud, everything throbs in his head. He has no idea what he's doing, is as clear-eyed as a gunman. His focus terrifies him. He blows out a long jet of air, his jaw clamped shut.

A hammering at the door.

'Neil? Bel? It's Ava. Help. I need help.'

He steels himself. A second, two. Come on, Neil. You have to do this.

He runs downstairs, inhales, opens the door.

'Have you got Abi?' Ava's face is a mask of total terror.

It is a mirror.

CHAPTER FORTY-TWO

Ava

Lorraine Stephens and Sharon Farnham are on the doorstep. Farnham cocks her head briefly towards next door. Matt reaches for my hand.

'OK,' Farnham says. 'Your neighbours have gone to a hotel. Are you sure I can't persuade you to spend the day with someone?'

'No,' I say. 'We want to be here. We want to be here when they find her.'

'Yes, thanks. We prefer to stay.' Matt lifts the knot of our hands to his mouth. I feel his tears on my fingers. I can't put my arm around him because we are tied together.

'Shall we step inside a moment?' Farnham says.

They follow us into the kitchen. None of us sits down.

'We knew she was in that house,' I say. 'At the party. We both sensed she was there.'

'That's understandable,' Lorraine says. 'Often what we almost know comes from lots of little things we haven't quite put together. It's possible part of you always thought your friend had something to do with Abi's disappearance, even where he might have hidden her. Some things are so unthinkable we… we don't or can't think them so they become feelings instead.'

'Will they be careful?' I ask.

'As I said last night, please be reassured that they'll be very careful,' Farnham says. 'They're experts, and remember she'll be protected by the bag.'

'But how will they know where she is? Exactly, I mean?'

'Mr Johnson—'

'Neil's going to be there?' Matt interrupts. I feel his body bristle; his hand tighten around mine.

Farnham shakes her head. 'No, he's drawn a plan of the kitchen and marked the place. Please try not to think about it too much. We'll be as careful as we possibly can, all right?' She looks at her feet, briefly, before turning to leave.

'Detective,' Matt says. 'Would I be able to talk to Neil? Can I call him?'

She shakes her head. 'No, sorry. It's… that would be inappropriate.'

He nods, too hard. 'Of course. Sorry. Yeah. And he won't be here at any stage?'

She shakes her head, her expression weary. 'As I said, we have the drawings and he's marked—'

'The place. Of course. You just said that. Sorry. Thanks. Thank you.'

'I'll see myself out, all right? I'll be in touch.'

Lorraine wanders over to the kettle, as if on autopilot.

Matt covers his eyes. He has a cold sore at the corner of his mouth. We have not slept at all – lying on the bed talking it over endlessly, trying to make sense of the surreal and grisly events Farnham relayed to us last night. There is no sense to be made. It is senseless. A tragic accident caused by our friend's negligence, a hand grenade he tried to throw away only to create a time bomb. That bomb has exploded now, of course. It has destroyed all of us and everything we were to one another.

My eyes drift to the black bin bag on the kitchen floor. In it, last night's rage: broken ornaments, a ripped dress of Abi's, a traditional teddy bear holding a heart cut into pieces with scissors, a smashed bottle of champagne, its contents left to glug, fizzing, down the drain. All gifts from Neil and Bella. There is a cracked picture frame in there too – a photograph of an Elvis impersonator with his arms around the four of us, taken at a curry house in Twickenham, dug out and ripped into shreds.

I did this, all of it.

If I had to say how I feel now, I'd say I don't know. Neither of us knows how we feel. Adrift is as near as we can get. Our daughter is lost. She is dead. And with her death, we have lost our friends, our life here.

Last night, when he was on his way to the spare room, I called to Matt.

'Hey,' I said. 'Sleep in here.'

'Of course.' He climbed in beside me and held me.

'This doesn't mean we're together,' I sobbed into his shoulder. 'I still hate you.'

'I know,' he whispered into my hair. 'I get it.'

'Best thing to do is stay as comfortable as you can,' Lorraine says now as we sit on high stools, burnt-out in the falling ash of ourselves. 'Let's go into the living room, shall we?'

We move to the front of the house, all of us tacit in the knowledge that the noise will come from the rear. Through the front window, we see the van arrive. Men in helmets and protective gear, ear defenders hooked around their necks, bring out electric drills. Matt draws the curtains closed. I don't stop him.

'Next door must have cleared out early,' he says. 'They're staying in a nice hotel, I suppose.'

No one replies.

When the rumble of machinery starts, we close our eyes. Fred is unusually restless. As if he knows what horrors are to be unearthed. I hold him close, let him suckle.

Later, another police car. Matt spies it through the crack in the curtains. Like a nosy neighbour, he turns to me and announces it with a sigh. I know how helpless he feels because he keeps telling me so and because I feel it too. We have never known such helplessness. Even that day, we were consumed – by fear, by hope. We were distracted by action. Now, this inertia is all there is. This waiting.

'Farnham,' Matt says. 'She's getting out of the car. She must've gone away and come back.'

I follow him into the hall. He opens the front door and is about to step out, but then, somehow, he is backing up, Farnham striding forward. She doesn't lay a hand on his chest, doesn't push him, but the whole thing unfolds as a kind of surrender. A second later and the front door has been closed and Farnham is showing us into our own living room, everything about her exuding an assertive calm.

'Let's wait in here,' she says. 'Let us do our job and let's make it as bearable as we can for everyone, OK?'

'OK.'

We are the guests. We are the strangers. We are the puppets.

A moment later, another rumble from next door. I have changed my mind. We should have got out of here today.

We should have gone to the park, to a café, anywhere other than here.

As it is, we sit. We do not turn on the television. Hours accumulate into minutes, minutes become seconds, until Farnham takes a call and leaves us.

I bury myself in Matt's arms. 'My baby. My little girl.'

Farnham returns, though I have no sense of how long she has been gone. Through my tears I can see she is trying to give nothing away, but the merest nod to Matt and the year we have lived in agony shrinks to no more than a flash.

'Have they found her?' I am on my feet.

'I know this is difficult.' Farnham is gently restraining me. Lorraine is sitting me down. Farnham is crouching in front of me as you crouch in front of a child who is hurt.

'Please,' I sob.

'I'm very sorry,' she says. 'They've found her.'

'I need to see her.'

Farnham transfers herself to the sofa beside me. Lorraine has hold of my hand.

'Let them look after her now,' Farnham says. 'They'll take good care of her, I promise.'

I can hear Matt crying. On his sheepskin rug, Fred kicks his arms and legs and coos.

After a moment, Farnham stands. 'I'll call you as soon as there are any developments. Best thing to do now is try to get some fresh air, try to pass the time if you can. You've got my direct line. I'll check my phone as often as I can, all right? We'll be in touch.'

CHAPTER FORTY-THREE

Neil

Neil rests the back of his head on his hands, the thin mattress hard against his shoulder blades. Outside the cell, the noise of a police station at night jangles and jars; the smell of disinfectant on lino makes his nose itch. Cigarette smoke drifts in through an open window; someone shouts abuse in another cell. But none of this distraction can keep him from the torture of his own crowding thoughts: Bella, Matt and Ava, his mum, his mates down the rugby club, his sister Bev, her husband, his family, his old school teachers, his clients… his entire town. Everyone.

There were so many awful moments. The crawl of the zip, Jasmine calling for him from the other side of the door, showing the copper round the work site, trying to keep it together. Testing the weight of the bag that afternoon when the dogs finally cleared out and he found a moment to return, rehearsing the excuse of securing his tools. He feels the weight of that bag, feels it now, as if the strap were still cutting into his hand. He can carry it without strain is what he's thinking; no, with the *right* amount of strain, that's the main thing. That terrible afternoon. It's 3 p.m. The dogs have sniffed his house, his shed, his van, and now he's here again, a place he'd prefer never to come back to as long as he lives. It's now or never. If he can get her into the van and stick his bike in, he can take the van up to Richmond on the excuse of leafleting a bit further out. Then all he has to do is cycle home and somehow sort the rest out later.

The chucka-chuck of a helicopter passes overhead. He thinks of Bella and begins to cry. He doesn't know if he can do it; doesn't know if he has it in him, and if he does, what that says about him, but he will never be able to give her a baby, a family, a home if he doesn't see this through. He will lose her. He will lose his life. Nothing he can do will bring Abi back. He loved her; he loved her like his own. But he can't save her. He can't make this right. Making this right will make everything else wrong.

In the hallway, he composes himself in front of the mirror, pushing back his hair, blowing out short breaths of air, over and over.

'Come on.' He squares his shoulders, tries to look himself in the eye. 'Come on now.'

And in that moment of utter loneliness, he wishes, bitterly and keenly, that he had known his father. Wishes he could call him now and ask him what to do. There was never anyone to ask; he's had to figure it all out for himself. He knows what he's doing is wrong, off-the-scale wrong, but what the hell else can he do? If he doesn't sort it, there is no one, no one else.

He grits his teeth. 'Come on.'

Another blast of staggered breath. He opens the door. Steps out onto the street. It is still raining, though not as heavily now. He pulls the Lovegoods' door closed and walks as slowly as he dares past Matt and Ava's house. Eyes front, head locked, he presses on towards his own house. No sign of the dogs. He just has to keep the bag off the ground.

Halfway down the road, twenty metres, no more, from his home, his throat blocks at the sight of two police officers coming out of number 58.

He recognises PC Peak, smiles and raises his free hand. 'Just dumping my tools in the van,' he offers. 'It's all open at the back, don't want them getting nicked.'

With a perfunctory nod, they carry on to number 56.

The urge to run is almost too much. His lips purse, as if to whistle, but he stops himself. At the van, he levels his key fob and clicks. The central locking clunks; the tail lights flash. It is all he can do not to look around. It is all he can do to put Abi inside the bleak metal shell. As if she were no more than this: a bag of tools, valuables to be locked away in case of thieves.

'I'm so sorry, baby girl,' he whispers. 'I'm so, so sorry.'

And later, much later, his beautiful god-daughter still in the cold van, his best friend's face looms over him in the dark and empty building site, eyes creased up in agony as he confesses.

'It was me. I left the door open.'

The thin, wet frame of the man in his arms, weeping for his fatal mistake.

'Don't tell her,' he hears himself say, astounded at how easily the words fall from him, as if they have in fact been spoken by somebody else. 'There's nothing to be gained.' And on and on – a sleight of hand with which he transfers the weight of guilt so that he can absolve himself of the larger blame and save his life: 'No police, no Ava, no one else. It ends here. Our secret. I've got your back.'

This – this is the moment he becomes a monster, he thinks. In the depths of his best friend's personal abyss, he sees only his own chance – to step in as the keeper of another's secret so that his own might remain buried. And then, later, in wild panic, when he realises he's left Abi's coat in the Lovegoods' washing machine, when he says goodnight to Matt on the pretence of going to bed, only to make a frantic dash in the dark, back across the splintering, cobwebbed fences, when he hides in the black scrubby garden of Johnnie Lovegood's dream home and sees the man he loathes at the loft window, leaning out, smoking a joint, floating above it all, riding his life like a luxury cruise while he, Neil, crouches filthy and sweating and crying in the shadows, he will see clearly the unfairness of it all. Johnnie, who is also to blame, smoking a bloody joint, enjoying his peace of mind in his soon-to-be state-of-the art show home, the home that Neil will build for him. He wants to run up there and punch him, hard, in his smug little face. But no.

Violence can't save him. Only stealth. He must get the coat into the river. He must try to somehow make it through this night. And tomorrow he will lay the bag in the trench and concrete in the steels. It is all he can think of. It is all he's got.

He grabs the coat, escapes once again over the back fence. Up to the lock he runs, lungs tight, the metal of blood in his mouth. Over the bridge towards Ham. No sign of the police. On the water, nothing stirs – not even an arrow of ducks disturbs the black water. The houseboats are mostly dark, one or two lit from within by the warm glow of an oil lamp. A damp, cold smell rises from the water. The breeze rustles in the scrappy branches of the spindly riverside trees. At least it has stopped raining.

Richmond is three miles away. He's not sure he can run three metres. His bones ache, his skin is freezing. He is so tired. He is so fucking tired. But the rest of his life depends on now. All around is silent. The loud, fast, foetal heartbeat he knows is coming from his own mind. A memory from an early scan, Bella's face lighting up in wonder. The galloping sound of life, of a family he almost had, only for that blessed noise to cease. Until now. Now, it has chosen to visit him, to torture him.

And so, tortured and snivelling, freezing and wretched, he runs the miles up to Richmond, where he drops his beloved god-daughter's coat, and weeps as it falls pale and blue into the deep black water.

It is 3 a.m. by the time he gets home. He has never felt so completely wrecked, so alone. Everything hurts, inside and out. And, like a child, he cannot stop crying. In the dark hallway, he strips. The washing machine is empty; his heart threatens to explode at the sight. Where are his overalls from this morning? He runs upstairs, naked, checks in the bath-room cupboard and almost cries out with relief to find them there, folded along with other clothes, airing in the warmth in a neat pile. Bella will have emptied the washing machine when she got in and put his stuff in the dryer. She won't have thought twice about it. Back downstairs, he loads his filthy jeans, T-shirt, raincoat, socks and pants into the machine and sets it to wash. Still shivering, teeth chattering now, he takes a long shower, increasing the temperature by degrees, warming himself through.

In bed, he curls himself around Bella's warm naked body. He presses his nose between her shoulder blades and breathes her in. She smells of perfume and the oily scent of her skin at night. Aromatherapy. She is what he needs. She is all he needs.

'Hey,' she whispers, stirring, then shifting, sitting up.

'We didn't find her,' he says, and it's enough to send her into floods of tears.

'Oh my God,' she says through her fingers. 'Oh my poor darling Abi. I can't believe it, I can't believe it. Poor Matt and Ava, oh my God.'

He rubs her back. 'I know. I know.'

There is nothing he can do but let her cry. He waits it out until at last she plucks a handful of tissues from the box on her bedside table and presses it to her eyes.

'You've been gone ages,' she says, blowing her nose. 'What time is it?'

'Late. Listen, there's nothing we can do now. Let's go to sleep, eh? We'll search again in the morning.'

She nods, her breath still shuddering in her chest as, dopey and obedient with tiredness, she lies down, rolls her back to him and pulls his legs to hers with the hook of her big toe.

I can't lose this, he thinks, wrapping his arm around her waist, returning his face to that place between her shoulder blades. *I'd do the time; gladly, I would, but I can't lose this. Everything I have done, I have done for her. For us.*

'I love you,' he whispers into her neck. And he feels it, oh God, he feels it.

'I love you too,' she slurs. 'You're my hero, you know that.'

CHAPTER FORTY-FOUR

Matt

Lorraine Stephens returns the next day to confirm. The body is Abi's. They will not be called to identify her. The police will use her DNA samples. Matt doesn't ask why. He knows why.

'Have they charged him?' Ava asks – these last days, she has become the stronger of the two of them, he realises.

'They've charged him with prevention of proper burial and with perverting the course of justice, but nothing else yet. We're still waiting for the post-mortem results, but we're looking at manslaughter on the grounds of professional negligence.'

Their daughter. Under post-mortem. Such a small mass.

'Try not to think about it,' Lorraine says.

She stays an hour or two before leaving them in the shattered peace of their new reality. Abi is dead. There is no doubt about that now, only horror and hope. Horror at what his best friend has done; hope that Abi did not suffer at the end. Neil killed their baby girl and hid her away. The fact of it is astonishing. It cannot be and yet it is. Neil. Matt can barely even remember a time when he didn't know this man, when he wasn't his friend. Friend goes nowhere near what Neil is to him – not even best friend can convey what he is, what they are. Was. Were. Friends no longer, just like that – a severing, a laser cut so precise the pain is yet to make its way through the fog of shock. A best friend will have your back, buy you a beer, turn up. But Matt trusted *this* friend with his daughter as with his very life, and now, feeling himself falling, what he has known bodily since he took the call his brain begins to frame in thought: Neil might not have murdered Abi, but Matt knows with total clarity that he can never forgive him for what he has done, that he will not, can never, see him again for as long as he lives, and that he will think of him and miss him every day for the rest of his life.

A little after seven in the evening, Sharon Farnham is sitting on their sofa once again. The light is falling. Ava has a glass of brandy in her hand. His own is on the coffee table, untouched.

Farnham is here to talk to them about the post-mortem. She addresses them as a couple still together, and there is no reason to tell her otherwise – that they share a roof, their grief, their son; that they have survived, and that is all. Out of the eye of the storm, Matt can see how careful these people have been with them over this time and wonders at how they can put themselves here, in the middle of other people's horror, for no other reason than to try to find the truth, whatever that truth turns out to be.

In the strange enforced intimacy, Lorraine brings in three mugs of coffee and a large glass of water for Ava. She is feeding Fred, as she has been for most of the day. He needs the comfort, she has said, more than once, though Matt knows that in reality it is Fred who is the soother here.

'Are you OK?' Farnham asks them.

'We're ready,' Ava replies.

Farnham brings out a notebook from her pocket, shifts her weight, seems unable to get comfortable on the sofa. A heavy exhalation and, with apparent physical effort, she begins.

'The post-mortem revealed that Abi died of a trauma to the head. This is consistent with the fall into the building trench. The trauma caused bleeding to the brain, which proved fatal.'

The air thins. Ava opens her mouth but just as quickly closes it again.

'Did she suffer?' Matt asks, glancing at Ava, who meets his gaze with silent acknowledgement.

'A blow to the head is quick,' Farnham replies. 'The concrete surrounding the bag preserved some tissues and remnants of her clothes. From those, we estimate she was buried approximately twenty-four hours after her death, which would tie in with Mr Johnson's account of events. He says he returned to work the following morning, having removed Abi from the site in the large tool bag and stored her body in his van, as I told you on the phone. He told us he parked on the Lovegoods' drive after they left for work the following morning, lifted Abi into the house in the bag and placed her, inside the bag, into the first trench as you come into the kitchen site. From there he was able to cover her under the pretence of concreting in the RSJ beams according to the building schedule. The lad who was labouring for him, when questioned again last night, believed Mr Johnson when he told him the site would be closed for a few days due to the police investigation.'

'So while we were looking at the picture of her coat,' Matt says slowly, aware that he is processing what he has just heard even as the words fall from his mouth, 'he was next door burying her in…'

'I'm so sorry.'

Matt smothers a gasp in his hands, his vision clouding.

'Sharon.' Ava's voice is no more than a croak. 'Can I ask you a question?'

'Of course.'

'Does this mean you'll be arresting Neil now for murder?'

The room stills. Matt makes himself look up. Farnham and Lorraine are not exchanging a glance, not exactly. It is smaller than that. They adjust their backsides forward on the sofa. And they do it at exactly the same moment.

'I was coming on to that,' Farnham says. 'The trauma to the head wasn't consistent with the angle it would have been had she simply fallen into the trench. There were also other internal injuries not consistent with the fall. And there was a small flake of paint found on her bracelet – I think it was a christening bracelet?'

'Yes,' Ava rushes in. 'It was getting too small.'

'We've sent it to forensics, but I don't have the results yet. We'll be in touch as soon as we do.'

CHAPTER FORTY-FIVE

Ava

Day one, we stay at the back of the house, watching movies on Matt's laptop, avoiding the press. My finger hovers over Farnham's number, but I don't call. My mother offers to come down, as she did when Abi went missing, but I tell her to stay put. This is too tough to watch. And there is nothing she can do. Once we know, I will call her.

In the evening, when the coast is clear of journalists, we order takeaway curry, to tempt ourselves. Most of it goes in the bin. We eat crisps, ice cream. We drink red wine to mute the world.

Day two, stir crazy and in need of air, we head out super-early to avoid the journalists. In Bushy Park we sit on a bench in the gated, secluded water gardens, away from everyone and everything. The weather is still warm enough to sit out in sweaters and jeans. We take sandwiches.

'We should eat,' we say to one another.

'Half each?'

We make bargains. A glass of wine later if you eat half a round. We nibble at the corners. We drink coffee from a flask. We have not dared risk a local café.

'You need to eat for Fred,' Matt says.

'Emotional blackmail is cheating,' I reply, and the smile we share feels like a small miracle.

We demolish a large bar of milk chocolate.

In the early evening, Farnham returns to talk to us, pushing past the press without comment and stepping swiftly into our home. We make her a cup of tea without asking how she takes it and sit in the kitchen, on the high stools around the breakfast bar. She pauses, with that slow drama of hers.

'We got the results from forensics,' she begins. 'From the paint.'

I inhale. Matt straightens his back. The clock on the mantelpiece chimes a soft quarter past.

'It was a dark orange colour,' she says. 'Like a burnt orange, you might say.'

My head throbs. Heat fills me. Farnham asks if I'm all right.

'Cayenne pepper,' I half gasp.

Farnham frowns. 'Sorry?'

'Porsche Cayenne,' I say, everything I have known falling backwards, rewinding, rejoining, like an explosion in reverse. 'The Porsche Cayenne, like cayenne pepper. Johnnie Lovegood's car.'

Farnham nods, her expression quizzical. 'Spot on. Lava orange is the shade officially. It's compatible with Porsches manufactured between 2013 and 2019 – this year. You'll find it on the 911, the Boxster.' She lists them on her fingers. 'The 718 Boxster, the 718 Cayman and the Cayenne.'

Matt exhales heavily. 'Oh my God.'

'We took the car in,' she continues. 'As well as your neighbour obviously. There was a small scratch on the front underside that had been patched up. A trawl through his bank statements established that he'd purchased a touch-up kit from an online retailer on the Tuesday following Abi's death, so he wasn't taking any chances. When faced with evidence of the paint, the scratch on his car, his bank statement, the injuries consistent with his vehicle, his own daughter putting them at the house at the same time Abi could have wandered out – well, you know all this – Mr Lovegood eventually confessed. Even then, he was keen to pin it on you guys, for leaving your front door open.'

'I can't take it in,' I say.

'It's a lot, I'm sorry.'

'Johnnie Lovegood killed her with his car,' Matt says, almost to himself.

'He killed her,' Farnham says. 'But not with his car.'

CHAPTER FORTY-SIX

Johnnie

Jasmine is fussing – something to do with her shoes. Johnnie feels his blood pressure rising, the blunt stab of pain in his oesophagus.

'I'll bring the car out,' he says, leaving Jen to it. She's better at handling that sort of thing. And they're late – well, they're going to be late if Jasmine doesn't calm down – and he has a client in Sunbury at ten for whom he hasn't yet completed the drawings. It's going to require some smooth talking and sleight of hand; the Armani jacket should do it.

In the bathroom he pops two omeprazole, then dips his head and glugs water from the tap. A quick glance in the mirror. *You'll be fine, Johnnie Boy; you'll be fine. You work better off the cuff.* Downstairs, a soft clank from the utility tells him Neil's here bright and early as usual. But he doesn't have time to catch up with him now. The RSJs are in – that's the most stressful part over. And after the embarrassing fuck-up with the measurements on Friday, the rather unpleasant argument that followed, Johnnie prefers to avoid him if he can.

He heads out and clicks on the remote. The garage door lifts. A little before eight and the street is quiet. He jumps into the Cayenne, starts the engine. The DAB blasts into life, the surround sound wrapping itself around him. Radio 6 Music. A grime artist, he thinks, turning it up. The name is on the tip of his tongue, but it'll come up on the digital reader in a second. He checks his hair in the rear-view and pushes it back, pulls one curl forward and runs his tongue over his teeth. Wonders about tooth-whitening toothpaste, whether he should tell Jen to put some on the Ocado order. He pulls forward, watching the display for the name of the artist. He can drop it into conversation later in front of the young graphic designer who shares the office space; he can casually—

A bump. He stops, but another second, two, passes before he takes it in.

He jumps out onto the driveway. Sees a little red ankle boot. A moment later, he is standing over the body of next door's child.

'Fuck.' He scans the road. There is no one. No one. He scoops her up. Reaches down once again. Grabs the plastic bag of bread she's dropped on the pavement. Into the open house he runs, heart thudding, head throbbing. From upstairs comes Jen's voice, soothing Jasmine, bribing her.

'OK, two more minutes. I'll put Cosima in the car then I'm coming back and you have to be ready, OK? No, Jasmine, not those shoes, please…'

The utility door is shut. The kitchen door is locked.

He throws the body over his shoulder. It is so small, so light. His fingers scrabble through his keys. Christ, come on, come on, there, thank God, the key to the kitchen door. He opens the site, eyes darting, scalp itching. The washing machine? No, too risky. She might not fit. No, she definitely won't.

Come on, come on, Johnnie Boy. You've got twenty seconds. The garden? He takes a step, his torso twisting left then right. Something falls to the ground – a cuddly toy of some kind. A monkey? God knows. Christ, he doesn't even know the child's name. But there's no time for this. There's no fucking time.

The trench.

She wandered in. She fell.

Good enough. It'll have to be.

No one knows he is here. No one.

He throws her, gags as her head cracks against the ridge before she falls, rolls, lands on her back, horribly, limbs all wrong. She stares at him, eyes glassy as a doll's. He throws the bag of bread in after her; it lands by her head, by her hand. It looks like she's fallen. Yes, she's fallen in. The bag has flown out of her hand. The new truth is already rehearsing itself in his mind. A tragedy.

The kitchen door beckons: come out, Johnnie Boy. Come out now. Run.

The utility-room door is still shut. No noise comes from within. No one knows he is here. No one knows what he has just done. If he leaves the kitchen door open, there will be no one to say it was him. Neil will come out and… Yes, Neil will come out and think there has been a terrible accident. This has been a terrible accident. She fell. The bag flew out of her hand. A tragedy.

It will be Neil's fault.

Professional negligence.

No one will believe the word of a builder over his. And on Friday, Neil was so aggressive with him, so keen to pin the mistake with the steels on him, like he had a point to prove.

An accident. A tragedy. Professional negligence. She fell.

It's not perfect. But it has to work. Johnnie cannot be anywhere near this. He's worked too hard to get this far. The mortgage on this place is a heart condition waiting to happen, and that's without the extension, the lighting, the hand-made units and the Cayenne. His throat is already stripped raw with acid reflux from all the stress he has to bear. If he admits to running over a kid, it will ruin him. There's Jasmine's care going forward to think about. Neil hasn't even got kids. He's young. He'll get two years, three, tops, whereas he, Johnnie, will never come back from this. He can't do that to his kids. He loves those kids. He loves Jen.

From the new truth, another truth grows: he's doing it for his family.

At his hairline, sweat prickles.

He slows to a walk as he steps out of the house. The chap from over the road is wheeling his green bin down his pathway. Christ. One minute earlier and he would have seen.

'Hello,' Johnnie calls out, waves, even though he doesn't usually. This chap can witness him, witness nothing happening, nothing untoward. Take a good look. 'Starting to rain, I think.'

'Looks like it.' The man raises a hand before parking his bin and returning via his side gate to the back garden.

By the time Jen comes out, Johnnie is in the car, engine running. He pushes the sweat from his forehead into his hair, wipes his face with a tissue from the glove compartment, drums the steering wheel to the music.

Jen is swearing at the car seat. Jasmine is still in the fucking house. *For God's sake, come on, woman*, he wants to say, but presses his lips tight. The radio blares. He's desperate to turn it down but daren't do anything he wouldn't normally in case she looks at him. Looks at him and says, *what the hell is wrong with you?* But she doesn't look at him; she is intent on the car-seat clip, which is fiddly at the best of times. He didn't check the drive. Oh God, he didn't check for blood. She wasn't bleeding. She wasn't bleeding, was she? Dead, yes – probably – but not bleeding. Oh God, he can't go down for this; he will not go down for a stupid accident that wasn't… and the thought occurs to him only now… wasn't even his fault. That's right. This is not his fault. He is not to blame. Who the hell lets their two-year-old roam around without supervision? The parents. It was the parents' fault, not his at all.

'Finally,' Jen says and heads back into the house.

He closes and opens his eyes. Closes, opens. God, the agony. The prolonged torture of it all. *Come on, Jen. Come on, come on, come on.*

A minute later and finally Jasmine comes out of the house.

There is still no one on the street. He's not yet used to suburbia. It's like no one even lives here sometimes.

Another minute or two and Jen jumps into the passenger seat beside him.

'Right,' she says, blowing good-humouredly at her fringe. 'Finally.'

'Did you see Neil, by the way?'

'No, actually.'

'Right.'

He pulls out. The garage door closes slowly. He drives into the longest day of his life.

He has no memory whatsoever of the 10 a.m. meeting. The rest of the day is a wash – colours, noise, a panic attack in a toilet cubicle. Liquid guts. All day, all fucking day, he was expecting a call from the police.

Mr Lovegood? I'm afraid there's been an accident at your property.

But nothing. It makes no sense. Hours-long tension of waiting, waiting, waiting. Rehearsing his story. There is no story. It's the truth now. He got up, fetched the car. Jen and the girls were last in the house. He saw nothing. Heard nothing. He thinks Neil might have been there but can't be sure – yes, best to be vague, he doesn't want to look like he's trying to pin it on anyone. Jen didn't see Neil. Best keep out of it all together. He doesn't know. He went to work. Literally nothing out of the ordinary. He had no idea. The less he says, the better. *My God, this is terrible*, he will say. *How did this happen?* He told the builder, told him… his wife had a lock fitted, had a key made for him. Totally irresponsible.

But no such call comes. All day, no call. He has no idea what this means, knows he will not find out until he gets home. Can't go home until he would normally.

Towards seven, he picks up Jen from the station, nerves jangling like loose change.

'Johnnie? John?' Jen is looking at him with concern as she buckles her seat belt. 'Are you OK?'

'I feel a bit sick actually,' he says. 'I think I had dodgy sushi at lunch.'

'Oh no.'

He lets Jen talk as he drives the short distance home. Today wasn't too bad actually. She'll probably have to work at the weekend though – there's quite a complicated case involving—

'Is that…' She breaks off. 'Is that a policeman at the end of our road?'

Yes. Yes, it is. Momentarily Johnnie thinks about revving hard, speeding off, away, away, before, guts folding, he slows the car. The guy waves at them to stop.

'What's going on?' Jen asks.

'No idea.' Sweat beading on his brow, he lowers his window and greets the cop.

'Has something happened?'

'Do you live here, sir?'

'Yes. We're just coming home from work. What's happened?'

'Little girl has gone missing.' He takes out a notebook. 'Can I ask you a couple of questions? We're talking to all the neighbours.'

'Of course,' he says. 'Sure. But we've been out all day. We were at work.'

'A little girl?' Jen says. 'Oh my God, that's terrible. Can you say who?'

The policeman hands Johnnie a leaflet: *HAVE YOU SEEN THIS GIRL?*

Yes. Yes, he has. But she wasn't missing.

Her name is Abi Atkins. If you have any information, please call…

His hand shakes. He hands the flyer to Jen.

'Do you know her?' he asks.

'Oh my God, I think that's next door's little girl!' She weeps, immediately, into her hand. How do women do that? 'Oh, poor, poor things.' Christ, she is sobbing. 'Oh my God, I can't believe it.' Her hand drops from her face and he can feel she's turned to look at him. 'It's next door's little girl,' she says again, her tone urgent. 'I didn't know her name but I think she's about Cossie's age. Oh God, how awful, how absolutely awful.'

'We've been asking all the neighbours if they saw anything at all. We believe she went missing at about eight fifteen this morning. Did you see anything around that time?'

'We'd gone by then,' he says, more quickly than he would have liked.

'Yes, we would have left by then, sorry,' Jen adds, thank God. 'We left at eight or so, didn't we?' She looks at him, concern already written on her brow. 'Did you see anything?'

He shakes his head. 'No. Nothing. Nothing at all. Nothing whatsoever.' *Shut up. Shut up, Johnnie.*

'And can I confirm that your builder, Mr Neil Johnson, wasn't at your property at that time?'

'He might have been,' Johnnie says. 'He probably was actually.'

'No.' To his immense irritation, Jen contradicts him. 'He messaged to say he'd be in later. He had to pick up some supplies.' Again, she turns to him. 'He put it on the WhatsApp – didn't you get it?'

No. No, he didn't. That's Jen's domain: organising the day-to-day. The details.

Jen's words filter in: *Messaged to say he'd be in later. He had to pick up some supplies.* That's not true. Neil was there. Johnnie heard him; could swear he did. And if the child is believed missing, then that means Neil has not taken the rap after all. The builder, believing himself culpable, has cleaned up the mess. This has worked better than he could have predicted.

'Do you need anything else?' Jen is asking the cop. 'Please don't hesitate if you do.'

'Could I get your house number?'

'Sure. It's number ninety. We're next door.'

They exchange thanks. Johnnie buzzes the windows up. The cop waves them on; Johnnie nods as he drives past.

Jen is fully weeping now and he feels himself bristle. Over-empathising to the point of neurosis. A bit OTT, frankly.

But as he reverses onto the driveway, the man whose daughter it is arrives home on his bike.

'Oh my God,' Jen says. 'That's him. That's next door.' She gets out as if ejected before he's even had time to brake.

'Hi,' he hears her call before she slams the car door.

His fingers tighten around the steering wheel. He too will have to get out. He will have to somehow get through a conversation. He steels himself and opens the car door.

Jen and the chap are talking. He offers his condolences, repeats what the cop told them moments earlier. It's all he can think of to say. More condolences – he can run off some posters if needed.

'Thanks.' The guy looks like a marionette whose strings have been cut. This is all so unfortunate. It's truly awful, really.

'We'll let you go,' Jen is saying, offering her number as if she has all the time in the world.

Unable to bear it a second longer, Johnnie walks towards his house, his hairline prickling. He resists the urge to wipe the sweat from his brow with the back of his hand in some cartoonish gesture of relief. Neil has not come forward. He has not held up his hand and claimed it. He must have hidden the body, disposed of it somewhere. But where?

Unless it's still there?

Dear God.

He slides the key into the lock. Creeps up the hallway. Just like this morning, he can hear his children upstairs, talking now to the nanny. He unlocks the site door with the stealth of a burglar. Once inside, he tiptoes forward, peers into the trench. She is not there; of course she is not there. A faint floral aroma – soap? Have the police checked the house? They must have. Neil must have moved her before they got here. A wave of exhaustion rolls over him, a great draining-down of relief. His knees almost buckle. Where has he put her? Where the hell has he hidden her?

The question pulses in his mind late into the night. Long after he has held his children all the tighter before settling them to bed with an extra story, an extra kiss, long after Jen has whispered to him that she can't sleep and he has taken her in his arms until he heard her breathing slow, long after he has smoked a celebratory joint out of his loft room window, been startled momentarily by a fox clattering against the back fence while he waited for the blow to kick in.

Only the next day does he understand. He is printing posters with Neil's rather attractive wife in his office when Jen texts to tell him they've found the little girl's jacket in the river.

The river. Of course.

I owe you, Neil Johnson, he thinks, still staring at Jen's message. *I owe you big time.*

CHAPTER FORTY-SEVEN

Ava

'He didn't kill her with his car?' I say, impatience rising. 'What do you mean, he didn't kill her with the car?'

Farnham drinks the rest of her tea and puts the mug carefully on the coaster.

'The results of the post-mortem showed that Abi died of the head injury sustained in the trench,' she says. 'She was knocked unconscious by Johnnie Lovegood's car but the car didn't kill her.' She glances up, her face soft and pained and sorry. 'She won't have suffered; she won't have known anything about it.' Another pause, as if it hurts her physically to carry on. 'But you see, she was still alive at that point. If Mr Lovegood had reported it when he knocked her over, it's entirely possible she would have lived. But he didn't do that.' She shakes her head. 'He didn't do that.'

'She was still alive,' I say.

'I'm so sorry. In the end, the whole thing came down to seconds. Literally.'

Matt, whose arm is around my shoulders, pulls me close.

'But don't those cars have sensors?' he asks.

'They do,' Farnham replies, 'but if you're listening to loud music or distracted… He wasn't paying attention, that's the bottom line. He wasn't driving with due care. Many accidents aren't caused by speeding as such but by manoeuvring the vehicle too fast in smaller operations such as three-point turns, reverse parking and, as in this case, pulling out of a garage. It really doesn't matter what car you drive, to be honest. If you're not careful.'

I close my eyes. Imagine Johnnie Lovegood, in his stylish clothes, sitting hunched in the back of a patrol car. I open my eyes to the man who is still legally my husband and the detective who has finally got her man. I wonder if she feels satisfied. Wonder how far removed you have to be from another's pain to feel something as uncomplicated as satisfaction.

'Protecting what's ours,' I say.

'What?' Matt is frowning at me.

'That's what this is all about.' I look back at him, at the man who is still, for now, my other half, letting tears drop from my chin. 'You lied because you were worried about losing me and Fred. Neil lied to save himself and Bella, and Johnnie lied to protect what was his. It's just a question of degree, really.' I look across to Sharon, who is listening, out of solemn respect or sympathetic indulgence it's hard to tell. 'Our daughter was murdered and her death kept secret because we stopped looking after each other. And if we don't look after each other, we're just hiding in castles, shooting arrows at our neighbours, aren't we? If you see a hat on the ground, you put it on the wall because that's what you'd like someone to do if they found your hat. If you hit a little girl, you call an ambulance because that's what you'd like someone to do if they hit your little girl, do you see? That day, no one stopped to think she was everyone's little girl… We're all connected, that's all, that's all I…' I am weeping into my hands, the sobs getting louder.

'Hey now,' Matt says, rubbing my back. 'Don't upset yourself.'

'I'm not upsetting myself. This *is* upsetting. Somewhere along the line, we've been so busy getting and having and getting more and more and more again until we have so much we have to guard it at all costs. We've forgotten – we've completely forgotten – to look after each other.'

Matt's arms fold around me. I feel his lips press on the top of my head.

'What are we going to do?' I sob into his chest.

'We'll be all right,' he says. 'We'll be all right.'

EPILOGUE

Ava

Four months later

Two days ago, in diagonal sleet, we moved to a cottage in a village not far from my parents' home. Unable to bear staying in our street, Fred and I have been living with them since a little after Abi was found, and now we are happy to be back under one roof with Matt. Matt has taken a lower-paid job with a firm in Manchester but intends to work his way back up. The houses are cheaper here, so I can have a separate room for my piano. I am quietly hopeful for this new start. I can live here safe in the knowledge that I won't be bumping into people who know what happened every five minutes, not to mention Bella or Jen, and this has brought me a great deal of relief.

After the trial, Bella texted to say how sorry she was and to reiterate that she knew nothing until after the party. I replied that I believed her, and that I thought she was a brave and special person. I wished her well. And I did, I do. She is the one who understood where the line is drawn between self-preservation and the right thing to do, and I will always admire her for that. What I didn't say, but what I suspect both she and Neil understand, is that we never want to see either of them again. The same goes for Jen, who posted a long and tenderly worded handwritten letter in her trademark purple ink, which Matt brought up on one of his visits. She and Johnnie are getting divorced. She was mortified by what happened and hoped I could find it in my heart to believe that she knew nothing whatsoever about her 'ex-husband's heinous actions'. I wrote back – the paper correspondence old-fashioned but somehow apt – that of course I believed her. I left out that this was only once I'd read her letter, because up until that point, I was unsure. But there the contact between us must end. I was fond of her, and I miss her, but I need this new start. We all do.

Neil was charged and convicted of prevention of lawful burial and conspiracy to pervert the course of justice. He was sentenced to two years but will most likely serve one, we are told. Apparently he and Bella are still together and are planning on moving to Guildford, according to an old school friend of Matt's.

Johnnie Lovegood was charged and convicted of manslaughter and conspiracy to pervert the course of justice. He is currently serving the maximum sentence at Her Majesty's pleasure in Wormwood Scrubs. I wonder how he finds the grey sweat suits, whether the cuisine is to his taste. He will, I know, find his punishment outrageous, a travesty.

'Have you seen the bedside lamps?' Matt asks, drumming on the living-room door jamb.

'In the kitchen. In one of the boxes on the table. It's marked "Bedroom Stuff", I think. Shall we have a cuppa though?'

'OK,' he says. 'I'll make it.'

'There are some biscuits in the cupboard by the kettle,' I call after him. 'Mugs are around there somewhere.'

From the box on the floor I pull out the framed picture of Abi, push the palm of my hand across it before placing it on the mantelpiece. We had a private family funeral for her a month after she was found. And whilst her life's end sounded the saddest possible note, it was a note less maddening than the hanging devil's chord, and I am able at last to sit with it and to hear it. My heart belongs to Matt and to my son, but it is still my daughter's too, still enmeshed with hers as hers is with mine. She is still part of me: my body, my tissue, my bones. She will always be part of me. Her death cannot change that. Nothing can change that.

'You can watch us from there, little monkey,' I say to her now, not minding the tears that fall.

Once we settle in, I plan to teach piano lessons. Eventually, I might return to the classroom; we'll see how it goes. I have played my mum's piano daily for months now, and together with my beautiful son, music has the power to bring me moments of joy. I still haven't mastered Chopin's Ballade No. 1, but that is a torture I have chosen for myself.

I no longer check the door four or five times every time I come home; my aim is to stop altogether in this new place. My sessions with Barbara ended when I moved north, but if I think I need help, I will make sure I get it. I know I must look after myself, in all respects, so that I can look after little Fred. Our son is seven months old now, sitting up – at this very moment, actually, napping in his new buggy in the hall. He is becoming himself, shouts 'Oi!' sometimes when he wants our attention, and this makes us laugh. I still have nightmares regarding him and Abi, but they are less frequent now.

So yes, here we are, Matt and I. We have survived. We are together. What he did was unforgivable, but love does not switch itself off so easily. A terrible act can define us or change us fundamentally; that is what I have come to believe – existentialism with a caveat, if you like. I believe Johnnie Lovegood's actions did define him. He was able to absorb what he had done and carry on. I believe that Neil's actions are not fundamentally who he is and that is why he was not able to exist as an authentic version of himself afterwards. I believe that Matt understands the consequences of what he did, that he understood them the night I told him there was no future for us. I believe the shock broke a pattern within him, and that night, he became a man strong enough and brave enough to finally take responsibility. I don't know exactly how I can be so sure, only that he seems, he feels, changed to me.

We all lie to one another, all the time. That day, that beat-by-beat morning, when seconds turned out to be the difference between life and death, the lies were flying around like bees. I too am to blame, and I know it more than anyone. If I hadn't gone upstairs for my phone, I would have seen Matt come back and stopped Abi from unclipping herself from her buggy. If I hadn't been on my phone, she might still have unclipped herself to follow her daddy outside, but I could perhaps have saved her from Johnnie Lovegood's car. If I hadn't been so glad of her silence, if I hadn't taken the break I thought I needed, she might still have been hit by Johnnie's car but I could have – perhaps, perhaps I could have – saved her from his callous and fatal disposal of her, his inability to see that she could so easily have been his own daughter, that in a sense, she was. But as Barbara would tell me, none of these things means I didn't love my daughter.

When they found her coat, I smashed my iPhone into little pieces with the hammer. But lately I've come around to thinking that my daughter's death is not really the fault of the material trappings of our lives: expensive phones, big cars, kitchen extensions, status symbols. To blame these things is too easy. For me, it is down only to how we act towards one another. So many people helped us that day, and showed such kindness in the weeks that followed; I can truly see that now, with distance. As for us, Matt and I plan to look after each other and those around us as best we can. It is all we have – this, and the seconds and minutes and hours of our lives.

It is all any of us has really.

A LETTER FROM S.E. LYNES

Dear Reader,

Thank you so much for reading *The Housewarming*. I really am so delighted that you did. If this is your first book by me, thank you for giving me a try and I hope you liked it enough to check out my others! If you've been with me since the beginning or have read me before, thank you for coming back, thank you for sticking with me – I really appreciate it!

My next book is well under way, and I hope you will want to read that one too. If you'd like to be the first to hear about my new releases, you can sign up using the link below:

www.bookouture.com/se-lynes

This story began its gestation in the summer of 2016. I was a very new debut author at the time and had gone along to the TBC party in Leeds (TBC is the not-so-secret secret Facebook's The Book Club, run by the famous and formidable book lover Tracy Fenton). I was researching my second novel, *Mother*, and had timed my trip to coincide with the party so that I could meet some of the readers I'd got to know online. There, I met Lorraine Tipene and her daughter, Rachel, who has Angelman Syndrome. I didn't really know anyone at that time, since my debut had only just come out, so I was a little nervous, but Lorraine was so friendly to me, as was everyone, to be honest, and at the end of our conversation I told her that one day I'd put Rachel in a book and make her the key to a mystery.

Lorraine has been a keen supporter of my work ever since, along with many other lovely people, and I never forgot our conversation. The problem was coming up with a plot. Then, at the beginning of this year, I got the niggling, nudging nugget of a new idea. I worked up some notes, a synopsis, a few chapters, then chatted to Lorraine over the phone – firstly to ask if she was on board and secondly to find out more about Rachel. The result is *The Housewarming*, a mystery whose resolution hangs on the words of a young girl with Angelman syndrome. If it weren't for Jasmine Lovegood, I'm not sure Abi would ever have been found and laid finally to rest. If it weren't for Lorraine and Rachel Tipene, I'm not sure this idea would ever have occurred to me.

I try really hard to write thrillers that linger in the mind long after the final page, so I hope *The Housewarming* gave you food for thought as well as providing an emotional and gripping reading experience. I began this book in January 2020 and finished it during lockdown, so I was quite far along with the process when it became apparent that Covid-19 was set to become an unprecedented and deeply traumatic moment in our global history. Matt and Ava's story was originally set in the late summer of 2020, but including coronavirus in the narrative felt too raw – both for me, the author, and for my readers. Also, given the scale of the virus, it would have been impossible to factor it into the plot without it taking over completely – such has been its impact. I therefore made the decision to move the story to a year earlier and to have the narrative finish before the impact of coronavirus made itself known.

However, the themes in my work usually come from all that I am feeling subconsciously, and *The Housewarming* is no exception. Very much informed by the time of writing was Ava's isolation, her anxiety, and her feeling of being contagious in her unresolved grief. The story is also underpinned by ideas surrounding individual and community responsibility – quite simply, the importance of looking after others, even when you yourself are not at risk. Even before official lockdown measures were put into place, it became apparent that protecting the vulnerable in society was a responsibility that belonged to all of us. This idea fed into the book: Abi was everyone's little girl, in the sense that we are all interconnected – the global pandemic has shown us that, no matter who we are, we all rely on each other to an extent.

Although the book centres around people looking after number one in a moment of extreme stress, I was keen to balance that with the wider sense of community, and with the kindness of others. The book is set in a fictionalised version of Teddington, where I live (I would ask anyone who lives there to forgive my artistic licence in terms of the local geography), and one of my abiding memories of my early years here is receiving a phone call from a woman I knew to say that she was in the local hospital with my daughter, then eleven, who had fallen in the park and broken her hand. This woman didn't call from the park but from the hospital, where she had driven my daughter directly. I was knocked out by this act of kindness, so I wanted to convey that people mostly do the right thing... but, hey, it wouldn't have been much of a psych thriller had my characters all done the right thing, would it?

I do need to acknowledge the inspiration of the most famous disappearance story of our time, that of Madeleine McCann. Like many people, I was very affected by that story, having two young daughters at the time, and, as with other cases of missing children, I have always felt very keenly how awful it must be to have your child taken and to never find out what happened to them. I wanted to explore that not knowing, the difficulty of not being able to grieve yet grieving every day. I didn't go too far into what it must be like to have suspicion fall upon you as a parent, because I was more interested in the existentialist idea of our actions defining us – at what point we cross the line and, because of one action, become someone else entirely; whether it is even possible to preserve one's sense of self afterwards. I took the narrative viewpoint of a year after Abi's disappearance because I knew I was working towards closure and resolution for Matt and Ava rather than a strictly happy ending. I hope Matt and Ava are now fixing up their house together and are forging their new life in love, honesty and relative peace.

Enough wanging on! If you enjoyed *The Housewarming*, I would really appreciate it if you could spare a couple of minutes to write a review. It only needs to be a line or two, and every review makes a difference. If you have questions about any aspect of my work, I am always happy to chat via my Twitter or Instagram account or my Facebook author page if you wish to get in touch. Any writer knows that writing can sometimes be a lonely business, so when a reader reaches out and tells me my work has stayed with them or that they loved it, I am truly delighted. I have loved making new friends online through all of my novels and hope to make more with *The Housewarming*.

Best wishes,
Susie

 facebook.com/Lynesauthor

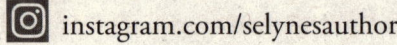 instagram.com/selynesauthor

ACKNOWLEDGEMENTS

First thanks go, massively so, to my new editor, Ruth Tross, who saw what I was trying to do, knew that I hadn't quite done it and valiantly set about helping me to do it. Thank you, Ruth, for your patience and sensitivity, your massive editorial expertise and for loving what we achieved in the end! I owe you a gin and tonic and a large packet of Tyrrells.

Thank you to my top agent, Veronique Baxter, for lovely lockdown chats and for the email that said *OMG I LOVE IT*. Always a good moment in a writer's life.

A huge shout-out and really enormous double thank you to Lorraine Tipene (née Stephens… if you remember a certain family liaison officer in this very novel). Lorraine, thank you for your openness, for your time, your support, for beta-reading an early draft of *The Housewarming* and making sure I hadn't messed up too badly in my portrayal of Jasmine Lovegood.

Thanks to my mum, Catherine Ball, who let me borrow from her fine art MFA thesis, explained the devil's chord to me and helped me develop it as a metaphor for the horrible unresolved nature of Ava's unimaginable loss. She also helped with Ava's piano pieces and, it needs to be noted, did play the *Moonlight Sonata* for me when I was little and having trouble getting to sleep. She is living proof that you can be working class, leave school at fifteen and become a master of fine art at seventy-five. In short, a legend.

Thanks to Jayne Farnworth for fab advice on police procedural and for beta-reading a truly awful first draft – really, you shouldn't have had to do that, I'm sorry.

Thank you to my local RNLI, particularly Paul Stallard and Jon Chapman, for providing me with valuable information concerning the river Thames and how and under what circumstances the RNLI is called upon. Book research aside, you guys do such an amazing job.

Thank you to the continually amazing team at Bookouture, particularly Kim Nash and Noelle Holten, the magnificent marketing duo, two phenomenal women, friends, and fabulous authors in their own right. Thanks to my copy-editor, Jane Selley, and my proofreader, Laura Kincaid, and a special shout to Jenny Geras, my former editor, who handed me over to Ruth as if I were a blown quail's egg, and who is now Bookouture's new top boss, woo-hoo!

Thanks to Tracy Fenton and all the team – Helen Boyce, Claire Mawdesley, Juliet Butler, Charlie Pearson, Charlie Fenton, Kel Mason and Laurel Stewart – at Facebook's The Book Club, without whom I would never have met Lorraine, not to mention many other lovely readers who, over the years, have become pals – roll on Harrogate 2021, I say! Thanks to Wendy Clarke and the team at Facebook's The Fiction Café, to Laura Pearson at Facebook's Motherload Book Club, to Anne Cater at Book Connectors, Mark Fearn at Bookmark and Iain Grant at the Stay-at-Home Facebook book club. Thank you, in fact, to all the online book clubs and the people who gather there to share their love of reading. If I've missed you out, I'm sorry, that's a mistake. I'm stressed about it even before I've realised I've done it, so do message me and I'll make sure to give you a wave in the next book, which I'll already be writing by the time you read this.

Huge thanks to flag-waving readers like Sharon Bairden (now an author in her own right, get in!), Teresa Nikolic, Philippa McKenna, Karen Royle-Cross, Ellen Devonport, Frances Pearson, Jodi Rilot, CeeCee, Isobel Henkelmann, Bridget McCann, Moyra Irving, Karen Aristocleus, Alessandra Nolli, Anne Burchett, Audrey Cowie, Alison Turpin, Theresa Hetherington, Donna Young, Mary Petit, Donna Moran, Ophelia Sings, Gail Shaw, Lizzie Patience, Fiona McCormick, Alison Lysons, Sam Johnson and many more not named here. Thank you. I read every single review, good or bad. If you don't see your name here, please give me a shout and I'll wave from my next book.

Huge thanks as ever to the amazing bloggers, who are unpaid and who work very hard spreading the word about the books and authors they love. I would like to thank the following bloggers, using their blogging names in case you wish to check out their reviews: Chapter in my Life, By The Letter Book Reviews, Ginger Book Geek, Shalini's Books and Reviews, Fictionophile, Book Mark!, Bibliophile Book Club, Random Things Through my Letterbox, B for Book Review, Nicki's Book Blog, Fireflies and Free Kicks, Bookinggoodread, My Chestnut Reading Tree, Donna's Book Blog, Emma's Biblio Treasures, Suidi's Book Reviews, Books from Dusk till Dawn, Audio Killed the Bookmark, Compulsive Readers,

LoopyLouLaura, Once Upon a Time Book Blog, Literature Chick, Jan's Book Buzz, and Giascribes… Again, if I have missed anyone, please let me know and I'll wave to you from my next book.

Thank you to the tremendously supportive writing community, particularly Emma Robinson, Judith Baker, Anna Mansell, Barbara Copperthwaite, Pam Howes, Patricia Gibney, Jennie Ensor, Carla Buckley, Joel Hames-Clarke, Angela Marsons, Zoe Antoniades, Eva Jordan, Vikki Patis, Marilyn Messik, Heide Goody, Iain Grant, Julie Cohen, Kate Simants, Louise Beech, Isabella May, Rona Halsall, Fiona Mitchell, Claire McGlasson, Callie Langridge, Tara Lyons, Paul Burston, Nicola Rayner, Emma Curtis, Lisa Timoney, Catherine Morris, Hope Caton, Robin Bell, Sam Hanson and my friend and first ever writing tutor, who always gets a special shout, lecturer and author Dr Sara Bailey. I will definitely have missed someone out and I am already sorry, but please let me know and I'll shout you next time.

Thank you to my gorgeous friends – you know who you are. I can't believe how many of you are still reading my books when they come out; you were only ever expected to read the first one.

Penultimately, thanks to my dad, Stephen Ball, who does in fact make his own pesto and bake his own bread and who is not a reader if you don't count *The Fisherman Magazine* but who has made an exception for me. Dad, I am writing them as quickly as I can, and thanks for keeping me in rainbow trout over the years. My kids, Alistair, Maddie and Franci Lynes – thank you for being the best lockdown gang ever and for not coming into the living room when I was working.

Finally, and as always, thanks to himself, Paul Lynes. There's no one I'd rather be locked down with, and yes, all right, if you hire a camper van I'll come to the next music festival with you. Now don't keep going on about it…

PUBLISHING TEAM

Turning a manuscript into a book requires the efforts of many people. The publishing team at Bookouture would like to acknowledge everyone who contributed to this publication.

Audio
Alba Proko
Melissa Tran
Sinead O'Connor

Commercial
Lauren Morrissette
Hannah Richmond
Imogen Allport

Contracts
Peta Nightingale

Cover design
Aaron Munday

Data and analysis
Mark Alder
Mohamed Bussuri

Editorial
Ruth Tross
Nadia Michael

Copyeditor
Jane Selley

Proofreader
Laura Kincaid

Marketing
Alex Crow
Melanie Price
Occy Carr
Cíara Rosney
Martyna Młynarska

Operations and distribution
Marina Valles
Stephanie Straub
Joe Morris

Production
Hannah Snetsinger
Mandy Kullar

Publicity
Kim Nash
Noelle Holten
Jess Readett
Sarah Hardy

Sales
David Murphy
Jess Harvey

Typesetting
Ramesh Kumar

RAISING READERS
Books Build Bright Futures

Dear Reader,

We'd love your attention for one more page to tell you about the crisis in children's reading, and what we can all do.

Studies have shown that reading for fun is the **single biggest predictor of a child's future life chances** – more than family circumstance, parents' educational background or income. It improves academic results, mental health, wealth, communication skills, ambition and happiness.

The number of children reading for fun is in rapid decline. Young people have a lot of competition for their time, and a worryingly high number do not have a single book at home.

Hachette works extensively with schools, libraries and literacy charities, but here are some ways we can all raise more readers:

- Reading to children for just 10 minutes a day makes a difference
- Don't give up if children aren't regular readers – there will be books for them!
- Visit bookshops and libraries to get recommendations
- Encourage them to listen to audiobooks
- Support school libraries
- Give books as gifts

There's a lot more information about how to encourage children to read on our websites: **www.RaisingReaders.co.uk** and **www.JoinRaisingReaders.com**.

Thank you for reading.